Flashman and
the Cobra

Robert Brightwell

Published in 2012 by FeedARead.com Publishing – Arts Council
funded

This book is dedicated to all the readers of my first novel and
particularly those who provided positive feedback on various
websites. Your comments were greatly appreciated and
encouraged me to continue with this project.

Introduction

This is the second instalment in the memoirs of the Georgian Englishman Thomas Flashman, which were recently discovered on a well-known auction website. Thomas is the uncle of the notorious Victorian rogue Harry Flashman, whose memoirs have already been published, edited by George MacDonald Fraser. Thomas shares many of the family traits, particularly the ability to find himself reluctantly at the sharp end of many major events of his age.

This second packet of the Thomas Flashman papers takes him to territory familiar to readers of his nephew's adventures, India, during the second Mahratta war. It also includes an illuminating visit to Paris during the Peace of Amiens in 1802. During Thomas's time, India was more of a frontier country for the British and, as he explains, the British were very nearly driven out of much of it.

The second Mahratta war saw Europeans and Indians fighting on both sides, including Arthur Wellesley, later the Duke of Wellington who fought his first battles there. As you might expect Flashman is embroiled in treachery and intrigue from the outset and, despite his very best endeavours, is often in the thick of the action. He meets many of the leading characters, from British governors and generals to Mahratta warlords, fearless Rajput warriors, nomadic bandit tribes, hairy highlanders and, not least, a four-foot-tall former nautch dancer, who led the only Mahratta troops to leave the battlefield of Assaye in good order.

Flashman gives an illuminating account with a unique perspective on both sides of the conflict. It details feats of incredible courage (not his, obviously), reckless folly and sheer good luck that were to change the future of India and the career of a general who would later win a war in Europe.

As editor I have restricted myself to checking the historical accuracy of the facts, which have been confirmed by several contemporary accounts. I have also added a series of historical notes at the end of the book on the characters and events that are featured.

The memoirs of Thomas's more famous nephew, Harry Flashman, edited by George MacDonald Fraser, are also strongly recommended.

RDB

Prologue – London, 1848

I was at a Waterloo Dinner years ago, the guest of his Britannic Majesty King George IV of Great Britain, Crown Prince of Hanover, Defender of the Faith, Prinny to his friends - or Fat George as he was universally known behind his back. For these annual events celebrating that famous day in 1815 the walls are lined with portraits of heroes from the battle. Naturally I don't feature, although with a debilitating deathcap fungus I might have done as much as anyone to help us win. In pride of place was a flattering portrait of George himself. I am not sure if he was literally mad like his father or just suffering from excessive toadying; but he had convinced himself that he had been present at the battle, when at the time his obese frame had not been closer to France than Dover. His delusions were such that he even claimed to have led a charge at Salamanca in Spain, disguised as General Bock.

Fat George sat in his reinforced chair at the end of the table in the uniform of the colonel in chief of one of the regiments of guards; but the closest thing to enemy fire he had experienced was when the French ambassador broke wind. In between stuffing his face he spouted on about ordering the charge of the Scots Greys and how he watched us beat back the Napoleon's Old Guard. "I have often heard your Majesty say so," intoned Wellington when looked upon for confirmation and we all sat there agreeing with him to protect our pensions.

Some years after the battle George insisted on travelling to Belgium to see first-hand the site of his imaginary triumphs. Wellington was ordered to accompany him as one of the guides and he brought me too for my own unique perspective on the battle. We rode around that bloody valley alongside the royal carriage for hours, but the king was not really interested in facts. It was the romance of battle he wanted to imbibe. After being taken around countless locations where hundreds of his loyal subjects had died showing great courage, the only time he expressed any emotion was when he was shown where Lord Uxbridge's leg had been buried. He bawled over it like a baby. Uxbridge still lives without his leg – he is Lord Anglesey now – so it was not even the loss of the man he was crying over, just the leg.

At this dinner Fat George asked Wellington if Waterloo was his finest victory, and after a moment's reflection the duke replied that no, he considered that the battle of Assaye was his greatest triumph. Without hesitation the royal fat-wit replied, "Yes, we certainly gave the

French a thrashing that day too, didn't we?" Wellington agreed that "not a Frenchman had been left alive on the field of battle", but his eye sought mine across the table and we shared a moment. We were the only ones at that gathering who had been at Assaye.

The enemy then had not been the French but a confederation of Indian warlords, and according to all the logic of warfare, the warlords should have won. In fact if it had not been for an error of judgement on my part, the battle would have been lost and Arthur Wellesley, as he was then, would have disappeared in ignominy. His first battle had ended in disgrace after half his force marched straight past the enemy in the dark and the rest got lost in some woods. He only retained command after that disaster because his brother was governor general of India and therefore commander in chief for the region.

Any rational person looking at the circumstances of Assaye would have concluded that it would have been suicidal to attack when Wellesley did. That was the obvious conclusion I made when a Mahratta warlord - who held me prisoner at the time - asked what would happen. I told them Wellesley would attack thinking it would persuade the Mahratta to hold their cavalry back and buy Wellesley time to withdraw. This was not selfless sacrifice on my part, you understand. I was only useful to them and worth keeping alive while Wellesley and the British East India Company army remained a force to be reckoned with. No one was more surprised than me when he did as I had predicted!

You will say that I am just claiming credit for the great man's work, but if you read the following memoir I think you will agree that I have suffered enough to earn some credit from the affair. This is an honest account of my life, and if I tell the truth about the cowardice, knavery and other discreditable acts, you can be assured that I tell the truth about the rest too.

I also played my part in Waterloo, which explains why Wellington always ensured I was invited to these dinners, as he was one of the few to know the truth. My presence at these Waterloo events puzzled many who could not recall me at the start of the battle, only at the end. The explanation was simple: I was with the French at the start of the day. For a few months I had held the rank of colonel in the French army, a higher rank than the major I achieved with his Britannic Majesty's forces. Wellington might have had more starch than a maiden aunt's drawers and he did not suffer fools, but he was loyal to people who served him well. I did him more than a few favours in my time. If he did not know that half of them were by mistake or for my own gain, well, there was no need to tell him.

But this account is not about Waterloo, it is about my first trip to India and how it was saved for Britain. It is about incredible courage, villainy and intrigue. It is about some astonishing characters, such as the tiny female general who saved the Mughal emperor, commanded some of the best soldiers I have seen and is now considered something of a Catholic saint. It also explains why I, the third son of a Midlands landowner with no title, am in Wellington's circle when he looks down on most people as though they were something he found under his shoe.

His cold demeanour is legendary. But a man cannot be all ice, and Wellington had heat between the sheets as all who have read the courtesan Harriette Wilson's racy memoirs will know. The silly bitch tried to blackmail him with them, which shows how well she understood him. He just sent a note back saying *Publish and be damned*. Like many others I paid up, but what she was planning to say about me was a lie. I was never that drunk and the bishop's billiard table was not ruined after we finished.

But even Wellington could not be that haughty when alone with me. He knows that I have caught him with his arse rising and falling over someone else's wife. I had found them by surprise as I had thought she was my mistress at the time. When we were in Spain I also pimped one of my pretty Spanish cousins for him, not that she complained as she did rather well out of the arrangement. Little of his affairs is mentioned in the memoirs of his contemporaries, for he would call them out to a duel if they did. But take it from me, his daily ride was not always on horseback.

I was also one of the few who had known him from near the beginning of his career. Few people rated his generalship at the start and he had to show that iron certainty to carry them with him. Mind you, there have been times when I have felt he has seen me as an inconvenient witness, which may partly explain some of the dangerous errands I have found myself being sent on.

But back to the story of my adventures in India, a tale which obviously starts... in Paris!

Chapter 1 – Paris, May 1802

There are parts of my life that I am proud of and other parts I don't normally mention. I suppose that my time in revolutionary Paris falls into the second category. The trouble was that too much temptation was put in my path, and if there is one thing I cannot resist, it is temptation. Mind you, I defy any red-blooded man to resist the bounties that were put before me then, and if I had been some bible-thumping God botherer with will power, well, we could have lost all India. Yes, strange as it seems those two weeks in France started a chain of events that would see me on the other side of the world with the fate of the empire in my shaking, sweaty palm. Your hand would be shaking too if you were being bounced from the clutches of a despotic prince to a ruthless female general, facing tigers and the insatiable Mrs Freese along the way.

It all started in such a trivial way with a handful of roses. The Tuileries royal palace gardens in Paris had lots of roses. They were apparently Josephine's favourite flower, and so to keep Napoleon happy the gardeners planted the finest blooms. To ensure that they looked beautiful when the first consul and his lady came by there were signs strategically placed around the gardens forbidding the picking of flowers. I know because I was deliberately standing in front of one when I suggested to Berkeley that his daughters would like nothing better than a bunch of blooms picked by his own fair hand. It was a childish prank, but I was now very fed up with Lord Augustus Berkeley, who had spent the last ten days ruining what would have been a very pleasant trip with his daughters if he had stayed at home. I was also bored as flower gardens are not really my thing and the ladies seemed to want to look at every inch.

Berkeley must have been fed up too or he would have ignored the suggestion. Normally if he could not bet on it or shoot it then he had little interest in anything, but he pulled out a small fruit knife from his pocket and was soon cutting through stems and snapping off thorns to have a bunch of blooms to present. He was being quite industrious and several Parisians were looking offended at this breach of the rules by a visiting 'roastbif'; I was sure one would go off to alert the park wardens. Not that the French normally obey rules themselves, you understand. Unlike the rigidly law-observing Prussians, the French see rules as guidelines for them and compulsory for other people. Soon a couple of agitated park-keepers could be seen in the distance coming our way. Murmuring something about going to look for a different colour, I slipped away, uncovering the sign, and moved out of sight down an avenue of hedges.

A minute or so later there was the sound of a heated altercation between the English aristocracy and French officialdom, two forces that rarely back down for anything. I found a gap in the foliage from which I could watch the results of my mischief and was not disappointed. The park-keepers had tried to confiscate the blooms and there was a shoving match going on between the parties. Berkeley was roaring in English that he was a British lord and guest of their country and would do whatever he damn well pleased while the parkies were jabbering in excited French and pointing at the sign I had hitherto been covering. With a bit of luck Berkeley would be hauled off to the park-keepers' hut and told off for a while, leaving me with some peace and quiet. My thoughts were already turning back to the two redeeming features of Lord Berkeley, namely his daughters Sarah and Louisa. Quite how such a short, fat, permanently bad-tempered cove had sired two such beautiful daughters was beyond me.

Unfortunately things escalated rather more than I had been expecting. As I edged away in the direction I had last seen the girls I caught another glimpse of their choleric father through the bushes. Two soldiers had arrived now but I thought he would probably still have got away with a caution if he had not hit one of them when they grabbed the Englishman's arm to calm him down. Flailing fists from all parties followed, and credit to the old buffer, he floored a park-keeper before a musket butt in the midriff put him permanently out of the fight. As I disappeared around a final corner more soldiers were coming and it looked like it was going to be a night in the cells now for this peer of the realm.

I passed several people I knew as I looked for the girls, for this was the surreal summer after the Peace of Amiens was agreed between Britain and France. The treaty had only been signed in March but nobody expected it to last long. A mass exodus in both directions had therefore begun to make the most of the opportunity before war was resumed. From France came Madame Tussaud and her first collections of grisly waxworks. The British public, having been horrified by tales of the 'terror' in Paris when thousands of (often innocent) people had been guillotined, were enthralled. A French balloonist also came over and, to the amazement of many, travelled from London to Colchester in forty-five minutes. He and his wife then both thrilled crowds by demonstrating a new device they called a parachute.

Leading the crowds in the opposite direction were ladies of fashion, for despite the revolution Paris was still seen as the centre for 'haute couture'. While French dressmakers were streaming across the Channel to sell their wares in London, many ladies were coming the other way to see French fashions first-hand for themselves. Others came out of curiosity. Revolutionary France had swept away its past, and with its radical politics and scientific institutes, it was seen as new and exciting. Top of the sightseeing list was the first consul of the French, Napoleon Bonaparte, whom everyone wanted to meet.

I was no exception, for general curiosity had brought me to France; I wanted to see how different it was. I was sure that the peace would not last, for I knew that the British had no intention of giving up Malta as required by the treaty. Despite my young age – I was just twenty then – I had a junior role with Lord Castlereagh who was in the Government. The British establishment was horrified by the thought of revolutionary France being seen as a success, for that would only encourage a similar revolution in Britain. But for both sides a temporary peace made sense, if only to give national economies a chance to recover from the high cost of war.

I had travelled to Spain and sailed around the Mediterranean the year before on diplomatic duty. I had been given that assignment because I spoke Spanish and could pass as a Spaniard with my black hair and slightly Latin complexion from my Spanish mother. I had returned with the undeserved reputation of being a capable agent, a sum in prize money and a taste for foreign travel. When the peace was declared it seemed a rare opportunity to see what was happening on the other side of the Channel. To add to my pleasure, when I announced my plans the Berkeley sisters from the neighbouring estate were keen to join me to see the Paris fashions, properly chaperoned, of course, as befit the daughters of an earl. They were pretty and good company, unlike their father, whose mood range spanned only from irritated to apoplectic.

His Lordship showed no interest in coming with us and so I happily agreed to escort the girls, and even if I could not shake off the chaperone, I was sure we would have a good time. Unfortunately a week before we were due to depart Berkeley changed his mind and decided to join the trip. A fact I believe not entirely unconnected with an American he had insulted who was subsequently seeking

9

satisfaction with a duel. In any event, he had glowered at us throughout the two-day journey to Dover, moaned constantly during the Channel crossing and then roundly berated every Frenchman he came across for all sorts of imagined slights. I was thoroughly sick of him and even his daughters were looking tense every time his brooding bulk came into view.

I found them at the far end of the gardens. They were chattering excitedly about a reception at the Austrian embassy that we had been invited to that evening. All the leading embassies in Paris were making the most of the window of peace to organise regular functions to encourage better relations and trade between their nation and France. A junior Austrian diplomat was staying at our hotel and, with an eye for pretty girls, he had provided invitations for the whole party. Not that we were intending that Berkeley or Mrs Fairfax, the chaperone, would come with us.

"Do you think Bonaparte will be attending the reception tonight?" asked Sarah. Her eyes gleamed with excitement. She was the younger of the two sisters, now aged eighteen.

"I doubt it," I replied. "They seem to be having these events every week now that there are so many people visiting Paris."

It was the first formal function we had been invited to since we arrived. There would be some members of the French government there, but the first consul seemed to stay away from these events, although he would make a few public appearances each week.

"It will give us the chance to try out the new French fashions," said Louisa, who looked unusually excited about the prospect. Louisa was the same age as me and my favourite of the two. I would have expected Sarah to be the most interested in clothes, but Louisa seemed quite flushed at the idea of her new outfit.

"That is assuming that Father does not find out. Where is he, by the way?" enquired Sarah.

"The last time I saw him he was at the other end of the garden," I replied, which was not untrue.

I wanted to enjoy some time with the girls without the old tyrant before we started the inevitable run-around to get him released. But my plans were immediately thwarted by a rotund, middle-aged woman who could be seen rushing towards us. She had the self-important look of someone who was bursting to share bad news, and as she was coming from the end of the garden where Berkeley had been arrested, with a sinking heart I could guess what that news would be.

"Ladies, ladies, your dear papa has been arrested! I saw Lord Berkeley being hustled away by some soldiers. He seemed wounded." She paused to catch her breath. "I asked where they were taking him and they said he was going to prison. You must go at once to the ambassador to get his release."

This announcement was greeted by gasps of astonishment from the ladies and a muttered curse from yours truly.

"What had he done to be arrested?" asked Louisa.

"They say he was fighting the soldiers. One of the men with them had a cut mouth and he kicked at Lord Berkeley when I asked. He kicked his lordship like a man would kick a dog, the villain."

"Father would not fight soldiers," said Sarah, sounding outraged. "Why would he do such a thing?"

Louisa gave me a glance that indicated that she did not think this possibility was as outlandish as her sister, but then a more suspicious look crossed her face.

"Did you hear Father getting arrested when you were at that end of the garden?" Louisa asked me shrewdly.

"Well, I did hear some shouting, but I did not go to investigate."

The fat lady tutted at my tardiness in protecting a fellow Briton, but Louisa gave me a hard look as she had seen instantly through the half-truth. We had known each other since we were children and she knew me far too well. She politely thanked the old lady, who walked back to her friends, and then, when the woman was out of earshot, Louisa turned back to me.

"I can't believe you let Father get arrested."

"He thumped a park-keeper and a soldier. There was nothing I could do."

"So you even saw it happen and you were not going to tell us."

"I would have told you... eventually... I just wanted to enjoy some peace and time with you without the old goat."

"That is our father you are talking about," cried Sarah hotly.

"Yes, the father you have lied to about going to the opera tonight, knowing he would not want to come, so that you can go to the reception without him. So don't play the dutiful daughters with me."

"All right, all right," said Louisa, holding up her hands in surrender. "We are all fed up with his constant complaining, but we can't leave him to languish in jail." She looked at me with those appealing eyes that I could not resist. "Please, Thomas, can you go to the British embassy and do what you have to do to get him released?"

"Couldn't we leave him in jail for just a couple of days?" I asked hopefully.

"You know we can't," said Louisa, smiling. "He is going to be really cross, so please, for my sake, try not to annoy him. I want you two to get on."

"I'll go, but you owe me some big favours for this," I said, trying to still look angry but failing as a wry grin crossed my face.

"Don't worry," said Louisa enigmatically. "You will get plenty of favours tonight."

Chapter 2

I took my time going to the embassy, first going back to my hotel to change into more formal clothes and then stopping for a pastry along the way. Paris was full of foreign visitors, some more welcome than others. The British seemed low down in the popularity stakes, with many French citizens seeing us either as people to be insulted or, like the pastry seller, to rob by overcharging. But even the inflated prices were no worse than London, and the pastries were infinitely better.

The British embassy, located on Rue Jacob, was a very busy place. It was a historic building, having been the site where Britain signed the Treaty of Paris back in '83 acknowledging the independence of the United States. Partly abandoned during the recent years of war, it was now a hive of activity with builders and decorators restoring years of damage and neglect while mixing with a throng of visitors and officials. The first three people I asked for help turned out to be fellow visitors, but eventually I found a harassed clerk surrounded by people asking questions who directed me to a room on the first floor.

As I was climbing the stairs I heard a voice call my name. "Thomas Flashman? Yes, it is you. Well, if this doesn't show the power of prayer I don't know what does. I have just been looking to find someone I know and trust in Paris."

I looked up, searching for a familiar face, and saw William Wickham smiling down at me from the top of the stairs. Then his last few words penetrated my consciousness and I felt a cold chill of alarm run down my spine.

Wickham was officially Britain's under secretary of state for the Home Department, but in reality he was Britain's spymaster. The last time we had met he had sent me on a supposedly simple courier mission. Instead I had narrowly escaped murder and been ambushed, half-garrotted, threatened with torture and rescued in one of the most audacious raids of the war. Along the way I had killed two enemy agents and, with my friend Thomas Cochrane, probably Britain's best seaman, had a series of other adventures. Wickham thought I was a resourceful agent and capable killer when in truth most of my actions had been driven by fear or anger or because the alternative was even worse. His need of someone he 'trusted' could only be bad news, but it would be hard to refuse without damaging my ill-gained reputation.

"William," I called. "I hope that does not mean that you have one of those straight-in-and-out jobs like the one you promised me last time."

He laughed, recalling the wild optimism of his previous mission briefing, and I smiled back. You could not help liking Wickham despite the fact that danger seemed to follow him around like a shadow. For a spy he seemed very open and engaging with those he knew well.

"What are you doing here?" he asked.

"One of the people I am travelling with has been stupid enough to get himself arrested for punching a park-keeper. I am here to try to get him out."

"Ah, Welling should be able to help with that. I will take you up to his office. Are you in Paris to see the sights?"

"Yes, I am here with Lord Berkeley and his two daughters. They live on the neighbouring estate and the girls wanted to look at the fashions, while I think Berkeley wanted to avoid some troubles at home."

"Ah yes, I heard about the problems he was having with the American." I was not surprised by this as Wickham was always up to date with news and gossip, despite spending most of his time on the continent. "I take it that it was his lordship who plugged the park-keeper?"

"Yes, the fool was arguing about picking flowers."

"Hmm, I never imagined him as the flower-picking kind. You are not keen on him, I take it." His eyes twinkled as he added, "I have heard his daughters are very pretty."

"They are quite easy on the eye," I admitted. I had no wish to get into my personal life with Wickham and so I asked, "Is Welling's office down there?" indicating a corridor that we had now reached.

"Yes, but I would like a private word with you first, if you don't mind." Wickham opened the door of another room, which was unoccupied but had some chairs and a desk. We both went in and sat down on the visitor side of the desk.

"What do you know about India?" he asked, getting straight down to business.

"Well, I know that Castlereagh suspects that the East India Company is not declaring about a million pounds of profit. I also know that the Company is in conflict with the governor general of India as the costs of the Company army are rising fast now that he is governing the province of Mysore in the south of India."

"Ah, of course, I forgot that you are still working with Castlereagh at the Board of Control."

Lord Castlereagh was president of the Board of Control, responsible for resolving disputes between the governor general of India, Richard Wellesley, Lord Mornington as he was known, and the East India Company with its avaricious board of directors in Leadenhall Street. He was also my patron in the Government, although there had been precious few opportunities for patronage of late. My modest income came from letting some properties that my father had helped me buy in London.

"Yes, from what I hear," I said. "Mornington is concerned by the French influence in the Mahratta states, but the Company does not care about that and just wants to maximise profits from trade."

"Do you know much about the French influence in the Mahratta states?" asked Wickham.

"Absolutely nothing, and before you start with another of your tempting offers of foreign adventure, I have to point out that I am escorting the Berkeley girls at the moment and their father has ably proved that he cannot be relied on to escort them alone."

"Yes, if he found another florist all could be undone," said Wickham, laughing. "No, I was just hoping that you could join me for a meeting tomorrow morning with an old French general who has served in India. He tells me he has information that I would find useful, but I am not sure why he would want to help us. You would be able to hear first-hand about French influence from someone who was there. Then you could pass back details to Castlereagh at the Board of Control when you are back in London."

"So you just want to use me as a courier to London?" I said, feeling very relieved. "Yes, I would be happy to do that," I continued. "It would be a pleasure. We are due to travel back in around ten days. Just as long as you are not going to try to send me to India afterwards."

"Well, someone will probably have to go. But don't worry, I appreciate that would be a big commitment, probably at least a year to get there and back." He grinned knowingly. "Who is to say whether the Berkeley girl you are after would wait for you."

"Well, I hope getting the old man out of jail will work in my favour."

"Yes, fate turns on the strangest things. Maybe the bruised nose of a French park-keeper will lead you to your heart's desire. We had better get you to Welling without delay, but thank you for your help tomorrow."

Welling, it turned out, was another harassed embassy official who was very familiar with the process for getting British visitors released from jail. While peace had been declared it seemed that old animosities took longer to die down and there had been various incidents and brawls across the city since the British visitors started arriving.

"Sometimes they are started by the British, sometimes by the French," he said. "It is only to be expected. After all, we have spent years trying to kill each other. You cannot simply expect people to forget and turn the other cheek over night." He gave a little sigh of despair at such naiveté shown by both governments. "We have been buying people out of prison as the most expedient way to solve these problems, and the French government has turned a blind eye as they do not want to damage the new friendship with court cases. But now I think some officials are seeing this as a money-making opportunity and we are seeing more British imprisoned for petty offences, all released for a fee."

He looked through some papers on his desk until he found the note he was looking for. "Ah here it is, the latest list that came in an hour ago: British citizen Berkeley arrested for brawling in royal gardens," he read out. "I am sure that this is a fabricated charge, sir. It is outrageous to think a gentleman would do such a thing."

I recalled the sight of Berkeley punching the park-keeper – it was a damn fine blow – but decided that describing it would not enhance his lordship's reputation with this fawning official.

"Good, that is him. Where has he been sent and how can we get him out?" I asked.

"He has been taken to the Conciergerie, sir."

I was surprised to hear this as even I knew that the Conciergerie was the main prison where they kept people waiting for the guillotine. Like many tourists, the other day I had been to look at it and then gone to the Place de la Revolution where the guillotine had been in daily use during the 'Terror'. The square was currently empty with just a stone plinth where a statue of Louis XV had once stood.

"Don't worry, sir," said Welling, seeing my expression. "The Conciergerie holds all types of prisoners and is often used to hold British people as it is in the centre of Paris, and because their detention is normally only for a day or two before payment is made."

"How much are they likely to want to release him?"

"The cash fee is likely to depend on whether they know he is wealthy, sir. They call all people citizens in official documents these days, but if they know he is a British lord then the fee will be higher. Do you think he will have revealed he is of the nobility, sir?"

I confirmed that I thought that was highly likely.

"That is unfortunate, sir. Then they will probably start negotiations at around a hundred guineas or the equivalent in gold in francs."

"Good grief!" I exclaimed as I did not have anything like that on me.

"Don't worry, sir, you can usually negotiate down to half of the figure they start with, as long as his lordship has not antagonised them in any way."

In that case we were probably up to two hundred already, I thought.

"If you need help getting the gold we can arrange that in exchange for a note on your bank, sir," Welling added helpfully.

I would get a note from Berkeley before negotiations were concluded so that he would pay his own damn ransom. I thanked Welling for his help, and as the embassy was only a ten-minute walk away from the Conciergerie I decided to go on foot. There were plenty of soldiers on the streets, and while I got the odd hostile look from some who guessed from the cut of my clothes that I was one of the many British visitors, I felt safe on the streets.

The Conciergerie was an intimidating medieval-looking building and its recent past made it look even more forbidding. The walk there had given me time to reflect and at this point I should declare to you, dear reader, that I have been less than honest so far in this account. I promised myself when I started writing this chronicle that it would be 'warts and all', as Cromwell once said, including the good and the bad, and so there is one more fact I must add here. My feelings for the Berkeley sisters, and Louisa in particular, are not as casual as I have made out. To start with I looked upon the girls almost as sisters as we have known each other since childhood, but once I came back from my Mediterranean adventures we spent a lot of time together and things changed. Louisa was a stunner and, as the daughter of an earl, would be a great match. While I was in no rush to get married, I was desperate to get her into bed but she was holding out at least for betrothal first. Traditionally I would have gone to Lord Berkeley to ask for her hand, but given his temperament and the fact that he rarely refused his daughters anything, Louisa sounded him out first. I turned out to be one of the rare exceptions. He absolutely refused to consider the match of his eldest daughter to the third son of a local landowner, describing our family background as 'murky at best'. It is true that the Flashman fortune has probably been tainted with piracy and even slave trading, but that was back in the past. Louisa was told by her father that she had to set her sights much higher, while I was filled with resentment at my lack of status in a very class-conscious world.

Now here I was facing the bitter irony that I had to get out of prison a man who felt I was too inferior to marry his daughter. There were some soldiers at the prison gates but I explained my business in French, which seemed to be understood, and I was shown inside. They gave me directions that led to a hallway with what looked like cell doors down one side. To be honest I did not need the directions for the final few turns as a familiar voice could be heard bellowing.

"Send another note to the British embassy! They should have got me out of here hours ago."

There was a pause followed by another shout: "Get me some food and wine! You can charge that to the embassy too."

As I turned the final corner I saw a weary grey haired army sergeant with a big, bushy moustache shaking his head at the tirade coming from the first cell in the row. The cell doors all had little barred windows in them. Berkeley's cell was the only one with a rag stuffed between the bars, in what seemed to be a futile attempt to muffle the noise.

The soldier looked up hopefully at my approach. He asked in halting English, "You are 'ere for ze prisoner?"

"Yes," I replied. "How much to release him?"

"In English gold it eez one 'undred guineas. I should charge two 'undred for he is a very bad prisoner and it is a serious crime. But I just want to get rid of 'im and his moaning, so it is one 'undred, in your guineas or French gold."

Berkeley must have heard us talking for now he suddenly bellowed, "Flashman, is that you? Where the hell have you been, man? I have been here for hours."

"I will need to speak to the prisoner," I said to the sergeant.

"Of course," he replied, getting up and detaching a bunch of keys from his belt. In a few seconds the cell door creaked open and there was Berkeley, staring at me all red-faced and belligerent.

"Well, you have taken your damned time. If you came when I called you in the gardens this would all have been explained and I would not have been arrested at all." The sergeant moved away to give us some privacy and I stepped into the cell. "You are bloody unreliable,

Flashman, always have been, whole family the same. Now what are you sitting down for? We have to leave."

My loathing for the man rose another notch. "Sit down, sir. You cannot leave yet. We need to pay them a release fee. They want a hundred guineas in gold."

"Bloody thieves and bandits, never mind your revolution," roared Berkeley so loud that the guard and no doubt half the prison could hear him. Then in a lower voice to me he barked, "Well, pay them, boy, and let's get out of here."

First the slur on my family and then treating me like some incompetent waiter. If I was not in love, or at least in lust, with Louisa, I would have told him to go to the devil. But instead I had to take a deep breath and admit that I did not have a hundred guineas to release him. "I will need a note from you to your bank for the gold that I can give to the embassy. They will give me the funds and then we can get you released."

"Huh," said Berkeley, reaching for a pen on the table; there was paper and ink there too, presumably for this very purpose. Dipping the pen in the ink, he started scratching away on the paper. As he did so he added, "What would you have done if you had married my daughter and she got arrested, eh? Left her to rot in jail because you did not have a hundred guineas?"

"I am sure I would have found a way to manage the situation," I said through gritted teeth.

"Well, you didn't manage it with me, did you? That is why her marriage to you is out of the question. It is a matter of breeding, Flashman, and you do not have enough of it." He handed me the finished note. "Now take that to the embassy and try to be back within the hour. I want to get out of here."

I walked out of the cell seething with rage. The guard shut the cell door behind me and checked the rag was still wedged in the little window to muffle the shouting. It did not stop me hearing Berkeley say to himself, "No bloody breeding at all."

The sergeant and I walked back to his desk. He asked, "You get ze money now?" He seemed very familiar with the routine. "Best to be back before dark as nobody likes to be in ze cells at night. The walls, they... 'ow you say... talk."

"What do you mean the walls talk?" I thought he had mistranslated the English.

"Those are the cells that ze condemned prisoners were kept in, before they were taken for ze ..." Here he made a swishing movement with a flat hand on the back of his neck. "Nobody likes to be 'ere at night. Too many ghosts."

An evil thought crossed my mind and I was just mulling it over when Berkeley helped make the decision by shouting, "Are you still there, Flashman? You have not got time to talk; get a move on."

I reached into my pocked and took out all the money I had with me, about ten guineas, and put it on the table. In a slightly quieter voice, so that Berkeley would not hear, I said, "We are only willing to pay ten guineas, take it or leave it."

"Ten guineas? Zat is not possible," said the sergeant, looking astonished. "Maybe eighty guineas, but no lower."

"Fine," I said, sweeping the coins back up and putting them in my pocket. "It looks like he will be staying overnight then, doesn't it."

I am one of the few people to walk away from the Conciergerie prison with a happy smile on my face. I decided that there was no point in taking abuse from Berkeley any more. He would never allow me to marry Louisa, which left elopement, and I was not sure she would go for that. Living on my current income would involve a significant fall in living standards from what she was used to. Still, I could make twenty guineas straight away by cashing in Berkeley's note and buying him out again for eighty guineas in the morning. To Louisa, I would blame French bureaucracy for the fact her father could not be released until tomorrow. As for Berkeley himself, I might tell him that my lack of breeding caused me to spend rest of the afternoon in an alehouse. It would be interesting to see how purple his face could get. Thinking about it, my best chance of marrying Louisa was probably to kill the old bastard by giving him apoplexy.

Chapter 3

Berkeley's daughters greeted the news of their father's continued detention with mixed feelings.

"At least we don't have to pretend that we are at the opera tonight," said Sarah.

"Yes, we do, at least for Mrs Fairfax's benefit," Louisa reminded her. "She is only allowing us out on our own because she thinks some other ladies are meeting us there." She turned to me. "Is Father's cell comfortable? He is not sharing it with criminals, is he?"

"Oh no, he has a room to himself and the prison was very quiet when I visited him. He has a bed, table and chair and a small window; he should be perfectly comfortable," I reassured them. It was early evening and still quite light, but soon it would be getting dark and I hoped those cell walls would be very talkative tonight.

The young Austrian diplomat, Alexander Hafenbredl, had organised a carriage to take us to the embassy. Two other couples staying in our hotel were also going and I chatted happily with them as we gathered in one of the hotel drawing rooms. The girls came down a couple of minutes before we were due to depart with carriage cloaks drawn tight around their necks that hid their new Paris dresses. Both of them seem quite flushed and red with excitement and I wondered if they had already been drinking champagne. The embassy was just a short carriage ride away and was a very grand and impressive building.

I can still remember now walking into that grand embassy reception room. The walls were bright with fresh colour – decorators had just finished restoring it to its former glory as it too had been abandoned during the revolutionary war. Great chandeliers blazed with light and then my gaze dropped to the crowd underneath the candles and my eyes nearly popped out of my head. Dresses were in what later became known as the Empire style, hanging straight down from below the bust, with often contrasting fabrics coming up from under the breasts and over the shoulders. However, at least in that Paris season, the ball gown fashion was for the upper fabric to be very diaphanous, in many cases almost completely transparent. The most daring of ladies had even gone to the trouble of adding rouge to their nipples so that there was no doubt what could be seen beneath the flimsy folds. My head whipped round to look at the sisters just as a footman took away the carriage cloaks from their shoulders, revealing what was underneath. They both looked stunning. While the tops of their dresses were not completely transparent, in the light you make out the curve of their breasts quite clearly.

Louisa smiled at me. "You like?" she asked simply.

Words failed me at that instant, but I nodded eagerly and noticed that Alexander Hafenbredl was staring with equally lascivious intent at Sarah. Louisa stepped towards me, still smiling, and with a delicate finger she pushed my gaping jaw up to close my mouth. Then she took my arm and steered me onto the dance floor. It was a magical night. As well as the revealing tops, fashion also dictated that corsets were out. So when dancing, instead of having your arm around the usual whalebone armour plate of a corset, you could feel the warm back of your partner through the fabric. All round, it was a far more intimate affair.

There was also a marked difference in the behaviour of the guests during the evening. The foreign nationals, more used to formal balls and dances, were more conservatively dressed and reserved in their manner, although several of the ladies were wearing variations of the new French fashions. In contrast, the French officials and their wives and mistresses had lived through the revolution with the subsequent 'terror' and seemed more determined to live life to the full. They were louder and many of the women dressed brazenly.

It was between dances that we literally bumped into Wickham and a very pretty lady whom he introduced as his wife. She spoke with a slight accent as it turned out she was Swiss and she seemed very friendly.

"Is Lord Berkeley here as well?" said Wickham, looking around. "Or is he still recovering from his period of captivity?"

"Unfortunately he is still in captivity," I said quickly, giving Wickham what I hoped was a meaningful look. "French bureaucracy means that he cannot be released until tomorrow."

Louisa shot me a look; she did not miss a thing even after four glasses of champagne.

Wickham responded smoothly, "Yes, those officials can be very dogmatic when it comes to paperwork, but I am sure he will be released tomorrow."

Before I was faced with any searching questions from my dance partner there was a disturbance at the end of the room. Like a wave, the word spread down the room: "Bonaparte is here." It was like an electric charge through the gathering as people strained to get a look at the first consul, who was evidently working his way around the room. The dance music continued for a while but nobody wanted to miss the opportunity of being introduced to the man who had conquered Northern Italy and then Egypt before finally restoring law and order to the Republic of France itself. With no one dancing, the band eventually resorted to some patriotic French tunes. The small group containing Bonaparte worked its way down the room towards us.

"He is an amazing man," murmured Wickham as we waited. "You feel that he can look right through you when you meet him, and he is very knowledgeable. He does not leave things to his officials; he likes to check everything himself and take personal control of every aspect of the Republic."

I looked down the room at Bonaparte for the first time. Later in life I was to get to know him quite well and I never ceased to be in awe of him. He gave off a sense of destiny, as though he could look into the future and see the difference he was making. His hair was cut short but it was already starting to thin on top and he was wearing a red coat with some military decorations pinned to it. But it was not his appearance that you noticed first about him, it was his energy. Three aides were with him and he was giving them instructions between meeting the groups around the room. On one occasion he stopped to read a short document one of them showed him. At the same time he was carrying on a jovial conversation with the ambassador, who was guiding him down the line of guests. His eyes were darting around the room and he nodded at a few acquaintances waiting to see him on the other side of the chamber. He seemed to miss nothing.

In a few moments he was up to us.

"This is William Wickham of the British Consulate," said the Austrian ambassador in French. The ambassador evidently knew Wickham and chose to brush over his real job title in the interest of diplomatic niceties. Napoleon shook his hand and smiled at the description. I had a feeling that he also knew exactly who William Wickham was.

"It is a pleasure to meet you, Mr Wickham," said Napoleon, speaking in French. "I believe I have heard of some of your exploits."

"It is an honour to meet you too, sir," replied Wickham.

"Is this one of your colleagues?" the consul asked, turning to me.

"This is Mr Flashman, sir," said Wickham, replying in the same language as I put out my hand to shake that of Bonaparte. "He was in the Mediterranean last year and was fortunate to be one of the few survivors of the sinking of the *Real Carlos*." Napoleon's brow furrowed slightly as he tried to recollect the incident. The *Real Carlos* and her sister ship had been two massive Spanish ships of the line. They had been part of a joint French and Spanish fleet, but in a night action they had caught fire, become entangled and had blown up.

Bonaparte's his brow cleared as the memory came to him. "Such a terrible loss for our Spanish allies," he said as he looked at me closely. "I recollect that there were only a handful of survivors?"

"Seventeen, sir," I replied, having hesitated a moment to remember the French for that number.

"Then you are indeed fortunate," the first consul said. "A lucky man will always beat a clever one, and so I am glad we are all at peace," he continued. He stared at me a moment longer; he seemed to be trying to memorise my face, and in that second I knew with certainty that we would meet again. I am sure he sensed it too, for he gave me the slightest nod and the ghost of a smile crossed his lips before he broke the gaze and swung his head round to look at Louisa. The smile broadened and he bent down to kiss her hand. "A pleasure to meet you, mademoiselle," he murmured before sweeping on to the next group in the room.

The rest of the evening passed in a whirl. We drank more champagne and danced until our feet ached and our heads span. For any red-blooded man it was a very distracting affair. Tits on display everywhere you looked, and the dance partner's warm, yielding flesh of in your arms. In dances where partners changed the French ladies were particularly daring, taking delight at shocking the visitors by grabbing or caressing them during dance encounters and then moving on, giggling, when some starchy Austrian official jerked away like a scalded stoat. With that and Louisa pressing her perfect breasts at me throughout the evening, I was becoming as horny as hell. Tight dancing breeches were not ideal clothes that night and I spent half the evening doing what an army officer once called the blue balls scuttle, trying to hide my obvious interest.

Eventually it was time to get back into the carriage and return to the hotel. Poor Alexander: after hours of enthusiastically courting Sarah, he was asked by his ambassador to stay on at the embassy. Sarah was furious at being denied her beau for the rest of the evening. Another couple shared the carriage with the three of us, and when we got back to the hotel another party was already underway. There was a large crowd in one of the drawing rooms and things seemed pretty lively. I was in no mood to go to bed and wanted to get to grips with Louisa in more intimate surroundings. She could not be caught in my room and I knew that a lady's maid slept in a dressing room between the bedrooms of the two sisters, and so I tried to steer her towards a quiet corner of the drawing room. The drunken crowd would not notice anything we were doing, but Louisa saw where I was guiding her and slipped away.

"I am going to bed," she said. She kissed me on the cheek while slipping a hand under my jacket and squeezing my arse.

"You cannot go to bed now, the night is still young," I cried.

In reply Louisa just winked at me as she ran quickly up the stairs. There may be some readers of this account that recognise that wink as a meaningful signal, but after a bottle and a half of champagne, I didn't. Given her need to protect her reputation and the lady's maid acting as chaperone in her room, this spelled the end of my evening with Louisa. I threw myself down on a nearby settee feeling thoroughly let down.

As Louisa's shapely rear disappeared around the top of the stairs her sister came over to me. To my surprise she leaned over and kissed me on the forehead, leaving her own virtually uncovered, perfect bouncers right in my face.

"Have you been left on your own too?" she whispered in my ear. "Why don't you come into the party with me?"

Well, you would have to be dead not to understand that 'signal' and completely stonehearted to decline it. Of course, had I been sober I might have remembered that of the two sisters I had always found Sarah to be spoilt, calculating and manipulative. But being drunk and horny and feeling abandoned, I did not give it a thought.

We went into the drawing room and joined a loud and raucous gathering. I was already tight but was soon swilling brandy with the rest. Two of the French women present had allowed their breasts to escape their diaphanous coverings and one was dribbling brandy down her left tit which was being eagerly licked off by a randy old Austrian count. Emboldened by this, I slipped a hand over Sarah's shoulder and had a fondle that would normally have resulted in my getting a slapped face. This time Sarah just nestled her head against my shoulder and rubbed her hand along my thigh. She certainly knew how to console someone her sister had rejected.

More solace arrived in the form of small glasses of green liquid; it was called absinthe. This green liquor is currently all the range in Paris. They make it in France now and its hallucinogenic properties have been blamed for all sorts of events, including a man murdering his entire family. But back then few people had heard of it, largely as it was hugely expensive, being made only in Switzerland. People drank it to show off that they could afford it as much as anything. It tastes foul but we were drinking it in small glasses like the Prussians drink schnapps. Soon a whole series of toasts were drunk with small shots of absinthe, first to the Austrian ambassador, then to Bonaparte, then to the ladies. I recall the brandy-and-now-absinthe-dribbling-lady's-left-tit had a toast to itself at one point, and then my recollections start to get a bit hazy.

Now I can hold my drink. Sure I can get leery in my cups, but never to the point that I do things that are suicidal to my interests. To explain what happened next I could tell you that while intoxicated I confused the two sisters and thought I was still with Louisa, but I didn't. I might have mixed their names once or twice, but I knew who she was. The truth was that with the absinthe and booze on board, I just didn't care. Sarah was ready, willing and eager and so was I. By now she had started caressing me though my breeches, which was putting a rare old pressure on the stitching.

"Let's go to my room," I whispered hoarsely.

"No, no, not there," she hissed. "We must go to my room."

"What about your maid?"

"Don't worry, she has been taken care of. By now she is as drunk as a pig merchant on market day."

We staggered upstairs, and I mean staggered. Whether it was the champagne, brandy or the absinthe, most likely a combination of all three, once we were moving we both found the co-ordination of limbs a bit of a challenge. We were pawing at each other as we went, and by the time we staggered past the drunken maid's bed to reach Sarah's room we were in a fine old state of anticipation. It was just as well that the maid was comatose as, locked in a fumbling embrace, I staggered into her bed on the way past. By the time we got inside Sarah's room we were tearing at each other's clothes and raring to go. Never mind making the earth move; for me the whole room was already moving and sometimes Sarah seemed a bit blurry too, but we both had an urgent need to satisfy. My body was a bit like an orchestra with the different sections slightly out of time, but the conductor wasn't waiting around and charged in with baton raised. It was a rare old romp, and afterwards we collapsed naked on the bed and within a few minutes I was asleep.

When I awoke the bedside candles had burned out and the room was dark. For a minute I could not remember where I was. I could tell it was not my room, but then I made out the naked form of the girl in bed next to me and memories started to come back. That sobered me up. Here I was in love with Louisa, thwarted by her father, who viewed me as untrustworthy, and now I found myself naked in bed with her sister after a strenuous bout of lovemaking. God we had made some noise and I suddenly wondered if the maid was now awake or even if Louisa had heard us from her room, which was on the other side of the maid's. Now that I listened for it I could still hear the lady's maid snoring, and if Louisa had heard her sister entertaining, hopefully she would not know it was me. From what I could recall we had not wasted time on conversation.

I had to move: I could not be found in there, it would be the hell of a scandal. Slowly I half-rolled out of the bed and started feeling around for my clothes. Five minutes and much searching around the dark floor later, I had found all of my clothes but just one of my shoes. I could not find the other one anywhere and could only hope that I had lost it somehow on the way up the stairs. I was soon dressed and moved to the door, opening it quietly. The maid was lying on her back with her mouth open, snoring, with a nearly empty bottle of brandy on the bedside table. To my left was the door to the landing and opposite was the door I presumed to Louisa's room. I thought briefly of paying her a visit, but I was in enough trouble. I eased out onto the landing and breathed a sigh of relief.

It was the middle of the night, the hotel was quiet and I could easily make it back to my own room without being seen. No one need know about tonight. Sarah knew her sister was in love with me and so I reasoned that she would keep quiet about our dalliance, and I was not going to tell anybody. The next few meetings might be awkward, especially if Louisa was around, but perhaps we could both just pretend that it had never happened.

I staggered down the hall, trying desperately to convince myself that I could get away with this. I came to my own room, stepped inside and stopped dead in my tracks. By the candles that were burning low in the candlesticks on either side of the bed I could see that it was already occupied.

"Bloody hell!" I said as I took in who was in my bed.

The figure stirred, waking up as she heard my exclamation.

"Thomas, what took you so long?" said Louisa, starting to sit up in the bed. "I gave you enough signals not to delay. Don't you want to taste forbidden fruit?" As she sat up the sheet fell away and I could see that she was naked. The conductor was starting to raise his baton again and this time it would be a full symphony.

I was a young man then and it turned out to be a full symphony and an encore before we finally fell asleep in each other's arms. I was clearly not the first lover of either of the Berkeley girls and I wondered idly who else there might have been. It was a more promiscuous age, but single girls still had to protect their reputation to at least appear pure for marriage. If they fell with child before marriage then foreign travel was normally arranged before the pregnancy showed. Naples was a favourite destination, with the child either adopted by a family there or discreetly brought back to England and left with a family where the mother could keep a maternal eye on its development, often by being the official godmother.

I awoke a few hours later as Louisa stirred beside me. "I need to get back to my room," she said sleepily. "I gave Rosie a full bottle of brandy to enjoy when we went out. She cannot hold her drink and was completely out of it when I came to your room, but she will be waking up with a hangover soon."

There had been a moment when I first awoke to find Louisa still in my arms when I had been blissfully happy. But mention of the snoring maid brought other memories back too, and in the back of my head a small alarm bell started ringing. If Louisa ever found out where I spent the first part of the night I was toast, but surely Sarah had as much to lose in her sister's friendship as I did. Still, it would be best if the girls did not compare notes about last night as one inopportune word from either of them could spell disaster for me.

I stroked Louisa's bare shoulder and asked, "Darling, you won't tell anyone about tonight, will you?"

"Of course not. Well, only Sarah. We share everything." As it turned out she was certainly not wrong about that!

"No, please, do not even tell Sarah. Promise me you won't tell her."

"Of course, if it means that much to you. Are you ashamed of me then?"

"You know I am not. I just don't want any complications. I want this to be just the two of us." For someone who knows me so well she can be extraordinarily trusting, and she reached down and kissed me. I had a quick fondle before she squirmed away, laughing.

"You just remember to get father out of prison this morning," she said as she slipped on her gown and moved towards the door. She opened it a crack to check the corridor was empty and was gone. I lay back on the bed with a stupidly happy smile on my face.

I was young and naive and actually thought I might have the ghost of a chance of keeping last night's events secret. Louisa had promised not to tell Sarah. I hoped Sarah would be too embarrassed to admit that she had made a play for the man she knew her sister loved. I really did not understand women or sisters, not having any of my own. If I had, I would not have been lying in bed grinning like a fool, but instead would have been packing and preparing to run from the cataclysm that was about to fall on me.

Chapter 4

The hotel was still quiet when I got dressed and left with a hundred guineas of Berkeley's gold in my pocket. I had arranged to hire a carriage for the morning. I planned to go to the Conciergerie early to spring his lordship and take him back to the hotel. Then I was going back to the British embassy to collect Wickham for our meeting with the French general. The streets were not busy and soon we were pulling up in front of the forbidding entrance of the prison. But I was still in high spirits and soon was past the guards and heading to the corridor where I had found Berkeley before. This time there was no shouting or bellowing coming from the cells. All was silent, and the desk where the sergeant had been sitting was empty. I thought perhaps Berkeley had been taken somewhere else and so went to the cell door and removed the rag still stuffed in the little window. Through it I saw an astonishing sight. Berkeley, whom I had only ever seen red-faced and angry, was sitting on his bed with tears streaming down his cheeks. His face was grey and his eyes were fixed on the opposite wall. His shoulders shook slightly as he sobbed. I was stunned. I didn't know what to say.

Then I heard footsteps approaching. I quickly put the cloth back in the cell door window to hide the shocking view and turned to find the old sergeant ambling towards me.

"Ah, Monsieur Flashman, you have ze 'undred guineas for me?" he asked with a smile as he sat back down at the desk.

"I thought we agreed eighty guineas last night," I replied, moving towards him. "And what have you done to him? He is crying in there."

The sergeant laughed. "We agreed eighty before I found out that ze prisoner 'ad given you a note for ze full 'undred. So now the price is an 'undred, unless you want me to tell ze prisoner that you are trying to steal twenty guineas from im?" The old soldier looked up at me with a knowing smile; he knew he had me. "I don't think your friend will stand another night in ze cells. We 'ave done nothing to 'im, but I told you that those walls talk."

"What about splitting the difference, ten guineas for you and ten for me?" The day was starting to take a downward turn and my early jauntiness was starting to fade.

"Why should I do that when I can 'ave the full 'undred?" The sergeant was still smiling like a card player with a handful of aces. "No, ze price is an 'undred, but because I like you I will throw in a quick tour of ze prison, to show you what it is that 'as quietened your friend down."

I could see I had no choice and dropped the bag with eighty guineas on the table and reached in my pocket for the twenty I had already taken out of it. The soldier was a wily old fox and must have seen every trick in the book. I should have guessed that he would have found a way to get Berkeley to confirm the amount he had paid. The sergeant put the remaining coins in the bag and then pocketed it.

"It is a pleasure doing business with you, monsieur," he said, getting up and patting his pocket. "If it makes you feel better, I normally charge five guineas to rich British visitors to show them ze sights."

"Oh, it is certainly worth a hundred guineas to get that old bastard to stop his constant complaining," I replied. "Especially as he is paying for it himself." The sergeant laughed and I smiled back; he was a rogue and he knew that I was a chancer too.

"These cells were all full in ze old days," he said as he started to lead me down the corridor towards the door at the far end. "This where we kept people who were about to be taken to the guillotine. It is near the main entrance where the carts collected them to take them to the Place de la Revolution."

"Were you here then?" I asked.

"Yes, there was a group of around fifteen of us and we used to 'elp 'ere and sometimes in ze square."

"You mean you helped with the guillotine?"

"Yes, the executioner was the one to always release the blade but we 'elped get people from the carts and strap them to the board that was then tipped under the blade." He opened a door at the end of the corridor and began to lead the way down some stairs.

"How many people did you help execute?" I asked. I was fascinated to speak to someone who was there at the centre of this political inferno.

" 'Undreds. I am not proud of it, but France was very different then. It was a crazy time. The revolution was being run by a group called the Committee of Public Safety." He gave a snort of derision. "They were more interested in revolutionary theories and philosophy than the people. In the summer of 'ninety-four they introduced new rules forbidding the use of defence counsels and the 'earing of witnesses. You just had to plead your case to the Revolutionary Tribunal and do it quickly before they tired of listening to you. The so-called Committee of Public Safety also introduced a law that made death the sole penalty for guilt. At the busiest time we were executing nearly thirty people a day, and that was just in Paris."

"Were they mostly aristocrats?"

"God, no. We used to put five in a cart and on average one might be what you would call an aristocrat, one would a merchant or lawyer and the rest were common workers." He opened a door at the bottom of the staircase and we stepped outside into a courtyard.

"You 'ave to understand, everyone was frightened then," he continued. "Anybody could accuse anyone of being a counter-revolutionary, and if you were accused, the chances were that you would die. People were accused to settle old scores or because the denouncer wanted to show their revolutionary fervour to protect themselves. I know one man who denounced nearly twenty people to show that 'e was loyal to the revolution. They were all killed, but it did him no good as 'e was denounced in turn and ended up 'ere. Even though we knew most of them were innocent, there was nothing we could do. If we refused to do our duties, we would have just been executed too."

I started to appreciate the full horror of the revolution. This had all happened less than ten years ago. The prison around me began to feel even more sinister. We were walking across a courtyard towards an open-sided wooden building on the far side. Walking towards us was a morose army officer who looked like he had the cares of the world on his shoulders. The sergeant threw him a salute but the officer did not seem to notice and walked past both of us, lost in his thoughts.

"That is Lieutenant Sanson," said the sergeant, as though the name should mean something to me. When I did not respond he added, "He is the son of Sanson the Great."

"Who is Sanson the Great?" I asked.

The sergeant seemed offended by my ignorance. "Most British people I show around have heard of Sanson the Great."

"Well, I haven't. Who is he?" I asked again.

"He was the royal executioner. His father and grandfather had been executioners before him. When the revolution happened he became the revolutionary executioner in Paris. He ended up executing his old employer, the king."

"Well, his son does not seem very happy about it."

"Ah, that is a sad story," said the sergeant. "Lieutenant Henri Sanson is the great Sanson's eldest son and his father wanted him to be his successor. But Henri did not want to go into the family business and so the younger son, Gaston, started to train with his father instead. But back in 'ninety-two the pair of them were executing some people, including an old woman who cursed the son. When the son held up the old woman's head to show it to the people he slipped on some blood and fell off the scaffold and was killed."

I could not help laughing at the irony of it. "You mean the old woman's curse killed him? I don't believe it."

"It is true, I was there. The old man, who 'ad spent his life killing people, was distraught. Henri then 'ad to become an executioner, the one thing he did not want to do. Since then he has been tormented by memories of everyone he has killed."

"How did the terror end?" I asked.

"The fear of being accused brought many people together and eventually a group working with some soldiers arrested Robespierre and his Committee for Public Safety. Robespierre tried to shoot himself at the end but the stupid fool missed and managed to shoot off half his jaw instead. They were all executed the next day. I was there for that too. We had to tie Robespierre's jaw on to his head with a cloth before we could execute him. He just seemed confused, as though he did not know what was going on. Most of those men who had ordered the death of hundreds went to their death shouting and pleading for mercy. Only the one called Saint Just, one of the most ruthless killers, showed any courage at the end."

We had now reached the open shed at the end of the yard. There was a tarpaulin, which the sergeant pulled pack to reveal what appeared to be a pile of lumber.

"What is this?" I asked.

"Can't you guess?" said the sergeant. "Here, let me give you another clue." He pulled off another cloth to reveal a large, angled blade. It was a dismantled guillotine. "This is the one that was used during the terror. That steel has taken hundreds of lives." He pointed to a wide board that had some straps on it. "That is the board we strapped people to; it stopped them struggling as we lowered them under what they used to call the National Razor. Often people started to panic when they saw the basket waiting to catch their head."

I shuddered at the thought. "I suppose at least the death was quick."

"Compared to hanging, yes. But you had to be careful as the heads would live for a few seconds after death. I have been bitten a few times picking heads out of the basket. If you called their name they would look at you for a few seconds before their eyes glazed over."

"Good God, so when you held up their heads to the crowd, their last glimpse in life was the crowd cheering their death?"

"I suppose it was, yes, if I was quick holding the head up."

We fell silent for a moment as I reflected on this horror, but the sergeant seemed unconcerned as he covered up the blade and dragged the tarpaulin back over the wood.

"Don't any of those deaths keep you awake at night?" I asked.

"There was one," he admitted. "It was a young girl; she was only fifteen, beautiful with blond hair. She had been sentenced to death with her parents and they all arrived together in the cart. I had to decide whether to give her a few minutes of extra life, but let her watch her parents die, or kill her first. I decided it would be a kindness to take her first. The mother was hysterical but we prised them apart. I can still see that young, tear-stained face. The poor girl was shaking with fear. I told her to shut her eyes and count slowly to one 'undred and it would soon be finished. She did what I told her and we got her on the guillotine quickly to get it over with. She had been counting aloud and I remember she had reached thirty-three when the blade dropped. When I picked up her head her eyes were still tightly shut and her lips were still moving slightly as though she was still counting. I often see that face in my dreams." His eyes were fixed on the door we were now walking back towards the cells and for the first time I saw him show some emotion. "I dream of her voice too, counting, but I always wake up as she gets to thirty-three. That is the only ghost that haunts me, but I know that it will follow me to the end of my days."

"I had no idea they killed children as well."

"They didn't normally. If the parents were killed then the children went to relatives or orphanages. If a woman was pregnant, she was held in prison until she gave birth and then she was executed, sometimes the same day. The baby would then go to family or an orphanage. After that girl was killed I asked around a bit because it was playing on my mind. The family were accused of being counter-revolutionaries, but that meant nothing. I spoke to a neighbour and she told me that the parents had turned down a request to give their daughter as a mistress to some revolutionary official. They should have run then but they didn't. The official had the whole family arrested and killed out of spite." He shook his head. "That was how it was then, people drunk with the power of life and death over others."

"Is that official still alive?" I asked as we started to climb back up the stairs.

The sergeant grinned. "No, that was one execution I made sure I was there for. I made certain he was last out of the cart too, so he could see the others die before his turn. He was kicking and screaming in terror right up to the end."

We had now returned to the corridor. "You had better get your friend now. I showed him the guillotine last night and made him touch the blade. I told him that anyone who touches the blade will feel the ghosts of the people it took. When I came in this morning there he was crying like a baby, but many do that when they know what the cells were used for. It's the walls, you'll see." He unlocked Berkeley's cell door and stomped away to another part of the prison.

[**Editor's note:** Shocking as the preceding paragraphs are, they are verified by contemporary facts. I will mention just one example here. There are several first-hand accounts of the death of Charlotte Corday, who was executed for murdering the revolutionary leader Marat in his bath. Her head was picked up immediately after being severed by a man named Legros, who then slapped her cheek. Several witnesses report an expression of "unequivocal indignation" crossing her face. The executioner, Sanson the Great, while happy to kill Corday was appalled at the unprofessional behaviour of Legros and had it made clear that Legros was not one of his assistants but a carpenter hired to make repairs to the guillotine. For poor Charlotte Corday the indignities were not over as the Revolutionary Council ordered a post-mortem to see if this unmarried woman was a virgin because they could not believe a woman would commit such an act of murder without a male lover putting her up to it. To their dismay she was found *virgo intacta*, i.e. a virgin, showing that women had also been encouraged to rise up against authority by revolutionary principles.]

I pushed the door open and Berkeley looked up at me, his bottom lip trembling.

"Get me out of here, Flashman, please," Berkeley whispered. I cannot look at those walls any more."

I stepped into the cell and looked at the walls. They had graffiti scratched into every stone surface. I had not looked at them closely when I was in the cell before, but I looked now. The walls were covered with names and initials and a few dates. Some deeply carved names had not been completed before the carver was dragged off to their death. Evidently many of the occupants had felt the need to leave a permanent reminder of their existence before that existence ceased. I was surrounded by primitive memorials carved by those who knew they were about to die. I now understood what the sergeant meant about the walls talking. Having just listened to his tales of the terror, I felt a chill in the room too and had no wish to linger. I helped Berkeley to his feet and guided him out of the chamber..

He was quiet all the way down to the carriage, but when we stepped out into the sunshine he suddenly stopped and gripped my arm. "God knows what the future holds, Flashman, but I want my daughters to be happy. If you make Louisa happy, I will not stand in your way." We climbed up into the carriage and he continued, "You won't get the title of course, that will go to my nephew, but Louisa will probably inherit the estate. Sarah will marry into money, she is a very calculating girl that one, but Louisa seems to have set her heart on you." He reached over and patted me on the knee. "You will be your brother's neighbour, and Flashmans will own half the county." He even laughed at the thought.

I began to wonder if the spirit of some executed French aristocrat had possessed him during that night in prison. However it had happened, this complete personality change seemed the best one hundred guineas of someone else's money I had ever spent. Suddenly the day was brightening up again. I had started it with Louisa in my bed and now I was looking at wealth and happiness for the rest of my days. We rode back to the hotel, and while Berkeley still looked shaken, my heart was singing. I had far less idea of the fate that was about to befall me than that poor girl counting to a hundred with her eyes tight shut.

I knew something was wrong as soon as I stepped into the hotel. Around a dozen people were in the entrance lobby, and they all stopped their conversations to look at us. At first I thought they were looking at Berkeley, who was still ashen-faced, but then I realised that it was me they were staring at. Some, particularly a handful from the party last night, half-smiled sympathetically, but others were looking at me in a decidedly hostile way.

"Your daughters are in the green drawing room, sir." A footman had come up to Berkeley and he guided the pale faced lord towards a door on the far side of the room. With a growing feeling of trepidation, I followed.

Sarah and Louisa were sitting together on a settee on the far side of the room. The only other occupant of the room was Mrs Fairfax, the chaperone, who seemed to inflate with outrage at the sight of me. Sarah had her arm around Louisa and they were both crying. Louisa's shoulders were shaking with sobs and I felt a sharp stab of guilt. Sarah dabbed at her eyes with her handkerchief and gave me what appeared to be a look of triumph as I entered the room with her father. In Sarah's lap was a black object that I recognised as my missing shoe from the pair I had worn last night; it must have been found in Sarah's room after all.

Berkeley saw his daughters crying and assumed that their grief was over his imprisonment. "It is all right, girls, I am back," he called. "There is no need to cry. Thomas here got me out of prison without any difficulty."

"How could you, Thomas?" cried Louisa as she looked up and saw me. "Wasn't one sister enough for you?"

Berkeley looked confused. "What, did you not want him to get me released?" he asked. Then, still looking puzzled, he added, "One sister?"

In the few moments I had been in the room I could see no way that this encounter could end positively for me and I began to edge back towards the door. I had a nasty feeling that Berkeley's benign personality change would only survive a few more seconds.

Sarah raised her arm and pointed at me with the portent of a Roman emperor giving the thumbs down to a gladiator and intoned, "Thomas got me drunk last night, raped me and then he seduced Louisa, all in the same night."

Both male jaws in the room dropped in outrage. I was expecting an ugly scene but this was ridiculous. "Rape!" I exploded angrily. "There are twenty witnesses in this hotel who will testify that you were all over me last night, dangling your tits in my face. As for seducing your sister, we both know that I found her naked in my damned bed."

I suddenly realised now what that little alarm bell had been when Louisa had told me she had got the maid drunk. Sarah had known the maid would be drunk, which meant she must have known of her sister's plan to wait for me in my bed. This explained why she was so keen to go to her room rather than mine.

"You knew that," I said, pointing an accusing finger back at Sarah, "which was why you were all over me the second Louisa was out of sight."

"You... you villain," gasped Berkeley hoarsely. The colour was returning to his face and he seemed to be struggling for breath. "You dare to sully my girls and then accuse them of playing some part in your foul designs." His voice started to rise as he got more into his usual stride. "I will ruin you. I will have you hunted down like the dog you are and whipped through the streets. I will put a price on your head big enough to get every cut-throat in London looking for you."

Berkeley was not the only one to get angry, as I started to realise that what I had thought were spontaneous acts of lust or love were in fact carefully planned by both of the sisters. It was as though I were an unwitting prize in a competition between them.

"Go to hell," I snarled at him. I turned to the girls and added, "I don't know what game you two were playing, but you both knew more about what was going on last night than I did. Now the pair of you have the nerve to sit there and accuse me of rape. Well, you can go to hell too."

With that I turned on my heel and tried to storm out. I yanked the door back to walk with as much dignity as I could muster from the room. Unfortunately that plan foundered immediately as I found my way impeded by about a dozen people who had all crowded up against the door to eavesdrop on the encounter. "Get out of the damn way," I shouted as I tried to push through. They sprang back like startled hares, trying to pretend they had not been near the door at all, but the delay gave Berkeley time to recover his wits. He started to move towards me, his face now puce with rage.

"You are a dead man, Flashman," he was roaring. "I will have you hunted down and killed. There is no place you can hide."

I was heading back out of the hotel but now devilment took me and I paused and turned around. "I suppose," I said in a voice of polite enquiry, "that this means that your offer just half an hour ago of your daughter's hand in marriage and inheritance of your estate is withdrawn?" Some in the eavesdropping crowd smiled at my effrontery. Berkeley was not a popular man and several had been at the party last night and had seen for themselves how ridiculous the rape claim was. I was determined to leave the hotel with my head held high. I paused, as though considering the matter, before I added. "I must speak to my lawyer. I might have a breach of promise claim there."

I am not sure what you call the shade that is darker than puce but Berkeley's face went that colour on hearing my final remark. He gaped like a fish, his knees started to sag and he would have fallen if others had not rushed forward to hold him up. I did not stay around but walked out of the doors and into the waiting carriage, outwardly calm but with my mind in a whirl.

Chapter 5

I climbed back in the waiting carriage and ordered it to the British embassy. Despite my casual air when leaving the hotel, my emotions were struggling to keep up with the pace of events. Just twenty-four hours ago I had been tooling aimlessly around the palace gardens. Since then Berkeley had been arrested and I had visited the British embassy twice to secure his release, been to the ball at the Austrian embassy, met the first consul, bedded both Berkeley sisters, seen first-hand the horrors of the revolution, released Berkeley, been promised happiness and a fortune, lost happiness and a fortune, been threatened with death and disgrace... Oh, and I had also got myself embroiled back in Government business too. I was still pondering the peccadilloes of life when the carriage came to a stop and I realised that we had arrived at the only building in Paris with the British flag flying above it.

Wickham must have been watching for me for he was out of the door almost before we had come to stop.

"What ho, Flashman!" he called as he swung himself up into the carriage. He called out an address to the driver and settled into the seat beside me. He looked full of beans and patted me on the knee in greeting. "I trust you are in fine fettle this morning. You seemed to be enjoying yourself with Louisa Berkeley last night. I take it she is the object of your desires?"

"Things have become a little complicated on the Berkeley front," I replied. But I did not want to talk about it just yet; the wound was still too raw. Wickham's ear for gossip meant that he would doubtless hear the news from other guests of the hotel before the day was out anyway. To change the subject I asked, "Who is this French general we are meeting?"

"Ah, his name is de Boigne, Benoit de Boigne. Have you heard of him?"

"No, is he a secret counter-revolutionary or someone Bonaparte has overlooked for command? Why is he talking to us?" Then another thought struck me. "Shouldn't we be doing this in a more clandestine way? I know we are at peace, but surely you are being followed?"

Wickham laughed. "Of course I am being followed. Fouché, the head of their secret police, has a whole team tracking my every move. But there is no need to worry. De Boigne is in favour with Bonaparte.

What we are going to talk about will be of little interest to the first consul, at least for the moment."

"So he is an experienced commander then?" I asked.

"Gosh, yes. He has built up and commanded armies of a hundred thousand men, won countless battles and made his master ruler of the region."

"A hundred thousand men," I repeated, astonished. "That is more than twice the size of the army that Bonaparte took to conquer Egypt. Why haven't I heard of him?"

"Because he did all of this in India, in Mahratta country, in wars between Indian princes. Our papers usually just report on events that the British are involved in, but make no mistake, he is a very capable commander. When the British arrived in India and started beating the native rulers with European tactics, many of the native princes quickly employed European mercenaries to train their armies in these new types of warfare. De Boigne was one of those mercenaries. He worked his way up until he commanded the army of one of the leading princes and then he steadily beat the armies of all his rivals. Along the way he amassed a big personal fortune and married a beautiful Indian wife in a Muslim ceremony."

"So why did he leave?"

"I am not sure; that is one of the things to find out. Initially he went to England with his wife, two children and Indian servants and bought an estate in Dorset. I think his wife was struggling to settle in England and so he left them there while he travelled to London. It seems that there he married again, possibly without mentioning the existence of his first wife, or perhaps he thought that a Muslim ceremony did not count in England."

I laughed. "Let me guess, the new wife is much younger and prettier than his Indian wife and claims to have married him for his personality and not the vast fortune?"

"That would be about the size of it. Adele, his new French wife, was sixteen when they met; he was forty-seven. She was a French émigré living in London, from a penniless but noble family who doubtless pushed her into the match." Wickham pulled out from his pocket a paper on which he had written some notes on de Boigne. "To be fair de Boigne is still providing generous support to his first family but his second marriage has not been a success. It seems that as well as being vague about his marital history he also gave the impression that he was of noble birth. He was born Benoit Leborgne and he was the son of a fur merchant. When his wife and in-laws found out they turned against him, while still taking him for as much money as they could. The age difference and rampant snobbery soon outweighed any affection there might have been and so he left England and came to France to escape them."

"How did he make his money? Was it loot from battles?" I asked.

"Partly. But the Indian princes pay well for European expertise and de Boigne, being a merchant's son, also did some trading on the side. He traded gems, gold, silver, silks and spices and made a fortune. Lots of Europeans get rich in India, which is why people go. If you are lucky, you can live like a king and come back with a hatful of jewels."

That got me thinking about my own prospects. My rental income was just about enough to live on but there were no government posts in prospect that would increase my wealth. On the contrary, I now had Berkeley's thugs to worry about as well. He would not want any public scandal involving his daughters, so there was no chance of a rape charge in the courts. On the other hand I should not have provoked him as he was rich and had influence. He could easily arrange for someone to disappear and smooth over any awkward questions from the authorities. He was now sure to hire some heavies to at least give me a beating and might even order me killed. I would have to be bloody careful when I went to London; I would not be the first person to be dropped, dead, in a weighted sack off a Thames bridge, never to be seen again. I needed to keep a low profile for a while, but going to India seemed extreme. I had no military experience to sell or skills in trade.

The carriage came to a halt in front of an expensive townhouse and we got down.

"You never did tell me what he wanted to talk to us about," I reminded Wickham.

"He was not entirely clear on that with me. He just said it was about India and would be to our mutual interest and could save lots of British lives." Wickham reached up to yank on the bell pull. "We will soon find out."

The door was opened by an Indian servant who despite the warm day was wearing an overcoat. "You are Wickham sahib?" he asked in halting English.

"Yes, and this is Mr Flashman, my colleague. Do you speak French?"

"I speak good French," said the Indian more confidently in that language. "Please follow me and I will take you to the general."

He showed us across a sumptuously decorated hall that had a tiger-skin rug and a huge range of what I took to be Oriental weaponry decorating the walls. Then doors were opened into a very comfortable study and a tall, thin, grey-haired man got up to greet us.

"Monsieur Wickham and Monsieur Flashman, General," announced the servant.

"Thank you, Kapil. Welcome, gentleman, welcome," said de Boigne in perfect English. "Please sit down," he said, gesturing to some comfortable chairs around a table. His back was ramrod straight and I could understand how his newest in-laws had thought he was from the aristocracy; he exuded a relaxed air of authority.

"It is a pleasure to meet you," said Wickham. "I have to say that your invitation was quite intriguing. You realise that I am likely to have been followed here by Fouché's agents. I trust our meeting does not compromise you in any way?"

"Fouché and his spies are amateurs in intrigue compared to the people I am used to," said de Boigne, smiling. "In any event, this matter is far too important to worry about that."

At this point, an elegantly dressed woman wearing a scarlet and gold sari entered the room carrying a tray with a teapot, cups and saucers and a plate of strange triangular-shaped pastries.

"Ah, tea," said de Boigne. "The pastries are an Indian dish called samosas; they are quite heavily spiced."

Tea was poured and I nibbled on one of the little triangular pastries. They were quite crunchy and initially all I could taste was vegetables but then a spiced heat built in my mouth.

"What took you to India?" I asked to make conversation.

"Well, I did not want to be a fur merchant like my father and so I joined the army when I was a young man, fighting for the French king in those days. I learned English then as there were regiments of Irish Catholics in the French army, and then I became a mercenary. First I fought in the Russian army of Catherine the Great against the Turks, but I was captured and was briefly a slave of the Turks. I was freed with the help of a British official, and hearing stories of the British in India, I decided to try my hand there. I was in the British East India Company Army for four years, but I was ambitious and so I decided to try my hand in the Mahratta states. Lots of British officers and other Europeans were doing the same thing and many were getting rich. The life was good: tiger hunting on elephants, servants to look after you and beautiful women – do you know that they even have temples dedicated to the art of making love?"

Well, I was not sure believed that last bit but India was sounding more attractive.

"And now you might fight again for the French?" enquired Wickham.

"Bonaparte has offered me the chance to be a colonel in his army, but I do not relish taking orders from some young pup general in his thirties who has been promoted more through luck than skill. I think it is retirement for me so that I can enjoy my wealth."

"Yet you are willing to help France's enemy? You must know that war will break out between Britain and France again soon."

"I am glad you are talking frankly," said de Boigne. "Let me return the compliment. What I want to talk to you about are things happening in India that have little to do with France. We all know that your British governor general is making threats towards the Mahratta states in India on the pretence of stopping French influence. We also know that France has very little influence in India. There are a few French officers there – I should know, I appointed most of them. But the majority are there to make money for themselves rather than as agents of France. Some are even royalists."

"We found some French officers and soldiers in the southern Indian state of Mysore when we captured that territory," said Wickham. "Who is to say that there are not more French troops in other states?"

"I am," said de Boigne flatly. "You know my history and I am telling you that there are no French troops stationed with the Mahrattas in India. I admit the first consul would love to extend his empire to India. That was partly what the Egyptian expedition was about, to open a new route to India. But we all know that it ended in failure. He may look at India again in the future but there are no French troops there now."

"Is that what this meeting is about?" asked Wickham. "To reassure us that there are no French troops in the Mahratta states? If so, I will be equally honest: I don't think this reassurance will stop the governor general."

"No, the meeting is about these," said de Boigne, taking a small, black velvet bag from his pocket and emptying the contents onto the table. Two black stone-like items fell out but they were lighter than stones. I reached forward to pick one up. I turned it over in my fingers and then, realising what it was, I dropped it back on the table with disgust.

"They are mummified snake or lizard heads," I said.

"Small cobra heads, to be precise," said de Boigne. "They are the calling card of a skilful assassin who calls himself The Cobra. One serpent was sacrificed for an unsuccessful attempt on my life when I was trying to leave India and one was sacrificed for a successful attempt on the life of my former master."

"What does that mean?" asked Wickham.

"I discovered whom The Cobra was working for when he tried to kill me," replied de Boigne. "It was the Mahratta Prince Dowlat Rao Scindia, who had succeeded to the throne of my former master Mahadji Scindia. I left Dowlat Rao's service because of his murders and intrigues, and when he wished me well, I half-expected him to make sure I did not work for someone else. I was staying in a guest-house halfway to Madras when one of my officers helped himself to a small jug of arrack that had been placed in my room."

"What is arrack?" I asked.

"It is the local strong spirit," de Boigne replied before continuing. "The poor man fell, gasping for breath. He died a few minutes later and we found one of those heads at the bottom of the jug." De Boigne reached forward and picked up one of the heads and smelt it. "It was this one; it still smells of the spirit.

"As soon as I saw this head I remembered where I had seen one before and only then did I realise just how treacherous Dowlat Rao could be. He was already Mahadji's heir but evidently he did not want to wait any longer to take power. The snake's head had been found next to Mahadji's body; he had been poisoned too. It is ironic really as he was already quite ill and would probably have died anyway. Only a handful of my officers know about the assassination of Mahadji. We put the word out that he died of his illness so that the killer did not get the credit for his dark deed."

"So what does this have to do with us?" asked Wickham.

"Revenge. I want to help you destroy Dowlat Rao and I want to do it in a way that will avoid the British battling the army that I spent years creating. Mahadji was a greatly loved prince while Dowlat Rao rules through fear and intimidation. It will only take a spark to turn his people and his allies against him."

He reached into a drawer and took out some letters and a ring. "What I have for you is a spark you can use. I am known in India as a loyal and trusted supporter of Mahadji. Here is an affidavit from me confirming my opinion that Dowlat Rao arranged the death of Mahadji. I am also giving you a ring I wore while in India that those close to me will remember, to prove the authenticity of the letter. I hear that the raja of Berar has joined forces with Dowlat Rao. If you can get the letter to him then he will make sure the contents reach those that count. He will see the opportunity to depose Dowlat Rao and lead the Mahratta confederation himself."

"How will that help the British?" Wickham asked. "We are just replacing one ruler with another."

"Berar has less influence with the other states and Scindia's forces will be trying to agree on a new leader. They will be less aligned and more amenable to negotiate. But warn your British friends not to push them too far or that will bring them back together. You must understand that the army I built is strong. With good leadership it could sweep away the British East India Company forces. They have ten times the men, the guns and the cavalry than the Company can put in the field and they can match European weaponry and tactics."

"You think the Mahratta forces can beat the British then?" I asked.

De Boigne smiled. "I know they can. I hear that the governor general has appointed his younger brother to command the Company forces. I know this young Arthur Wesley was involved in the capture of Mysore, but from what I heard the only fighting he personally commanded was a disastrous night action. He has no significant experience of battles or fighting in India. My army would take him apart."

Wickham smiled back. "I understand that Lord Mornington, the governor general, has changed the family name to Wellesley now as it sounds more refined. So our young general is called Arthur Wellesley. He has proved a good governor of Mysore since we captured it."

"Pah," said de Boigne dismissively. "He should worry about his fighting abilities not his name, and being a governor of a captured state is a lot different to being a general and doing the capturing."

"Didn't you change your name to sound more refined too?" I asked mischievously.

De Boigne laughed. "Yes, I did, young man, and little good it did me. The Indians did not understand the significance of the change, and back in Europe it attracted the wrong sort of people."

I thought he was referring to his new in-laws and so let the matter drop.

"So," said de Boigne, becoming serious again, "will you take my message to India? Your governor will know people who can reach the raja of Berar. I just need someone who can put the letter safely in your governor's hands." He looked pointedly at me and added, "I imagine that the courier will be well rewarded for his work and India offers many rewards of its own."

"We will certainly take it," said Wickham. "But Mr Flashman has agreed just to take the letter to London. There another courier will be found to take it on to India."

"Actually," I said, "I have a mind to take it to India myself. I imagine that it will have more impact with the governor general if I can talk first-hand about what was said in this meeting."

"It would. But are you sure, Flashman?" asked Wickham. "It is a four-month sail there and another four months back. You would be away for nearly a year. What about courting the lovely Louisa?"

"Duty first, old boy," I said, trying to sound like I meant it.

But Wickham just looked at me with an arched eyebrow, doubtless remembering that the last time he had sent me abroad I had been hiding in a Turkish-themed brothel.

"Oh, all right," I conceded. "The Berkeley situation has got a bit complicated. It would be best for me to be out of the country for a while."

I had made up my mind during the earlier conversation. A short trip to India would give everyone a chance to calm down, and if Berkeley sent heavies or killers to hunt for me around London, well, he would be wasting his money because I would be on the other side of the world. The deciding factor was that I would not be required to deliver the letter to this Berar chap in what sounded like rebel territory. All I had to do was turn up and deliver my packet and then I could explore the delights of the safer parts of India for a few months before catching the next fleet home. I had heard stories of elephants, tigers, jungles and exotic palaces; this would be a great opportunity to see them. De Boigne had mentioned that there were beautiful women and temples to the art of lovemaking to explore too, which was the icing on the cake. I had visions of beautiful priestesses doing the dance of the seven veils while weaving through the congregation and wondered idly why the religious types in Britain thought it was necessary to send missionaries to India. Indians should be encouraged to send missionaries to us. The Church of England would not stand a chance with that kind of competition.

Map of India 1802

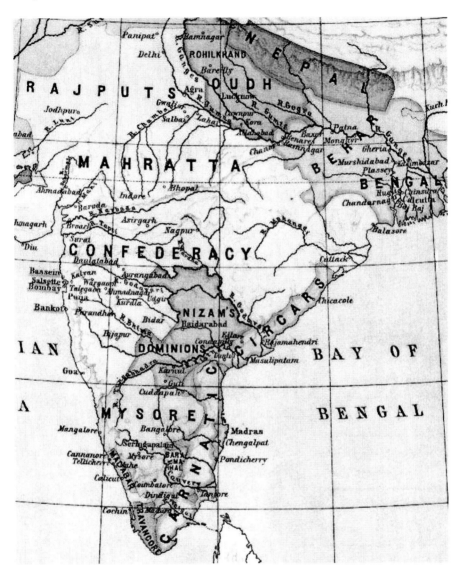

It was hard to distinguish between the cloud on the horizon and the hazy blur of land underneath it, but the passengers on the East India Company ship crowded up on deck and forward to the rail as soon as word spread that land had been sighted. I had been on deck when the call came from the masthead and had already studied the strip through a telescope borrowed from an officer. At this distance little could be seen and so instead I watched the passengers. One of them was a thief, but during the time of the voyage I had not been able to discover who it was.

Over four months had passed since that meeting with de Boigne. I had returned swiftly from Paris to London and briefed Castlereagh on what was discussed. What had shocked me was the level of mistrust between the East India Company and the government. Castlereagh was convinced that the Company even had spies in his own office and warned me to keep the letter secret. The Company was determined to do all it could to stop the governor general's plans to expand British influence and all agreed that the Wellesley brothers could not attack if the Mahratta stayed united. The Company would therefore try to stop anything with the potential of dividing them reaching the shores of the continent. The problem for me was that the only way to reach India was on an East India Company ship. They were called indiamen and they sailed in fleets for protection, with one fleet just about to depart.

I sent a cab to get the possessions I needed from my rooms and had them delivered to the Board of Trade offices. The driver reported seeing a group of heavies watching the building at either end of the street. Berkeley was not bluffing with his threats and so my final act before leaving was to send a letter to an American with the address of a Paris hotel that he might be interested in. My passage on one of the ships in the fleet was arranged by Castlereagh and within a week of arriving back in Britain I was on an indiaman as it sailed down the Thames, bound for the Orient.

Everything had changed three weeks into the voyage: the letter given to me by de Boigne was stolen from underneath my locked trunk. The captain had asked all passengers to hand over any valuables for him to keep in his strongbox. I had given him some gold and some other letters to look after but I did not trust him with de Boigne's message. He kept pressing me for more as though he knew I had other things of value with me, and even mentioned documents specifically.

"The men smell valuables, sir, be they gold, jewels or even documents," he told me one morning. "They are good men, sir, but I don't want temptation put in their path. Even if they cannot read, sir, they knows that some letters will have value, and so I urge you to put anything you hold dear in my strongbox. They will be as safe as the ship in there."

I was all too aware of the warnings I had been given in London about not letting the East India Company know what de Boigne had provided. As the Company owned the ship and the captain was their employee, there was no guarantee that either he or his clerk would not open the letter and copy its contents or steal it. I had to keep it to myself. I couldn't keep the letter on me: in the tropics at sea we only wore shirts and breeches, no jackets. Keeping it in the large sea chest was too obvious; it would be the first place a thief would look. The mattress must have been used to hide things by a previous passenger as there was a strip of newer stitching along one of the seams and so evidently that was also a common hiding place. The trunk was held in place by large nails banged into the deck to stop the heavy casket moving in a rough sea and so I hauled up one end of it and slid the letter underneath. I then used a brass candlestick to bend a couple of the nails to make it hard to lift up again.

I thought I had been pretty clever until I entered my cabin on the third week of the voyage to discover it had been expertly searched. The trunk was locked as normal but when I opened the big chest I could see that things were not exactly as I had left them. To check whether someone had searched my possessions, I always left the buttons of a folded jacket exactly aligned with the buckles for some shoes. Now the buckles were a couple of inches out of alignment. There were other signs too: the layers of clothes underneath were if anything slightly neater than I had left them, and later I noticed that the newer stitching on the mattress and been unpicked and replaced. But of course the first things I looked at when I realised someone had been in my room were the nails in the floor. They were still bent over the foot of the trunk but they also looked slightly different. Without a hammer it took me nearly an hour to get the heavy nails bent back so that I could lift the trunk. I knew what I would find before I hauled the end of it up. The letter was gone.

I spent nearly three months trying to get it back. I learnt how to pick the cabin door locks by practising on my own door from the inside. Then, chatting to the passengers, I tried to draw up a list of likely suspects. Chief among these was the captain himself, and while I did manage to get into his cabin while he was holding a Sunday church service on deck, I found nothing apart from the locked strong box, which easily defied my new lock-picking skills. The captain was a dark, taciturn fellow who made no effort to get on well with his passengers. In fact the weekly church service was the only time you could guarantee he would be out of his cabin. The other officers were friendly, and when they discovered that I had been with Cochrane when he took the *Gamo* the previous year I was given a standing invitation to the wardroom, which was a more relaxing place than the saloon used by the other passengers.

One officer who went out of his way to be friendly was Lieutenant Harvey, the third officer. He was new in the ship too and confided that the other officers were wary of him until he had proved himself. We spent a lot of time together, me relating my adventures with Cochrane and him talking about his voyages in other indiamen. Eventually I felt I could trust him and confided that my cabin had been searched and that an important document had been stolen. He was all interest of course, and particularly keen to know why the document was important, but I was a bit cagey there. He offered to help search some of the officers' cabins as he knew when they would be on duty. Between us over the second half of the voyage we must have discreetly searched most of the ship, but not a trace of the letter was found. I still had de Boigne's ring, which I wore on my finger, and I told nobody about that. I cursed myself for not keeping the letter on my person now. I had thought that four months of sweat stains and creasing would make it barely presentable to an Indian raja, but a stained and creased document was better than none at all.

Before I talk about arriving in India, I should mention briefly the near-four-month trip in an indiaman ship. There was a mixed group of passengers: a returning Company colonel and his wife; several single ladies looking for wealthy husbands in India – the colonel's wife guarded them like a mother hen; some scientific fellow; and a couple of merchants. I recall one evening when the scientist had regaled us with stories of the mosquito and how it bit you in the night and sucked up your blood through its proboscis or nose. In truth he was quite an interesting chap with facts about cobras and how tigers do not climb trees, and later he brought out a picture book from his cabin. This was passed around until suddenly there was a scream and one of the young ladies fainted to the ground. When she came round she gasped that she had no idea mosquitoes were so big. Puzzled, we looked at the picture book and found she had been looking at a picture of an elephant!

The ladies were very mercenary in discussing their marital value; it was clear that love would play very little part in their liaisons. I recall the colonel's wife insisting that in the army they should settle for nothing less than a major in rank, and then only from one of the better regiments. The sailors looked on in wry amusement and I asked one of them if de Boigne's claim of temples to lovemaking were true. This they confirmed with relish, describing temples with wall paintings and carvings that would make eyes and other organs bulge.

People have often asked me how I coped with the heat in India but this was something that you got used to on the journey so that by the time you arrived it was barely noticeable. As we travelled down the coast of Africa it got hotter and hotter, until we were becalmed for a week in the Doldrums. This area of sea is notorious for its sudden lack of wind and merciless heat. We were there for a week and it was like living in a wooden furnace without any cooling breeze. I can well understand how people have gone mad and blown their brains out when forced to stay there longer. One of the frustrations is that you do not know when the wind will come back. A couple of people jumped in the sea to cool off, but no sooner had they done so than two large, evil grey shapes appeared and started to close in. The swimmers came back up the sides of the ship almost as fast as they had flown down them. When the ship had been moving, some of the passengers and crew had tried spearing porpoises and dolphins as they had raced alongside the bow of the ship, but I had not joined in. They seemed such happy creatures it was a shame to try to kill them. But I had no such qualms when it came to shooting at the sharks that calmly circled the ship in the Doldrums, as though they were daring another person to jump. Between us we must have fired a barrel of powder and ball at them with muskets, but either their skin was armoured or the water slowed down the shot. Apart from a nicked dorsal fin, they seemed to take no harm at all.

The weather got cooler around the Cape of Good Hope and then the heat built slowly again as we approached India. The captain was keen to get to Madras by September to miss the worst of the monsoon season. After nearly four months at sea any land would have been a welcome sight, but the Coramandel coast just south of Madras was particularly beautiful. The early monsoon rains had made the vegetation lush and green. At first it was just a green smudge, but then as we got closer we could see a long, green coast with coconut palms and a range of low mountains behind. Later we saw the buildings of Madras with St Thomas's Mount in the background and we knew we had finally arrived. Catamarans and massuli boats and other native craft swarmed out around the ship as we dropped anchor out in the bay.

Chapter 7

Everyone was keen to get ashore and there was a queue at the captain's cabin while we retrieved our valuables. With trunks and sea chests to follow, the passengers dressed to make a good first impression on the local populace and swarmed over the side to the waiting native craft. I carried just some spare clothes and my razor with my letters of introduction and money. I was intrigued by the narrow canoe craft with a V-shaped mast arrangement that seemed to move with particular dexterity over the waves. I found one alongside the ship and offered the crew a silver coin to take me ashore. They were delighted, as I subsequently discovered I had massively overpaid for the trip, but to me it was worth every penny. A skilled man makes what he is doing seem easy and the two lads with that canoe made the trip ashore look effortless as they shook out their sail and with their flimsy outrigger poles we sped towards the shore. We moved with exhilarating speed over the surf and within minutes we were beached on the sand. I reached over the side and picked up a handful of Indian sand from the warm sea and had a brief moment of triumph: I had arrived in India. But before I could enjoy the experience further the canoe was surrounded by a crowd of shouting locals.

Even before I was out of the boat I was the subject of an argument. Around twenty people seemed to be haggling about me rather than with me, although a few broke off to brandish papers in my direction. A wily cove climbed into the boat over the bow and, patting the two oarsmen on the shoulder as he passed them, he sat down next to the rear-most oarsman as though part of the crew.

"They are arguing over the right to be your dubash, sahib," he called over the din. "You look a rich man and they will rob you blind before you learn the price of things in India. If you tell them you already have a dubash, I will meet you with a palanquin at the top of the beach."

"And you won't rob me blind, I suppose?" I asked with a grin.

"No, sahib, I want to serve you for long time, not just the first days. I show you round India, you buy bungalow, I be your housekeeper." He grinned back. "I make many more rupees from you than them if I serve you long time."

Well, you had to laugh at his audacity, and that was how I first met Runjeet, my dubash, factotum, butler, housekeeper and local guide. India would not have been the same without him, and although he claimed he worked for me, there were times when it felt the other way round.

There was a heck of a row when I got out of the canoe and headed up the beach without hiring the dubash who had won the debate. It served them right for thinking that I would not have a say in whom I hired. But there, where the ground was firmer, was a palanquin with a grinning Runjeet alongside it. A palanquin is a bit like a sedan chair; you could lie in it or sit and bigger ones like this had four bearers, one at each corner. As soon as I was aboard we were off, leaving the crowd behind. I did not really feel comfortable lying down so I sat cross-legged like an Oriental, watching the new sights slide by. The houses on the outskirts of town were mostly of the rundown mud-brick variety, and we soon had a crowd of children and dogs running alongside, shouting for coins. The children were shouting, of course, not the dogs, which reminds me that instead of the variety of dogs we have in England, virtually all the dogs there looked the same, being medium sized and sandy-yellow in colour. We passed various market sellers and a butcher who was hacking with a cleaver at the massive side of an ox. Instead of a sea breeze there were land smells in the wind now; dung featured prominently in the aroma with all the animals about, but I also thought that there was the smell of spice in the air. Certainly Indian settlements had their own distinct smell, which was different to that of a British town. Runjeet ran alongside to assure me that he was having me taken to an excellent hotel that was run by his cousin. As I was to discover, Runjeet had a huge number of cousins, and I should know as I seemed to end up employing most of them.

The hotel turned out to be a small two-storey affair near the fort. It was also reasonably priced, which brings me to a top travel tip for any reader planning to go to India. Always take two purses. In the first put an amount of money appropriate to a man of modest means and keep the rest hidden away. I had mine stashed in hidden pockets sewn into my leather belt. The prices your dubash will charge are directly related to the amount of gold he thinks you have, with the aim of bleeding you dry during the term of his employment.

Runjeet and his cousin now showed me up to my room, which was the best in the place. It had a terrace with an awning to keep off the sun and a view of the sea and the fort. There were half a dozen ships out in the bay and I could tell mine by the flurry of boats still pulling back and forth from it. Fort St George looked impregnable with various triangular buttresses so that it must have been star-shaped from above, and there were various outworks, moats and drawbridges to keep out unwanted visitors.

Having settled in, the hotel served luncheon, or tiffin as they called it, which comprised mulligatawny soup and grilled chicken with rice. As I ate I reflected on what to do next. Now that I was in Madras I could not put off reporting to the governor general and I would have to admit that I had allowed the important despatch I was carrying to be stolen. This seemed a major faux pas for a diplomatic courier and there was the irony that I still had all the less important documents that had been put in the captain's strongbox. I called for a pen and ink and wrote a brief report of the loss of de Boigne's letter to add to the papers I had to present. I knew what these diplomatic types are like, you see: they are paper shufflers at heart and like nothing better than more papers to shuffle. The meeting would not go well, but delaying it would not help, and so after tiffin I dressed in the best clothes I had brought with me and headed to the fort with the documents I did have and de Boigne's ring.

As I stepped outside and approached the fort I could feel the heat of the afternoon reflecting off the stone surfaces. The pavement of the approach road had been in full sun all day and I could even feel it through my boot soles, which explained why most of the natives wore sandals. But despite the temperature being up in the nineties the soldiers of the garrison were dressed and behaved as though they were in Horse Guards on a chilly day in London. Thick woollen coats were buttoned up to the neck, sentries wore their leather stocks to keep their heads erect and belts were pipe-clayed a gleaming white. The officers were all similarly dressed and were stiff with starch and their own importance. Two other passengers from the boat were already waiting to meet officials but my letter of introduction for no lesser person that the governor general meant that I jumped the queue and I was led by a lieutenant to a grand office on the far side of the fort. I handed all my documents to a clerk and then waited in a stifling anteroom for nearly an hour before I was finally shown into the presence.

Richard Wellesley, known as Lord Mornington and governor general of India, sat at a large desk. Sitting at another table nearby was a man who bore a striking similarity to Richard whom I learned from the introductions was his brother Henry.

"Welcome, Mr Flashman," said Mornington. He gestured at the papers in front of him. "I understand from both Castlereagh and Wickham that you are a capable agent and so it is, er, 'unfortunate' that the letter from the de Boigne fellow has gone missing. Unfortunate for us and dangerous for you."

"Dangerous for me?" I asked, feeling slightly alarmed.

"Certainly," replied Mornington. "The only evidence of Scindia's betrayal is the letter and your account as a witness to the meeting with de Boigne. If, as you suspect, the letter is now in the Company's hands then it is either being destroyed or being sent to Scindia himself. When Scindia learns of it from his spies in the Company or from receiving the letter, he will certainly want any other evidence of the meeting destroyed too. That would include you, sir."

"You mean he could be sending bands of snake-decapitating killers after me even as we speak?" I asked. I was trying to keep my voice normal and calm but this was absurd. I had taken this trip to avoid being hunted down in London, and here I was less than a day in India and I might be about to be tracked down by an even more lethal band of killers.

"Oh no," said Henry Wellesley. "They won't be sending assassins after you now." But before I could relax more than a fraction he added, "It will take six, maybe eight weeks to get a message to Scindia and for his response to reach Madras."

"You must be used to this in your line of work, I suppose," added Mornington, giving me a quizzical look, and I remembered that he had just been reading the references on me from Castlereagh and Wickham. I had indeed been pursued by foreign agents in London last year and had escaped their clutches more through panic than cunning. Now it seemed that they expected me to shrug off bands of assassins with the ease of losing a coat.

But then I saw a glimmer of hope. "Wait a moment," I said. "I haven't written an account of the meeting. As far as anyone is concerned I am just a courier; no one else knows I was at the meeting with de Boigne."

"That is probably the only reason you were allowed to live on the indiaman," said Henry Wellesley. "But now we do need you to write a detailed account of the meeting and sign it. I will witness it and my brother will add his seal. We must have an official account of the meeting to give to the raja of Berar. The ring on its own will not serve. Even with your statement he might not believe it, but I suspect that he will start to make enquiries among his people to find out the truth."

They were coolly asking me to write what was effectively my own death warrant. I had been expecting a roasting over losing the de

Boigne letter but this was far worse. I could not flee straight back to Britain as the heavy monsoon rains were coming and no ships would be leaving for at least a month. I was trapped in India and in the not-too-distant future this Scindia fellow would be sending agents to kill me. Obviously I could not show any alarm to the Wellesleys; I had my reputation as a capable agent to consider. In any event it would have made no difference to the situation if I had run around their office screaming like a virgin in a barracks.

At least I had some warning this time and an opportunity to make some preparations. Maybe the lack of imminent danger helped, for I was feeling strangely calm in the circumstances. India was a big country with thousands of Europeans in it and hardly any of them knew me. I had wanted to travel a bit in India, and now I realised that the best way forward was to change my name and still travel. Perhaps up the largely British held coast to Calcutta, although that would take me closer to Mahratta territory. Or I could go across the country to the new British protectorate of Mysore; I may be able to catch a ship home on the west coast. So I agreed to give them the statement and offhandedly said that I would just have to make sure that Scindia did not find me.

"Oh, you should have at least six weeks to enjoy yourself in Madras," said Henry helpfully. "In the meantime we can arrange for some papers in a new name and some funds to help you lie low for a bit before you sail home."

Well, I was ahead of him there. I was not going to wait like a lamb for the slaughter under a false name that Scindia's spies would doubtless discover. I would take the money, though. My mind was busily considering options as we spoke. If there is one thing that focuses the attention it is preserving one's skin.

Chapter 8

I met Henry Wellesley several times during the next two weeks. He was working on his plans and I was working on mine. We had sat together as I wrote the account of the meeting with Benoit de Boigne and he was most interested to hear about life in Paris. I discovered that he and his sister Anne had been captured by the French on a ship in the Bay of Biscay and they had been prisoners in Paris during the 'terror'. At one point they were held in the Conciergerie and Henry talked about the prisoners he saw and mentioned that once he saw a whole family carted off to be killed. I wondered if that was the blond girl that the sergeant had talked about, but I did not ask questions as I was still struggling to get that poor girl out of my thoughts.

Henry arranged for me to receive a letter of introduction from the governor general to the nizam of Hyderabad, a British ally. I had suggested Hyderabad as it was the one place I had no intention of going. The letter introduced my official alias George Thompson as a wool merchant looking for trade opportunities. Henry also gave me fifty guineas in gold, which would enable me to live like a king in India for the time I planned to be here, but annoyingly he also insisted on giving me a draft in George Thompson's name for another twenty as emergency money and to back up my identity. Cashing that would be a risky business.

Meanwhile Runjeet and I were making our own preparations. I had hired a boat and gone back to the ship to recover my other luggage. Runjeet had warned me that there was a thriving extortion racket run by the owners of small boats exploiting newcomers to India, or 'griffins' as we were called then. Essentially they would wait until you had all your goods in the boat and then, just as they were about to run in through the surf, they would announce that the fare had doubled and demand it in advance.

"Threaten to put a ghoolie through the side of their boat," he advised, obviously offended that someone other than him should take money from me.

"What is a ghoolie?" I asked. It turned out that ghoolie is an Indian word for pistol or musket ball.

I chose a boat that was manned by both an Indian and a European, thinking that they might be less likely to try to gull a griffin, but sure enough as we approached the waves the pair of them breached the boat side onto the surf so that it rocked dangerously and demanded a double fare. With Runjeet's warning I had already taken my pistols from trunk and had loaded them ready in my pockets. Without saying a word I simply pulled one out, cocked it and put the muzzle to the side of the boat on the waterline. Rowing to the shore resumed promptly.

In many ways, such as climate, India was as I expected, but in others it was totally different, such as the easy way between Europeans and Indians. Recently I saw my young nephew Harry who has earned fame in India, and from what he says things have changed considerably now. He happily bragged of having to thrash his servants on a daily basis. In my time some beatings did happen but the chief justice at Madras, Sir Henry Gwillam, was doing all he could to ban the practice. When I was in Madras there was a lot of gossip about a Major Cavendish who was known to beat his servants. One had apparently threatened to complain to Sir Henry and the gallant major had arranged to meet him in a small bungalow on the edge of his grounds. Boasting that he had ensured that there would be no witnesses to support a complaint, the major started to set about the servant with a cane. The servant, being bigger and stronger, responded by seizing the cane himself, and as there was no one nearby to come to the major's aid, gave his master a proper thrashing and then disappeared. I saw the major myself and he was still carrying the bruises then.

The difference between India in my time and now is down to women. There were few white women in India when I was there; they were only just starting to arrive. So Europeans would mix with Indian women and then they would start having children with them, and sometimes they would marry them, either in native or Christian ceremonies, and often Europeans would adopt some Indian ways. Why, old Sir David Ochterlony who was our 'resident' or ambassador in Delhi, dressed like an Indian and had thirteen wives who would promenade around the walls of the red fort each evening on the back of their own elephants. Because they were living with each other or in business together, Europeans and Indians understood and respected each other much more than they do today. Now they live in separate communities and an English officer would be shunned socially if he married an Indian woman. These days the British treat the Indians with contempt, and mark my words, sooner or later the Indians will bite back.

Getting back to my time in India, Runjeet was proving to be a very able dubash, introducing me to the ways of the country. I had given him some money to cover ongoing expenses and the cost of the hotel, which was as good as any in town. That is not to say that it was entirely comfortable. We had got used to the heat on the boat but not the mosquitoes. The bed had a mosquito net, but I swiftly discovered that this acted like the doorman at some exclusive dining club. It kept out the riff-raff insects while leaving your body at the mercy of the more experienced bugs that had the foresight to wait for you within its folds. The food left something to be desired too: breakfast was typically green tea and fresh fish while all other meals seemed to comprise a version of mulligatawny soup and grilled chicken and rice.

When I complained at the lack of variety Runjeet suggested that I rent a bungalow and chef; naturally he had a cousin who could serve in this capacity. I dismissed this at first as an absurd extravagance as I was only planning to be in Madras for a few weeks. Then, as I thought about it, I decided that this would add to my cover. It would show that I was planning to return to Madras after my trip to Hyderabad, which may stop people looking for me elsewhere. I was completely sold on the idea a day later when Runjeet showed me a beautiful little bungalow set in its own tropical garden. It was well maintained with a veranda running around all four sides and came furnished. It was owned by another of Runjeet's relatives and had previously been let to a Company captain and his wife, who had provided much of the English furniture. The wife had died in childbirth and the captain now preferred to live in the officers' quarters. As I looked around I regretted that I would not be able to enjoy living there for more than the few weeks that were left before I was due to depart, but Runjeet had me swiftly moved in on the same day.

By that evening I was enjoying a splendid spiced curry in my own dining room and afterwards I strolled through the grounds enjoying a cigar. You could very easily live like a lord in India. The cook was, as Runjeet promised, excellent and I noticed during the meal that I had also acquired a serving boy to bring food to the table. Then when in the garden I noticed that I now had a gardener too. When I asked Runjeet about this he informed me that both were his cousins and came at very favourable rates of pay. He also told me that in addition to these I had employed a syce or groom to look after the stables, even though I did not own a horse at this point, and two cleaners and a cook's assistant would be starting tomorrow. When I calculated the wages and rent of the property from ruppees into guineas it did indeed seem very reasonable and I gave Runjeet some more money for expenses. I discovered later that I was paying around double the local market rate, but to be fair the people Runjeet hired, whether actual cousins or not, did an excellent job.

The next morning, after a breakfast of eggs, bacon and proper toast made with yeast-leavened bread, not the normal flatbreads, I stepped outside to find that overnight I had acquired a fine horse for myself and a smaller pony for the syce and headed into town. For the next few weeks I appeared all over Madras visiting barbers (the hubs of male gossip the world over) barracks, hotels and all manner of other places on the pretext of settling in and telling as many people as I could of my plans to travel to Hyderabad. If Scindia's men did not try to follow me there, it would not be through lack of effort on my part.

Henry Wellesley arranged an invite to the officers' mess of the local Company regiment at the fort one night, which demonstrated the excellent value of a good syce. I had arrived at the officers' quarters at around seven in the evening, just as the drummers were playing 'Roast Beef of Old England' across the barracks to signify that dinner was being served. The officers were gathered on the veranda of their mess enjoying the sea breeze. All were tanned, strong characters, apart from the bruised major, whose forehead and one cheek were still a riot of colour from his beating. He claimed of course that he had fallen off his horse, but his servants had done a fine job of spreading gossip to the servants of half the garrison, many of whom gleefully told their masters. Most present were clearly Europeans; some could have been Anglo-Indians. Given my Spanish blood, I probably could have passed for Anglo-Indian myself.

Madeira wine was passed around and then we were called into the dining room, with various silver trophies down the table and a servant standing behind each chair. Fish and soup courses were served and then they brought in the largest turkey I had ever seen (at least they said it was turkey) and a huge ham to match. The servants brought you whatever food you desired; there were several curry dishes as well and they topped up your glass after virtually every sip. It was therefore hard to judge what you had taken on board.

After dinner there was the usual round of twenty-odd toasts to the king, the duke of York and the army, General Baird and the heroes of Seringapatam, other senior officers and officials in the region and then down to some of the people present, such as the surgeon. To cut a long story short, by the end of the evening I was drunker than a Catholic priest on St Paddy's day. Normally riding a horse, or even finding my horse, in such a state would have been a challenge, but my able syce, seeing me stagger from the mess, was up in a trice and helping me to mount. Then before I could fall off, he was on his own steed and, with a hand firmly grasping my belt to keep me in the saddle, he steered us both back to my veranda. Now you don't get that kind of service from grooms at home!

We were nearing the time of my departure when I received another big invitation, which was to a ball being thrown to welcome the single ladies who had arrived on my ship and one that had docked a week or two after us. Well, they said it was a ball, but it was also a bit like a civilised slave auction. All of local society was there and so it was an excellent place to expound my cover story. Once everyone had arrived a fanfare of sorts was played by the band and the crowd broke apart to leave a corridor down the middle, and one by one the new ladies were led down it to be formally welcomed by some local bigwig. Unlike slave auctions in America, he did not ask them to strip naked, examine their teeth and stand on a block for sale, but he didn't stop far short. Each girl was asked a series of questions, ostensibly to introduce her to the crowd, but highlighting her genteel background and social skills. The colonel's wife, who had coached the ladies on our ship for this display, flapped around like a proud overseer. I recalled her coaching the girls to not accept offers to dance from anyone under the rank of major, apart from plain Jenny Graves, who had a squint and whom she thought would do well to claim a captain.

The dancing resumed, and a few senior officers and wealthy local merchants who were obviously confident that they reached the minimum standard went to claim dances and view the merchandise in more detail. Junior officers, wary of a very public rejection, stood back or danced with the married ladies, who being so claimed could be much more relaxed with their dancing favours. It was at the punch bowl that I met one of these wives. Eliza Freese was a small, very pretty woman with dark hair in long, curled ringlets. She was in her mid-twenties then with a curvaceous figure, having given birth to her second child earlier in the year. A young lieutenant who was pouring her a glass of punch introduced us.

I was pleasantly surprised when she responded, "Ah, Mr Flashman, I hear you are about to leave us to go up country to Hyderabad." It was good to hear that news of my departure had spread to people I had yet to meet. "Will you be away a long time?" she added.

"Yes, quite a while," I confirmed. "Certainly several months."

"Ah, I will have moved on myself by then, so this looks like the only time we are destined to meet. Perhaps you would do me the honour of the next dance."

We danced and chatted together happily. She asked me why I was in India and I was vague about selling wool and she told me about how she missed her husband whom 'dear Arthur' had been obliged to send away to where he was most needed. Her husband had been sent by Arthur Wellesley to Seringapatam before her son was born, and while the baby had a wet nurse Eliza did not want to travel until the child was older. As she let slip that her father was General Stuart I guessed that she was well connected and used to doing what she wanted

At the end of the dance as I made my bow she leaned towards me and whispered, "Perhaps you would save the last dance for me too. I love the last dance, and after four months at sea I'll wager you are a keen partner." With an archly alluring smile she then swept away to some other officers' wives who had been taking turns to dance with the more junior officers.

Well, there was no mistaking her meaning there, and she was right, now that she mentioned it I did have an itch I needed to scratch. Since my arrival in India I had been so wrapped up in plans for my own survival that I had not given women a thought. I had been surprised at her approach, but she evidently wanted a quick fling with a handsome young man (and I flatter myself I was that then) who would not be around afterwards to cause complications. Now that I looked again around the hall where the event was being held, I guessed that there must be affairs going on all the time. There were a relatively small number of white women in Madras and men were frequently sent away for months at a time. Many, particularly the junior officers, were looking on with lustful eyes, especially at the new arrivals. The prettier girls froze them out with looks of haughty disdain, which resulted in them sitting out many of the dances. In contrast, the plain girl with the squint was enjoying a lot of attention. I suspected that when matches were made hers was likely to be the happiest as she had more choice. But as one of the sailors on the indiaman had said on the voyage over, "You don't travel halfway around the world to marry for love."

The last dance was finally announced and I went to claim my prize. Everyone who could dance was getting up for this final hurrah of the evening, but Eliza steered me through the throng. "Let's leave now," she said, "while the crowds are distracted."

We slipped out through the door and there, waiting nearby, was her carriage. My syce and the horses were also nearby, but the discreet fellow, seeing I was with company, stood back. I helped her into the carriage and then got in the other side. The only people watching were native grooms and drivers, with just flickering torches around the entrance to the hall, so I was half-hidden in shadow. As soon as the carriage had moved off into the darkness she was at me like a dockyard whore on a paid-off sailor. Within moments my britches were unbuttoned and she was astride and giving the coach springs as well as me a proper workout.

As we arrived at her bungalow she climbed off, initially sated, and called out to the driver, "Sardul, take us around to the side entrance." Then she turned to me and whispered, "There is a side door that leads straight to my bedroom, so we can be discreet."

I never cease to be amazed by how people think that their servants know only what they tell them. You just knew that once he had finished unhorsing the carriage old Sardul would be in the house recounting how the mistress was acting the trollop again. Doubtless my syce would be seen and invited in to give his views on the situation too. Mind you, it is the same in England: some duchess will confide her most intimate secrets to her lady's maid in the morning and they are all over the household by luncheon and shared with most of the local tradespeople by dinner.

That is by the way, but she was a noisy lover and her servants would have had to have been deaf as well as blind not to know what was going on. I might have been without a woman for four months, but I think I made up for that all in one night. I was a hollow husk when Eliza Freese had finished with me. No sooner had I collapsed into an exhausted and well-deserved sleep than she was nudging me and whispering that I should leave before the servants saw me.

It was well past dawn as I staggered out of the side door. As I stepped off the veranda my grinning syce stepped forward, holding my horse and his pony.

"Good morning, sahib. Can you still ride?" he asked with a mischievous chuckle.

Many would have damned his impertinence but in the circumstances that seemed absurd, and so I just grinned back and said, "Only just."

I mounted and we trotted down the drive. The syce turned to head home but I stopped him, remembering we had somewhere else to go first. Eliza Freese was not the only person I had met at the ball last night.

Midway through the evening I had run into a Henry Davis of the Boulton and Watt Steam Engine Company. Mr Davis was an evangelical, not of religion but of the power of steam. He was nearly fifty, fat and balding but his enthusiasm on his subject was irrepressible. He had waxed lyrical to me for a quarter of an hour on the benefits that steam would bring to the world. Already, he told me, they had done trials using steam to drive boats, and soon ships would be powered with it without the need for wind. Steam was doing the work of hundreds in pumping out mines and its potential was huge. He presented me his card and even showed me a pamphlet on engines produced by his company at their Soho works in Birmingham, and that is what gave me the idea.

When I travelled I was not going to use my own name and I certainly was not going to use the George Thompson name provided by the governor general. I was sure that Scindia's spies would know of both names very soon. I was going to assume a third identity but I had no documents to support it. As I did not plan to meet anyone at the other end, I was originally going to fake some letters of introduction, but now a much better opportunity beckoned. I had made up my mind to act when I learned that Henry Davis was staying in the hotel owned by Runjeet's cousin and that he would be attending a breakfast levee held by the governor general this very morning.

We trotted slowly into town to arrive after the levee had started. I pulled up at the hotel and asked which room Davis was in and went upstairs. I already knew I could pick the hotel locks as I had practised my new lock-picking skills on them in an idle afternoon while I still stayed there. Within a couple of minutes I was inside Henry Davis's room. He was evidently not the tidiest of men but there on a table was what I was looking for: a leather folder containing over a hundred brochures on steam engines and a greater quantity of business cards. I took twenty of each, which would be enough to support my use of his identity for the brief while I needed it. I had liked the man and felt a twinge of guilt at stealing from him, and so on an impulse I reached into my pocket and pulled out my wallet. Inside it I kept the bill for twenty guineas in the name of George Thompson. Picking up a pen on the desk and dipping it in the ink, I endorsed the bill over to Henry Davis and signed it George Thompson. I could not use the money and it was a shame to waste it. As Henry Davis looked nothing like me he was unlikely to be confused with the young courier from England by Scindia's agents.

I left feeling well pleased with myself. I had a new identity, Runjeet was making the travel arrangements to leave in three days' time and I had enjoyed a damned good gallop with Mrs Freese. In fact we had made arrangements to have a final meeting the next day, to give me time to recover. She was going to take me out to see some of the temples in the area after I asked whether there really were temples to lovemaking as the sailor had told me.

A day later and with an Indian guide for propriety, Mrs Freese and I set off once more. My head was soon swimming with the Indian pantheon of gods. There were human ones, humans with multiple arms, animal ones such as monkeys and then mixtures of animal and humans such as Ganesh who was human with an elephant head. He seemed to be the god of parties, wine and having a good time, which made him my favourite. But it was the carvings that took your breath away. There were several temples like tall pyramids with flattened tops that had every inch covered in intricate stone carvings. Some had been painted in colour too and they looked astonishing. Westminster Abbey looked like a road mender's hut in comparison, and when you went inside the detail was similarly impressive.

The Indian guide seemed to know what we wanted, and he took us to one temple and directed us to a particular corner while he retired outside. Well, it was an education for both of us, I think. There were carvings there that would have made a sailor blush. Every conceivable position was featured and some that I could not conceive, unless Indians are routinely double jointed. There were couples and groups and some seemed to include several of the human and animal gods. Mrs Freese seemed very excited, and to avoid alarming her servants we spent the afternoon and evening at my bungalow. To cries of "No, Thomas, the monkey god had his ankle on the girl's shoulder" and "Well, the elephant-faced god could manage it from there" we worked our way through several yards of wall carvings.

To be honest, you can have too many instructions even for lovemaking. I am a big believer in making it up as you go along and so I was not sorry when Mrs Freese left that evening. My back was aching, I had nearly dislocated my shoulder when we fell over during one contortion and I was looking forward to starting my journey the next morning. I wanted to be well gone before Scindia's men got here. While Runjeet had gone on ahead to make transport arrangements, he had promised that there would be a surprise waiting for me the next morning to start the journey.

Chapter 9

I found the surprise on my lawn the next morning. It was a four-ton elephant called Tara. My bungalow was on the road from the centre of Madras towards Hyderabad and so, having announced that was my destination, I had to be seen leaving in that direction. However, we then had to cut across the jungle to get onto the road to Seringapatam, which was my real destination. The elephant was Runjeet's idea as it would make sure people noticed me leaving town and was also the ideal transport for moving through the forest between the two roads. With Tara came her mahout and his family: a wife, a five-year-old girl and a baby the wife carried on her hip. The syce was on hand too with his pony and my horse in case we needed to go a bit faster than the four- to five-miles-an-hour speed of an elephant. A couple of Runjeet's cousins were also there on horseback and well armed as bodyguards. I had a pair of pistols tucked into my belt too, just in case Scindia's men somehow caught up with us early.

Compared with what was about to follow, the start of the journey seemed idyllic. I was absurdly pleased to be able to ride an elephant as it was something I had wanted to do since I decided to come to India. The household was lined up to see the master off and I noticed that there were now a dozen of them, including at least two I would have sworn I had not seen before. The mahout had a bamboo pole with some rungs drilled into it to help me mount the beast and into the howdah that rested on her back. This consisted of some more bamboo poles lashed into a square to stop me sliding off, and some cushions.

If you ever get the chance to ride an elephant, I can strongly recommend it. The view is excellent, the platform is steady and if the animal could only go a bit faster, it would be perfect. We lumbered off up the street with the mahout and his family walking alongside and the little girl darting ahead to snatch favoured shoots from nearby bushes that she fed to the elephant. Despite the fact the child was only five, she was easily able to keep up with the elephant, which gives you some idea of the speed we were going.

Still the elephant was doing what I wanted her to do, make my departure memorable to those who saw it. When killers came looking for Thomas Flashman Esquire they would soon learn that he was seen heading out of town on the road to Hyderabad. My new neighbours grinned and waved as they saw me riding like a raja out of town and they doubtless joked it would take me months to get to my destination.

Once we were out in open country the mahout started looking for a path to our left, and when he found it he gave a shout to the two horsemen and swung himself up to sit on Tara's neck. We turned into the jungle. The path had not been used for some time but the elephant easily pushed her way through, trampling or snapping off the strands of jungle that had tried to reclaim the track. The mahout's family now followed the elephant. The horsemen, having cut bushes and bent branches to obscure the path entrance, brought up the rear.

Various whoops and calls came from jungle creatures as they warned of our approach and I could see monkeys jumping around in trees and shrieking. You feel very safe on the back of an elephant, but when we reached a clearing one of the horsemen came alongside and passed up a musket. "For tigers, sahib," he said. That brought me up short, but I recalled the naturalist chap on the boat had insisted that no animal would attack an adult elephant. I did feel slightly uncomfortable looking at the little girl still foraging for the elephant and just the right size to make an ideal kill for a tiger. But dammit, I had paid for the elephant and I had not asked her to come and so we pressed with just me in the howdah.

Mid-afternoon we reached a lake and it looked like the mahout was planning for the elephant to wade across. His woman passed up the baby to him and then the girl climbed up piggyback style on her mother. It was a big lake and I had no idea how deep it was but I had heard that huge water snakes and crocodiles lived in Indian rivers. I looked to the horsemen to get a hint of what was expected, but they were pointedly looking away. The only thing giving me a clue was the elephant, which kept looking around at the woman and child and flicking her trunk up her side to point at me.

Well, I could not enjoy the journey with a child drowning or being eaten nearby, and so I called for the wife and child to join the father and baby with me on the elephant. The mother sat demurely in the corner of the howdah but the five-year-old chattered at me in her language and was soon pointing out animals that I would not have seen. There were deer and oxen drinking from the shore of the lake and shoals of small fish, and then she pointed up above our heads. Just twenty feet above us and staying exactly over the elephant was a massive sea eagle, black with a white head and yellow talons. I had seen them before but never so close and so still as it glided above us, staring at the water around us. Through mime the little girl explained that it was watching for the movement of fish that were disturbed by the elephant's feet. That was the thing about riding an elephant: other animals seemed to see the elephant but completely ignore any humans on its back. We made camp that evening in a clearing and the syce told me that we should rendezvous with Runjeet the next morning on the road to Seringapatam. But before I leave my elephant I must tell you one more incredible thing which had I not seen it myself I would not have believed. When we made camp the elephant was secured with a rope around her foot to a stake in the ground. The mahout cut a pile of favoured foliage for the creature's tea and then set out to find more. The wife then went off with the little girl and left the infant on the ground next to the elephant. She said something to the beast as she left and patted her on the trunk. As I watched it seemed that the baby was left in the elephant's care. I would guess that the child was near his first birthday and was capable of crawling. First he crawled into the elephant's tea, whereupon the elephant's trunk delicately wrapped around the intruder and deposited him nearby. Then the child crawled between the elephant's legs but, moving her feet carefully to feel for the child, the elephant turned so that she could keep an eye on her charge. When the child looked like he would exceed the range of the elephant's tether, she reached forward and picked up the child again and put him back in his starting place. Throughout, the child showed no alarm at being picked up by the huge, grey behemoth. It was astonishing to see the gentle intelligence of this massive creature, which truly was part of the mahout's family, being also its source of income.

The jungle is a noisy place at night and I did not sleep well. But the next morning we found the Seringapatam road and after a mile or so we found Runjeet. He had a caravan of men and animals ready for the next part of our journey. Here I exchanged Tara the elephant for three evil tempered camels that were burdened with tents, a collapsible bed and table, clothes, cooking equipment, wine and another half-dozen more of Runjeet's cousins to manage the camp. The cousins were mounted on ponies and I reverted to my horse, which the syce had brought along.

The day with the elephant had been dry, but it was now the height of the monsoon season and on most days there would be torrential showers. On the positive side it was so hot that your clothes would soon steam themselves dry afterwards. Well, perhaps not entirely dry, for it was a hot and humid season, with swarms of insects. In short, it was not entirely pleasant – I spent most of my time damp with sweat or rain and swatting flies that swarmed around humans and animals like black clouds.

"The rains will stop soon, sahib," Runjeet assured me. "Then you will see India at her best with lush, green forests, plump, well-fed animals and sweet fruits for you to eat."

The fruits in India had been a disappointment. Because oranges and other tropical fruit are rare in Britain, coming from hot houses, one of the things I had been looking forward to was an endless variety of new and sweet tropical fruits in abundance. The reality was that sweet, tasty mangos were a rarity and other native fruits were often revolting. They had a big, round thing called a jackfruit, which tasted like boiled socks. There was also something called a durian fruit, which smells appalling, but if you can get over the stench it does not taste too bad. I had hoped for oranges, but the only citrus fruits in the region were at a place called Saughur, one hundred and twenty miles from Madras, where they were grown by the Nabob of Arcot.

We rode on for three days, moving considerably faster than we had with the elephant. We camped either on the roadside by the big water storage ponds called tanks that were filling fast in the rain or at purpose-built roadside shelters called choultries that the Company maintained along routes between its main garrisons. It was at one of this choultries that my fortunes changed again.

We were just getting ready to start the day's ride, in a light rain, when a half-company of red-jacketed Company cavalry pulled up outside. A few moments later more cavalry appeared and a knot of British officers was among them. It was my first glimpse of Arthur Wellesley, and in many ways it summed him up. He was riding alone, ahead of the group, not slumped but sitting straight in the saddle. He was wearing a Company redcoat with few marks of rank, but he exuded a sense of authority. On his head he had a tall, leather East Indian Company Army hat. Judging by the mud spattered on his breeches, he had ridden partway through the night, but he swung easily down from the saddle.

Without waiting for his companions, he strode towards the shelter of the choultry, where I was standing on the balcony. We were the only other party there and I was the only other European. He looked at me coldly, taking in my damp, brown civilian coat and wide-brimmed straw hat, which had already seen better days. For a moment I thought he would walk straight past. But at the last moment he seemed to decide to introduce himself.

"Wellesley, Major General," he barked at me. "And you are?"

I came within an ace of giving him my real name, but remembered in the nick of time. "Henry Davis of the Boulton and Watt Steam Engine Company," I replied.

If anything his look of disdain grew and he nodded a curt greeting and walked past me to where two Indians were serving hot tea from a boiling kettle.

I was just congratulating myself on maintaining my disguise when a voice called out, "Good God, Thomas Flashman. What on earth are you doing here?"

I looked round and some beaming cove was running up the stairs towards me and holding out his paw to be shaken. For a moment I could not place him at all and I was starting to say hesitantly "No, I think you are mistaken" when through the whiskers and suntan I saw the boy I had once known at Rugby school, Teddy Carstairs. The last I had heard he had joined the dragoons, but now here he was, nearly pulling my arm out of its socket and exclaiming, "Flashman, old fellow! Why, I haven't seen you in years. What the deuce are you doing here on the Madras road, and are you still in touch with the old crowd? What is George Berkeley doing these days, and what about his charming sisters? You must give me all the news..."

Before I could answer any of this avalanche of questions Wellesley's harsh voice called out from behind me, "You told me your name was Davis."

Now another, older officer coming up behind Carstairs said to Wellesley, "Flashman... ain't that the name of the courier your brother wrote about who lost his message?"

Suddenly I was surrounded by three questioning faces, one friendly, the others looking decidedly curious.

"I am Thomas Flashman, but I am trying to travel in disguise." I turned to Wellesley. "Your brother, Lord Mornington, arranged it."

"You are a courier who lost his message?" asked Carstairs, grinning.

I felt my face redden with embarrassment and then, like a fool, I added, "I am not just a courier but a government agent. I was in Spain last year and I was in Paris at the meeting with Benoit de Boigne this spring when he accused Dowlat Rao Scindia of murdering his great uncle."

I turned to face Wellesley. "Your brother believes that Scindia will want me dead, so he asked me to leave the country in disguise."

It was rank stupidity and I did it not to impress Wellesley but Carstairs. When you meet a fellow from your school you want to show that you are making something of your life, and I did not want him to think I was just a failed courier.

"Damned right he will want you dead," said the older officer. "Major Jock Malcolm," he said, introducing himself. "I am one of the political wallahs. If his people started to believe that story, he would never be able to keep his throne. He will want to personally destroy the letter and anyone likely to talk about it."

"If an East India Company agent stole the letter, do you think the Company will pass it on to Scindia then?" asked Wellesley.

"Definitely," said Malcolm. "Those penny-pinching bastards in Leadenhall Street want to earn favour with him and are terrified of you starting another campaign that would make the Mysore affair look like an economy drive. They want peace, trade and profit. If the Mahrattas are united and strong, they do not believe you would attack them. If they fall apart then they know you and your brother will be on them like wolves, costing the Company a fortune to extend Britain's interests."

"So we need to make sure that the message gets through to other Mahratta chieftains, such as this raja of Berar," said Wellesley, smiling wolfishly. "We have not got time to wait; my brother wants them beaten before he is recalled."

I looked up sharply at that, for the word in the barracks back in Madras was that it was young Arthur, the major general yet to have a victory, who desperately needed war, not his brother, who was seen by everyone apart from Leadenhall Street as having done a good job.

"Your brother has sent him a sworn witness statement and de Boigne's ring," said Malcolm.

"Yes, but will that be enough?" mused Wellesley.

I had a nasty feeling about the way this conversation was going and was just about to take my leave and get the hell out of there when that infernal blot Carstairs piped up, "Flashman could tell him about the meeting personally. He has been an agent before in Spain; I am sure he could get through."

Dammit, I could have punched him, and to make matters worse I think he genuinely thought he was doing me a favour: giving me another opportunity to earn laurels in my field. I had to stop this idea taking hold, but without losing what little credit I had.

"Well, obviously I would like to try," I lied. "But with so much at stake we need to be sure I can succeed. In Spain I could speak the language, but I have only been in India a few weeks and have not had time to learn the customs or any of the languages."

"He is right," agreed Malcolm to Wellesley. Inwardly I sighed with relief for just a second before he added, "He would stand out like a sore thumb on his own. But if we sent a troop of native Rajput cavalry with him then I think he would stand a reasonable chance of getting through."

"Hold on," says I. "Look, I am keen to do what I can, but I am the only witness to that meeting and your brother thinks that trained killers are already on the prowl. Surely if I go roaming around the countryside even with these 'raj pot' fellows, I am just making life easier for the other side? Perhaps it would be better for me to sit in Fort St George and write some more witness statements that you could distribute to all the Mahratta princes?"

If I had to go back then I was going to make damn sure that I was in the hardest place for those killers to find me, but I was cursing the fates that had brought Carstairs across my path. There I was minding my own business, having got myself out of one tight spot, only to be landed in the soup again.

"Unsupported statements would be seen as weak propaganda and discredit the governor general," said Malcolm. "I think we need to concentrate on getting Flashman to the raja of Berar. He will have the ring to back up the claim and if we can convince the raja to investigate then we might make a difference. It is risky, though."

"Yes, but by risking one life we might save thousands," said Wellesley.

I stared in horror as the situation closed in around me. I wanted to scream at them that it was *my* bloody life they were talking about risking. But it would make no difference arguing now. I would have to find some other way to slip out. The monsoon on the south-east coast of India around Madras would soon be ending, which meant that the port would reopen. I could stow away and then claim the Company had shanghaied me.

My face was set in grim determination. They were not to know that it was to escape their designs, for I was sure that certain death waited for me there. They assumed the expression was born of my resolve to do my duty, as I toadied up with, "I would be proud to be of service, sir." Then I added, "I will turn my little caravan around and I should be able to join you in Madras in a few days." Well, it was worth a try, but they were not falling for that.

"No, you must come with us at once, sir," said Wellesley. "Take any necessaries you need and leave your household to follow."

An hour later I was galloping down the road back to Madras a lot quicker than I had come up it. Wellesley was riding alone ahead, while I was now in the group of officers behind, with the idiot Carstairs alongside, gushing at what an exciting life I must lead compared to his as a second lieutenant in the dragoons. He explained that Rajputs were a people from north-west India with a fearsome military reputation. "You can rest assured, Flashy, that if they are assigned to protect you, they won't let you down. Why, every last man will fight to the death." Well, that was some comfort, but I did not expect assassins to come in a pitched battle; they were more likely to slip in at night and cut your throat quietly before making their escape.

Chapter 10

If I had been jumpy before I got to Madras, the news there did not make me feel any better. For all the talk was of a murder, not just any killing but an abduction of a white man who had been taken a mile or so out of the city and there tortured to death. His corpse had been found on the morning of my arrival back in the city. Everyone was speculating on who he was and why he had been killed. His face had been horribly mutilated and various parts of his body cut off while he was still alive, and it was clear he had died in agony. But no person had been reported missing. I entertained the hope that the poor devil might have been mistaken for me somehow and that the killers were now heading home thinking that their mission was complete, but I did not really believe it. I am not that lucky.

Some of the provosts and a doctor had been out to where the body was found to investigate the killing. I loitered in the adjutant's office when we arrived. I did not want to go to my bungalow in case it was being watched, or be seen about town. It was better for most people to think I was still on my way to Hyderabad. I was reading some back copies of the *Madras Courier* when the medical officer came to report.

"I would guess he is between forty-five and sixty," said the sawbones. "The deceased was overweight so not a physical labourer, and the bits of his hand that I found were not calloused. The only clue to his identity is this leather folder we found in the undergrowth near the body. It has the initials HJD on it."

Even though the room was stiflingly hot, I felt a chill run down my spine. I was out of my chair at the mention of the word 'folder', and sure enough it was the leather folder that had once held the brochures and business cards of Henry Davis of the Boulton and Watt Steam Engine Company.

"Oh God," I said as I looked at the folder, which still had dark blood stains on it. For I realised why Davis has been tortured. Someone here in the fort had told the killers about the bank draft and then they must have found out from the bank who had cashed it. They would have tortured Davis to find out what he knew of the mythical wool merchant George Thompson. Of course he had no idea who had given him the draft as I had left it when I had broken into his room. Even if they had tried asking him about a man called Flashman, if he did remember me from the party, he would only remember a man planning to go to Hyderabad.

76

"His name is Henry Davis," I said. "We stayed at the same hotel when I first arrived in Madras. I remember seeing him with that case."

I did not add any information about why he might have been attacked. I felt a bit sick. What I had thought was an act of generosity had ended up getting the man killed in the most appalling way. The death also proved that Scindia really did have spies everywhere; even the fort was not as safe as I thought. I was not going to be given time to stow away either as I had been told that the Rajputs would arrive the following morning. I was trapped.

I had been finding out a bit more about the Rajputs, though, and it seemed that they really were brave as lions and with a strict honour code. One officer told me a story of an attack on a small hill fort occupied by just twenty Rajputs. The British force was over five hundred men and the officer commanding the vanguard who knew about their ways offered to let them withdraw with honour and their weapons, which they started to do. Unfortunately the general commanding whole column countermanded this order and insisted that they surrender as prisoners. Massively outnumbered as they were, the Rajputs calmly returned to their fort and defended it to the last man, taking sixty British lives with them.

Henry Wellesley also got me thinking by saying that if we could convince the raja of Berar to investigate Mahadji Scindia's death, then killing me would become less important to Dowlat Rao Scindia. My death would not stop the investigation. Strange as it may seem, actually doing my duty may be the least dangerous of a lot of dangerous options. I just had to stay alive that night to meet up with my capable bodyguard.

They gave me a room at the fort and invited me to dine in the mess, but I was too jumpy for that. There were too many native servants with access to the fort and I had already had one European betray me on the ship, stealing the letter in the first place. They may have other agents here among the garrison. I needed somewhere I could stay for one night, where no one would think to look for me. One option sprang to mind.

As the officers went in for dinner I went into their mess and picked up a cloak and hat to hide my features and then slipped out to the stables. A few minutes later I was on horseback and trotting across the drawbridge and into town. Several times I stopped to check I was not being followed, but no one seemed to be paying me any attention. I carried on, taking a road out of town, until I reached a familiar bungalow. I walked the horse through some trees and left it tied to one of them. As I moved to the private side door I picked a bunch of flowers from the well-tended flowerbeds. I had already checked that John Freese was not among the officers returning with Wellesley, and so I was all set to give Eliza an unexpected visit as I swung open the door with my flowers in hand.

"Surprise, I am back," I called as I moved into the room. But whatever else I was going to say died in my throat as she had a far bigger surprise for me. With astonishment I saw from the candles that she was not alone and white buttocks were moving rhythmically up and down above her. She screamed when she realised I was there and covered her head with a pillow. Major General Arthur Wellesley, however, turned to me with a look of angry indignation.

"Flashman, what the devil are you doing here?"

For a moment we both stared at each other in astonishment as the implications of the situation sank in. Eliza's shoulders started to shake and at first I thought she was crying, but then she moved her pillow and we both saw she was laughing.

"I am sorry," she said between giggles. "I am so sorry, my poor John," she added, referring to her absent husband. "I am a terrible wife, but I just so hate to be alone."

"You mean you and Flashman..." said Wellesley as the penny dropped and he climbed off the bed. He was naked and looked around for something to cover himself. Eliza had pulled the sheet up to her chin and so he picked up her robe and wrapped himself in that.

"I'm sorry," she said, "but you sent John away and then went away yourself for months. I met Thomas last week and he was going away too. I didn't think I would see him again."

Well, they gave us some etiquette classes at Rugby, how to greet royalty, that sort of thing. Strangely this situation was not included. I mean, what is the correct behaviour when two men meet while intent on rogering the wife of someone else? Do you both withdraw or form an orderly queue?

Wellesley stared at me across the bed. Whenever he is being too starchy I think back to him at that moment, hair dishevelled and looking more than faintly ridiculous in a robe that was too small for him and embroidered with flowers. Eliza was smiling nervously at him, but to my surprise he grinned and shook his head at the absurdness of the situation. "Flashman, give us a few minutes, would you."

"Of course," I said and, leaving my flowers on the nightstand, I turned and went out the way I had come in. As I stepped out in the grounds I saw that old Sardul, the coachman, had untied my horse and was taking it to the stables, muttering as he went. Doubtless he was complaining that his mistress had the morals of a Bengali bazaar whore, for he was shaking his head in disgust. When he saw me he stopped to see if I wanted the horse returned; he seemed only slightly relieved that Eliza was not taking clients two at a time. I had nowhere else to go and so I waved the horse away and went out to the little summer house on the lawn to collect my thoughts.

A few moments later Sardul re-appeared with a tray on which there was a decanter of brandy, a glass and some cigars together with a candle. He would have made an excellent knocking shop attendant that one; he really knew how to look after the patrons. It was as he was pouring the brandy that we first heard a squeal. It seemed that after I had gone Wellesley had got back in the saddle. Sardul moved to one side, muttering again. I had said before that she was a noisy lover and she must have woken the household again that night. Over the next ten minutes her cries and groans rose to a crescendo that only just managed to drown out the grinding teeth and growls of her disapproving retainer.

I was halfway down the cigar when Wellesley joined me. Sardul fetched him another glass and we sat there for a while smoking and drinking brandy in silence, neither of us sure what to say.

"I would be grateful for your discretion, Flashman," started Wellesley. "For the lady's, I mean Eliza's, reputation as well as mine."

"Of course I won't say anything. I am a gentleman, you know."

"Yes, yes, of course. I didn't mean to imply..." Wellesley tailed off. "I did need to send John to Seringapatam, you know, it wasn't just so that Eliza and I could, er..." and he tailed off again. "It's all bloody embarrassing," he finished.

"She is a striking woman," I replied.

"Was it you that she took to the temples?" he asked, looking directly at me for the first time. "She mentioned that she had been there recently and thought we ought to go."

"Yes. The wall carvings were somewhat educational."

"I see," he said.

But I was not sure he did, so I added, "There is a position involving an elephant-headed god that she was keen on. If you value your back, I would not risk it."

"Good grief!" he said as he fully understood and then took a large swig of brandy.

We sat in silence a while longer. I was twenty one and he was thirty-three, a major general in the Company's army who was yet to win a battle. His rank had been either bought for him or appointed by his brother, and he was desperate to prove himself. In that private moment you could almost sense that hunger in him.

"I am grateful for your help with the raja of Berar," he said at length. "Richard's enemies will see him replaced soon and if I, I mean if we, have not subdued the Mahrattas by then, there may not be another opportunity."

"You do know that there are no French troops among the Mahrattas, don't you?" I said, remembering de Boigne's comments.

"Yes, but if they stay unified, they could beat us aside. Their army has beaten us before, you know. If a French army ever gets to India, the number of French mercenaries amongst the Mahratta will mean that they will side with the French against us. British interests in India will not be secure until they are subdued. Of course, all the Company sees is this year's profits; they refuse to take a longer-term view." I sensed that this statement was one that both Wellesley brothers had rehearsed to justify their actions, which were as much about achieving or securing rank for themselves as protecting the nation's interests.

We chatted, smoked and drank in this vein for a while, but as the brandy took hold Wellesley was more open. He admitted that he knew many of his subordinates had more battle experience and that until he had won an action his men would not fully trust him. He talked about his first battle, which had been a disaster, and swore he would never fight a night action again, and he never did.

In the end he offered me a bed for the night at Government House. I don't think this was generosity on his part; he was just worried that I might try that side door again if he left me behind. Knowing Eliza, even after everything that happened, she would probably have let me in too!

Chapter 11

I spent that night in the most comfortable bed I had been in since I arrived in India and had one of the best dreams too. There I was back in Eliza's bedroom, with her welcoming me dressed just in her flowery robe. Behind her, outside the window, there was Wellesley in a monsoon shower shouting "Mr Flashman, Mr Flashman" and knocking on the glass. Why he was being quite so formal I could not tell or care, as Eliza was slipping off the robe and I was growling in anticipation. Now, somehow, Wellesley had got into the room and was shaking my shoulder shouting "Mr Flashman, your escort is here", which seemed deuced strange, and then with a start I awoke to find that some elderly Wellesley family retainer was indeed shaking my shoulder and saying the same.

I am always in a bad mood when woken from a deep sleep, especially when such an enticing fantasy has been interrupted, and so I told him to go the devil and tried to turn over. But the infernal pest persisted and explained that my native escort was waiting outside, ready to set off with me on my journey. Well dammit, I was a guest of the governor general and not someone at the beck and call of some insomniac corporal. I told the old duffer to double down to the escort and tell them that I would be down when I was good and ready and I wanted my breakfast first. He squeaked in alarm at this, but I told him to get moving and then tried to settle down again between the covers.

I couldn't sleep again now and noticed from the window that the sun already seemed quite high in the sky. My earlier anger was slowly replaced with a nagging doubt. Whoever this escort commander was, I should not antagonise him as my life would depend on him for the next few weeks. I crept out of bed and took a quick peek from the side of the window. The governor's mansion was a two-storey affair, and looking down from my room I saw fifty cavalry men all drawn up in four ruler-straight rows with their commander sitting on his horse, front and centre. My God, they looked a businesslike bunch too, with yellow turbans, long, red Company jackets with sashes and swords around their waists and everyone holding a razor-sharp lance. You could not tell expressions as they all had glossy black beards, but they sat damn tall and proud in the saddle. As I watched, the retainer trotted out and gave the commander my message. I was regretting that now. The commander looked furious and glared up at the windows. I ducked back as quickly as I could but I was not sure if he saw me. Well, the die is cast now, old boy, I thought. You have set yourself out as some aristocratic martinet; you will have to see it through or lose face.

Things were not getting off to a good start when I looked at my clothes. They were the ones I had been riding in for the previous two days and the hat and cloak I had stolen from the officers' mess yesterday. All had seen better days and would look shabby against the spotless perfection outside. Just as I was wondering if I could borrow some clothes from the Wellesleys there was a knock at the door. That little hero Runjeet had tracked me down and stood there with a small valise of clothes and my two pistols, which I had left behind when I had been abducted from his company earlier in the week. He asked for some money to pay off the caravan and keep the bungalow going, and I was so grateful that I broke my 'golden' rule and took some of my hidden gold coins from my belt in front of him. His eyes glittered at the sight of them but I didn't care. The way things were, I would be mightily relieved if I lived long enough to have him drain me of the rest by the time I came back.

I felt much better with a fresh set of duds, and went down and enjoyed a hearty breakfast too. From the clock in the morning room I discovered it was now half past ten, which was mighty late in those parts as people liked to do things before the heat of the day, but it was too late to worry about that now. Deciding I would continue as I started, I sent Runjeet off to ask the leader of my band of cavalrymen to join me for coffee so that we could discuss the route. I thought that might help me assert some authority. As I waited I looked out of the window and nearly choked on my toast, for there among the roses was a pair of the aforementioned fearless warriors wandering through the flowers, holding each other's hand. It seemed their leader had given them permission to fall out and they were enjoying the surroundings. No matter how long I spent in India I never got used the sight of men walking together holding hands. They do it quite naturally and it doesn't signify that they are of the more 'artistic' persuasion. But it looked deuced odd, especially when you saw two fierce soldiers at it.

The leader of my escort arrived a few minutes later. He was taller than me by several inches, broader too, and he had black eyes that glittered dangerously. He introduced himself as Risaldar-Major Poorun Singh and was stiffly formal. He saluted so sharply he could have cracked a walnut in his elbow joint and refused my offer of a seat and coffee.

"Is the sahib now ready to leave?" he asked stiffly.

"Soon," I replied. "I just wanted to discuss the route first. Do you have a map?"

He looked coldly at me and replied, "I do not need a map, I know the way well." Then, as a challenge to me, he added, "Do you know India well?"

"I think we both know that I have only been in the country a few weeks," I retorted. Then, to regain control, I said, "But I do know enough not to go riding out into strange lands without a pretty good idea of where I am going and why. Perhaps you would be good enough to show me our route using this map on the wall."

He had to loosen up a bit after that as he struggled to understand the English spellings of some of the landmarks and we had to work together, with him saying place names and me finding them on the map to be able to chart our route. I quickly realised that as well as being as proud as Lucifer, he was a capable man and had thought out the route carefully.

Berar lay to the north of the province of Hyderabad, which was friendly to the British. The nizam of Hyderabad had provided soldiers to help with the Mysore campaign and had pledged to support any action against the Mahrattas. The nizam was a Muslim and the Mahrattas were largely Hindu, but the split was not along religious lines as most of the nizam's people were Hindus too. The rift was due to the fact that the Mahrattas supported *pindaree* bandits. *Pindaree* were tribes of nomadic thieves who lived off the land and robbed farmers of crops and raided towns and villages. The Mahrattas tolerated them because in times of war the *pindaree* leaders would bring hordes of horsemen to serve as cavalry. I had heard earlier from an army colonel that these horsemen lacked what he called 'bottom'; i.e. they would not attack a strong hostile force. But if an army was in disarray or retreating then they would charge in to loot and kill, like the robbers they were. To protect their own people the Mahratta leaders encouraged the *pindaree* to raid their neighbours such as Hyderabad, which explained why the nizam was keen to help the British.

Poorun Singh thought that Scindia could have sent the *pindaree* out to look for me and so he suggested that we avoid the main routes through Hyderabad and go the backcountry way. He clearly described the route, which he evidently knew well. Once we were near Berar he had the name of a trusted man we could use to arrange a meeting with the raja. That was the bit that worried me, but we had the best part of eight hundred miles to ride first, which would take nearly a month.

83

When he had finished explaining the route Poorun Singh gave another of his nut-shattering salutes and said, "We are ready to leave immediately." With a dark, unreadable face, he strode from the room. I had thought the Flashy charm was starting to win him round, but clearly he had not forgotten my earlier offhand orders.

As I prepared to leave, putting on a smart blue coat and black hat, I heard a trumpeter sound some signal. Judging from the speed at which the hand-holding Flora and Daisy sped from the flower garden to the front of the house, it was the recall. Well, if Singh wanted to play the punctilious soldier I could continue the martinet role and he would have to take the consequences. So I strolled out of the front door of the governor's mansion, determined to show that I could keep these natives in their place, only to stop dead in astonishment. Runjeet was leading away my fine thoroughbred horse and in its place a trooper, or sowar as they were called in the Company cavalry, was leading forward a wiry pony, similar to those that the other soldiers rode. Before I could say anything about that I noticed that by my feet was a pile of well-worn clothes, a sowar's uniform.

Poorun Singh looked down at me from his horse. "A troop of Company cavalry with a British civilian will be noticed and remembered, especially if people are looking for a British civilian. No one will remember just a troop of Company cavalry out on patrol." It was hard to tell with the beards, but I was pretty sure that he and the rest of them were smirking at the thought of this arrogant white man being forced to join their ranks.

"You want me to wear these?" I asked, moving the clothes with my foot. They were well worn and in some places patched but at least they looked clean. There was a uniform coat, breeches, well-worn riding boots, a sash, some other long strip of cloth that I took to be a turban from the colour and a sword belt with a heavy sabre in it.

"If you want to live, it would be wise," replied Poorun Singh. "But the choice is yours," he added, as though he did not really care if I lived or not. Well, he certainly knew how to appeal to my basic instincts and what he said actually made a great deal of sense. Hardly anybody knew I was back in Madras; many thought I was still on the main road to Hyderabad. Leaving in disguise would buy us a lot more time, and if these *pindaree* people were in on the hunt too then I needed all the help I could get. So, after a moment's hesitation, I picked up my new costume and headed back into the house.

If I suspected that the sowars were smirking when I came out the first time there was no doubt about it when sowar Flashy emerged a little while later. They roared with laughter. I nearly tripped over my sabre coming down the steps and my turban, which resembled a cloth cow turd, was already starting to slip down my ears. There are times to stand on your dignity and also times to recognise that your dignity has sailed without you. This was one of the latter occasions. I knew I looked ridiculous and that this was Poorun Singh's victory, but if he kept me alive then it did not matter. I turned to find him grinning in amusement as my turban slid down to cover my left eye and I asked with heavy irony, "Are you sure this getup will not attract attention?"

He gave some orders and a sowar sprang forward and took the cloth turd off my head and within a few moments was expertly tying it into a proper turban. I saw that all the soldiers had badges on the front of their turbans and asked if I should have one too.

"They are for proper soldiers," said Poorun Singh in a tone that indicated there was no room for debate on that point. The sowar adjusted my sabre belt so that the sword did not keep falling between my legs and then I thought we were ready to go, but Poorun Singh barked out more orders. Now the sowars I knew as Flora and Daisy were coming forward. Flora had a pot with a brush in it and Daisy was holding what appeared to be a bundle of shaved pubic hair. "You must have a beard too," explained Poorun Singh as Flora liberally laid about my chin with his glue brush. I was more worried about the hair and asked where it had come from, miming my suspicion. The troops roared with laughter again, evidently thinking I was quite the comedian, but Daisy used his fingers to indicate the horns of a goat and bleated. Wherever it came from, the hair and glue combination stank, and despite Daisy's best efforts it was not likely to fool a child at close quarters. Even Poorun Singh suggested that I stay in the middle rank when he saw the finished result.

Eventually the troop of fifty-one Company cavalry headed down the governor's drive and out onto the main road. I did not have to worry about controlling the horse as he kept himself in perfect station with the mounts around him. Few people paid us any attention. I even spotted one or two people I knew as we rode out of town, but they just looked up and saw Company cavalry and went on with what they were doing. Nobody noticed the strange fellow in the middle.

A few miles out of town we turned off the main road to go down a jungle path, but Poorun Singh knew his business when it came to avoiding a tail. He ordered us to halt and dismount on the main road and we walked our horses off the road and down the first few hundred yards of the trail to avoid the hooves hacking up the grass by the side of the road. Then a couple of sowars were detailed to cut down some foliage and use it to block the path entrance. Finally he left one sowar behind to watch for someone trying to follow. Then we set off again. Fifty horses leave a trail that is not hard to track, but soon we reached a large, shallow lake similar to the one I had crossed with the elephant; indeed it might have been the same one, as it was in the right area. This time we did not cross it but, wading the horses knee-deep, we went some distance along the shore to come out by a small temple that stood alone in the jungle.

There at last Poorun Singh called a halt. They were soon starting fires to make tea and sharing flatbreads and other food. A corporal or jemadar called Lal, who had ridden alongside me for the afternoon, invited me to join his section, which also included Flora and Daisy. I thought I had nothing to offer but discovered that my saddlebags were filled with rations too. I was not sure what some of it was, but after four hours in the saddle I was hungry and thirsty. I noticed Poorun Singh set himself apart from his troop to eat alone. The horses were left to crop grass and many of us rested in the shade from the trees dotted around the lakeside. Daisy, it turned out, was a bit of a fisherman and sat at the edge of the lake. He obviously knew where to find fish for by the time we left he had five plump trout in his saddlebag.

We stayed there until the trooper we had left by the road came splashing along the lake shore to report he had waited two hours and there had been no sign of us being followed from town. We started off again then, riding for another four hours to higher ground away from the lake to camp for the night. The evening campsite had fewer mosquitoes, as the air had been black with them by the water. I followed the men's example of looking after my horse first and then campfires were burning again. For Lal's section, including me, there was grilled trout and rice for dinner.

Again Poorun Singh sat apart from his men, and as I had given him no cause to like me I steered clear and stayed with my section. Lal spoke some English and we managed to communicate, with me learning some Hindi along the way. Flora and Daisy only spoke Hindi but we got by with mime. There were no tents; people just settled down on the bedrolls that had been tied to the saddles. But I found a mosquito net in my saddlebags and planted some sticks in the ground to make a tent of it over my head and shoulders. I slept well, although my glue-stained cheek kept sticking to my saddle, which I was using as a pillow.

That first morning with the troop I remember waking up and watching monkeys jumping around in the tree canopy above me and thinking life was not all bad. I won't bore you with a daily account of that journey. We generally rode two stretches a day for at least four hours each, and after getting stiff for the first few days, I soon got used to it. Each morning the men would wash if there was a stream and in the evenings some would wash clothes to dry overnight. Despite the journey they kept themselves spotless and there was an inspection each morning. I excused myself from that and Poorun Singh did not insist on it, but I tried to keep myself as clean as the others. God knows what they put in that glue but the stuff on my face took days to wear off with tufts of black hair still attached. I was not shaving and slowly my own beard growth replaced the fake.

The country changed from jungle to more mixed forests and clearings, and we went through various small villages with no one taking much notice. Despite my circumstances, I found I was enjoying myself. Lal, Flora and Daisy were constantly chattering away and I was picking up Hindi quite quickly and was soon able to have halting conversations. While they found my translations hilarious, they seemed to know what I meant.

At one point we came across a large river that we needed to cross. There was no bridge or ford but we went down the bank until we came to a village which had half a dozen large, round coracle-type craft made like a huge wickerwork basket and covered with bullock hide. They were like shallow dishes, but they took four men together with their saddles and kit and a ferryman. Once they were floated we tied at least four horses to each one and the horses swam across the river, taking us with them. The ferrymen paddled boats back to bring more men across.

On we went into the territory of the nizam of Hyderabad, but the country could still throw some surprises. I remember once filling my water bottle at a stream and looking down to see a huge feline paw-print in the mud. It was much bigger than my splayed-out hand and Lal confirmed my suspicion that it was a tiger-print. He pressed the print; the mud was soft.

"Tiger drinking. He hear horse come. He watch us now," said Lal in his halting English and grinning at what I thought was pretty alarming news. I went back to my horse and got out one of my pistols, checked the priming and fired it into the air. The crack and smoke sent several birds up into the air, but I did not hear the sound of a larger animal charging off into the jungle.

"What on earth do you think you are doing?" asked Poorun Singh, riding up.

"I was trying to scare off that tiger," I said, pointing at the huge footprint in the mud.

"A pistol will not scare off a tiger. They survive by staying absolutely still unless they are sure you have seen them, and then they will often attack."

"So it is still out there then?" I asked, looking closely at the nearby forest.

"Of course, and you will never stop a tiger with a pistol anyway." He looked down at me from the saddle and, in a slightly sneering tone, he added, "You had better hope that the tiger does not like the taste of white meat." With that he trotted back to the head of the column.

Well, that was easy for him to say, but when you come from a country where the most dangerous animal in the wild is an angry squirrel, it comes as a shock to find that you are not the top predator. I reloaded my pistol anyway and kept it in my hand until we were well past that place.

One evening Poorun Singh had us practise sabre drill. I had used a cutlass with Cochrane the year before and had even disabled two Spanish officers with one. But those victories were down to some dubious tactics taught to me by a Swedish bosun and a large helping of good luck. The sabre has a heavy, curved blade, longer than a cutlass and is designed to be used on horseback. The front edge is sharpened, as is the top third of the reverse edge so that you can cut backhand.

I was set against a sowar who, Poorun Singh told me, was the weakest swordsman in the company. Well, he might have been the weakest, but the sword was long and unfamiliar and he nicked me twice in the first five minutes. The trouble was that as part of the drill you had to keep your distance, whereas old Eriksson's favourite trick was to sweep in close and kick your opponent in the balls. Not only had he caught me twice, but the lightweight little pipsqueak was getting cocky. Lal and his section were cheering me on, but my opponent kept darting out of range. I realised that I was not going to beat him with speed and that I would have to beat him with cunning.

He stepped back a few paces and opened his guard to encourage me to attack. I darted forward, but pretended to slip, going down almost on one knee so that my left hand could pick up a handful of dirt. In he charged, squealing with delight at the thought of another easy win against the white man, but I was up in a flash and throwing the dirt in his face. It distracted him for a second and that was all I needed to get in close, kick his legs out from under him and then fall on his prostrate form with my sword poised over his neck. My squad cheered with delight and I pretended not to notice Poorun Singh shaking his head in disgust.

We rode on for another three days, passing villages where we sometimes stopped to buy food, but we always camped out on our own. Poorun had taken to sending scouts on ahead of the column and they would reconnoitre any villages we came across first, to ensure that there were no *pindaree* bandits in the vicinity. On the fourth day one of these scouts rode back to say that there was a dozen of the nizam's soldiers at the next village, investigating the disappearance of a local woman. We rode in and came to a halt in the village square, where Poorun Singh had a long discussion in Hindi with the commander of the soldiers. He turned and shouted some orders to the men, who suddenly looked pleased and excited and were dismounting from their horses and hefting their lances. "Tiger!" shouted Lal, pointing to the trees and grinning. I could think of nothing involving a tiger that would make me grin that happily, but now Poorun was walking towards me to explain what was happening in English.

"The nizam's men want our help," he told me. "A woman is missing and one of the villagers says he saw a tiger dragging a body into the forest to the west of the village. There is a clearing on the far side. They will wait there with muskets and they want us to drive the tiger towards them."

"I thought you said that they stay still unless they are certain they have been seen and then they often attack?" I was appalled: it was bad enough being watched by an unseen tiger, but now they were expecting me to march straight towards where one, a man-eater at that, was supposed to be waiting.

"This is how you hunt tigers," Poorun said simply. "There is no other way. You have lots of men to make noise and then wait for the tiger to break cover."

One of the nizam's soldiers came running over with a musket and cartridge belt and handed it to me.

Poorun smiled. "Given how you fight with a sword, I have arranged for you to have a musket. It is better at stopping tigers than a pistol."

I pulled the belt over my shoulder so that the bayonet holster rested on my hip and checked the priming of the gun. It was loaded. I felt happier with a proper weapon in my hands, but it would be a cold day in hell before I voluntarily went nose to nose with a tiger. The other soldiers were gathering at the end of the wood with their lances and some villagers with sticks and pans or anything else to make a noise were joining them. Soon nearly a hundred people were lined up on the edge of the forest, with yours truly in the middle. A hunting horn was blown and everyone started to move forwards. Well, when I say everyone, there was one white man with a musket who seemed to be holding back. Oh, I stepped into the woods all right, but just a bit slower than everyone else. Gradually the line crept ahead of me, first five yards and then ten. You could hear animals fleeing from the din ahead and I caught a glimpse of a deer darting through the trees. What I did not spot until I nearly stepped on it was a huge black snake that had slithered through the gap in the line that should have been filled by me. The damn thing reared up, hissing, and I stepped back a few more paces to allow it to make its escape through the undergrowth. I got the bayonet out after that and put it on the end of the musket and used that to probe the ground in front of me.

We had been walking through the woods for nearly half an hour. The rest of the line was fifty yards ahead, close enough for me to rush up when the coast was clear but far enough away for them to flush out anything stripy before it reached me. It was hot and humid and I needed a break. A huge fallen tree now blocked my path and so, before I struggled to climb over or around it, I leant my musket against the trunk and unbuttoned my flies to take a piss. I had just finished when a big droplet of sweat ran down my cheek. I went to brush it away and to my surprise found it was blood and not sweat. Well, I must have been bitten by fifty insects since I had walked into the jungle and so I was not unduly concerned. I picked up my musket and stood back just in time to see another droplet of blood fall to the leaf litter at my feet. I looked up and felt a cold chill run down my spine. There, several feet above me, resting in the branches of the fallen tree, was a huge lump of meat. There was flesh and bone and swarms of flies, but between all of this were a few shreds of cloth to confirm that this had once been human.

It had to be the missing villager but my mind was already whirling: if the body was here then surely the killer might be close by too. I sprang back a few feet and looked around. I remembered the scientist on the ship out saying that tigers could not climb trees like leopards. I raised the musket and moved round, looking at nearby bushes. But wait, if tigers do not climb trees, how did the body get up there? Was the kill stolen by a leopard? Would a leopard steal from a tiger? I wished I had paid more attention to the naturalist on that boat now. Then a second later I realised that would have been a waste of time, as the scientist was a lying bastard.

There, just a few yards away in the tree, two yellow eyes were staring at me. To be fair the trunk of the tree was so thick that my aged Aunt Agatha could have climbed it, but back then I was more worried about the tiger getting down from the tree than how it had got up. It was in the foliage and as I watched I could make out the black, white and yellow of its face, which was camouflaged perfectly with the leaves and shadows from the branches above. I slowly took another step back, while equally slowly I swung the musket around in its direction. The tiger did not move; it just stared at me without even blinking. We looked at each other. The beast knew I was there and that I had seen it. There was no fear or alarm in those eyes; the creature was the king of the jungle and was certain it could kill me any time it wanted. It must have sat up there and watched the others go past and then seen old Flashy blunder in its direction. It was probably mildly annoyed to see me piss my scent all over the bottom of its tree as though marking it as my territory. Well, I was happy to give up any rights to the tree.

Slowly I started to take another step back, but this time it quietly growled its disapproval. I froze. I knew I could not turn and run, for it would be on me in a second and I sensed shouting for help would invoke a similar response. I was only still alive because the beast was curious and wanted to look at me. It was, I guessed, ten yards away and the only weapon I had was a musket designed to hit a group of men at eighty to a hundred yards range. I didn't need to just hit the tiger, I had to kill it. If it was wounded it would still tear me apart.

I slowly raised the musket to my shoulder and tried to aim the musket between its eyes. The long, heavy weapon wavered and it was difficult to hold the aiming point at that exact spot. There were so many factors that could affect the aim: I had never fired this gun before, it could pull to the left or the right, the ball could be misshapen, affecting the flight, or the powder could be damp and it would not fire at all. No, I could not think of that. I lowered my aim to the crouching body to give me a bigger target.

Suddenly, with a grunt, the tiger got up and started to move down the tree trunk, from my left to my right. I tried to track it with the gun but it disappeared behind some foliage, and for a brief second I thought it might have jumped away. But no, it reappeared next to its grisly kill, not even bothering to look at me as it padded down the sloping trunk. With feline grace, it dropped the last few feet onto the ground and turned those yellow eyes back in my direction. It dropped back into a crouch, still around ten yards off, but it felt closer now that the creature was at my level.

I had to take my chance with the musket; it was now or never. They say aim low, as muskets kick up, and so I aimed for the middle of its chest, took a deep breath and started to pull the trigger. It must have sensed my intent, or maybe it heard the click of the hammer, but suddenly the animal exploded forward. As the musket crashed into my shoulder there was a snarl and an orange-and-black blur of movement towards me. God knows where the ball went, but it did not hit the tiger and I did not even have time to scream in terror. I tried to stumble back, but my heel caught in some root and then I was falling and the tiger was springing through the puff of musket smoke. It all happened in a split second, but to me everything seemed to happen in slow motion. I was still holding the musket and falling backwards, those huge teeth and claws were coming towards me and I knew with absolute certainty that I was going to die.

My back hit the dirt at the exact moment that the great beast blocked out the sky above me. There was a deafening snarl and its claws were swinging in. The only reason I did not piss myself in terror was that I had just watered the tree. I shut my eyes, not wanting to watch the final moment, and braced myself for the first rip of my flesh. But it did not come.

There was a groan from the creature and claws bashed my right shoulder and left side. My face was filled with its putrid breath, but I still lived. I opened my eyes and must have whimpered in terror for the nose of the tiger was no more than a few inches above my face, the head hanging down and those terrible great yellow eyes staring directly into mine. For an insane moment I thought that it had been waiting for me to look before it killed me, but then some blood gushed out of its mouth and I felt its claws twitching against me. Something was holding it up. It started to fall to one side and the musket was wrenched from my hand and suddenly it made sense.

When I had fallen backwards over the root I had still been holding the musket with its seventeen-inch bayonet on the end. As the tiger had pounced on me it must have impaled its heart on the bayonet, pressing the butt of the weapon into the ground so that the creature was suspended above me. Now I lay next to the huge cat, which stretched a good three feet longer than me. It still twitched but its eyes had lost their fire, and if it was not dead, it soon would be. The bayonet was embedded right up to the socket. I heard shouting and people crashing back through the trees towards me.

From a distance I clearly heard Poorun Singh's voice call, "Flashman, what are you doing back there? Why don't you answer? Have you accidentally shot yourself?"

The damned cheek. Well, I would show him. I reached over and tried to tug the bayonet out of the cat; it was stuck hard between its ribs. In the end I had to stand and put my boot on its chest to get the thing free. Then, holding the weapon as casually as I could, I called out, "Over here. I have killed your tiger."

They came crashing through the trees even faster after that and suddenly four sowars including Lal were with me, staring in astonishment at the tiger's corpse that I now rested my foot on. They started shouting in Hindi that the tiger was dead and to come quickly and soon even more were there, first a dozen and then thirty people, all looking in awe at the tiger and the man who had killed it.

Poorun Singh pushed through the crowd to stare himself. "Flashman, how on earth did you do that?"

"He ducked the ball and so I had to kill him with the bayonet," I said casually, gesturing to the blood-soaked blade at the end of the weapon. The response was instantly translated by Lal into Hindi and spread around the still-growing crowd. It was to be repeated all over the village by nightfall.

"But that is impossible. No one can kill a tiger with a bayonet. You must have shot it first, surely?" Poorun simply could not believe it. He had already built his opinion of me, and it was probably pretty accurate. Coolly bayoneting a charging tiger did not fit it at all. But here was the evidence at his feet.

"The only wound you will find on the tiger is from this," I said, gesturing again at the blood-covered steel point at the end of the musket."

Blow me if he didn't get down on his knees and check. He swiftly found the fatal injury and could clearly see the L-shaped cut that matched the cross-section of a bayonet blade.

I thought I would add some embellishment to my tale and added, "I noticed that there were a lot of flies in this part of the forest and so hung back to investigate. I found the body of the villager in the tree and the tiger soon after."

Several people followed my glance up into the tree and there were gasps of horror as they saw the half-eaten remains of the poor woman. My hands were starting to shake slightly, from delayed shock, I think, and so I leant the musket against another tree and slid them into my pockets, looking cool as be-damned and feeling pretty pleased with myself.

"I misjudged you, Flashman huzoor," murmured Poorun Singh, getting to his feet again. It was the first time he called me 'huzoor', which was a mark of respect. He reached a hand into one of his pockets. "I think it is time you wore this on your turban, for you are truly worthy." And with that he pinned the same regimental badge that the other sowars wore onto my turban. It would be easy to mock his gullibility, but I won't. For bearing in mind what happened over the next few days, that gesture was one of the biggest, if undeserved, compliments I have ever received. Aye, and that tiger nearly had the last laugh and got me killed then too.

Chapter 12

That night for the first time in our journey we stayed in a village. A feast was given in our honour. Simultaneously the village celebrated their liberation from the tiger and a funeral pyre was lit for the remains of the poor woman. The tiger itself was tied to a pole and brought down for all the villagers to see. I claimed it as a trophy and paid two of the locals with a cart a handsome sum to take the carcass back to Madras to have it skinned for a rug. I have that rug still and you would doubtless expect me to have romped various women on it, but I haven't. Well, I tried once and got a claw scratch on my left buttock, which shows what happens when you get a tiger skinned on the cheap. But mostly when I look at that skin I remember those fiery yellow eyes both when they were gazing at me in the tree and then when I opened my eyes and found them inches from my own. Those types of thoughts put you off your muttons, and so now the skin is in the study to remind me of my time with those fearless Rajput warriors.

God knows what they put in the village brew but I awoke the next morning with a hell of head. I sobered up pretty fast. I had to, for I was dragged into consciousness by Poorun Singh shaking my shoulder and whispering, "Flashman, wake up. It is grim news. We are being hunted."

"Go away, damn you," I moaned before his words sank in, but he persisted.

"I have been speaking to the village headman. There is a price on your head. It is literally worth its weight in gold and he wants us gone before someone tries to claim it."

"What the hell are you talking about?" says I.

"Come to the headman and hear for yourself," he replied.

So reluctantly I got dressed and what I heard flushed the hangover out of my body in moments, only for it to be replaced with nauseous fear.

The headman's hut was only slightly less of a hovel than the rest of the buildings in the village, but he made us welcome: he had his woman serve us tea and then made her and the rest of the family leave the hut entirely. He explained that two days since they had got word that Scindia had sent huge groups of *pindaree* horsemen into the Nizam's territories, ostensibly to forage for food but the word was that they were also looking for an English spy.

"This spy is called *Iflassman*," said the headman and the word sent a chill down my spine.

We had been riding steadily for weeks now and I had begun to believe that we had shaken off any pursuit from Madras. Well, we had, but Scindia had just set up a new obstacle between us and our destination.

"I know you are English but I do not want to know if you are this *Iflassman*," said the village headman; although the look of horror on my face must have given him a pretty good idea. "We are grateful to you for killing our tiger, but there is a great price on your head, just your head, and soon people will think about this gold. You must leave before people are tempted."

"What do you mean 'just my head'?" I asked and almost immediately wished I hadn't.

"Scindia has said if you are found then you are to be killed immediately and he will pay in gold the weight of your severed head. Several heads have been sent to him already, but he has someone in his palace he says who will recognise the true head."

I reeled back in shock. Things don't get much more personal than your own head and that much gold would provide a powerful incentive to any bandit or villager. Perhaps even to one of the Rajput troopers? I wondered. No, I could not believe that. They were so obsessed with pride and courage that the rest would feel dishonoured and hunt down anyone who tried it. Scindia was cunning, you had to give him that: his means of payment meant that nobody would keep me alive and he did not run the risk of my being able to spread the rumour.

"How many *pindaree* are there ahead of us?" I asked.

The village headman named some of the leaders and Poorun Singh, who knew some of their bands, turned and said, "There must be around five thousand."

Jesus Christ, five thousand bloodthirsty bandits and countless more poor villagers all around us, all looking for my golden noggin. I thanked the village headman for his warning and Poorun and I stepped outside to talk in private.

"Surely we must go back?" I whispered to Poorun.

"No, huzoor, the rumour will have spread behind us; it will even reach Madras. You will not be safe there. We can still complete your assignment. The size of the *pindaree* bands mean that they cannot stay long in one place or they will starve. They are moving from east to west, so we will go more to the east to go behind them. Your skin is getting darker and your beard strong. From now on you must just speak Hindi when we are with strangers and no one will know that you are British."

Well, it was true that I had cause to be grateful for my Spanish mother's complexion; I probably could pass for a native on sight. But while my Hindi was coming on strong, it would still give me away at the moment.

Poorun slapped me on the back and grinned. "For a man who can bayonet a tiger, this is nothing!" And with that he strode off to get the troop ready to leave.

Well, you can imagine how I felt. Having by chance earned the admiration of our gallant commander, he now assumed that I was braver than one of those ancient British warriors who used to attack the Romans while naked, painted bright blue and high on narcotic mushrooms. Even if I showed my true colours and begged and pleaded for him to take me to a British port, I suspected he would still take me, willing or unwilling, to Berar to complete his own orders. And what was the safest option? Striking out on my own would be fatal. It would be open season for poor Flashy with every bandit, villager and itinerant beggar on the lookout for the chance to cut off the head that paid its weight in gold. Staying with the troop offered my best chance of maintaining my disguise, but word would spread from the village we were in that a strange Englishman was travelling with Company cavalry and we would have to stay ahead of that rumour to stand a chance.

We were saddled up and ready to go within the hour. The family of the woman who had been killed came over to give their final thanks for killing the tiger. I was already getting jumpy and checking their belts for knives and making sure some troopers were around me. The sowars had evidently all heard the rumour, but Lal, Flora and Daisy and several others came up and assured me that we would get through or die trying. I really wished they would not keep going on about the dying bit.

We left the village, heading west. Before we set off, Poorun had waited until some villagers were nearby before discussing with his corporal, or daffadar, how long it would take us to reach another town to the west, so that there was no uncertainty as to the direction we were going. In fact we did travel to the west for a full day. Poorun explained that fifty horses are easy to track and if we turned east too soon the villagers may find the trail and pass it on to others trailing us. We reached a river and wading our horses in, turned eastwards and trotted on through the shallows for several miles until we found a ford and crossed.

We headed north-east for another week, skirting around villages and sometimes travelling at night so that we would not be seen. Poorun now sent four men as scouts ahead and left four men behind as a rearguard, with proper pickets on duty every time we camped. Lal, Flora and Daisy worked hard on helping me improve my Hindi and I was now able to have basic conversations if they spoke slowly. As we travelled the country changed; there were fewer trees and big expanses of plain.

On the sixth day we came across a village that the *pindaree* raiders must have been through before. It was completely deserted. Poorun said that there would be villagers hiding out in the surrounding scrub who would have run away when they first saw our scouts. We pressed on and came to a wide, arid-looking plain that we had to cross. We all felt dangerously exposed on that featureless expanse. Poorun assured me that there was a hill fort in the middle of it and we hoped to get there by evening so that we could at least water our horses before moving on.

Late afternoon one of the forward scouts rode back to say that he had seen no *pindaree* bandits and that the fort was empty. You could see it by then in the distance, built on a huge lump of rock standing up from the plain. These hill forts looked impressive, often standing on sheer-sided rocky outcrops, but the walls were dangerously exposed to cannon. This one was small but it still looked impressive close to, at least to me. We walked our horses around it to the north side where a large, stone-rimmed water tank had been built in the shade of the rock to hold monsoon water drained from the rock and some of the surrounding fields. There were water wheels and abandoned irrigation systems and crops that were dead in the fields. The occupants must have left when they heard that the *pindaree* bandits were coming. We watered the horses and relaxed in the shade before starting the final climb to the fort.

"Would this be their only water?" I asked Poorun. "Is that why they deserted the fort, because they have no water supply inside?"

"No, it is too deep to dig a well down to water underground from the top of that rock, but they will have cut down a channel to below the level of this tank and then another tunnel to the water. The tank acts like a cistern so that there is always water at the bottom of the well in the fort."

"So why did they abandon the fort?"

"This is the only water and good vantage point for miles. If a large number of *pindaree* were coming this way, the people in the fort would expect them to come here. If the garrison was not strong enough to defend the ramparts then the sensible step would be to abandon it. *Pindaree* are nomads; they would not stay here. They would soon move on and, when safe, the people will come back."

The truth of these words was evident when we got to the top of the rock. The big gate had several holes it in, which must have come from a small, horse-drawn cannon that the *pindaree* had brought. One ball had evidently smashed the locking bar on the gate and the *pindaree* must have stormed in. We found evidence of this inside as the fort had not been completely abandoned. There were around twenty bodies of soldiers piled up around the walls and some other bodies of elderly inhabitants who had been too old or ill too travel. All had been slaughtered and the bodies were in an advanced state of decay. The stench was appalling.

We took doors off some of the buildings inside, loaded the corpses on those and carried them outside the fort, then unceremoniously tipped them off the cliff. Some of the bodies burst on impact and even fifty feet above them the smell of released putrification made you gag. After one body-run, to avoid doing another, I volunteered to draw water from the well to wash down where they had been lying. Mind you, it was bloody hard work hauling the huge well bucket full of water up over fifty feet.

We had been so busy we did not notice the little dust cloud to the south when it first appeared on the horizon. But it was still miles away when one of the sowars was sent up onto the ramparts to scan the horizon. "A small group of horsemen," he reported. Poorun and I went up to take a look in the fading light of the evening. He studied the cloud with his telescope.

"Do you think they have been following us?" I asked.

"Possibly, but from the size of the dust cloud there are no more than twenty of them. They won't reach here before morning, and if they try to get in our way then we can sabre them aside."

We scanned the rest of the horizon and it was clear, although there were various little ravines or dry river beds they called nullahs across the plain to carry away the monsoon water when it came.

"We should be all right tonight, but I will be glad to get away from here in the morning," said Poorun, putting away his telescope. "I've got an uneasy feeling about this place."

Well, if there is one thing a windy beggar like me does not need to hear it is comments like that, especially when he is effectively carrying a bank vault above his shoulders. I stayed up there a bit longer, scanning the horizon, but saw nothing other than that distant group of horsemen.

I don't know what woke me up that night. I had managed to find a rope bed in one of the abandoned rooms and had been sleeping fitfully under my blanket. Suddenly I was awake and it was not just the night chill that made the hairs on the back of my neck stand on end. For a while I listened, but I heard nothing. I tried to convince myself that I had just been unsettled by Poorun's words, but I could not get back to sleep. I decided I would get up and check everything was secure. Then I would be able to sleep, I told myself, slipping my feet into my boots. I reached into my saddlebags and took one of my pistols and slipped it into my sash and then stepped softly outside.

An unfamiliar abandoned fort can seem sinister at night, especially when you have spent part of the afternoon tipping the previous residents off a cliff. There seemed to be no one about. The sentry post above the south-facing gate was abandoned, there was the screech of some animal out in the dessert and as I crept quietly forward my heart started to race.

"Huzoor."

"Jesus!" I shrieked, leaping about three feet vertically into the air as the voice sounded just behind me.

"Are you all right, Flashman huzoor?" said some grinning white teeth in the gloom, trying to stifle a chuckle. Into the dim light stepped one of the troopers. "I have been sent to find you huzoor. The havildar-major would like you to go to the western rampart."

If I thought that the voice in the dark had given me a shock, I was in for another one when I reached the western rampart. There, across the darkness, were half a dozen lights.

"Please tell me that they are powerful glow-worms," I muttered to Poorun as I stepped up beside him.

"I wish I could, but I fancy these have a more powerful sting," he replied. "They have been appearing for the last hour. I think they have been approaching in the nullahs, but now that they are closer they have come up onto the plain."

"Shouldn't we be trying to get away?" I asked.

"We would need to light torches to see our way, and if they are hostile, they would see us and we would be caught in the open. Their horses should be tired after a night ride. I think we would do better to break out with fresh horses at dawn. They might not even be hostile," he added. "They could be the rest of the castle garrison returning now the *pindaree* have left." I could not see his face in the dark but I don't think either of us believed that.

"How many do you think there are?"

"It is impossible to tell. One torch could be leading one or two horses, or a string of twenty. I wish now we had not stopped for that tiger or that you had not killed it. Word will have got out that an Englishman was with us." He paused and stared south. "I think at least that group to the south may have been on our trail. The others could be *pindaree* returning from the west if they have heard the rumour of the Englishman killing the tiger. But most people who cross this plain stop at this fort, so they could be traders. Any less than a hundred and we should be able to cut our way out with fresh horses."

Well, I was not going to sleep now. That bloody tiger; if we had just got past that village like all the others then they would not have had a clue where I was. I paced up and down the ramparts while I considered my options, and there were not many. I could cut out on my own but probably would not last the day as a single Company cavalry sowar with a dubious grasp of Hindi in country where at least one group of horsemen was likely to be after my head. Staying with the troop seemed best, and Poorun's plan of breaking out at dawn with fresh horses seemed sensible if there were not too many hostiles outside.

But over the next two hours those six lights increased to ten. I kept looking towards the eastern horizon, praying for the dawn that would enable us to get on our way and reveal what waited beyond the walls. It is strange: when you are tucked up under a blanket with a pretty young bint keeping you warm then the sun is up in a moment, but when you are desperate for it to appear, it takes forever.

Eventually I must have settled myself in a corner of the ramparts and managed to doze for I remember a sowar shaking my shoulder and saying simply, "Look."

It was the grey of dawn. I was cold and stiff, but I forgot that in a moment when I looked out over the ramparts. The area to the west was still in shade, but I could see shapes moving to the south and north and there seemed to be hundreds of them. I ran around the ramparts to look over the east wall and there were yet more there, and in the better light I could see that many were walking their horses to keep them fit for any pursuit. They were fighting men all right, not traders, and while I had never seen a *pindaree* bandit before, I was pretty sure I was looking at hundreds of them now. We were never going to be able to fight our way out through this lot and survive. To confirm my suspicions, when I looked down into the courtyard Poorun was there with around a dozen troopers building a barricade behind the shattered gate in the entrance to the fort.

I went down to meet him and must have looked ashen-faced for he turned to me and said, "Don't worry, Flashman huzoor, we will not give you up."

It says something about the inherent courage and honour of the Rajputs that not for one moment had I thought that they would. I had assumed we would try to survive as a group.

"How are we going to get out of this?"

"We cannot ride through them. They are jackals; they love to chase down and kill when they have an enemy on the run. But they may think twice about attacking us in the fort. There is only one way in and we can match them man for man at the gate." He paused, looking pleased with himself, before he continued, "At the English school I went to they taught us about a battle that some old people had fought where three hundred warriors had held off a mighty army in a narrow pass."

"Thermopylae, the Spartans against the Persians," I said, remembering the same lesson at Rugby school.

"Exactly," said Poorun, grinning. "We will be the Spartans."

"They were all killed in the end," I reminded him. "And they were buying time for the Greek army. Is anyone likely to rescue us?"

Poorun looked a little crestfallen; he had evidently been pleased to show off his education in the classics. But his example had filled me with horror.

"It is the best I can do, huzoor," he said quietly. "If we fight well, they may give up or run out of food, and if word of where we are has spread then maybe the nizam will send soldiers to help us. We are still in his territory." He put his hand on my shoulder. "I am sorry; you must be worried for your mission. I fear I have failed you."

My mission was the last thing on my mind; I was just thinking of survival. Jesus, given the choice now, I would have shouted that I had bedded both Berkeley sisters in one night from the middle of Parliament Square and taken my chances with his lordship's thugs. One randy night had started the whole chain of events that had ended up in this wretched little fort surrounded by hundreds of bandits determined to separate my head from my shoulders. It was not even as if I had raped or seduced either of them; if anything, they had seduced me. I couldn't die here, I simply couldn't. I had to find a way out.

"Could I hide somewhere in the fort and then continue my mission after they have... er attacked... do you think?" It was awkward talking about the time that they would all be dead defending me, but Poorun was all for it.

"You are a brave man, Flashman, thinking of how you can complete your mission even at a time such as this. I will give you a couple of men to help you find a hiding place and then at the last we can help you hide. If you reach Berar, the man you should speak to is the chamberlain to Manu Bappoo, the raja's brother. He can arrange a meeting with the raja. If you manage to split the alliance then we will not have died in vain and the Company army will avenge us, yes?" He patted me on the shoulder again and detailed two men to help in the search.

For a while my hopes rose. Now at least I had a ghost of a chance of avoiding death and decapitation. There must be a hiding place in a fortress and we set to our search with enthusiasm. It was Daisy and Flora who joined me in the hunt for a safe hideaway and I would like to record in this account their proper names, but they were long and unpronounceable. They did not resent helping me search for a hiding place that would enable me to survive the battle in which they would die. Indeed, if anything they seemed excited about the prospect of the coming battle.

It made no difference anyway for there was no hiding place. You can be assured that I went over every last inch and you could not have hidden anything much bigger than a mouse. The granary was empty, the buildings had been swept clean of virtually all furniture and much of what was left had been chopped up for firewood. The walls were of stone and there were no attics, just a range of fairly basic rooms surrounding a central courtyard. Even the stables had no hay to hide behind. At one point I seriously found myself considering whether I could hide behind a large door, but even a child would have found me there if he had entered the room. And of course when they did not find an Englishman amongst the bodies they would search every inch of the place until they had.

I sank back in despair and climbed up the ramparts, and then really wished I hadn't. When I had last looked out the light was still dim and hazy, but in the time we had searched the sun had got well up in the sky. It was a bright, sunny morning – almost certainly my last sunny morning, I thought, as I looked down on the plain. There were literally hundreds of *pindaree* down there. As I walked around the walls, feeling increasingly sick with fear, I saw that there were herds of horses tied to lines around the tank on the north side of the fort where they were being fed and watered. To distract myself, I tried to count them. An old drover I knew had taught me to break a flock down into half and then quarters and then eighths, count those and then multiply up. I tried that and calculated that there were around three hundred horses down there. I saw their owners when I walked around to the gate. There were still at least a hundred mounted men waiting at the bottom of the narrow path leading from the fort in case we decided to make a break for it, but more were on ropes that were hauling a small cannon up the path. I guessed it was the same cannon that had broken the gate down before. It would make short work of the barricade, and if they had grape shot it would decimate any charge of horsemen. Evidently some more of the men had settled in the rocks around the cliff path as a musket ball ricocheted off a battlement near me and a chip of rock flew in the air. The fort was a bottle, and it was well and truly corked.

Chapter 13

People react differently when they only have a few hours of life left. Some of the sowars sat in corners chanting or praying quietly to themselves, other more practical souls spent it sharpening every weapon they had to a razor edge. Thomas Flashman Esquire spent his last hours in that fort running around the battlements in an increasing state of funk. My last hope was that by some miracle we could hold out until nightfall and then I could somehow lower myself over the ramparts and down the precipice below. I craned over the battlements to try to see what the rock was like beneath and where I might possibly climb down. It was hopeless: the walls were fifteen- to twenty-feet high, on top of fifty feet of rock. I would have no rope, be in the dark and would only have that chance only if we could hold out until nightfall. The futility of hoping we could survive the day was demonstrated a while later when there was a sharp crack outside and a round shot bounced off the ground outside the fort and smashed through the gateway barricade, sending a shower of splinters across the courtyard.

Oh, Jesus, I thought, they are starting the attack; this could my last few minutes of life. I am not a religious man, but I prayed then all right, although quite what miracle I expected God to provide I am not sure. The best I could hope for was a swift end. I had a sudden memory of Paris and wondered if my last sight on this earth would be from my own severed head and of cheering *pindaree* before the world went black.

Some of the sowars were gathering at the battlements above the gate and I went to join them. Having got our attention with the cannon shot, a small deputation of six *pindaree* leaders was coming forward under a flag of truce. They stopped thirty yards off and one of them shouted, "We know you have the Englishman called Iflassman. Give him to us alive or dead and we will leave. There is no need for further bloodshed today."

You can guess that if it was anyone else that they wanted I would be all for handing him over. Save fifty lives for the price of one, when we would all die otherwise? Well, it makes sense, doesn't it, especially when one of the precious saved skins was mine. I looked around the men to see if any were considering it, but they were all laughing at the *pindaree* leaders.

"Listen to the wind coming from that baboon's arse," said Lal loudly enough for the bandit to hear.

While they chuckled at that Poorun shouted down, "We do not all have the morals of a mutinous pi dog. If you want Flashman huzoor, you will have to fight for him, and many of you will die in the attempt."

Far from being cowed, this set off a great cheer amongst the *pindaree* who now had confirmation that the man with the 'golden head' was here to be taken.

"Come, brother," said Poorun to me. "It is time to get ready to send these jackals back to Shaitan or whatever other devil they believe in."

I looked over the parapet one last time. The *pindaree* leaders were going back and the gun crew were making ready to fire while the other *pindaree* crowded up behind the gun. They were still cheering, with some waving their swords or muskets in readiness for the attack.

We lost our first man a few minutes later. The gun crew were sending a cannon ball into the barricade every couple of minutes, and once it had smashed through the wood, the ball ricocheted around the stone walls of the courtyard. There was no way to guess where it would go and it moved too fast to avoid. There was just a bang, a crash and then a shower of stone where it struck. One of the sowars was standing in the wrong place and the ball struck him in the chest, killing him instantly. His long hair was in the blood, for now that the Rajputs knew they were going to die, they chose to die like the warriors they were. They took their turbans off, leaving their long hair to flow down their shoulders and many took off their red jackets. Several were even bare-chested. One or two started some traditional chant and soon they were all joining in, and to me it seemed to turn into a song that they were all bellowing. I don't know if they scared the *pindaree*, but they alarmed me. The neat uniforms and familiar cavalry ways had been replaced with keening warriors and incantations that I could not understand. They were not the same men I had spent the last month with.

Poorun saw me staring at them in astonishment and he laughed. "Sing, Flashman, sing to your god like we do to ours. It will help you make your sword sing when they attack."

Well, it might help them, but I couldn't imagine a quick chorus of 'He Who Would Valliant Be' would give me any backbone. I was still sick with fright and suddenly feeling very alone. It was my head that was the prize in this battle after all.

But before I could worry about that there was a fusillade of musket fire through the barricade from outside and then a burst of flame. Looking round, I saw two more of the Rajputs falling, hit by the musket fire. The cannon had evidently not been destroying the barricade fast enough and so now the *pindaree* had set it alight. Judging from the roar of the flames, they had also poured oil on it first. It was emitting thick, dark smoke that was getting blown into the courtyard, making us cough and our eyes sting. We had a choice: to stand either side of the gate to avoid the musket fire, which was still being fired blindly through the flames from the other side, and choke on the smoke, or go out into the courtyard and risk the bullets. Some went up into the battlements, but the smoke was still curling around the walls. The only cover from the bullets in the courtyard was the stone surround of the well and I ran to crouch behind it.

I had my sabre and my two pistols; they were the only firearms we had as the sowars had just sabres and lances. I put my powder flask and some pistol balls on the top of the well so that I could reload quickly. I heard a crashing sound as the *pindaree* used something to try to batter down the barricade. The horses in the stables were whinnying in panic as they smelled the smoke. There was shouting and yelling on the other side of the gate, chanting and singing this side of it, and somewhere someone was whimpering in terror. I realised who that was and clamped my jaws shut.

The courtyard was almost completely full of smoke and I could no longer see the gateway. There was another crash from that direction and suddenly someone was looming out of the smoke towards me. I picked up one of the pistols and fired. The ball missed, which was just as well for I saw when the figure got closer that it was one of the Rajput sowars. He waved his sword at me and grinned, oblivious of the fact that I had nearly killed him.

I did not smile back, as I was cursing at the wasted shot. Now I had just one loaded pistol left and I had been speculating whether at the last I would use that on myself. It would ensure a quick death, and if I blew my brains all over the yard, I would have the satisfaction of depriving the murderous bastards of most of their gold. But I doubted that I would have the courage to go through with it. I had to reload the used pistol quickly. My hand shot out to grab the powder flask, but with smoke in my eyes and the rush I managed to knock it instead. I watched, agonised, as it skittered across the stone... and then dropped down the well. I got to my feet and put my head back and screamed at the heavens in frustration every profanity I could think of. I was beyond caring now. I stood and ranted at the sky. Musket balls whizzed past my head, but I did not give them a thought. It would be mercy if one of them killed me. I cursed God with every invective I had ever heard in taverns, brothels, ships' foc'sles and the House of Lords.

"That is the way, Flashman huzoor, lash them with your tongue." Poorun loomed now out of the smoke and grinned at me as he moved on towards the gate. He was lucky I had not accidentally shot at him as well, but I did not answer him, for suddenly my prayers were answered.

It was just a thought, an idea, and I immediately sprang into action, hauling on the rope to lower the bucket down the well as fast as I could go. There was no time to think things through – another splintering crash against the barricade and renewed shouting from that direction meant that there were only seconds to spare. Again there was a crash from the barricade and this time a big cloud of sparks could be seen through the smoke and a loud cheer signalled that the *pindaree* were coming through the gap.

"Flashman huzoor, they are through. Come and wet the blade of your sword," called Poorun from a few feet in front of me as he ran forward to meet the charge.

"I will be right with you," I shouted back as I grabbed hold of the rope and swung my legs over the edge to drop down into the well.

I dropped six feet and then the rope held, caught on the spindle that was used to raise the bucket. I had been ready, holding it tightly with my hands and feet so that I did not slip, and now I went down it hand over hand. For at that very last minute I had remembered what Poorun said about the well when we had watered our horses on the northern side of the rock and how it was joined to the tank by a channel. I had no idea if that channel was just a pipe or a passage I could get through, or if it had been barred to stop people getting in or out of the castle. It was just an idea, a hope, which was more than I had before. The noise of battle continued above me but sounded even more eerie echoing down the stone shaft. I heard the clang of metal on metal and a blood-curdling scream above the general noise of the mêlée.

Suddenly my feet were wet and I kicked the bucket out of the way and dropped into the water. I was starting to sink; I was still wearing my heavy cavalry sabre and a woollen coat that was now heavy with water. I had to hold on to the rope while I unbuckled the sword, took off my sash and shrugged off the heavy coat. I looked up and saw a small circle of sky which looked strangely peaceful in contrast with the continuing noise of battle above me, but at least no one was looking down the well. I had hoped that there would be a light showing where the tunnel was but it all seemed dark. Would I drown down here or would I be hauled up, defeated by the *pindaree*, only to be beheaded? I had to keep calm. There had to be a water channel of some kind. I held on to the rope and started to work my way around the wall of the well, feeling with my hands and feet for a break in the stone.

I was just starting to panic when my foot kicked at nothing: there was a gap! Feeling with my hands and feet, I found it was big enough for me to get through. I took a deep breath and lowered myself underwater to see. I thought the distance from the well to the outside wall must be around sixty feet; it was hard to judge that in the tunnel, but there, at the end of it, was a dull green glow. I surfaced again and looked up. There was the circle of blue sky above me and the noise of battle was still raging. Waiting would serve no purpose. I had to act. I took three slow, deep breaths and on the third I dived and kicked into the tunnel.

There was room to pull myself along by grabbing the walls but not room to turn around if I got stuck. I tried to concentrate on counting slowly to a sixty to keep calm while I steadily pulled away on the sides of the tunnel. A third of the way along a rock had fallen from the ceiling, but I managed to squeeze over it without wasting too much time. Now the light ahead was looking stronger and I could see that there were no bars or other obstructions between me and the daylight. I was only halfway into my count when I came to the end of the tunnel and saw that plants and reeds were partly obscuring its entrance.

I surfaced in the foliage and concentrated on not making a noise. For a minute I just lay in the plants with my mouth wide open, gasping silently like a fish. The noise of battle was continuing fifty feet above me. Hopelessly outnumbered as they were, the Rajputs were clearly putting up one heck of a defence. Well, if I had anything to do with it, their efforts would not go to waste. I peered through the plants. There were rows of horses but initially I could see no people. Then I spotted a crowd of old men and young boys standing halfway up the path to the fort where they had a better view of the battle. I only saw the other old man as I nearly trod on him to get out of the tank. He had been dozing in the shade against the wall but was now coming awake as I had splashed him with water. I had no weapon and if he gave the alarm then the others would come running and I would be finished.

Desperation can drive you to do terrible things. I reached down to the floor of the tank and picked up a large rock. As the old man struggled to turn round to see what had splashed him, I brought it down on his head with a sickening thud.

I knew he was dead. I had heard the skull crunch under the rock. Now I might not be the bravest man you will meet, but I reckon that I can think pretty fast when death's hot breath is blowing down the back of my neck. For I saw at once that this old man's demise could actually help me escape. In a moment I was pulling off the dirty turban from his head, before it became soaked in blood. It was one of those lose ones with a tail that you can wrap around your face. I tore off my own turban and I quickly put his on to hide my features. Then I was hauling off his sword belt, loose coat and pyjama trousers. I was well hidden by the strings of horses and even someone looking down from the fort would not have seen the body hidden by the tank wall. I could not leave the corpse to be found, which was now stripped down to a loin cloth and some boots that were too small for me, and so I dragged him up over the tank wall. A few moments later I was pushing the body back up the tunnel towards the well and moving the plants to hide the tunnel entrance. Still I had not been seen, but I needed to get moving.

I put on the old man's clothes on top of my wet ones and looked for a good horse among those tied around the tank. I found a likely mount; it had a full water skin and a fodder sack tied to the saddle. I was just about to leave when I noticed something gleaming on the ground. It was the Company regimental badge by my old turban. I picked up the cloth and the shiny badge and swung myself up in the saddle and started to walk the horse away.

When you are riding off in disguise from a bunch of hostiles, and I have done it more than once, it is important not to rush. Amble off looking casual as though you want to empty your bowels in private and you will earn little or no attention. I did hear someone call from the crowd on the path, but I did not look round and just gave a vague wave of my hand and kept plodding on. My heart was racing, though. I was slumped in the saddle like an old man, but my ears were straining for any sound of pursuit or further challenge. I could not risk looking back in case someone who knew the old man was looking in my direction.

I headed north, directly away from the fort, and saw a short distance away one of the nullah river beds heading away in that direction. I ambled the horse across to it and we found a shallow slope to climb down. Now just my head and shoulders were visible above ground level and I risked a glance back. The fort was some two hundred and fifty yards away and the sound of fighting seemed to have been replaced with the sound of shouting. The old men and boys were now walking up the path towards the fort, which had evidently been subdued. I kicked the horse into a trot and lay down low in the saddle so that I could not be seen.

I had made it! I had got away, and if you ask me whether I felt a shred of guilt at running out on Poorun and those gallant troopers, well, I didn't then and I don't now. If I had stayed and died with them, it would have made no difference: they would still be just as dead and some bandit leader would have been richer by the weight of my head in gold. I found out much later that after the *pindaree* had finally slain all the Rajputs they fell to arguing amongst themselves. They were not all from the same band, you see, and when I was not found among the dead they started accusing each other of hiding my corpse and head for themselves. One enterprising villain even decapitated one of the younger Rajput corpses and gave it a European haircut and tried to claim the money, but it did him no good.

But you can't spend six weeks with a group of people and not mourn their loss. I felt very alone as I rode away and found myself turning the turban badge over in my hands as I thought of them. It says something that I have that badge still. I managed to hang on to it despite everything that followed and it rests now in a little box of mementoes that I have on my desk as I write this.

Chapter 14

I really should have checked what was in that water skin before I set off. To this day I don't know what it was, but it smelt appalling and tasted worse. I nearly tipped it away when I first gagged on it, but luckily I didn't, for I would not be here now if I had. It was mid-December then and the rainy season had ended there a couple of months ago. There was still green foliage around for the horse to graze on but the bed of the nullah was dry. For the first day we rode north inside the nullah, following it where it went. It kept us out of sight from the rest of the plain and I was convinced that a pursuit would soon start.

It was cold at night, but that first evening I could not risk a fire and I kept warm by walking on with the horse alongside me. At dawn I climbed out of the nullah and onto some nearby rocks to survey the ground around and particularly to the south, where any pursuing riders were likely to come from. Initially I saw nothing. Then, after a while, I did see some clouds of dust, but they were moving west as far as I could tell. I stayed up there, watching and resting and warming myself in the dawn sun. Eventually I saw another smaller dust cloud moving east, and while I could not see it, I guessed that another was moving south. They were ignoring the north as only an idiot would head towards Mahratta country.

That idiot was considering his options. Berar also lay to the north but I had no intention of trying to complete my mission. Scindia's spies and killers would be all over the place. No, just getting out alive was my goal. I was not sure precisely where I was. I thought I was still in Hyderabad. There was a big river on the border and we had not crossed one. Going north or south would take me to enemies and west was where most of the *pindaree* were heading. East seemed the safest option: the east coast was friendly to the British and I should be able to get a boat to Madras and beyond. But as I took another swig of that foul liquid in the water skin I knew that water was my first priority and then food, for there had been nothing in the saddlebags for me to eat and I was starving.

I stayed up on the plain for the next day and headed east. It was rough country with rocky ridges and outcrops and every now and then a nullah to cross. It was another cold night but I sheltered between some rocks and managed to sleep. The horse was struggling; it had not drunk for two days, the fodder sack was now empty and there had been few plants for grazing. I walked him at dawn and spotted a cart track heading north-east. A track meant people and it might lead to a village or a river where we could get food and water.

I saw the first corpse an hour later. It was lying by the side of the road, or at least some of it was as jackals had torn the body apart. It was impossible to say how the man had died, but from the look of his remains it must have been at least a week ago. I saw two more bodies as I continued along the path during the next hour. At the second half-eaten skeleton we found, two jackals ran off into the scrub at the sight of us. As the sun climbed and the day warmed, three vultures could be seen circling in the air ahead. Finally, as we breasted a hill, I saw the little village spread out below us. I paused and studied it closely.

I suspected that the bodies we had passed had been running from something and that thing would have been in the village. Now, though, the place was as still as a grave and, judging from the vultures I could see on the ground, that could be exactly what it was. We had to go in. I was parched as the foul stuff in the skin had run out the previous day and I had not eaten now for two days. I mounted the horse and we trotted down the hill, the horse picking up speed as it got closer. There was a well in the village with a stone trough beside it and both man and mount flung themselves beside it and drank greedily.

After slaking my thirst I looked around. The village had around twenty buildings and several looked like they had been ransacked, with possessions strewn about. In the dried mud around the well there were lots of hoof-prints and more human remains were scattered around including those of a woman and two children. It was then that I noticed the three survivors. They were sitting on the ground with their backs to the wall of one of the huts and they were not far from death. The three men all looked middle-aged but it was hard to tell. Their eyes were sunken and their hollow stomachs and emaciated frames showed that they had not eaten properly for ages. Another corpse lay near them and it would not be long before they joined him. They took no notice of me, just staring blindly into the distance. It was only the movement of their chests and the visible pulse on the neck of one them that told me that they were alive.

"What happened here?" I asked them in my best Hindi.

Two ignored me completely, but the third slowly turned his head as though it was taking all his effort and fixed me with a pair of immensely sad black eyes. "*Pindaree*," he croaked softly before fixing his gaze back into the distance.

Looking around, it all made sense. A band of *pindaree* must have raided the village, taking all the food that they could find and anything else of value. Some villagers must have fled ahead of them on the road I had come in on and the rest were either killed or left to starve. The three men were just sitting there and waiting to die.

What made no sense at all, though, was the thing that suddenly moved between two of the huts towards us. How could people let themselves starve to death when there was half a tonne of prime beef in the form of a lame ox there for the eating? Oh, I know cows are sacred to Hindus, but they ain't sacred to Flashy. With a cry of delight, I sprang forward, drawing my sword as I went. The weapon was razor-sharp and I was so hungry I did not hesitate. Getting alongside the ox, I swung the blade up and across the beast's throat as hard as I could. I half-expected the villagers to give some protest, but they made no move at all as the oxen staggered after making a truncated bellow at my attack. Blood was gushing from the deep wound, but it took a full minute to sink to its knees. I didn't waste the time, but started hacking at the wooden wall of one of the nearby huts to gather some firewood and pulling dry straw off the roof for kindling. I had a flint and steel in my pocket and very soon I had a fire going. A search of the nearest hut brought an iron skillet and some earthenware bowls and by the time the ox had breathed its last I was on it again with the sword to cut myself a hunk of meat.

If I was served the same mystery cut of ancient ox now in my London club, I would box the waiter's ears and demand to see the maître d'. But then, not having eaten for two days and watching it roast in the flames, it was the sweetest meat I had ever tasted. I trimmed off the corners with my sword as they looked cooked and cut myself a large slice as soon as it was ready. I sat there gorging myself with the meat juices running down my chin. I was feeling much better.

Then I looked up and saw those three faces staring at me and suddenly I felt angry. How dare they just give up on life? I cut them hunks of meat and put bowls of it before them. They didn't even look at it and then I really lost my temper.

"The beast is already dead, you stupid bastards," I raved at them. "It won't do it any harm if you eat it now."

They just ignored me and I kicked dust at them in frustration. It still makes me angry years later the way that they just gave up when things looked bleak. In my long and eventful career I have looked certain death in the eye an alarming number of times. I had done it twice already on that trip. I may have faced most of these times in a blind funk or panic, but I never gave up and just waited for death. That is the human spirit: to keep fighting to the end. An old India hand once told me that of all religions he thought that the Hindu was the bravest in facing death, with many showing absolutely no fear at all. Certainly the Rajputs showed no fear, but they at least went down fighting.

I slept fitfully that night, with gut ache as my stomach struggled to cope with the sudden change in its diet. I had the fire for warmth and cooked more of the ox, cut into strips that I planned to take with me when we left. As dawn came up I looked at the three survivors. They were still alive, now covered in dust and with the meat still untouched at their sides. I felt a twinge of guilt and took the meat away. Having interrupted their decline into oblivion, I knew that as soon as I left vultures and jackals would descend for the rest of the ox. I had only kept them away in the night by lighting more fires around the carcass. Thanks to me, the last sight the survivors would have on this earth was likely to be a foretaste of what would happen to their corpses when they died.

I didn't mount the horse as we left, as unlike me it had not eaten well. I had scavenged around the abandoned vegetable patches of the village and found it about half a bucket of useful food and it had found some light grazing. The water skin was full now with fresh water and I had also found a pottery jug and bowl so that I could water the horse. We set off again, following the road north-east.

In the next three days we found two more villages like the first, only these had nothing alive in them and in one the well had been filled with rotting bodies. The horse was now on its last legs, and while I was better in body, my mind was despairing of the endless territory we were crossing that had been scoured of life. In five days I had heard just one word from another human: *pindaree.*

As the midday heat built on the third day, the horse and I found some shade beneath a rocky overhang and settled down to rest. I don't know about the horse, but I certainly did not hear the other horsemen as they approached and slowly surrounded where I was sleeping.

"Good afternoon," a voice said in perfect English as its owner kicked my foot to wake me.

"Eh, what's that?" I said, waking. Then automatically I said, "Good afternoon to you too..." But these final words tailed off as I realised that I was surrounded by armed men and had just given away the fact that I was an Englishman. I stared around in alarm and gave a slight groan of despair. All that effort to escape but now my head would be taken anyway.

"Don't worry," said the stranger. "I am sure that you are not the person whose head my master seeks." And with that he winked at me. "But I have heard tell of another brave Englishman who bayoneted a tiger to death and then escaped five hundred *pindaree*. So I thought, when I cross into Hyderabad, if I see this man, I will recruit him. For being here on his own, he is surely looking to enlist into the Mahratta army, like many Europeans before him." Now he gave me an encouraging smile and added, "Is that not so?"

Once again my brain was struggling to keep up. Quite why I was being recruited instead of being killed I did not understand, but I knew the right response to the question. "Absolutely, old boy, desperate to join up I am. Just show me the way to the recruiting office."

"Steady," said my new friend, suddenly looking grim. "Understand this clearly. While I may not always approve of my master's methods and I respect men of great courage, I have taken my master's salt and given my oath to serve. If I find out you are this Flashman, I will be obliged to have you killed. So, my friend, what is your name?"

"Teddy, I mean Edward Carstairs," I said without hesitation.

"Welcome to the army of Daulat Rao Scindia," said my new friend, putting out his hand for me to shake. "I am James Skinner."

Nowadays all India hands have heard of James Skinner, the famous leader who set up his yellow-jacketed cavalry regiments known for their courage and skill, but back then he was just another of Scindia's officers.

[**Editor's note:** The regiment known as Skinner's Horse has survived to this day and is now an armoured unit in the present Indian army.]

He knew full well who I was, but while I gave him scope not to know, he could choose to ignore the blindingly obvious fact that I was the man with the golden head. I wasn't so sure about his men, though, for a few of them were giving me deuced odd looks. One of them was also looking closely at the markings on my horse and shouted something to Skinner, who barked a reply back. A moment later there was a gunshot and the horse was dead on the ground.

"It had *pindaree* markings that would have been difficult to explain if people saw them," said Skinner. "We will give you a horse and clothes to match your status as one of Prince Scindia's officers."

Within moments a fresh mount was provided and a new uniform jacket to match those of the rest of the troopers. I stripped off my *pindaree* rig and gathered what few possessions I wanted to keep. I was still wearing my Company cavalry breeches and shirt and so soon looked more like a soldier.

"Ah, that is better," said Skinner. "Now we can resume our journey. Come and join me at the head of the column and we can talk."

So began one of the more bizarre conversations I have ever had.

"I was wondering," said Skinner, "if by chance you had spoken to this Flashman fellow? For I heard that he met my old commander, de Boigne, and I would be interested to know how the general was."

"I did meet him, yes," I replied. "And he told me that the general is well. De Boigne has married again and lives in Paris now, where he is much respected by the French government."

"That is good to hear. My master is trying to stop a rumour but there are enemies in his household and the rumour is already abroad. There were previously stories that my master tried to kill the general when he left, but now there are stories that my master was responsible for the old Pateil's death too."

"Old Patiel?" I asked, puzzled.

"Apologies, patiel means village headman; it was how my previous lord, Mahadji Scindia, liked to be known. He never forgot his humble beginnings despite uniting the whole Mahratta confederacy with de Boigne."

"Yes, that is what de Boigne said, at least according to the Flashman fellow, and I think he can be trusted on that point."

We rode on silence for a while and then Skinner said, "It does not matter that this Flashman did not complete his mission, for the rumour is already out and there are already enough rifts among the Mahratta. Have you heard of a chief called Holkar?"

"No, I haven't."

"He is a cowardly jackal, but he is shrewd and already he has broken with Scindia and says he will not fight the British. I suspect he hopes that the British and the other Mahratta will fight and weaken each other so that he can then take more land."

We rode in silence a while longer and then Skinner continued, "These men are my personal escort and each of them can be trusted. I think it would be best if you became my escort commander; that way you can stay close. I have recently visited my sister, a Mrs Templeton in Calcutta, I have two other sisters also married to Company officers

117

and my father lives in British territory. I like to visit them regularly. As my escort commander you would naturally accompany me. If you chose to stay once we are there, it would be entirely understandable."

"Are we going to one of your relatives now?" I asked hopefully.

"For you, sadly not. I have been given command of a regiment based in Meerut and that is where we must go. It is about a hundred miles north-east of Delhi," he added, seeing that the name of the town meant nothing to me.

"But that is in the heart of Mahratta country," I croaked.

"Indeed," smiled Skinner. "Which is why I thought it best to keep you close. But you are free to strike out again on your own if you prefer."

Of course I didn't. I would be safer with Skinner and his men than on my own. I was feeling damn nervous about going into the centre of the enemy territory, but it seemed I did not have a choice. I just had to hope that if I kept my head down then in time I would be able to make my escape.

Chapter 15

The journey to Meerut was in many ways similar to travelling with Poorun and the Rajputs in terms of routine. I rode up alongside James Skinner for most of the way and found out a lot about him. His father had been a Scottish officer in the East India Company army who had married a high-ranking Rajput woman. Together they had six children, three boys and three girls. James's oldest brother, David, had gone to sea, but his younger brother, Robert, was also a soldier, serving another warlord. Tragically the gulf between the cultures of his parents proved too much. While his mother had been happy for her sons to have an education, her husband wanted an education for his daughters too. In Rajput culture it would dishonour a girl to be seen outside the care of her female relatives. When the girls were taken to school their mother felt that they had been violated and so killed herself. James was twelve when this happened and it must have had a big impact on him. He was educated at boarding school for the children of Company officers but was also given an education in his Indian culture too. As a result he could read and write in perfect English, Hindi and Persian.

His father had ensured that he had a good understanding of both cultures and he seemed remarkably well-balanced as a result. He was a man of great personal integrity, which is why he had kept an eye out for me on his return journey to his regiment. Professing to be a Christian, in a battle a few years ago he had taken a vow to build a church if he survived. When I knew him he was yet to carry out this undertaking but he mentioned it to me as something he fully intended to do. He did it as well and was later buried in his own church. But his Christian faith did not extend to matrimony where he took a more Indian approach, taking numerous wives and fathering many children. He truly was a man who bridged two cultures.

On the journey to Meerut I also gained a greater understanding of the Mahratta army. The *pindaree* were certainly not representative of Scindia's forces and indeed the professional soldiers despised these bandits, who were as likely to rob their own side as the enemy given the chance.

"The only places that are truly safe from their ravages are Gwalior and Sardhana," Skinner told me one day.

"What is so special about those places?" I asked.

"Gwalior is Scindia's original base before he moved to Delhi. As for Sardhana, that is the begum of Samru's territory and she would have their balls for kebabs if the devils raided there."

"Why would a woman frighten the *pindaree*? Wouldn't they see a woman ruler as a soft target?"

Skinner laughed. "There is nothing soft about the begum. I know for my brother Robert works for her. Oh, there must have been something soft when she was a girl, for the story goes that she was a nautch dancer. She had something soft to attract a mercenary called Walter Sombre. She was fourteen then and he was forty-five and a commander of a mercenary army that was for hire to local warlords. There were four battalions totalling about 2,000 men. They married, and despite her age she won the respect of all the key commanders in her husband's army and often used to advise Sombre. She was just twenty-five when her husband died but she was so well-established that she was accepted as the new commander of the army."

"Did she not remarry?"

"Oh, she tried, but the army mutinied at the thought of their commander marrying one of her French officers. There are lots of rumours about what happened next. Some say she was fleeing to the British and some say she tricked her new husband to get rid of him and stay in power."

"What happened?" I asked, intrigued.

"Well, Robert says they were married but the army caught up with them when they were trying to make their escape. It seems that they had agreed a suicide pact in case they were captured; at least her new husband, called Le Vassoult, thought they had. As the soldiers crowded round she brandished a knife and screamed and then there was blood on her clothes. Le Vassoult thought she had killed herself and blew his brains out with a pistol. It turned out she had just scratched herself and in a few days she was back in command of the army."

"A cunning lady then. How does she get on with Scindia?"

"He is wary of her. He knows that she would make a very dangerous enemy. The old Mughal emperor also views her as a daughter after she helped quell two rebellions against him. No, Scindia does not need any more enemies. You will get a good idea of how unstable things are when we get to Meerut."

He was not wrong there, for even before we got to Meerut we had started to hear rumours of a battle at Poona. Holkar, the Mahratta leader who would not join the Scindia alliance against the British, had accelerated the break-up of the Mahratta Confederation by attacking another Mahratta leader called the peshwa, who had fled to the British for protection.

"Mr Carstairs, your friend Flashman could not have done a better job of breaking up the Confederation or giving the British an excuse to invade," murmured Skinner with a grim smile when he heard the news. "The sooner we get to Meerut, the better, but it might be a while before I am able to visit my family again if war is imminent. But then if the British attack the Mahratta states, it might be easier for you to cross the lines."

We had been travelling in the Mahratta states for two weeks by then and once we were out of the north of Hyderabad the countryside was less ravished by *pindaree* and looked more prosperous.

One morning Skinner woke me up by saying "Happy Christmas, Edward Carstairs" and he gave me a small cloth-wrapped gift. It was a gold ring, a typically generous gift from this big-hearted man, and I regretted that I had nothing to give him in return. He brushed this aside and said that my friendship was enough of a gift in the circumstances. I realised that I had then been travelling for two months, with various bands of companions. Thoughts of Christmas brought memories of home too. This was my first Christmas outside Europe, and fleeing across a strange country under a false name and in fear of my life did not seem an ideal way to partake of the festivities. That said, it was only slightly less dangerous than the traditional Boxing Day hunt at home. Tearing across the countryside amongst a huge crowd of drunken horsemen with a massive hangover and yapping dogs. There were falls and broken bones every year and two riders have been killed in my time alone. I cannot remember us ever taking a fox. Mind you, I normally dropped out to water myself and my horse at an inn early on in the proceedings.

At Skinner's suggestion I changed my appearance again on the journey. European officers did not normally have beards, but going back to clean-shaven may remind people of any descriptions of Flashman that had been issued. He proposed that I shave off the beard but retain a moustache and side whiskers, which I did, and judging from my reflection in a scrap of mirror I borrowed, I looked damned dashing as a result.

We reached Meerut in early January and the town had the appearance of a kicked hornet's nest, with everyone bustling about but no obvious order. The latest news was that the peshwa had signed a treaty the previous month, ceding territory and power to the British. The peshwa was the nominal leader of the Mahratta, although in practice the power was with more powerful warlords like Scindia and Holkar. The Mughal emperor was old and blind and in effect he had no power either these days. Yes, Mahratta politics were damn confusing, as the people who had the titles of rulers such as emperor and peshwa didn't or couldn't actually rule. The real power was held by a crowd of smaller princelings and warlords who were now also fighting amongst themselves.

Dowlat Rao Scindia was only twenty-four then and Holkar was twenty-seven. There had been a longstanding feud between the two families which the new young rulers had continued. Holkar had destroyed one of the armies Scindia had sent to attack him, while Scindia's forces had raised to the ground Holkar's capital of Indore. Scindia was not the only one to use *pindaree*; Holkar sent hordes of these bandits against both Scindia and the peshwa. In return Scindia had captured a member of the Holkar family and had him executed by being crushed under the feet of an elephant.

Holkar had sworn revenge and to my mind he seemed to be playing the far smarter game. He had a much smaller standing army, having to rely largely on *pindaree* and other bandit tribes from the north. By staying out of the Mahratta alliance and then engineering a situation where the other Mahratta would have to fight the British, he was effectively weakening all of his potential enemies. Once the British and Mahratta had fought each other to a standstill then his bandit armies could sweep in and plunder their territories at will and Holkar would replace Scindia as leader of the Mahratta.

Everyone now expected war but it would take months for the British to gather their forces and more importantly the logistics that could support their army on the long march north. This all meant that I would have to lie low amongst Scindia's army for several months before I could make my escape. Initially this seemed a worrying prospect, but as we arrived at the Skinner bungalow I could see that it would have its attractions. For three of the prettiest women I had ever seen rushed out and greeted James Skinner very warmly. Whether they were all his wives I was not sure, but from the strength of their greeting I was pretty certain that they were more than good friends. He introduced me as Teddy Carstairs and they greeted me more formally, although one seemed to pass an appreciative eye over me and my new whiskers. Hello, thinks I, maybe this new face furniture will serve as something more than a disguise. It did too, and that very night, although it left an awkward situation afterwards.

After months on the road Skinner turned in early and his little harem disappeared with him. It seemed his brother officers had tactfully stayed clear on the first night of his return. So apart from a few servants, I tooled around the rest of the bungalow alone. I drank brandy and smoked on the veranda and tried to ignore the occasional ardent noises coming from the back of the house.

We had been passing through Mahratta territory for weeks now and I had got used to playing the part of Teddy Carstairs with Skinner to back me up, but nobody had paid me much attention. Now, though, I was in one of Scindia's main garrison towns and people would look at me more closely. Scindia himself was less than a hundred miles away in Delhi. There were still people looking for Thomas Flashman; the price remained on my head. But finding me was now less important as Holkar's actions had done more than I ever could to break up the Mahratta confederacy. Whatever happened, I was going to be in the heart of Mahratta territory for several months, one of their most-wanted men disguised as a new officer recruit. I was going to have to act the whole time and a single slip could be fatal. Of course since then I have acted many parts, from a colonel in Napoleon's army to a Spanish guerrilla and even a Patagonian llama farmer (and try saying that after a skinful of fermented Patagonian llama milk). But back then my only acting had been of a Spanish peasant while acting as a courier in Spain. That had ended disastrously after half an hour as my mission had been betrayed in London and my enemies were waiting for me. So you can understand my apprehension as I strolled up and down that veranda and speculated on the future. I could survive but I would have to be damn careful and lucky to carry this off.

When things had quietened down I retired to my room and it was a delight to sleep on a proper bed again. I must have been sleeping soundly as it was only when the girl climbed into the bed beside me that I woke up. The room was totally dark, but in the moment of awakening I was able to determine that the intruder was female, as slim as any of Skinner's harem and wearing nothing but a veil. She giggled as she ran her hand over my body, but she said nothing at all. After months with nothing to ride but a horse it took but a moment for her to coax me to attention and then she was astride and writhing away in a most diverting manner. Now fully awake I decided to show off what I had learnt from the Hindu temples with Mrs Freese and she was soon stifling muffled squeals of delight as we rolled around the bed. Then we upset a bedside table as I tried the monkey god position with just one foot on the floor. She must have seen the same carvings for while I could only feel her body rather than see it, she managed to contort her limbs in the most amazing manner. She had a leg halfway up my back while she bounced around like a jumping Maasai warrior with a scorpion in his loincloth. The delicate bedside table was little more than matchwood when we had finished.

I hauled myself back onto the bed, exhausted, and tried to pull her after me for a lingering post-coital fondle, but she slipped away. A moment later I heard the door close and she was gone. I was left with nothing more than an appealing flowery scent on my body and the bed to prove that she had been there at all. There is nothing like a good rattle to pick up your spirits, and as I dropped off to sleep again I was thinking that staying with Skinner might not be so bad after all.

To this day I do not know which of Skinner's lovely harem it was. I watched them closely for some secret smile or favour the next day, but they all looked as cool as bedamned, often with a knowing smirk in my direction. Skinner looked pleased with himself too, which was not surprising with those girls at his beck and call. He grinned when he saw me and I am not even certain that my nocturnal visitor was one of his harem and not some native nautch dancer he had arranged on my behalf. But I did not get time to ponder that as a steady stream of visitors arrived with news that was all bad for Skinner, but more mixed for me.

Morale in the army, particularly among the officers, was very low. Scindia's chief minister was his father-in-law who used his daughter and other concubines to distract the prince with as much debauchery as he could. With Scindia out of the way the minister could run the country as he liked. Oh, it was a tough life being a prince in those days and it is amazing Scindia lasted until he was forty-eight. The father-in-law was a cunning weasel who had got rid of most his rivals back in '97 when there had been a rebellion against the new ruler. He took the chance to have most of Old Patiel's ministers rounded up and executed. Two were blown from the mouths of cannons, three had their heads crushed with tent mallets, two were poisoned and one lucky soul was blown apart by rockets, a means of execution that the father-in-law devised especially for the occasion. Since then, apart from the few times his son-in-law staggered, exhausted, from the boudoir for a rest, he had been ruling the roost. As a consequence, things were going to hell in the region. Most of the surviving men of consequence from Old Patiel's days had wisely taken themselves off out of sight, so the only counsel the prince got was from his father-in-law.

Meanwhile, in the army de Boigne's successor, General Perron, was inadvertently going about destroying the army. While de Boigne had promoted on merit, Perron, who spoke poor English, showed great favouritism for French officers above all others. This caused huge resentment amongst both native officers and those of other nationalities, including the British. I found this out as various officers came to complain to Skinner over the next few days. With his mixed parentage, Skinner was seen as part of the British contingent, although I think he saw himself as Indian. He certainly had no qualms then about fighting the British if necessary; he had taken an oath to serve the Scindia family and that he would do. Skinner introduced me to the various visiting officers as Teddy Carstairs and they all greeted me warmly and showed no suspicion that I was someone else.

I quickly realised that Skinner was highly revered in the Mahratta army, and if he said I was a loyal new recruit, no one was going to question it. A lot of the 'British' contingent of officers were born in India, usually of mixed parentage like Skinner. They often asked me what life was like in Britain, and most did not seem alarmed at the prospect of fighting the 'old country'. Two did, though: a Captain Stewart, who had been born in India, and a Captain Carnegie, who had been born in Scotland and had come to India to seek his fortune. They were not comfortable at all with the thought of fighting British soldiers and sought out my views. Of course, I had no intention of fighting the British army either, but I could not attract attention by leading a revolt and so I assured them that I thought the situation would be resolved by negotiation and that there was little to worry about.

I am bound to report that these two honourable men did resign their commissions when war came. Perron used this as an excuse to dismiss the entire British contingent including Skinner, which explains how Skinner later found himself leading his horse regiment for the British, although he always refused to fight against Scindia. But all that is later in my tale.

One of the more interesting visitors we had in those first few weeks in Meerut was James's brother Robert. He came down from Sardhana, the begum of Samru's province, which was about three days' ride away. He had set off as soon as he heard that his brother was back to hear news about their sisters and father. The begum had given him ten days' leave and so he was only able to stay for four days with the journey time, but it was fascinating hearing them talk about their childhood. Their father had loved his wife but had wanted the best for his children and that included an education. The loss of their mother when their sisters went to school had been a terrible blow for all of them. Having had schooling, they now appreciated why their father had felt it so important, but it had forced them to become more westernised. "Mother was a Rajput princess," explained Robert. "She had grown up knowing just one culture. She could not bend and adapt as she learned about western ways. She needed to be flexible to get the best of both worlds."

"You mean like the begum?" asked James Skinner, laughing. "I don't think anybody else could be that flexible."

"What is the begum like?" I asked Robert. "I have heard stories about her, but you must know her well as you work for her."

"Nobody really knows the begum of Samru," said Robert. "She makes herself a different person for different people; she even uses different names. For the Mahrattas, her soldiers and the Mughal court she is Begum Samru. Begum is a Muslim title meaning lady, and Samru is derived from her first husband's name of Sombre. It reminds them that she and her first husband are accomplished warlords and that she has helped them win many battles. For Hindus living in Sardhana and elsewhere she is Farzana or Zebunissa, an impoverished nautch dancer made good and either from Kashmir or from a Mughal family. Some say she is the daughter of a Hindu dancer or sold as a slave, take your pick."

"But is she a Hindu or Muslim now?" I asked.

"I have seen her do rights for both faiths," replied Robert with a grin. "But it does not stop there. She was baptised as a Roman Catholic twenty-five years ago, and when she is with Christians she uses the name Joanna Noblis. She truly is all things to all men, which makes it impossible to guess her real mind."

"Well, that is certainly being flexible," I said, starting to understand how this woman had survived among the warlords. "Where does she stand if there is a war between the Mahratta and the British?"

"Oh, her army will fight for who can pay her the most for their services," says Robert. "That will be Scindia, as Holkar cannot afford to pay for armies. He has to rely on banditry that fights for loot. She is raising another regiment now to have as many troops as possible to sell, but those recruits will never be ready to fight in time."

"So she serves Scindia then?" I asked.

"She writes to both Scindia and Holkar and various other warlords besides. I think that both Holkar and Scindia are very wary of her. She has been involved in intrigues for much longer than them. She is fifty now and has been ruling on her own for over twenty years. Her power comes as much from what she knows and her influence with other warlords as from her formidable army. You can bet your last coin that she has plans for all eventualities."

There followed a debate on the readiness of various regiments which I will not bore you with. In fact, I will speed over the rest of my stay in Meerut, which lasted nearly three months. I was given a smart uniform of a yellow coat and red sash and a tulwar sword, but this was just for form's sake. The tulwar swords were strange; at first I thought mine had a child's grip as there was only room for three fingers within the guard, but they showed me that you held the forefinger wrapped around the guard for a better hold. They were razor-sharp too. James Skinner explained that most were made from better-quality Damascus steel than the Sheffield steel used by the British. While the metal was softer than the British weapons, they could be ground to a much finer edge, and as they did not keep hauling the blades through the throats of their scabbards in salutes, they stayed sharp. Some officers swore that their blades must taste blood every time they were unsheathed. Obviously I did not have that rule, but I can confirm that if you test the edge of your tulwar with your thumb as you would a British sword, you end up with a cut thumb.

I was not required to do any actual soldiering. From what I could see, though, Scindia's army was a formidable force. There were parks of artillery, which when they fired a salute on one occasion seemed very well served as they reloaded and trained the pieces quickly. The infantry marched well and could fire volleys; they seemed slightly slower to reload than British infantry, but it was hard to be sure as I had not timed either with my watch.

Sadly none of Skinner's harem troubled me again after that first night, which was a frustrating disappointment as I was staying in the same bungalow as those beauties. I still remembered the scent that my night-time visitor wore, but frustratingly all three of them seemed to use it. Skinner once caught me inhaling it as one of the dusky maidens served me food.

"Carstairs, are you smelling my wife?" he asked in a voice of mock outrage.

"I am just getting a whiff of a most enchanting scent," I replied. I could not afford to offend Skinner, as without his help I was lost, but I could not resist a tweak at whichever of his harem had visited. As they were all present I added, "I have smelt it before around the house and it will always remind me of the exceptional hospitality you and your ladies have provided."

"Well, if it will stop you sniffing at my women, I will get you a bottle," said Skinner with a wry grin.

But he must have wondered about the wisdom of keeping a horny Flashy under the same roof as his little ménage, and two days later he led me down the road to a smaller bungalow in the officers' quarters. "I thought it was time you had some space of your own. We are likely to be here some months yet. Will this serve?"

It was a very pleasant little place, not as nice as my bungalow in Madras, but some of the best officers' quarters in a garrison I have ever had, and it was about to get better.

Skinner rang a bell and into the room walked a beautiful young woman in a red sari. The wanton look in her eye as she appraised me completely outweighed the other demure aspects of her appearance. "This is Fatimah, your new housekeeper," Skinner announced with a grin. "She cannot cook, clean or manage a household, but you may be able to find a use for her." And with that he left us to get acquainted.

Chapter 16

Skinner was wrong about us having months to wait in Meerut; well, he was wrong for me anyway. While the events that followed were terrifying at the time, looking back I think that they might have kept me alive. Fatimah made Mrs Freese look frigid. I am pretty sure I lost a stone in weight purely through fornication in my six weeks in her company. Whereas Mrs Freese had only studied the wall carvings once, this beauty had been brought up with them and countless other material besides. It was the first time I had heard of a Hindu text called the Kama Sutra, which is all about sensual pleasure. It is in Sanskrit and so I could not read it, but apparently it has one thousand, two hundred and fifty verses. My lovely Fatimah must have studied it to a level where she could have lectured on it at Cambridge, and boy wouldn't she have packed the lecture halls.

That I was not a dry, desiccated shadow of my former self towards the end of March was some kind of miracle. When Skinner asked me to accompany him on a trip to a place called Oojeine, I welcomed the opportunity to recover my strength and did not enquire as to the purpose until I joined him outside the garrison stables. I was surprised to find nearly a hundred other men from Meerut also waiting to set off. Looking around, I saw that all the European and native officers from all the regiments were present together with virtually all the non-commissioned officers from corporal or jemadar upwards. Like me they were all in uniform and most had a brace of pistols tucked into their belts as well as their swords. Skinner appeared and, mounting his horse, he gestured for me, as the commander of his bodyguard, to ride alongside.

"What is happening?" I asked him.

"Scindia and his father-in-law are planning to kill General Perron and his European staff at a meeting they are having in a place called Oojeine. But all of his officers, corporals and sergeants are going there to make sure this doesn't happen," he replied calmly.

"You mean I am going to be in the same place as Scindia, the man who wants my, I mean my friend Flashman's head?" I whispered hoarsely at him so that we could not be overheard.

"Don't worry, there will be over three hundred officers and men by the time they have been gathered from all the regiments. You will be lost in the crowd, and if you stayed behind you would have aroused suspicion. Scindia has spies in all the army camps. Anyway," he grinned, "you look like you could do with a rest from Fatimah. Now you understand how Scindia's father-in-law can distract him from government."

"Why do they want Perron dead just before they are about to go to war?"

"Probably because the father-in-law wants the army under his control to help him consolidate power. Palace politics is a dirty business." He looked over his shoulder to check that the rest of the company were following in good order. "Perron has been out of favour for a while in court; there is no trust between him and Scindia. Recently they summoned him for a meeting and then kept him waiting for hours while they flew kites of all things. Now he has been summoned to a council meeting, but someone has tipped him off that Scindia has hired five hundred Pathan warriors to kill those who attend."

"Five hundred to kill just one man?"

"All of the European officers have been invited to the meeting, including you and me. They plan to kill us all and then leave one of their men in command of the other Indian officers."

So while I was thinking I was safe and busy rogering myself away to exhaustion, others were plotting to kill me and around thirty other Europeans or half-Europeans in the army. It made no sense as these were among the most experienced officers they had and all would be needed if it came to war.

"Do we have enough to fight off five hundred Pathans?"

"Look around us: everyone will sell their lives dearly. But I doubt it will come to that. Scindia is not stupid enough to kill all his officers and non-commissioned officers just before a war."

Killing any of his officers just before a war seemed daft to me as it would destroy the morale of the army, but as we rode our band increased with the men from other regiments and so did my confidence. Unsurprisingly Scindia was not popular amongst his men, at least this group of them, and they were all sure that it would not come to a fight.

The council meeting, or durbar as they called it, was held outside the town. They would normally be held in a palace or large tents, but because of the numbers involved this time it was out in the open. Despite my apprehension I wanted a glimpse of the man who had been so keen to arrange my death, although I made a point of staying amongst a crowd of tall junior officers as we approached. A long, expensive carpet had been laid out on the grass. At one end of it under a richly embroidered canopy was a throne in the centre of a row of chairs for other dignitaries. Sitting on the grass down the far side of the carpet were five hundred of the most evil-looking villains I had ever seen, who were scowling malignantly at us as we approached. Skinner went to sit with leaders down at the front while many of our party started ostentatiously loosening swords in scabbards and checking the priming in pistols as they sat down. Your correspondent was searching around for likely escape routes if fighting erupted while sitting himself in the middle of the thickest group of soldiers.

It took five minutes for everyone to settle down. Suddenly a crowd of richly dressed people appeared from behind the throne and started to take their seats. The man I took to be Scindia, dressed in extravagant silks and cloth of gold, sat down in the central throne. Next to him sat what appeared to be a clean-shaven dwarf with a turban and plainer robes. On his other side sat an older man who seemed to be continuing a heated argument with Scindia as they took their places. The man next to me told me that this was Surjee Rao, the father-in-law. I was starting to get very uneasy as from the body language it seemed that the father-in-law was urging restraint, and losing the argument. Scindia was looking petulant and angry. He waved the old man aside and glared imperiously in our direction.

"General Perron," Scindia barked, "I believe I commanded just you and your European officers to attend this durbar." I heard the words clearly, and if I missed any of the Hindi I could hear the translator turning the words into French for the general.

The general rose slowly from a chair that had originally been set for him nearest the Pathans and which some of his officers had moved closer to the centre of our group. "I brought my entourage in accordance with the custom agreed by myself and your great uncle." He spoke clearly and without a hint of fear.

Heated whispered debate resumed between Scindia and his father-in-law but suddenly the dwarf spoke. "You fool, they will kill us all if you do." The voice was sharp and while the face had a prominent nose that could have been a man's the voice was undoubtedly that of a woman.

Scindia lapsed immediately into silence and seemed to sulk. The woman, who could not have been much more than four feet tall, looked at us with black, glittering eyes. There was no hint of fear in her face, but instead a look of mild amusement.

Looking around, I could see nothing amusing. The front ranks of both contingents glared at each other across the carpet, just a few yards apart. Whether Scindia gives the order or not, I thought, it will take just an ill-judged gesture or insult from either side for this to explode into violence. Surjee Rao, the father-in-law, must have thought so too, for having got Scindia's consent he ordered the Pathans to withdraw. There was a furious growl from that side of the carpet but Surjee Rao shouted at them again and reluctantly they started to get up and move away. They looked at us hungrily like gluttons dragged away from a feast, while those on our side of the carpet laughed and jeered in triumph.

Without his protection Scindia appeared more conciliatory, and food and drink was served for all and gifts exchanged between Scindia and the senior men of the army.

We all started to relax, and while I declined the betel leaves that were passed around for chewing (disgusting stuff that tastes foul and involves a lot of spitting), I did partake of some skins of arrack that were also circulated among the crowd. After the tension at the start of the meeting the sense of relief now was almost palpable. My travelling companions had been proved right: we were not going to be attacked. Amongst them, even with Scindia just a few yards away, I felt deceptively safe and drank more than I should. Little did I know that I was not nearly as safe as I thought.

"Who is the short person sitting next to Scindia?" I asked one of my companions.

"Why, that is the begum of Samru. Where have you been not to know her?" said a stout havildar beside me.

"I am new here, but I have heard of her, of course, just not seen her before. I had not realised she was quite so short."

"Aye, don't be fooled by her size for she has courage that one. More than once she has led her troops to victory when heavily outnumbered. She can be ruthless too, for I heard she once had two servant girls buried alive for displeasing her."

"Ha," said his neighbour, "she is small like a scorpion with a sharp sting, as her second husband found out when she tricked him into blowing his brains out for her."

At this they all laughed at her cunning.

"She is good to her troops, though," added another from the group. "Unlike Lord Scindia, she actually pays them occasionally and she does not waste their lives in pointless folly on the battlefield."

This comment kicked them off into a long debate on soldier's grievances, for pay in any army is invariably in arrears, if it comes at all. I drank more arrack and watched those at the end of the carpet. Scindia was back to looking petulant and bored, but the begum sat there still with her amused smile and her eyes were darting amongst the men sitting on the carpet. Occasionally she would give a nod of greeting and twice men got up to salaam back at her in return. There was clearly a lot of respect for her amongst the soldiers, and if there had been a riot with the Pathans, while Scindia might have been killed, I had a shrewd suspicion that she would have been spared.

It was starting to drift into the evening before we were finally given leave to go, but at this the general stood up and went to stand in front of Scindia and, taking off his sword, still sheathed, he laid it at the prince's feet.

"I have grown old in your service," the general said loudly for us all to hear, "and it does not become me to be disgraced by dissolute knaves and bullies." Here he gestured broadly at the courtiers around the prince, although we all knew he meant the prince himself. "I will therefore take my discharge." He turned to the men and said clearly, "From now on you must look to the Lord Scindia for guidance."

On hearing this both Scindia and his father-in-law gave a smile of triumph. Scindia stepped forward and embraced the general, insisting that he regarded him as an uncle. With the five hundred Pathans still milling around the outskirts of the town he even had the nerve to say that he was sure he had no idea what could have offended him. But neither the prince nor the father-in-law made any attempt to change the general's mind.

We all got up and started milling about to find friends and make a general movement towards where the horses were tied. A number of the courtiers were mixed in with the throng and at first I walked past him without noticing. You must have done the same: walked past someone and then a pace or two later your brain tells you that you know that face. In this case my brain knew the face, and suddenly a whole lot of other things fell into place too. Of course if I had any common sense I would have just kept on walking while my mind worked it out and hoped that he had not noticed me. Unfortunately I was not that smart, and before I knew what I was doing I was turning around to stare. He had turned around too, and for a moment we both looked at each other in astonishment. Now I knew how the letter had disappeared on the indiaman ship from England. I also knew why I had not managed to find it searching cabins and why Scindia knew about it and was so confident in recognising my head. For there, standing in front of me wearing robes and a turban, was Lieutenant Harvey, the indiaman officer I had thought was my friend on the ship.

"Flashman... my God, it is you behind those whiskers."

Even then I might have tried to bluff it out if I had thought fast enough, but I was still in shock. "Harvey!" I gasped, thus sealing my fate.

"Guards! Guards!" shouted Harvey, recovering first. "Arrest that man! He is the British spy Thomas Flashman."

If I thought my army comrades would come to my rescue then I was destined to be disappointed. They started to shrink back, leaving a space around me as though I were still at school and accused of farting in chapel. One man did not shrink back, though: pushing through the crowd came James Skinner.

"Leave that man alone!" he cried. "He is Edward Carstairs and he is the commander of my bodyguard."

Of course Skinner had to maintain the pretence to protect his own position, but he showed no hesitation in coming forward. Seeing his approach, the other soldiers stopped shrinking back, but they did not impede the royal guards who now pushed through them in my direction.

"His name is Thomas Flashman," replied Harvey. "I know as I was at sea with him for four months. He is the man with the golden head and now I am going to claim my prize."

The guards grabbed me by the arms and it was then that I started to panic. After all I had been through – the weeks with the Rajputs, escaping the *pindaree*, having to travel to the enemy heartland just to survive – now I was betrayed by the wildest of coincidences.

I started to struggle. "Let me go! I am one of you, I am Edward Carstairs.... Oh Jesus, they can't kill me now."

They were dragging me towards dais where Scindia and the others still sat, now staring curiously at the disturbance.

Suddenly Skinner was alongside me, pushing the guards back. "Listen, you must show courage. They will have no pity for the weak," he whispered at me. "You must be strong. Tell them that you are a man of influence, a friend of the Wellesleys, that the brothers will avenge you if you are harmed." The guards dragged me on closer to the dais. "It is your only chance," Skinner called after me.

We were through the crowd of soldiers now, and looking up, I could see Scindia, his father-in-law and the begum all staring in my direction surrounded by their courtiers. They had been preparing to leave as well but now settled back down to see what this disturbance was all about.

"Sir!" shouted Harvey as he pushed past me. "Lord Scindia, I have found the spy Thomas Flashman. He was here disguised as one of your officers."

"Are you sure?" asked Scindia in astonishment. "He was hiding in my own army?"

By now I had been dragged in front of them and one of my guards swept away my feet with his leg as he pushed me so that I sprawled before them in the dust. I could feel my face burning; it went red when I was terrified, which people often mistook for anger. Luckily I looked up before I spoke, which may have saved me. I had not really been listening to Skinner as he had shouted at me as I was pulled through the crowd; my mind had been paralysed in terror. But now his words came back to me as I looked up at the faces of those who would decide my fate. I saw not a shred of mercy would come from that quarter. The begum was looking annoyed at having her departure delayed and glared at me stonily. Scindia coiled himself back into his chair and licked his lips while smiling in anticipation. His father-in-law grinned and rubbed his hands in delight and leaned over to whisper something to Scindia which made them both chuckle malevolently.

Skinner's words came back to me then: bluff was my only hope. So instead of begging, pleading and grovelling for them to spare me, I stayed silent. The guards who had released me stood either side but did not move to stop me as I got back onto my knees and then stood up, brushing the dust from my clothes. I gazed at them red-faced and sweating but tried to look as cool as I could with my guts churning in terror.

"This is him, sir, definitely Thomas Flashman," said Harvey again.

I ignored Harvey and looked Scindia in the eye, playing my part of the fearless British officer.

"Are you really Thomas Flashman?" Scindia asked quietly.

For a moment I weighed up whether to try to continue claiming to be Carstairs. It might buy some time while they checked that the real Carstairs still lived, but then I would be dead for certain. Looking at them, I did not think they would wait to check. They would believe Harvey whatever I said because he told them what they wanted to hear, which just happened to be the truth.

"Yes, I am," I replied and there was a gasp of astonishment and murmuring from the surrounding soldiery. "I am a trusted aid to Lord Mornington, the governor general, and his brother, General Arthur Wellesley. If you harm me they will hear about it," I said, gesturing at the three hundred soldiers watching this encounter. "The Wellesleys will not forget such an act when preparing for war or negotiating a peace. On the other hand," I added hopefully, "I would be happy to take a message from you to the governor general." I looked at their faces to see how this was going down but Scindia was staring past me into the crowd.

"Colonel Skinner," he called. "Come and explain to me how a notorious British spy came to be commander of your bodyguard."

Skinner marched forward a few paces to stand beside me. "He told me his name was Edward Carstairs, sir. He never gave me reason to think otherwise."

"And where did you meet him?" enquired Scindia with exaggerated politeness.

"On the Deccan Plain. He was on his own, riding to join our forces," said Skinner stolidly.

"And you did not think to connect this lone English horseman with the English spy who had escaped the *pindaree* nearby just days before..." Scindia's voice now rose to a shout: "And who all my forces should have been looking for!"

"No, sir," said Skinner woodenly. "He gave me no cause to doubt his identity."

"Then you are either a liar or a fool," hissed Scindia angrily. He sank back in his chair, reflecting on us both, and then glanced up at the sky where the sun was sinking towards the western horizon. Then he turned to me. "You wanted to help me send a message to the Wellesley brothers, didn't you. Well, so you shall."

You would think that my spirits would have risen at this, but they didn't. There was a malevolence emanating from Scindia that left little room for hope. Every fibre of my being wanted to throw myself to the ground and beg for mercy, explain how I had been tricked and trapped and how I had wanted no part of the dastardly scheme that had got me in this mess; but looking at Scindia's face, I knew that to do so would be pointless and fatal. I looked across at the others on the dais. The begum was showing complete disinterest and was whispering to one of her aides while the father-in-law was grinning in anticipation. Skinner had said that my only hope lay in showing courage; perhaps he was planning a jail break or knew people planning a coup. It did not seem much of a chance but it was all I had, and so I stood tall and looked him in the eye.

"We will send a message to the Wellesley brothers by executing you in the morning," announced Scindia loudly to the crowd.

I heard a murmuring spread through the watching soldiers but at that exact moment I felt nothing; my mind went numb. I had been half-expecting it. After all, he was unlikely to have offered the keys to the local bun shop or a pardon after his forces had been trying to kill me for months. But if, dear reader, you are ever in the unfortunate position of being sentenced to death, and I speak from experience here as it has happened to me at least three times in my life, let me tell you it takes a while to sink in. I just stood there in shock and disbelief, as they then discussed the means of my despatch.

"Let me see now," said Scindia, grinning at me and obviously waiting for some sort of reaction. "Shall we use an elephant or perhaps a tent mallet?"

"Rockets?" suggested the father-in-law hopefully. "We have not done that for a while. We have some here and they certainly make an impression."

"Yes, rockets," said Scindia.

He looked disappointed that I had not started raving and begging for mercy yet. Looking back, I am surprised myself. If he had said 'hanging' then that may have brought back memories of executions I had seen and triggered a reaction, but talk of elephants and tent mallets made the scene surreal. I just continued to stare at him while my mind tried to fully comprehend 'execute' and 'tomorrow'.

Scindia evidently decided to give my imagination some help. "We will tie your left arm and right leg to one rocket and your right arm and left leg to the other. Sometimes two limbs are torn from the body, but if you manage to hold the rockets together in their cross, you are killed when the shells inside them explode."

"What about the head?" asked a voice. "I need the weight of that in gold."

I looked and there was Lieutenant Harvey in his robes talking about weighing bits of what would remain of my body and suddenly my mind seemed to catch up in a rush. The theft of the letter... Harvey, betrayal to Scindia... Harvey, enabling my head as a prize... Harvey, delivering me to Scindia... Harvey, and now here he was just two yards away arguing about the resulting offal from my destruction.

The rage welled in me like a volcano, completely out of control. The guards who stood either side were no longer holding me and were completely unprepared for what happened next. One moment I was standing still and erect and the next I had launched myself at Harvey with an animal growl. We fell to the ground and I got my hands around his throat and I crushed it for all I was worth while roaring at him, "You treacherous little bastard! I'll rip your god damn head from your shoulders!"

It took four guards to pull me off him and I was still raving and kicking out like a mad thing. In the end three of them sat on me and to stop me shouting one of them shoved a gag in my mouth and rapped the back of my skull with something hard. I think I blacked out for a moment, but when I came to I remember seeing Harvey being helped to his feet. He was making choking noises and massaging his throat, while beyond him Scindia was laughing in delight at the reaction he had prompted. I was vaguely aware of chatter and shouting from the ranks of the army behind me, but no one seemed to intervene.

Eventually Harvey stood free and, having cleared his throat, he gave me a look of utter hatred and then turned to the dais. "Lord Scindia, I would like to ask permission to light the rocket fuses at the execution tomorrow."

"No," said Scindia, suddenly becoming serious again. "That will be done by Colonel Skinner, and if he refuses, he will be tied to another rocket cross himself." He looked with a hint of contempt at Harvey before adding, "I might let you light them both if that happens."

His final words were almost drowned out by an even louder chorus of shouts and cries from the soldiers behind but I don't recall any more as I think I passed out again.

Chapter 17

I came to alone in some strange, stone-built, bottle-shaped cell, which must have been part of one of the buildings in Oojeine. There was a small barred window high up on the wall and I saw that the sky was now dark with the first few stars visible. I had been woken by the sound of a terrified scream which had been cut off suddenly with a choking gurgle. It had come from nearby and I shrank back, terrified in the darkness, listening to scuffling outside my cell door and the sound of two low voices muttering. Finally there was the noise of what sounded like a body being thrown on the floor. I wondered if it was some rescue party organised by Skinner, but that scream had sounded truly awful and I could not bring myself to call out. If it was a rescue party, they would call for me... and they didn't.

It is strange what you find yourself grateful for at times. At that point I took some comfort from knowing that as I was due to be spectacularly blown apart by rockets in the morning, I was unlikely to be murdered by Scindia's men in the night. It was not my first time in a prison cell and it would certainly not be my last. Bizarrely it was not even my only stay in a bottle-shaped cell, for they seem to be quite popular in some places. But whatever happened, it was destined to be one of my shortest spells of incarceration.

Now awake, I began to pace my cell and stare up at the small square of stars visible through the window. You have probably done the same in dire circumstances, wondering if you would see them again and if they were also shining down on someone you know. My only hope of rescue was some kind of revolt by the army officers, but they had shown no interest in stopping my arrest and had only expressed outrage at the idea of Skinner being blown up too. They would not put themselves out to save a British spy from a rocket-powered evisceration. If he had any sense, Skinner would touch off the fuses. I knew I would in the same situation.

I let my mind dwell on how I would die for a while and was nearly sick at the thought of it. The jets of flame burning my limbs while the awful rockets tried to tear me apart and all the while burning down to the explosive shells inside them. I had no idea what force a rocket could generate and whether I was likely to be blown up whole or in several pieces, and believe me when I say that it did not bear thinking about.

I only spent a few hours in that cell but I truly believe I would have gone mad that night if my stay had not been interrupted. With the terrors I have been through in my life, it is a miracle I have not ended up in the blue devil factory like one of my brothers.

I had been pacing around, desperately trying to take my mind off the rockets and listening for any sound of rescue. Surely James Skinner would attempt something, I reasoned, but all I heard was the sound of the odd owl screeching or the dying squeal from its prey. I was not even sure if James Skinner was still at liberty. He could have been arrested as well, to ensure that he was there to light the fuses in the morning. Then suddenly I heard more noises in the corridor outside my cell. There was a slight scuffling sound and I wondered if the men from earlier were back or if I should call out this time. Before I could make up my mind a voice whispered urgently, "Flashman, are you here?"

I could, and probably did, weep with relief. It was rescue. "Yes, I am here," I whispered back, knocking on the cell door.

In novels the cell door always swings open at this point, but in reality there was a delay of what seemed an eternity but which was probably just a couple of minutes while they found the right key. It gave me time to cuff any tears of relief from my eyes and then get stressed again worrying that the key would not be there and it was not rescue after all. Finally, after muttered cursing on both sides of the door, they found a key that worked and the door swung open. There were the familiar Skinner features but a strange uniform and it was only when my rescuer stepped into the patch of moonlight in my cell that I realised that it was Robert Skinner and not his brother James.

"Surprised to see me?" asked Robert, grinning. "Had to get you out or my foolish brother would have refused to light your rockets and you would both have been blasted to the heavens."

I stood there gaping at him, for I had only met Robert once when he visited his brother for a few days when I first arrived in Meerut and now here he was saving my life. Little did I know that the surprises of that night were only just beginning.

"Well, let's get a move on," he added. "Unless you want to stay for the fireworks after all?"

That sparked me into action and I was through the cell door and down the passage, which was lit by flickering torches. I could see a couple of Scindia's guards lying tied up at the far end with another of Robert's men guarding the entrance. But before I reached them there was a big black patch on the stone which I realised was pooled, sticky blood and there, thrown against the wall, was another body. It was a white man and it took me a second to realise that the face, frozen in a contorted look of terror, was that of Lieutenant Harvey.

Robert must have seen where I was looking for he murmured, "It wasn't us. Scindia evidently felt he had outlived his usefulness."

I couldn't feel sorry for him, the bastard had got what he deserved, but it brought home the treachery of Scindia and his father-in-law. Rather than pay him, they had just arranged for him to be taken down in the dungeons where a couple of villains had cut his throat. His body had been dropped in a corner like rubbish, to be buried in the morning.

We emerged out of the corridor into a small courtyard. Robert's men led the way silently around the shadowed sides until we reached a small door in a larger main gate that led onto the street. I stepped through to find two of Scindia's men tied up and gagged and watching me, white-eyed, with more of Robert's men standing over them. In the street was an opulent-looking palanquin, one of the two-seater affairs with eight bearers, all dressed in some sort of uniform with two on each pole.

"Your means of escape," said Robert, gesturing to it.

It would only take minutes for Scindia's guards to discover I had been broken out and this looked the worst vehicle possible for a fast and discreet escape. Christ, a rickshaw pulled by blind beggars with bells could not attract more attention.

"I don't want to sound ungrateful, but wouldn't something a little less ostentatious and faster, like a single horse, be better?"

Robert grinned at me. "Don't worry, it is the begum's personal palanquin. No one will dare stop it and there are enough of her bodyguard around if they try. It will take you to the city gates where horses waiting for you."

I looked again and now I noticed that the palanquin bearers had swords and there were more armed men loitering in doorways and at either end of the street.

"Go quickly. We don't want to hang around," urged Robert.

Well, no one has ever accused me of being slow to run away from danger and that wasn't going to change now. I bounded across and climbed in through the curtains of the palanquin and dropped into the forward-facing seat and immediately it started moving. I peered out of the curtained window. Soldiers were moving out from doorways to run alongside; there must have been twenty visible down the side I was looking. I was ducking back into the dark interior of the palanquin to look out of the other side when a woman's voice just beyond my knees said, "You need not worry. We will not be stopped."

How my heart has survived the shocks it has experienced in my life I will never know, but it must be at least as strong as the fabric on top of the palanquin, which my head slammed into as I jumped in alarm.

The woman chuckled in amusement. "You seem a little jumpy, Mr Flashman," she said in perfect English.

"Is it any wonder after the last day I have been through." I squinted into the other side of the palanquin but could not make out the figure I was sharing the compartment with as thick curtains blocked out the light. "Who are you? Are you one of the begum's servants?"

A curtain on the other side of the palanquin was pushed back and moonlight flooded in. Two twinkling black eyes stared at me from a face that I had last seen beside Scindia's the day before. There in front of me was the diminutive figure of the begum of Samru.

"I suppose I should be grateful that you did not sit on me when you jumped into my palanquin," she said. "What are you doing? There is no need to climb out again. If I wanted to harm you, I would not have just saved you from certain death, would I? Just sit down and stop rocking us about."

My first reaction had been to bolt from the vehicle and I had got one leg out before the import of her words got through the fresh burst of panic. She was right: if she wanted me dead, she had only to wait. But for the life of me I could not understand why she would want to rescue me, and I must have said so.

"Really, Mr Flashman, you must learn not to take things at face value, especially with the Mahratta. We are much more complicated than that." She settled herself back in the centre of her seat and regarded with me with a look of mild amusement. She may have been only four feet tall but in that confined space she did not seem small at all. "Just because I was at Scindia's durbar, you should not assume I am just in Scindia's party. As a ruler of a small province I need to balance many friends to maintain my independence."

"So why were you at Scindia's durbar?" I asked, still trying to work out what was going on.

"Why, to see what would happen, of course." She gave another little chuckle. "Who do you think warned Perron what Scindia had planned? I even suggested what he should do about it." She paused, shaking her head at the memory. "Mind you, even I did not think Scindia would be stupid enough to consider letting the Pathans attack all his officers. That would have torn his army apart."

I was sitting back and watching her carefully. I remembered what Robert had told me before about how she adopted different personas to give people the impression she wanted them to see. I was just twenty-one then but I was already learning that people do you favours for a reason. This was a very canny woman who had ruled for over twenty years because she was cunning and ruthless when she needed to be. She had not rescued me just out of goodwill, and now she was telling me how she manipulated the Mahratta rulers and generals. There would be a price to pay for my rescue.

"Wouldn't the destruction of Scindia's army be beneficial for you? Surely it would drive up the price of your own troops?" I asked.

"No, it is a matter of balance. If Scindia's army was destroyed or broken up then Holkar, the other leading Mahratta ruler, would attack and win and then he would be all-powerful. The Holkar and Scindia families have been battling each other for generations; they hate each other. They both think I favour them, but in reality I and other smaller princes work to keep them balanced. That is in our best interest as then they both look to us for support."

"Rescuing me will not help maintain the balance, so I have to wonder why you have done it."

"Can't a humble Catholic woman do a favour purely out of Christian charity?" She gave me an innocent smile and I grinned back.

"From what I have heard about you, lady, there is usually at least one good reason for anything that you do. You did not rescue me as an act of human kindness."

She laughed again. "Maybe I have my reasons," she admitted. "Holkar is the enemy Scindia is really focused on. Scindia's troops have beaten the British before and he is confident that they will do so again. They vastly outnumber the British and now that they are trained in European ways they are a formidable force. But I am not so sure of their victory. The tiger-loving Tippoo Sultan of Mysore was a powerful ruler with a strong army and the British beat him. Scindia is also doing a great job of destroying the morale of his own troops. So I am thinking that it might be wise to have someone to help negotiate with the British if they do beat the Mahratta."

"You mean me?"

"Precisely. Of course Robert Skinner believes I am doing it to save his brother. James was set to refuse to light your rockets and would have been killed as well in the morning. James Skinner is far too principled a man to fight for a ruler like Scindia, who does not understand the concept of honour."

"But won't Skinner be punished when Scindia finds out I have escaped?"

"No, that is why I collected you with my uniformed men and left the guards alive to see them. Scindia will learn it was me who broke you out and he may guess it was to save James, but he won't do anything about it. Right now he needs my army too much to risk losing it to kill a British spy."

"What happens if Scindia does beat the British?"

She looked me in the eye as she replied. "Well, then it will be difficult for me to refuse him if he asks for you back, and to be frank, you will be of little use to me then." Perhaps 'straight talking' was another one of her qualities that she wanted me to report to the British if the time came, but right then I would have welcomed the 'reluctance to cause offence' approach more typical to Indian culture.

So there it was: I was relatively safe with the begum while the British remained a threat to the Mahratta, but that issue would take months if not years to resolve. This was a lot better than my explosive prospects back in the cell.

Before I could consider the matter further, the palanquin came to a rest at the city gates and there waiting for us were around fifty fast horses. The begum had evidently planned ahead for my rescue, sending her carriage and baggage on ahead late that afternoon, and had just stayed behind with her bodyguard. The palanquin was now abandoned and we all mounted and set off down the road to her province of Sardhana. For all her talk of 'Scindia needs my army and so would not dare challenge me' I noticed that we went off at a fair gallop. She was a good horsewoman and her tiny frame sat like a jockey on a powerful horse which she handled with ease.

She led our column and I rode alongside. Soon the turban she had been wearing had slipped off her head and her long hair was flying in the breeze. I remember looking across at her then as she rode. Despite her fifty years, I started to see how she had attracted her first husband and his entire army to her control and caused her second husband to kill himself rather than live without her. In the moonlight she looked years younger and the soft lunar glow revealed the beauty that must have enchanted men in her earlier years. She was still full of energy and enjoyed the company of her soldiers, joining in some of their banter. When one of her bodyguards suggested that she ease up as the road was rough and the horses could trip and fall, she cajoled him for being an old woman and rode even faster. The soldiers laughed in delight at her recklessness and you could tell that they adored her. She was a woman who had been getting men to do what she wanted all her life, and while her physical attractions may have faded, she had plenty of other tools in her armoury. She caught me studying her once and, as though reading my mind, she smiled and said, "Don't try to understand me, Mr Flashman. Many have tried and all have failed."

As the sun climbed over the eastern horizon we caught up with the carriage and baggage wagons that she had sent on in advance the previous day. Her ladies fussed around her and she disappeared into the carriage, presumably to conduct her toilette. Her soldiers and I rested outside, watered what few bushes there were and ate a breakfast of boiled rice and a strange green spicy paste. I noticed that guards were posted for any sign of pursuit; they were not taking chances. But none was seen.

After an hour we prepared to set off again, but as I was about to mount up I was invited by one of the ladies into the begum's carriage. In daylight she was travelling in a manner more fitting to the ruler of a province. I climbed in and sat opposite her and she gave me a smile of greeting.

"When we are alone you must call me by my Christian name of Joanna. May I call you Thomas?"

"Of course. Where did you learn to speak English?"

"One of the best soldiers I have ever commanded was an Englishman called George Thomas. He helped me learn my craft. He was a great man who went on to rule his own province before Scindia's men destroyed him." She paused and looked out of the window and then added thoughtfully, "I owe George a lot. I nearly married him, but when I chose Henri Le Vassoult instead, he came back and helped me regain command of the army and secure my lands again." She looked back at me. "I take it you have heard the story of my second husband?"

I nodded as I thought back to the story Robert had told me of the possible suicide pact and the cackling soldier talking about it just the previous day. "Yes, I have heard the story," I confirmed.

"It is the only time that my courage has failed," she said wistfully. "I don't regret it as I have done much good since, but I do regret what happened to poor Henri. I should never have married him." She seemed to shake off the memory and her black, glittering eyes bored into mine as she asked, "What other stories have you heard about me?"

"A soldier told me that you once had two servant girls buried alive. Is that true?"

"Yes, it is. Are you shocked?" she asked as I must have shown some surprise that the little lady in front of me was capable of such a thing. "It was just after my first husband had died and I was trying to establish my authority. Some soldiers thought I was too weak to rule. These servant girls had soldier lovers and they tried to steal my jewels and burn down a house with soldiers' families in it to mask their escape and hide their crime. They were caught and I had to make an example of them."

Once more she looked out of the window as though recollecting the scene before continuing. "I chose to bury them alive, which was a lot more peaceful death than some wanted. A pit was dug in the courtyard and they were thrown into it. Some planks were wedged against the sides of the pit to form the roof of a space around the girls and then the earth was piled back above them. The pit was never re-opened."

She looked back at me. "It sounds cruel but it saved many more lives in the long run. People were more shocked that I had killed women and it gave me a reputation as a ruler not to be crossed. The army was stabilised and peace reigned in Sardhana for many years. I would have had to kill many men to get the same effect. After all, this happened over twenty years ago and the story is still being told."

She had a point. This was an age when people were executed by tent mallets, elephants, even blown apart by rockets, and yet her reputation for ruthlessness was based on some executions that happened two decades ago, just because she was a woman executing women. I later found out that her first husband had been involved in the massacre of some English prisoners, but there was no evidence that the begum was involved. Not that this little detail stopped some of the old timers amongst the British in India having a very jaundiced view of her. As I subsequently discovered, they would believe any black tale about her and her army, but I am here to report the truth as I saw it.

What I found at her province of Sardhana when we got there was a well-run country and people who greatly respected their ruler. They appreciated that while there were lots of soldiers to support, these ensured that their lands would not be ravaged by *pindaree*. The begum sold the services of her soldiers astutely so that the cost of the army was partly covered from this income, although wars requiring mercenary armies did not come with regular frequency. While I was there, though, war with the British, and possibly later with Holkar, was fully expected. All available troops were being drilled and equipped. As well as her veteran regiments, who looked as tough as teak, the new regiment of recruits was being trained so that they would be ready for hire in the coming conflict.

I spent five months in Sardhana as the guest of the begum. Technically you could say I was a prisoner as I was not able to leave, but as I was given rooms in her palace it was the best incarceration I have ever experienced. I had complete freedom to go where I liked, but if I went to the stables to borrow a horse, a couple of her cavalry sowars were detailed as an escort. There was no real need for an escort as the province was peaceful and so I could only assume that they were there to deter me from trying to make a run for British territory. The fact that we were surrounded by lands controlled by Scindia, where I was still a wanted man, acted as a far greater deterrent.

As the weeks passed I began to relax and feel more comfortable as all the news we received of the wider world was positive from my perspective. In April the British advanced to a place called Poona, which was where the exiled peshwa, nominal ruler of the Mahratta, had his throne. The Mahrattas had planned to burn the city before they abandoned it, but the British captured it intact in a surprise attack. By May the peshwa was back in his palace and firmly under British influence. Of course the real Mahratta power still lay with the warlords and they were still confident that they could drive the British back. The British marched out of Poona in June and Mahratta armies gathered menacingly on the nizam of Hyderabad's frontier as negotiations continued, but it was not until early August that war was finally declared.

Throughout that time I saw little of the begum, who was busy ruling her lands, preparing her army and travelling to see other princes. She would invite me occasionally to join her for dinner and sometimes she would ask me to join her for mass on Sundays. I had mentioned my Spanish mother and so she assumed that I was a Catholic. Given the broad lexicon of religions she had already, I did not have the heart to mention I was Church of England. In fact I saw her once leaving a Hindu celebration and took the opportunity to ask what her true faith was if she had to choose one. She just smiled and said, "Sardhana, Thomas. I will worship any god for my people of Sardhana." It was a typically ambiguous begum answer, but she certainly took her

Catholicism seriously judging from the time she spent at mass and with her priest, who incidentally was called Julius Caesar! Later she built a huge Catholic basilica. Some accused of her of being a Catholic to win favour with the British, and it certainly helped her do this, but to be fair to her she was baptised in 1781, long before the British had influence near her lands.

In August, following the declaration of war everything seemed to change. The British moved swiftly to Scindia's great hill fortress of Ahmednuggur. It was one of the strongest bastions in India and right on the frontier of the nizam of Hyderabad's lands. After a four-day cannonade the garrison surrendered. I was delighted: if this was a sign of the resistance that the Mahratta could put up then I naively thought that they would be beaten easily after all. At the same time we heard that some British officers in Scindia's army had refused to fight the British and consequently all of them, including Skinner, had been expelled. Scindia was now marshalling his force to resist invasion from the British and this included the begum's regiments. We were ordered to march south and so, wearing a new uniform of the begum's army, I rode reluctantly to war.

This time the cavalry sowars were constantly on hand as I rode as part of the begum's personal escort. She went to war on horseback, leaving her carriage behind, and slept in her tent each night, served by a couple of her ladies. The veterans marched in the vanguard of our force while the new recruits brought up the rear, doing little more than guarding the baggage.

Scindia's army was well spread out as it marched and to some extent we lived off the land we passed through to supplement the supplies we carried. Consequently we rarely saw other Mahratta units. They had been preparing for this march for months, and even though we were just a small part of the army, our column of men and supplies stretched back for miles. As well as the infantry and their supplies there were the great guns, which were pulled by elephants or oxen. For each gun there was a further caravan of wagons containing powder and shot. There were also traders called *bhinjarries* travelling with the army who sold food, drink and other supplies, even women, to the men as they marched.

I had mixed feelings about going to war. Of course I would not be expected to fight, but my fate very much depended on the outcome. Scindia himself was up ahead, leading a great swarm of cavalry, and word was that he lived in a huge tent palace that was kept apart from his soldiers. The chances were that I would not run into to him to remind him of my existence, but I had reverted to a growing a full beard to fit in with some of the native officers and hide my face. I knew that Scindia's officers were demoralised and that they had surrendered quickly at Ahmednuggur. But the begum had not been there and her soldiers did not look they would give up as easily. I wondered often if she really would hand me over to Scindia if the British were beaten. While I think she liked me and thought I would be useful if the British remained a force in the field, she ruthlessly protected her interests. If she was prepared to bury servant girls alive to protect her lands, then it would be rockets for poor Flashy without a moment's hesitation.

My hope was that Scindia had forgotten about me in recent months or that the British would either win or remain a force to be reckoned with. They had split their forces into two, which seemed reckless while they were heavily outnumbered by the Mahratta. Arthur Wellesley commanded the largest column and the other was commanded by a Colonel Stevenson. The guides for both columns seemed to be Mahratta men as we had reports not only on where the British were, but the routes they were taking next.

It took over a month to march south. The begum had five battalions in her army, totalling nearly five thousand men, supported by a dozen cannon.. But with men leading the various oxen teams, camp followers and the *bhinjarries* the number on the move was closer to seven thousand. Some sporadic monsoon rains had started again which made the few roads muddy and difficult to move the guns along, but we made good progress. Other Mahratta forces had been shadowing the British for some time, but it was past mid September when we finally caught up with the main body. I was relieved to discover that Scindia had got frustrated leading his cavalry and, being unable to bring the British to battle, he and the raja of Berar had withdrawn to one of their palaces. After Perron's departure the army was now being commanded by a genial Hanoverian called Anthony Pohlmann whom I had met before when with Skinner.

Pohlmann was a shrewd and experienced commander, and it seemed to me that he had been waiting for Scindia to depart before he planned the destruction of the British. As soon as the ruler had gone he started to gather the army into one place while he launched plans to lure the British into a trap. We had received word that the two British columns had met at Budnappor on the twenty-first of September and the British had received intelligence that the main Mahratta army was at a place called Borkardan. It wasn't; presumably this was misinformation from an agent of Pohlmann, who seemed to be leading the British a merry dance. Wellesley decided to keep his army in two and march his columns either side of a range of hills to trap the enemy at Borkardan. It was nearly a fatal mistake, as I discovered the next day.

Late on the twenty-second of September we crested a rise and saw the rest of the Mahratta army stretched out before us. It was next to a village that has since become famous all over the world. It was a poor, scrubby place called Assaye.

Battle of Assaye – 23 September 1803

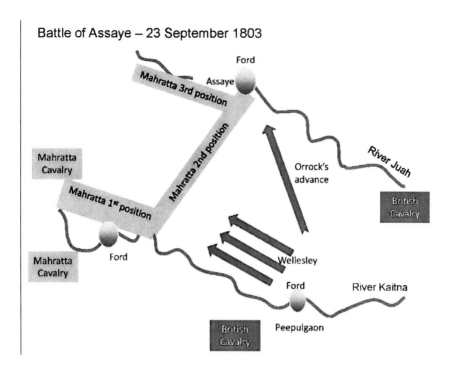

There was mounting excitement as the army gradually pulled itself together in a single place. Even I had a feeling of apprehension as we saw other dust clouds on the horizon moving in the same direction. There was a strong sense that the shadow war with Mahratta cavalry and the British evading each other was coming to an end and that a proper battle was coming.

We were among the last units to gather, and as I crested that final hill before Assaye I remember my jaw dropping in astonishment for the army was far bigger than I had imagined. The camp stretched fully two miles from left to right and including the camp followers there must have been close to one hundred thousand men in that valley. They had set up camp in the fork of two rivers with the cavalry off to the right, where the fork widened to give more grazing, and the infantry to the left, where the rivers joined. On the opposite side of the valley was an undulating plain leading to some more steep hills in the distance.

To beat this massive army the British had a force of less than twenty thousand. The idea that they had split to trap the Mahratta seemed ridiculous. It was a bit like two mice stalking a cat. The Mahratta had gathered because they had the British where they wanted them. They knew Stevenson with his half of the force was isolated on the other side of the distant hills and that soon Wellesley's column would be spread out before them on its way to attack the mythical Mahratta forces at Borkardan. The real Mahratta forces, and in particular the forty thousand cavalry, planned to sweep in the next day to make a surprise attack on Wellesley's column. You did not have to be a general to know that forty thousand cavalry would destroy an army of less than ten thousand strung out marching along a road. Particularly with another thirty thousand infantry, much of it well trained, in support. That would just leave Stevenson's column to deal with, and if that 'mouse' had any sense, it would run south as fast as it could go.

We marched through the ford at the village of Assaye, crossing the northern river called the Juah to join the rest of the camp between that river and the Kaitna half a mile or so further south. The recent rains meant that the rivers were already fast flowing and around chest height for a marching man. Apart from at the fords the banks were quite steep. Climbing the further bank of the Juah, we found that nearest space to have room for our battalions was near the fork of the rivers and so we made camp there. This was upwind of the rest of the camp as already the fields had a strong smell of where thousands of men have been living and defecating for several days. It was colourful, though, with tents of every hue for all the leaders, together with flags and other banners to mark out the camps of the various Mahratta tribes. Officers and men had more basic shelters from the occasional heavy rains or slept under the stars. At the far end of the camp where the space between the rivers widened there were thousands and thousands of horses tethered in rows, and looking to the northern horizon there were still more troops joining the gathering.

That evening the begum invited me to join her retinue to attend a council of the Mahratta chieftains. She said she wanted my opinion of the discussions from the British viewpoint. The council took place in a large tent with cushions for the various leaders in a circle and space for their retinues to sit and stand behind. I was there with Colonel Saleur, the deputy commander of her army. I had planned to slip quietly into the back of the tent unnoticed, but one of the officers from Skinner's old company came over to greet me warmly.

"Flashman huzoor," he said, "did you hear that the treacherous snake of your people who betrayed you was found dead the day after your escape? May Shaitan roast his balls to eternity. How are you, old friend?" He pounded me on the back.

"I wasn't sure how welcome I would be amongst Scindia's officers after what happened," I replied.

"The Mahratta always respect courage. Now we know you are the Flashman who bayoneted the tiger and escaped the *pindaree*, and did we not see you with our own eyes stand up to our prince?" He glanced around to check that we were not overheard before adding, "Who even now, on the eve of battle, prefers debauching with his women rather than fighting with his men." He gave a snort of disgust. "Be wary of the *pindaree*, though, Flashman for they are here in number and feel that they have a score to settle with you."

I looked around and sure enough there was a group of swarthy coves without uniforms on the far side of the tent who were glaring maliciously at me.

"Thank you for the warning, my friend. How many of them are there here?"

"Many thousand, huzoor. They come here like jackals, sensing an easy kill. They will be the last to charge and the first to the plunder as usual."

Several other of Scindia's officers whom I knew caught my eye and gave me a smile in greeting. Even Pohlmann, whom I had met only twice before, gave me a nod of recognition when one of his officers made introductions around the group as we sat down.

After the usual courtesies and introductions Pohlmann opened the meeting by reminding all present of the British position as I have detailed earlier. There were divided, deceived, and half of the army was expected to march across our front tomorrow morning, unaware that we were on their flank and not at Borkardan where they expected. There was no discussion as to whether the Mahratta would win; given the facts, that was the only conclusion conceivable. Pohlmann was congratulated for his cunning and ingenuity, and from what I saw, despite what followed, he was a skilful general.

The debate then turned to the manner of the attack and that is where the arguments started. The British were in the habit of starting their marches very early in the mornings so that they reached their destination before the peak of the afternoon heat. This meant that they set off before their scouts could reconnoitre the route in daylight. The plan was for the cavalry to cross the southern river, the Kaitna, in the morning and launch a surprise attack as soon as the Mahratta scouts signalled that the British column was marching along the road opposite our position. The slower-moving infantry could then follow up the attack and mop up any resistance. It seemed sensible, but it set off a howl of protest among the infantry regiments, who were also in part here for plunder. They knew that they would arrive at the battle long after the regular cavalry and *pindaree* had taken absolutely anything of value for themselves.

Pohlmann tried to calm the situation by suggesting that there would still be British units holding out and plunder for the infantry to find, but no one believed that the British could withstand such overwhelming numbers of cavalry for long. He then suggested that the infantry would be leading the attack against Stevenson's column, but again no one believed that this column would stay around to be attacked. It was clear that there was a big division between the cavalry, consisting of a lot of independently minded leaders and large numbers of *pindaree*, and the more regimented and European-trained infantry. In recent weeks, before I had arrived, Scindia had been leading his cavalry on various sweeps in fruitless efforts to trap the British. While they had failed to bring the British to battle they had already gathered some plunder. In the meantime all the infantry had done was slog over hundreds of miles of muddy roads dragging cannon and supplies with them. Now they thought it would all be a wasted effort.

Despite having no cavalry and commanding around a quarter of the foot soldiers present, the begum had taken no part in the arguments at the end of the council meeting. She just sat there impassively, watching the infantry and cavalry officers around her hurling insults at each other. Once, when her opinion was sought by one of the other infantry commanders, she just smiled enigmatically and said, "We must serve Lord Scindia the best we can to ensure victory." Pohlmann thanked her for her wisdom and support and shortly after that the meeting broke up with other infantry commanders still feeling very resentful.

As the begum and I left the council tent and started to walk back to our own part of the encampment, she turned to me and asked, "What did you make of that?"

In truth I could see nothing then but a disaster for the British. Mahratta spies seemed to be feeding them false information and acting as their guides as well. They were hopelessly outnumbered and had foolishly divided their forces. But to say so may have convinced the begum that I was of little value to her if Scindia's men came calling for my return. So I played for time while I desperately hoped that Wellesley had a surprise of his own up his sleeve.

"Wellesley is no fool, he may not do as you expect," I said but with very little belief.

"He will have to be a remarkable general to avoid defeat tomorrow," said the begum. "Our cavalry are confident that they can beat him alone if they catch his force unprepared on their march. Of course I shall pray tonight for my soldiers and for the opportunity that the whole army will be able to share the spoils of war. You must make your own prayers, Thomas."

But the following morning everything changed and both our prayers were answered, although I suspect the begum's had more earthly assistance.

Chapter 19

I did not sleep well that night. While I had a bed in a tent, it was stifling in there sharing with five others in a space that did not fully lose the heat of the earlier summer day. I took my blanket – and my mosquito net, as there were thick black clouds of the insects so close to two rivers – and laid out under the stars. I remembered the night I had spent in the cell at Oojeine looking at the same stars and wondered if I was much safer than I had been before. If the battle was lost then either the *pindaree* would hunt me directly or remind Scindia of my presence. In either event the begum would not risk conflict with the then all-powerful Scindia to protect me. I had hoped before that if battle came I could slip my captors and join a retreating British force, but the way things were looking, the British would be massacred and there would be no orderly withdrawal. I lay there all night tossing and turning, and yes, even praying, while swatting at insects that had somehow got under the net.

As the grey light of dawn crept across the eastern sky the massive camp started to come alive. I rose early to wash in the stream and saw that the first troops of cavalry were starting to stir and get saddled up for what they expected to be a day of killing and looting. Some of the Mahratta mounted scouts were already splashing through the southern river Kaitna using the ford that was directly opposite the camp. They would ride south to give us the first news of the British advance. Despite the early hour two of the begum's sowars were on hand to make sure I was not tempted to slip away, but with the British likely to be destroyed and *pindaree* on the prowl, safety still lay at that point with the begum. Gradually more people started to move around the camp but no one was in a rush, the British were not expected until late morning. Cooking fires were lit and soldiers started to wash and dress in their best clothes and uniforms for the battle ahead. Soon troops of cavalry started to splash through the ford, to jeering and insults from the infantry. These horsemen gathered on the southern shore of the Kaitna so that they were ready for the ride south.

It was a group of *bhinjarries* that started to unravel the Mahratta plan. They sold information as well as goods, and so when a British cavalry patrol found them that morning, for a fee they revealed that the Mahratta were not at Borkardan, but much closer just across the river Kaitna. It was mid-morning by the time the news reached Wellesley and by then his army had already marched fourteen miles to a village called Naulniah, which was just five miles south of Assaye. As soon as he was told, Wellesley set off to investigate, taking nearly all his five thousand cavalry with him. Leaving a sepoy battalion as rear guard, he ordered the rest of his four and a half thousand infantry to follow him.

The first that the Mahratta knew of these events was when some scouts came riding fast over the hills from the south. A stream of scouts had been arriving all morning with news of the progress of the British march, but as these two riders came splashing full tilt through the ford on sweat-lathered horses, it was clear something was not right. I tooled on over to Pohlmann's tent to find out what. If I was expecting consternation, I was to be disappointed, for Pohlmann was laughing with delight and several of the other commanders there, including the begum, looked equally pleased.

"This is excellent news," boomed Pohlmann, giving one of the messengers a hearty thump on the back. "Now the British come to us, we are in a strong position, and both infantry and cavalry can share the victory and the spoils. Let us break camp and have our guns lining the southern shore so that we can give them a hot reception when they arrive."

The begum saw me standing there and came over. "Well, Thomas, one of my prayers has already been answered, but you should not blame God if he does not listen to you today. To beat the combined artillery, infantry and cavalry after a twenty-mile march, now that would take a real miracle." She looked up and saw someone waiting for her. "Now you must excuse me. I have some business to conduct," she said as she walked away.

She walked over to one of the *bhinjarrie* chieftains and I saw her hand over a large purse. I did not think anything of it at the time, as we bought lots of materials from the *bhinjarrie*. Only days later did I discover how Wellesley had learned of the Mahratta position. Ever since I have wondered whether the begum relied entirely on God to deliver the British to the combined Mahratta force or whether she arranged some more practical help through the *bhinjarrie*.

A short while later the British cavalry arrived on some high ground overlooking our camp around a mile and a half south of the Kaitna. They stood watching what must to them have seemed an ant's nest of activity as tents were struck down, guns dragged by elephant and oxen to be lined up on the river shore and infantry organised into two solid ranks behind the guns. Despite the fact that they outnumbered the British horsemen ten to one, half of the Mahratta cavalry, including many of the *pindaree*, decided to cross the river again back to the Mahratta shore. They had been insulted by the infantry when they had headed south but were now greeted with howls of derision from their own soldiers for their timidity in front of such a meagre force.

"Why look at these brave horsemen who would run to hide behind our skirts at the sight of an angry washerwoman," cackled one sergeant. Others started throwing turds at the retreating cavalry. Soon there was some jostling and I saw some cavalry sowars and *pindaree* using the flat of their blades none too gently to push their way through the heckling crowd with several cut heads as a result. Infantry and cavalry officers moved in to restore order but clearly no love was lost between the two forces.

I looked for the begum again and found her where the command tent was being dismantled with a gaggle of other officers including Pohlmann. They were gathered around two large brass telescopes on tripods.

"Ah, Flashman," said Pohlmann in his slight Hanoverian accent when he saw me. "Come and tell us whether the officer in front is Vellesley."

All I could see with the naked eye was a dark crowd of officers on a distant hill, but they made way for me around one of the telescopes, which was a fine instrument. While you could not see the faces, the positions of the leading officers told me all I wanted to know. There, as when I had first ridden with him back to Madras, was one tall, erect officer sitting out alone, using a telescope to stare back in my direction. A few yards behind him was someone in native dress whom I took to be a guide and then a gaggle of senior offers standing back a few more paces.

"Yes, that is Wellesley," I confirmed, watching as he now swung his telescope to his right to stare at something beyond the Mahratta left flank.

"Vat is he looking at?" asked Pohlmann, who was watching Wellesley through the other brass telescope. I stepped away so another officer could look.

"He is looking at the village of Peepulgaon down the river," said the other officer.

"There is another ford there, isn't there?" asked Pohlmann.

"Yes, but it is smaller than the one in front of us, and anyway, his guide will tell him that the one in front of us is the only crossing of the river. You see, sir, the guide is pointing Wellesley back down in our direction."

Pohlmann gave a grunt and then said, "Flashman, take another look. Vat do you think?"

I stepped up to the second telescope again and looked. I did not realise it then but I was watching what was probably the pivotal moment of the battle. The scout was indeed saying that the ford in front of the gathering Mahratta ranks and cannon was the only one in the area. Wellesley, looking down at the steep banks, chest-high water, massed guns and twenty thousand cavalry still on his side of the river waiting to pounce, saw that a frontal assault with his meagre force would be suicidal. But looking to his right, he saw the village of Peepulgaon on the river bank with another village on the opposite bank and he reasoned that the two villages would not be so close on opposite shores of the river if there was not a ford in between. He also realised that if he could get his men across onto the narrow neck of land between the two rivers then he could attack, with the rivers stopping the Mahratta outflanking him. Not that I appreciated any of this as I watched, but I was just in time to see him send a group of his officers off in the direction of Peepulgaon to confirm his suspicion of the existence of the ford.

"Vill he attack now he has seen our forces?" asked Pohlmann.

"He cannot possibly consider it," snorted one of the cavalry leaders. "Our cavalry outnumbers his ten to one and our scouts say he has only four and half thousand infantry following him against our eleven thousand trained infantry, and we have another ten thousand warriors not to mention over a hundred cannon."

I turned away from the telescope in time to see one of the *pindaree* leaders stare wolfishly at me and say, "The British are beaten before they even fire a shot. They have to retreat, and when they do we will tear them apart." Then, looking me directly in the eye, he added meaningfully, "We always settle our scores with the British."

"Vat do you think, Flashman?" Pohlmann repeated.

"He will attack you, sir," I asserted, sounding as confident as I could. "He knows his army would be destroyed if he tried to retreat and he is desperate for a victory as a general."

"Nonsense!" exclaimed the cavalry commander. "This knave is just trying to stop you releasing the cavalry to ensure their destruction. Even now we could destroy their infantry before they get here."

While the commander of the regular cavalry was still keen to attack, his forces were only a small part of the whole and I noticed that the *pindaree* leader was less enthusiastic.

"Let them waste themselves on our cannon first," the *pindaree* chieftain said. "Then we will sweep in on what is left."

I turned back to the telescope and watched the British, who seemed tantalisingly close through the lens. Wellesley was desperate for a victory; indeed, I heard later that he had said that if had not attacked at Assaye, there would have been nothing for him to do but hang himself from a tent pole. But desperate or not, I could not see how he could secure a victory against such overwhelming numbers, even if Stevenson came to his aid. Perhaps his appearance with cavalry was a feint to allow his infantry to slip away? But no, our, that is the Mahratta scouts, had seen his army also marching in this direction. But surely once he had seen what he was up against he would change his plan? My thoughts were interrupted by Pohlmann.

"I agree with Mr Flashman. Vellesley will attack." There were general shouts of disbelief at this, although the begum stayed silent, her dark eyes darting between Pohlmann and me. "He may be young but he is no fool, this general," continued Pohlmann. "Despite the efforts of his guide I think he has already guessed there is a ford at Peepulgaon, and if he can, he will cross his men there. We will then fight him on the land between the rivers. It is no matter: while we will not be able to outflank him, his men will have no alternative but to march right into the mouths of our guns. They will be lucky if any actually reach the lines of infantry behind them. When they break, both the infantry and cavalry will share the spoils."

He walked over to a map table. "We will stay lined up on the river for now, but I want some of our lighter horse-drawn guns taken upriver to cover the ford at Peepulgaon. They can pound the British while they are vulnerable crossing the river, until they have too many men on this bank and then they can withdraw. Once they are committed to crossing at Peepulgaon we will redeploy our forces in a straight line between the two rivers."

He turned to the begum. "Lady, I would like you to command the left of our line with your men, anchoring it against the village of Assaye. I will command the centre and the right with Scindia's forces." The begum nodded her agreement and Pohlmann continued, "The plan of battle is simple. The cannon are to be spread out evenly in a straight line between the rivers and the infantry formed up behind the guns. Use solid ball in the guns to start and canister shot when they get close. If any survive the guns, the infantry can finish them off."

It was a brisk and efficient plan from the experienced Hanoverian. Its simplicity meant that there was less to go wrong. Try as I might, I could not see how it could fail. When Wellesley moved to explore the other ford, I had wondered if he had a chance, but now his prospects seemed as bleak as ever. For while a less organised army might be caught while redeploying from facing across the southern river to facing across the neck of land, Pohlmann was making sure that this was not going to happen to him. Already elephants and oxen were being allocated to each gun so they were ready to move. Officers were being detailed to mark where the guns were to go in our new front line and space for the various regiments was allocated. None moved yet in case the British found the ford too deep or were bluffing and were planning to swing back across the ford by the Mahratta camp.

I could not think of anything to give me a glimmer of hope. If Wellesley managed to get his men across the river, he would find that they were all exposed to a lethal bombardment of one hundred guns. There would be nowhere for them to hide. I paced around, trying to keep out of the way, and after a while heard a cry that the British infantry were in sight. I managed to get a quick glimpse through one of the powerful telescopes and suddenly I knew the day was not yet lost.

They had already marched over twenty miles that day, carrying their packs, muskets and ammunition. The last five miles had been in the heat of the noon-day sun. It was a march that would leave most men exhausted, and yet these soldiers, knowing that a battle waited for them at the end of the day, marched resolutely on. Despite seeing the huge host arrayed before them, they did not stop and falter in any way as they crested that final hill, but just kept on marching in. There were two British Highland regiments and four regiments of Indian sepoys. The Scots wore white breeches as the climate was too hot for thick woollen kilts. Apart from their officers who also wore breeches, the sepoy troops wore shorter white leggings that finished down their thighs. It seemed that these men were just going to work and their next customers were in front of them. Even from a mile and a half away they collectively exuded confidence and gave the impression that they did not for one moment consider that they could be beaten. For the first time I sensed a ripple of unease spreading through the Mahratta camp. They all saw the infantry coming and knew that the best-trained Mahratta infantry would probably have hesitated if they had seen the same massive odds facing them. Pohlmann sensed the disquiet, and even though the range was extreme for hitting infantry, he ordered the row of cannon to open fire on them.

Commands were shouted and soon the guns began to fire with great plumes of smoke obscuring our view of the enemy. This was my first great land battle, but I had already seen sea battles and knew a little of gunnery. The Mahratta cannon were a very mixed bag covering all shapes, sizes and calibres from workmanlike artillery pieces to much more decorative guns that seemed to have been taken from palace courtyards. The standard of gunnery was similarly mixed. Because of the smoke I could not see what damage they were causing to the British, but it was clear that some of these guns were much easier to serve than others. Some of the large and decorative siege guns had crews of up to a dozen men who took nearly five minutes to sponge out, load and then position the gun again.

For nearly a quarter of an hour the guns blazed away, creating a huge pall of gun smoke that was slow to drift away in the light winds. I suspect that they did not do much damage as most of the gunners were firing almost blindly into the smoke. Pohlmann, unable to see anything, mounted his horse and rode along the bank towards Peepulgaon to see how the British were progressing. His officers and staff called for their own horses to follow, and as the begum mounted up one of my sowar escorts passed the reins of another horse for me. We all galloped down the river bank after Pohlmann, and by the time we reached the end of the Mahratta's main line of guns I could see that the infantry were nearly at the Peepulgaon ford. Some of the British cavalry were also now approaching the ford, but roughly half remained on the high ground opposite the initial Mahratta position. They were mostly lancers and could charge down into the flanks of the near twenty thousand Mahratta cavalry who were still on the British side of the river if they attempted to interfere with the crossing. Lancers always terrify other cavalry, especially from the flanks, as there is nothing you can do until you are past the point. More than once I have been chased by them and dreaded the white-hot pain of a steel lance point slicing through my back. Clearly the Mahratta horse, many of them *pindaree*, were content to let the guns and the infantry do the hard work. The Mahratta cavalry was saving itself for attacking the British when they fled back across the river in defeat.

We rode on towards the small group of light horse-drawn guns that had been set up on a rise covering the ford at Peepulgaon. They were two-pounders firing with a sharp cracking sound and with a small escort of regular cavalry amongst which Pohlmann was now standing. We drew up with them and stared across at the ford. Men were now streaming across. I saw Wellesley on our side of the river with a knot of officers encouraging the men across. The group proved a tempting target for the gunners and there was a puff of dirt just in front of them where a ball pitched into the ground and then bounced into the air over them. Then I saw that it had partially decapitated one of the dragoons riding next to Wellesley; I discovered later it was his orderly. The man's horse reared in panic as it smelt the blood but the body stayed in the saddle, held there by map cases and other accoutrements. The men around tried to catch at the horse's reins but it reared again and this time the corpse fell directly under the horse's falling hooves. The horse continued to plunge about, and while we were too far away to see, we could imagine the blood and brains being spattered about by the way the other officers moved away in disgust. Wellesley was ordering his officers forward to survey the space between the two rivers and one disturbed a fox that now ran in our direction.

"Ah, they are committed," said Pohlmann, watching as the first infantry reached the opposite shore of the ford. He turned to the begum. "It is time to redeploy our forces, Lady. I know I can rely on you to hold our left."

"You can indeed, General," replied the begum, "and I wish you good fortune this day. It is a shame our lord is not here to witness his victory, but perhaps better that the battle is left to professionals." They laughed at what seemed to be a private joke between them and then the begum wheeled her horse about and we rode towards Assaye.

Chapter 20

It took an hour for the British to cross the river and get ready to attack. It seemed that their original plan had been to march in strength in a double line of infantry along the bank of the Kaitna and catch the Mahratta in the flank. But when they saw how quickly the Mahratta had redeployed they were forced to change their own disposition. The Mahratta frontline now stretched nearly a mile from one river to the other and was thickly manned with guns and men. Wellesley only had enough men to attack half of it, with just a single line of infantry.

I positioned myself on the flat roof of a house in the village of Assaye which was the begum's command post. One of the brass telescopes that Pohlmann had been using was placed on the tiles and, combined with our elevation, gave an excellent view. Pohlmann had the other large telescope with him on an elephant in the middle of the Mahratta line. The begum's men had turned the village into a small fortress with barricades across the ends of streets and all of the windows and roofs lined with men. The line of Mahratta guns started in front of the village and stretched away to our right and they were already inflicting a terrible punishment on the British.

Wellesley had sent the cavalry who had crossed the river to the rear to act as a reserve. The British had managed to get a dozen small cannon across the river and they started an artillery duel with the Mahratta guns. The British guns were outnumbered and much smaller than many of those against them. A hail of fire from the Mahratta lines soon saw the British guns dismounted and many of the men and oxen that had been bringing the ammunition killed. More fire rained on the infantry, who were being organised into lines. Cannon balls would whip through files of men and leave holes of flesh and gore before the sergeants shouted for the men to close up. Wellesley had to order the attack straight away or his men would have been slaughtered where they stood.

Five regiments marched forward in a line with their left flank against the Kaitna and directly towards the right-hand third of the Mahratta line. The rest, a regiment of Highlanders and a sepoy detachment of all the advance guards, set off diagonally across the field towards Assaye. For the next hour the battle was broken into two halves, with very different results.

I swung the telescope round to watch the five regiments. They had the shortest distance to travel and would reach the Mahratta first. It looked a pitifully thin line of red-coated soldiers marching abreast straight towards the barrels of fifty cannon directly in front of them. Wellesley and some of his staff officers rode behind the line as the guns to their front fired death and dismemberment at them. Sometimes you would see a puff of dirt where a ball pitched short and bounced over their heads, but all too often you would see a sudden spray of blood and guts and a gap in the line appear. Slowly, man by man, the line began to shrink. I could not imagine the courage required to continue pacing towards those guns, knowing that thousands of men waited behind them, but not once did they hesitate. Steadily they tramped on, covering the yards that took them closer and closer to the muzzles facing them.

The earlier cannonade across the river now started to take its toll as I could see some of the Mahratta gunners running out of ammunition. Wagons were racing back to the powder and ball stored back at the camp, or at their original firing positions on the river bank. This meant various carts trying to break through the lines of Mahratta infantry behind the guns, and the infantry soon started to become disorganised. Pohlmann was there with his officers, trying to organise some channels through the men for the carts, but I saw that some of the cannon, particularly the ornate ones which probably took specially cast balls, had stopped firing. Until now the guns had been firing solid shot which, if it hit the red line, rarely took out more than one man at a time. But now, as the red line crept closer, some of the gunners switched to canister.

When the guns fired the space in front of them was filled with gunsmoke, but during the couple of minutes that it took the gunners to reload and lay their guns this dissipated and so the infantry could see when the gun was going to fire at them again. With canister, instead of a single man disappearing in spray of gore, a whole group could be sent spinning away, dead and wounded, and a gaping hole in the line would be left. Now I saw several groups of men throw themselves to the ground as they saw the gun in front of them about to fire, but only once did I see a sergeant have to prompt them to get up again.

Closer and closer they marched; not one man broke or ran away or even tried to. Wellesley later referred to his men in the peninsula as the scum of the earth, but even he admits that he never saw a nobler sight than that thin red line marching stoutly to those guns.

As they got closer the Mahratta gunners tried to reload even faster. They were now starting to panic. One fired while the rammer was still down the barrel, others out of ammunition began to creep back to the safety of the infantry behind them. They had expected the British and Indian sepoy soldiers to break long before now, but even though their numbers were thinned, the line still consisted of over three thousand men.

The red-coated infantry was just a hundred yards away from the guns when they were finally released into a charge. Even from nearly half a mile away I heard the guttural roar as they shouted their challenge at those who had tormented them. Through the telescope I watched as they sprang forward with their glittering bayonets outstretched to take their revenge on the gunners who had been killing their comrades, making them sweat with terror. Many of the gunners did not stay around to contest the issue but ran. Others tried to hide under the wheels of their guns as Wellesley and the other officers rode forward and urged the soldiers on past the cannon and into the waiting infantry beyond. A few redcoats stayed to hunt down the gunners but most swept on.

The Mahratta soldiers had been told that at most a few shattered and disorientated redcoats would stagger through the line of guns. They did not for one moment expect a serious fight on their hands. First their lines were broken by ammunition carts and then, instead of destroying the enemy with a final barrage of canister, the gunners started to run back to them in panic. They were followed by thousands of well-trained professional killers who had been driven mad with anger and fear and who were now filled with bloodlust. The Mahratta line rocked back with the impact of the redcoats. They had roughly the same number of trained soldiers as Wellesley, but their untrained, irregular infantry got in the way as they tried to fight back, often with the irregular soldiers pushing through the Mahratta ranks to get away. There were no organised volleys, just a steady crackle of musketry from both sides, and then they closed to fight with bayonets and swords. A skilled man with a bayonet will beat a swordsman every time as the bayonet has a much longer reach, and now the redcoats started to plough through the Mahratta ranks. As I watched in astonishment, more and more of the Mahratta started to slip away from the fight or step back to avoid the stabbing blades, and suddenly their whole line began to curve back.

Pohlmann tried to order in reinforcements but men were retreating faster than they could be replaced and many seemed to hold back in the hope that the Mahratta cavalry further behind them would come to their rescue. The horseman showed no inclination to intervene. Many were *pindaree* and this was no strung-out baggage train full of loot to attack. There was a good chance of being killed by these deadly red-coated men and little hope of plunder, and so they stood back. Perhaps they remembered the angry jeering of their own infantry earlier in the day and decided that, as their infantry were double the number of the enemy, it was time for them to earn some respect.

Wellesley, riding past the guns, must have been shouting encouragement at his men, but the presence of the enemy commander proved too tempting a target for the Mahratta gunners who were hiding near the guns. One charged him with a pike. Wellesley saw the man just in time and turned, but the pike went into his horse's chest and it fell, trapping Wellesely's leg underneath the animal. More gunners ran forward to kill him, but a redcoat sergeant who had been hunting the gunners saw what was happening and ran over and fought furiously to hold them off until Wellesley got free and his staff galloped over to rescue him.

There was no doubt about it: despite the huge disparity in numbers, on the far side of the battlefield the British and sepoy forces were winning. I was astonished and jubilant. Then I took my eye from the telescope to look at how the other British and sepoy troops who were marching towards Assaye were doing and my heart lurched again.

I later learned that Wellesley had ordered their commander, Colonel Orrock, to join his soldiers to the end of Wellesley's men to extend the line of attack. Orrock, being possibly the stupidest man on the battlefield, had seen all of Wellesley's troops form a long line. When his orders arrived to 'extend the right of the attack', he misunderstood and marched his men straight at the strongest part of the enemy line. At some point his staff officers, seeing the rest of the army march off in a line, may have questioned the wisdom of the attack or his orders, but as none survived we will never know. Orrock was brave, though, riding a white horse among the middle of his men while the remaining fifty Mahratta cannon were now trained in his direction. Things would have been better if he had extended his men out in a longer line to give them a thinner target to aim at, as Wellesley had done. But instead, he kept them in a double line with the sepoys still as an advance guard at the front. Behind them were the 74th Highlanders with their colours flying, drummer boys to the fore and a piper doing his best impression of the sound of a pig castration.

Shot was soon whistling through this red slug of men, who marched slowly across the full width of the battlefield, leave a trail of dead and dying in their wake. Instinctively men closed up, taking comfort from being part of a large group, and so when ball hit it would pulverise three of four of them together. When I finally turned my attention to this group I could see clearly the route of their journey towards me from the line of broken bodies that they had left behind. They were now about four hundred yards off, having lost around two hundred men on the march: little more than six hundred left against half of the entire Mahratta army.

"What does the fool think he is doing with such a small force?" asked the begum, who had now joined me on the rooftop after organising her forces down below. I had heard her cursing and swearing in a very soldier-like manner when the Mahratta right had fallen back under Wellesley's attack and at the cavalry's failure to respond. She had sent messages to get a detachment of the more reliable regular cavalry to support her forces that were even now forming up behind her line of infantry. She took the telescope and studied the Mahratta right in more detail. It was slowly swinging like a gate in the Mahratta line but the 'hinge' in the middle was also now starting to retreat. Soon the Mahratta would be lined up with their backs facing the shore of the northern river, the Juah.

"We must sweep these fools away quickly," she said brusquely. "Then I can swing my forces round to catch Wellesley in the flank. Let's see how he does fighting proper soldiers. If our cavalry find their balls then they can charge him on the other flank and we can destroy him between us."

I looked again at the redcoated group in front of us and saw a sight that will live long in the memory. There was a battery of four of the begum's guns in front of us which had taken to firing simultaneous salvoes to dishearten the enemy. They now roared again at what was for them almost point-blank range. The balls tore through the tightly packed men. One of the little drummer boys and about a dozen soldiers just ceased to exist. I saw a leg spin into the air, bent at the knee; I think it was the boy's and now every time I see the Isle of Man flag with its three-legged wheel I have a flashback to that spinning leg.

The sepoys had reached a small rise in the ground at about three hundred yards from the Mahratta line. It gave some shelter and there they faltered and finally stopped. Orrock roared for them to go on as the Highlanders were just a few yards behind them.

"Release the cavalry on them!" shouted the begum to one of her officers who ran to pass on the command.

"Leave them, look they are stopping," I shouted back as the Highlanders also started to hesitate to climb over the last bit of cover between them and the guns.

"Do you think I am a fool?" demanded the begum, her eyes suddenly blazing. "I know of your soldiers' courage. Have I not just seen them attack twice their number and guns? I am not leaving redcoats alive on my flanks." Her words were interrupted by the call of trumpets and a large squadron of Mahratta cavalry poured through a gap in their infantry ranks. "Release the second regiment to attack!" the begum now shouted over the parapet and I realised that the 74th and the sepoys who were with them were doomed.

Colonel Orrock, miraculously still mounted on his white horse, gaped uncomprehendingly as the two hundred or so horsemen streamed out of the lines in front of him and spread out to charge his line of men. His other officers were quicker shouting for the men to form a square to defend themselves against cavalry. The men on the extremity of the redcoat line stood little chance of reaching the relative safety of the square before the cavalry reached them. A number were cut down by the lethally sharp swinging blades and some threw themselves to the ground in the hope of not being trampled. But one flinty-faced sergeant armed with a spear-like weapon called a spontoon that was normally used to defend the regiment's flags or colours from horsemen swung his blade up and caught a cavalry man square in the chest with it. I watched with astonishment as, with a grunt of effort, he used the weapon to lift the horseman off his saddle and slam him into another rider, who was then knocked off his horse. The sergeant freed his weapon as the rest of the cavalry rode on to turn for another charge and then jabbed its blade through the throat of the second man he had dismounted. Then, with enemy cavalry wheeling to his right and enemy infantry beginning to march in from his left, this cool character marched towards his square, shouting at some of the men in it to adjust their facings and pausing only to help a sepoy soldier who was hobbling back to the square with a blood-soaked leg.

"My God," I said to myself, "even now they don't think they are beaten."

Cavalry charged the ragged square from one side and infantry from the other. The cavalry struggled to make progress against the tight hedgehog of bayonets that held them back and there was soon a pile of dead men and horses on their side of the square. The begum's trained infantry made more progress because they concentrated their fire on just one side of the square. After several rounds of volley fire from men who massively outnumbered the defenders on that side, the ranks of Highlanders and sepoys facing the Mahratta line were shot to pieces. The begum's men fixed bayonets and went in for the final kill just as the rest of the square began to fall apart, its officers desperately tried to find men to face this last assault. I remember pounding the parapet around the edge of the roof with my fist in frustration at the slaughter before me. I was cursing at the begum and imploring her to show some mercy because within moments these redcoats would be slaughtered to the last man.

I did not expect the begum to listen; she was a soldier at heart and she had a good military reason to destroy this force. But suddenly she seemed to take notice and I heard her calling for the soldiers to be recalled. It was not pity; she had seen something I had not. Through the gun smoke ahead of us she had glimpsed more horsemen coming. At last, whether under Wellesley's orders or that of their own commander, Colonel Maxwell, the British cavalry reserve was coming to the rescue.

There had been no British trumpet calls so the two thousand horsemen of the 19th Dragoons and the 4th Native Cavalry caught their enemy completely by surprise. Sweeping forward in two ranks, the horsemen were a majestic sight with flags flying and sabres glistening in the sunlight. The remaining Mahratta infantry and cavalry around the 74th Highlanders and sepoys were ridden down and slaughtered. This task needed only the squadrons of horsemen closest to the northern river and the rest of the red-coated riders swept on towards the Mahratta line. The begum's remaining infantry and artillery stood firm in their tight ranks, partly protected by the village, and their guns roared their defiance. But Scindia's troops further along the line began to panic. Those at the middle of the Mahratta line were already in a confused state as they joined the begum's troops, who still faced east with the rest of the Mahratta line, which was gradually moving back to face a southerly direction. Now these soldiers saw a large contingent of enemy cavalry riding towards them while they were deployed in a vulnerable and disjointed line. Some of the better-trained infantry tried to change into a square formation, but the irregular infantry got in their way and began to stream back towards the northern river. Seeing the confusion his men were causing, Maxwell veered his men away to charge at the 'hinge' in the Mahratta line, which dissolved before him.

I have seen the moment a semi-orderly withdrawal becomes a rout in battle many times, but rarely have I had as good a view as from that rooftop. As the hinge of the Mahratta line broke before him, Maxwell wisely did not allow his men to chase the Mahratta fleeing towards the river. Instead they rode on to the now-exposed flank of the next section of the Mahratta line, which broke in turn and so they continued along the line. Within a few moments thousands of Mahratta were abandoning weapons and running for their lives. Some ran for the river, but many of the better-trained troops ran for the safety of the begum's lines of infantry who now began to extend around in an arc towards the river so that the remaining Mahratta line formed a bow shape with one end at the ford at Assaye and the other against the river a quarter of a mile along the bank. These remaining soldiers were pretty much all the European-trained infantry and I could see Pohlmann, who had abandoned his elephant for a horse, giving orders and sending staff officers off to get the troops in order.

The rest of the Mahratta infantry who had broken were running full tilt for the river, chased by the sepoy troops and 78th Highlanders on the far end of the original line of attack. They showed no mercy and were shooting and bayoneting any stragglers as they pursued the enemy from the field. With the redcoats scattered over a wide area with their backs to the Mahratta cavalry and the British cavalry blown and disordered from their prolonged charge, it would have been an ideal time for the Mahratta cavalry to launch an attack of their own. They still outnumbered the British horsemen ten to one, and if they had charged, they could have saved the day for the Mahratta, as most of the British cavalry and infantry were exposed. Instead the Mahratta horsemen, who were mostly *pindaree*, decided that the battle was lost and it was time to save themselves. With their enemy vulnerable before them, rather than attacking they turned their horses to ride west, away from the battle. I watched as Pohlmann sent a couple of riders, presumably to order them to attack, but I knew that this desperate measure would prove fruitless.

The begum had been watching the cavalry through the telescope to see if they would attack, and when she saw them turn away she issued a volley of curses and insults that she must have learned in her early days as a nautch dancer, for they would have made the coarsest ship's bosun choke on his grog.

"It seems you are of use to me after all, Thomas," she muttered, still looking slightly shaken by the speed of the change in Mahratta fortunes.

"You mean I am free to go?" I enquired eagerly, realising that after months of risk and danger, safety might now be at hand.

"Not yet, I need to write a letter for Wellesley. Wait here a few minutes and then we will let you go."

She disappeared down the stairs to the room below and I watched as Wellesley tried to regroup his forces. His main infantry line had chased the enemy to the northern river bordering the battlefield, the Juah. While some blazed away at the Mahratta, clambering on each other to get over the steep, muddy northern bank, the majority of the redcoats were more interested in slaking their thirst, even if the water was tainted with enemy blood. They had marched over twenty miles to get to the battle, had fought long and hard in the baking heat of the afternoon and had spent some of that time biting down on paper cartridges containing salty gunpowder. With the enemy defenceless in the river before them, there were dozens of redcoats lying flat on the bank and trailing their canteens into the water to fill them. There would be no moving them until all canteens were full again. Their officers realised this and moved their men quickly away from the river when their wooden flasks were full so that others could get at the precious water. Slowly the men with water began to outnumber those still pushing to get to the riverbank.

During this lull in the battle Maxwell had taken his cavalry to the south where the original Mahratta camp had been, opposite the largest ford across the southern river, the Kaitna. This gave his troopers the chance to water their horses and themselves in the river. The presence of his horsemen together with those left south of the Kaitna persuaded the remaining Mahratta horsemen on the southern bank of the Kaitna to withdraw in the same direction as their comrades, to the west. After the furious fighting of the last few hours both sides were regrouping.

As I watched I heard heavy footsteps come up the stairs and there on the roof was Anthony Pohlmann, looking hot and harassed.

"Ver is the lady of Samru?" he asked me.

Before I had the chance to reply she also appeared, climbing the stairs behind him. "I am here, Anthony."

They made an incongruous couple. He was around six feet tall, broad shouldered and wearing a general's uniform covered in various decorations. She was just over four feet tall and wearing a loose-fitting sari and a hooded turban on her head. She exuded calm and confidence while the general looked nervous and anxious.

"Vould you give me one of your regiments to help defend our right flank?" he asked without hesitation.

"No, Anthony," she said calmly. "My men will not go further away from the ford here at Assaye. The battle is lost. We must look at how we can retire and protect our forces."

"But our infantry is as good as the British and sepoy battalions, and half of it has not been used," he protested.

In the tone of voice that a mother might use with an upset child she said to him softly, "Anthony, we have lost most of our guns and our cavalry will not fight. If we move away from the river, we will be outflanked by their horsemen. We have no choice but to retire."

Pohlmann walked to the edge of the roof and stared out at the ground where once his great army had looked so certain of victory. Now there was just an arc of nervous infantry remaining and thousands more troops on foot and horse fleeing in the distance. The abandoned line of cannon, marking his original defensive line, highlighted just how badly the battle had gone. Suddenly his shoulders seemed to slump in defeat as he accepted the inevitable and in a quiet voice he asked, "Vill you support me and tell Scindia that I did all I could?"

"Anthony, you cannot think of going back." She walked over to where he was standing and, reaching up above her head, she pulled his shoulder round so that he was forced to look at her. "Every one of his spineless cavalry will swear that you lost the battle and so there was no point in them attacking. Scindia will believe them because he loves his horsemen. If you return to him, you will be killed. Retreat with your men, take what treasure you have with you, but tonight set off on your own with any men you trust. Head south, change your name and appearance and go home."

"Vat will you do?" he asked.

The begum gestured at me. "I am making my own arrangements," she said.

"You are a true friend," Pohlmann said, his voice breaking slightly, and he reached down and kissed her hand. He looked out across the battlefield. Slowly his back straightened and he looked like a soldier again. "You know," he mused, "they have withdrawn so far off that I think we can recover some of the nearest guns. That should help us hold them off until nightfall. I have heard that Vellesley has sworn he vill never carry out another night attack and his men will be truly exhausted by then." He looked round, grinning again. "If we must be defeated then at least we can march the trained infantry away with its colours flying and unbroken." He slammed his big fist into his palm "Dammit, ve are not beaten yet, yes?" And without waiting for an answer he walked over to the stairs and, shouting orders to his aides, disappeared out of sight.

Chapter 21

The begum watched Pohlmann go and then turned to me. She held a sealed letter in one hand. "My first husband once told me a story about a brave lion outwitted by a cunning jackal. I cannot remember the details now, but Pohlmann is a lion, brave but foolishly assuming everyone is as brave and honourable as he. I have had to be a jackal to survive this long and I am not sure about you." She gave me a half-amused smile before adding, "The man who leapt in the air when he found me in my palanquin does not seem to be the same man who would coolly bayonet a tiger."

"I didn't have a lot of choice with the tiger: it was him or me."

"Well, now you do have a choice. You can denounce me to the British as another heartless Mahratta leader or you can take this letter to Wellesley." She held out the document, which had been wrapped in ribbon with a wax seal impressed with the ring she wore on her finger. "The letter describes how I saved you from certain death and warned the European officers of the plot to murder them at Oojeine." She looked me in the eye and continued, "So that you emerge with credit from the affair, I have also confirmed that you escaped from five hundred *pindaree* bandits and had Scindia's men looking for you for months. I also describe how you stood up to Scindia at Oojeine and that your example inspired some of the British officers to leave his service. Your reputation will be considerably enhanced with this letter if you support it."

She paused and looked out to where her army waited in disciplined ranks. "All I want is for Wellesley to allow me to withdraw my men in good order. In exchange I offer peace and friendship with Sardhana. You can doubtless tell him what a useful friend I can be amongst his enemies."

Well, she could have marched her forces away behind the town band for all I cared, although I was not sure that Wellesley would be so amenable. But she certainly had my measure: anyone who offers me a route to safety and some extra credit for my undeserved reputation gets my vote every time. Of course if I had known that for me the worst part of the battle was yet to come then perhaps I would not have been so quick to kiss her hand and make my escape, but I did.

"Good luck, Thomas, and when this is over, come and see me again," she said as I left.

At the time I thought that there was more chance of my visiting Timbuktu than seeing her again, but I did. She lived another thirty-three years to the ripe old age of ninety and died in 1836. Years later when I revisited India, I went back to Sardhana and she welcomed me back as an honoured guest which, given what happened subsequently that day, was a pleasant surprise.

I went down the stairs accompanied by one of her staff officers, who steered me through the Mahratta lines and arranged for me to be given a stick with a white neck-cloth tied to it. The only British troops nearby were the remains of the 74th Highlanders and the sepoys who had marched with them. They were three hundred yards off and so I walked in their direction. Their battle had looked a grisly affair from the rooftop, but close to the carnage left from the slaughter was terrible. Nobody took any notice of me as I approached; the begum's troops had already helped their own wounded away. The ground was littered with the dead of both sides and wounded redcoats with some able-bodied soldiers moving amongst them, offering aid. The corpses were so thick on the ground that I had to step over them and I jumped when one suddenly spoke to me.

"Have you come to surrender your forces?" I looked round and there, just a few feet away, a young British lieutenant was watching me. He was lying with his head on the thigh of another body and with both hands he was trying to hold into his body what looked like a knot of purple snakes. His guts must have been laid open with a horrendously deep sword cut and his white breeches were blood-soaked down to the knees.

"I have a letter seeking terms to withdraw, yes," I said, staring aghast as a spasm gripped his body and one of the purple snakes escaped his clutches and slithered down to his thigh.

The lieutenant shut his eyes for a moment as though gathering his strength and then when he spoke again blood dribbled from his mouth down his chin. "Thought so, didn't think they would want to tangle with us again."

From where he lay he could not see all of the slaughter around him and doubtless he was more focused on his own fate. Four-fifths of both forces that had marched with Orrock had been killed or wounded. I found out later that of the five hundred 74th Highlanders who had marched towards the begum's part of the line all the officers had been killed or wounded apart from a Major Swinton. One hundred and twenty-four other ranks were killed and two hundred and seventy wounded. Only eighty-nine soldiers were left fit. Of Orrock's picket detachment, the only able bodied survivors were Orrock himself and seventy-five men.

"You'd better see Major Swinton," said the lieutenant, his voice getting hoarse.

I looked down at him. The wound was truly terrible and proved what I had been told about the sharpness of Mahratta swords, for he was nearly cut through to the backbone on one side. "Can I get you help or give you some water?" He was dying and he knew it, but I could not just walk away.

"Thank you, no. Water just made it worse." Another spasm gripped his body and more blood gushed from his mouth. He opened his eyes again and looked at me. In a voice just above a whisper he added, "I would take that Mahratta coat off if I were you. It is not too popular around here." And then his eyes shut again. He still seemed to be breathing as I took his advice; with the stick in my teeth I shrugged off the green Mahratta coat and then, with white shirt and breeches, I stepped forward towards the thickest pile of bodies, where the 74th had made its final stand.

Around twenty of the able survivors were marching back from the river, each holding half a dozen canteens of water. The fearsome sergeant I had seen earlier was looking up at vultures that were now circling in numbers above the battleground. The noise of battle had now died away and the birds were getting lower as they surveyed the feast of dead meat below them.

"McTaggart," the sergeant called to one of the corporals who were standing near him. "Take six men and go back the way we came across the field and shoot any of those black bastards," he gestured at the birds above, "that try to get near our dead and wounded."

"Shouldn't we try to keep the men together, Sergeant?" asked a cultured English voice from the crowd of men beyond him.

"Why is that, sir?" asked the sergeant with more than a hint of aggression in his voice as though he was just holding in his temper in the presence of an imbecilic child.

The officer stepped forward. He was a thin, immaculately dressed major with the exception of a cut to his head that despite having a rough bandage was still bleeding profusely down his cheek and neck and onto his shirt. He was polishing a pair of spectacles which he now put on and squinted at the battlefield around him. "In case they try to attack again?" he asked uncertainly.

The sergeant made a point of looking around at the hundreds of dead and wounded men who surrounded them and then turned back to the major. "If they attack again, we are all dead men, sir."

This seemed my cue to step forward and confirm that the Mahratta were not looking to attack again and so I took a few steps forward towards the major.

"There's far enough."

The voice behind me accompanied by the unmistakeable click of a cocking musket, which was a convincing argument to stop. I slowly moved the stick out to one side so that the man behind could see it clearly.

"I am here to speak to your commanding officer," I called loudly. "I was a British prisoner of the Mahratta."

"Aye, so you say," the voice behind me snarled, "but they had British officers, didn't they. So perhaps you're some bastard traitor."

I started to turn, "Now look here, I want..."

The sharp point of a bayonet cut into my back, causing a stab of pain, and I felt warm, wet blood on my back. "You so much as twitch, you treacherous fucker," the voice behind me snarled, "and you will have a foot of cold steel through your innards."

"That is enough, Private Gilray," barked the sergeant.

"I saw 'im taking off a Mahratta coat back over there. 'E was talking to Mr Collister," protested Gilray behind me.

"I have a letter from the Mahratta commander for General Wellesley," I called, waving the sealed letter in the air so that the major could see it. "They are seeking terms to withdraw and are not planning to attack you again."

"Thank God," muttered the major. "Gilray, step back and let the prisoner pass." He stepped forward to meet me and held out his hand. "Major Swinton, 74th Highlanders, and you are?"

"Thomas Flashman." I paused – what was I... a courier, a spy? I couldn't just say 'a gentleman loitering behind enemy lines'. "The general sent me into Mahratta country nearly a year ago to try to split up their alliance," I finished.

"I see," said Swinton, looking around again at the carnage as if to imply that I had not been that successful. "I suppose I should introduce you to Colonel Orrock as he is the senior officer, but he is somewhat broken up at the moment." He gestured to a man some yards off in a red coat stiff with gold braid. The colonel was sitting cross-legged on the ground and on his lap rested the head of a white horse which had a wicked wound in its side but judging by the twitching legs was still alive. The colonel was openly weeping and crooning to the animal. "I gather the colonel had raised the horse from a foal," said Swinton apologetically. "He is struggling to cope with what has happened to his command."

"He should be shot," grunted the sergeant, although from his grim expression it was not clear whether he meant the horse or the colonel.

Swinton gave the sergeant a nervous look as though he too was unsure of the meaning of the remark. "Thank you, Sarn't Fergusson. If we are not to be attacked again, perhaps we should get the wounded organised so that when the surgeon arrives they are all in one place. And round up some of the loose horses, please, we need to get this message to the general."

"Yes, sir," barked the sergeant and turned to issue a stream of commands to the men.

The major led me away to one side as various soldiers started making battlefield stretchers out of their muskets and jackets to move the wounded. This essentially involved unhooking and crossing the shoulder straps of two muskets so that they formed a cross of leather between the weapons. Then the sleeves of a coat were threaded over the barrels of both guns so that the back of the jacket lay over the straps and the shoulders of the garment provided further support. The same was done with another coat over the butts of the weapons and then their owners went off looking for passengers. It was rudimentary but effective. Some more men were quietly approaching some of the nearest horses who were looking very jumpy.

"Who commands these forces?" asked Swinton, gesturing at the hundreds of men watching us from just a few hundred yards away. "Is it Prince Scindia or one of his mercenary generals? We heard that a Hanoverian was commanding the army."

"These particular troops are commanded by the begum of Samru."

"Ah yes, I have heard about her. Some frog shot himself when in love with her, didn't he?" His Adam's apple bobbed as he gave a loud gulp that could have been heard in Assaye before he added, "I say, is she very pretty then?"

Judging by the lascivious look on his face, he was already imagining an Indian Helen of Troy and I did not have the heart to tell him that she was only four feet tall with a nose you could open barrels with. "She was once," I confirmed. "But don't be fooled into thinking she is soft because she is a woman. Her mind is as sharp as that bayonet your man just jabbed in me." I was reaching back to feel the wound, which was soaking blood into the back of my shirt.

"Sorry about that," muttered Swinton. "Gilray's brother was blown to pieces by a cannon shot as we marched across the field."

We both turned as we heard hooves pounding the dirt behind us. A British staff officer and a couple of cavalry troopers as escort reined in beside us. I didn't recognise the officer whose face was covered with dust and sweat and several days' growth of beard.

"Holy Mother of God," the officer exclaimed as he surveyed the carnage all around. He turned to Swinton. "The general's compliments, Major; he sent me to find out how you fared."

"We have around a hundred and fifty men still standing, sir," said Swinton grimly. "But this officer has come from the Mahratta army with a letter for the general seeking terms to withdraw."

"Has he now. Well, he may be too late as I have just left Wellesley who was massing his remaining infantry for a final assault on their line. Now we have them beat there is no reason to leave their army in a state where it can challenge us again." He looked coldly at me and added, "Now, Major, I suggest that you send this rascal back to his army with the news that their terms are being considered, rather than exchanging idle gossip."

I bridled at that. I had spend the best part of a year risking my precious skin for my country and when I finally got back to my own side I was insulted. But the major got in before I could say anything.

"But, sir, he is not a Mahratta officer. He claims to be a British prisoner who was held by them. He says he was sent to the Mahratta by General Wellesley himself."

"A likely tale told by a turncoat renegade, I'll be bound. Your name, sir?" he barked, looking down at me.

"Thomas Flashman," I said coldly, "and I would be grateful if you would arrange for me to meet General Wellesley at once or you will answer for the consequences."

My answer seemed to affect him like a stunning club on an ox for his eyes bulged in astonishment and his jaw sagged as he just stared at me, dumbfounded. "Flashman," he gasped at last. "That ain't possible. Flashman is dead."

"I can assure you he isn't, although it was a close-run thing on a number of occasions."

"My God it is you, I can see it now. You did not have a beard when we last met."

"We have met before?"

"Yes, when Arthur, I mean General Wellesley, and I caught up with you on the road to Seringapatam and took you back to Madras. I am Jock Malcolm."

Looking through the beard and grime, I could now see the genial political officer who had helped talk me into this mess in the first place.

"We heard that you had been trapped in a hill fort with your escort and that you had all been massacred."

"No, I escaped from that but was caught again later and sentenced to death by being tied to a pair of rockets." I paused to allow for their gasps of horror and astonishment. "But I was rescued by the begum of Samru, who commands this part of the army," I said, gesturing to the nearby troops. "She is not just seeking terms to withdraw, but offering to be an ally of the British amongst the Mahratta states."

"Interesting, but I don't think it will stop the general driving their arms from the field by force. They still outnumber us two to one, and if their cavalry ever find some courage, we could yet be in trouble. Give me the letter and I will take it to Wellesley, and when this is over you will have to tell me all about your adventures. If we can find you a horse, I will take you back to the staff officers. The general will want to see you as soon as the battle is over."

A Mahratta cavalry horse had been caught and I swung myself aboard. We trotted along the abandoned line of guns towards a distant knot of officers. From the added height of the saddle I looked across to my right and saw the ranks of the remaining 78th Highlander and sepoy regiments marching abreast towards the waiting Mahratta troops. Cannon suddenly crashed out from the Assaye end of the Mahratta line where they still had big guns and you could see some of the balls whip diagonally through the red ranks. Smaller galloper guns that had moved with the Mahratta troops fired as lines got closer together and then, when they were only a hundred yards apart, the Mahratta infantry opened fire. They had organised themselves into three ranks to receive the redcoats and were firing by rank to send a steady stream of balls into the soldiers facing them. They were doing it damn handily too, reloading as fast as any troops I had seen. Slowly through the musket smoke you could see the redcoats falling back.

"Damn," said Jock Malcolm, who was watching them with me. "Wellesley won't want to see that. Generals think that they command armies, Flashman, but the common soldier on both sides can see the situation here. If the Mahratta break now, they are finished, trapped between the river and our bayonets. On the other hand, our soldiers know that the Mahratta will slip away come nightfall, so there is no need to get your head blown off rushing them. There is only an hour or so to dusk now anyway. Go and rest in the shade of that tree and I will get your message to Wellesley."

He rode off and I trotted the horse slowly towards a big peepul tree. The horse was limping; it was lame, which was probably why they had managed to catch it in the first place. I got down from the saddle and sat with my back against the tree, trying to apply some pressure to my bayonet cut to stop the bleeding. I was facing the distant Mahratta line and could hear renewed volley firing from my left as the British officers tried to force the infantry forward against the Mahratta line again.

Sitting on the ground you could not see the hundreds of bodies that were scattered over the battlefield but there were now dozens of vultures circling above to confirm they were there. This was my first moment alone and safe for nearly a year and I almost had to pinch myself to believe it. After countless dangers I was now back with my own people. Not only that, but once the begum's letter had been read I would emerge with some credit, which I would downplay in a way that could only earn more admiration. Most importantly I had escaped the bloodbath of Assaye without a scratch, unless you count a bayonet jab from my own side. I was sitting there feeling mighty pleased with myself. I even started planning my return to Madras; with Wellesley still out in the field I would have a clear run at Eliza Freese until the next boat for home came in.

As I watched, the British infantry attack fell back again, but it did not matter for the Mahratta had finally decided to leave the field of battle. Scindia's remaining troops broke and ran to the river, but there was no such indiscipline amongst the soldiers of the begum. Their whole line gave a smart left turn and began marching in neat ranks with their galloper guns towards Assaye and the ford to cross the river. The battle was at last over... or so I thought.

Now I am not sure whether there is one god as us Christians believe or a whole crowd of them as the Hindus and others support, but what I can tell you is whatever deities there are, they enjoy tormenting us mortals. For while I was relaxing in the shade they were busy working the fates to get my bowels churning in terror again. The first I knew of this was when the ground began to shake. The hooves of two thousand horses slamming in the dirt create quite a vibration and I got up to see Colonel Maxwell bringing up the cavalry that had rescued the 74th Highlanders and broken half of the Mahratta line. I did not know whether Wellesley had got the begum's letter, but her army remained a considerable force and he wanted it destroyed. The begum's troops were strung out in a marching line and anyone with an ounce of military knowledge knew that the only way infantry could defend themselves against horsemen was in a square formation, otherwise they would be destroyed. I could see several of Wellesley's staff officers riding over to join the cavalry for this devastating final stage of the battle. Well, they weren't getting me to join in; I had done enough and I had no wish to see the begum's destruction. She had saved me from certain death, and while I would not trust her further than a bankrupt stockbroker, she had always treated me fairly.

The horsemen lined up for the charge just twenty yards in front of my tree and several saw me and invited me to join in but I waved them away. Jock Malcolm rode over to join the throng and he called out to me too: "Flashman, after all you have been through I would have thought you would have wanted to join the last hurrah." At this one of the dragoons looked round and positively goggled at me. I saw it was my old school friend Carstairs who had not recognised me with the beard.

"I would love to ride with you," I lied. Gesturing to my horse I added, "But I can't. My screw is lame, so I will have to miss out."

"You can have Fairfax's horse," called out Carstairs. "He was shot off it earlier but it still rides with the herd. Here, I will bring it over."

Bloody Carstairs, it was showing off to him that helped me into the soup in the first place, but with everyone watching I could hardly appear reluctant now. I certainly could not resist due to my wound as several of the horseman were carrying much worse with an arm in a sling or other bandages visible.

But wait, I could still wriggle out of this yet. "Hang on," I called, "I don't even have a sword. What do you expect me to do, get up close enough to bite them?"

Malcolm laughed. "I have just read the begum's letter and from what she says of you then you probably would get close enough to bite them if you had to. But I am sure we can do better than that. Has anyone got a spare sword?"

The nearest cavalry troopers were looking at the strange, white-shirted civilian with renewed respect at Malcolm's words and I admit I felt a twinge of pride at my growing reputation. Well, they could get me to join their charge and I would shout "View halloo" as we went as loud as the rest, but I would just take care to ensure that my shouting was from the back.

An officer rode over and handed down a gold-and-jewel-encrusted sword. "I picked this up from a corpse earlier and I shall want it back, but I prefer my usual weapon for the charge." Holding the sword with one hand, I reached up for the reins of the horse Carstairs had brought with the other and swung myself into the saddle. Too late did I notice that the previous rider had left blood and gore over the leather and neck of the horse.

"I say, Flash," said Carstairs, "I heard that you had been killed by a *pindaree* bandit gang and that there was a prize on your head. You must have had some adventures escaping that lot, eh?"

"That is how it is in my line of work," I said coolly. "I take it the previous owner of this horse did not survive?"

"God no, he took a bullet in the guts and then they damn near decapitated him. But it is a good cavalry horse and it should run well with the rest of us." He gabbled on: "Gosh, today has been the first really interesting day I have had since I arrived in India."

"Interesting!" I almost squeaked the word in dismay. "If this is just interesting, what do you fellows do for real excitement then?"

Carstairs just laughed and rode away to join his troop. He always had been a bit strange at school, what the masters called attention seeking and what the rest of us called half-mad. He had been completely fearless then too; he once climbed the chapel tower and then ran along the top of the chapel roof for a dare.

The cavalry was formed up in two ranks. The front rank was all cavalrymen while the second rank was also mostly troopers but included all the staff officers and other extras. I trotted my horse into the second rank and before I had a chance to say anything to my neighbours there was a trumpet call. I did not know what it signified but the late Mr Fairfax's horse did, and I suddenly found myself at the walk and moving in an exact line with all the other troopers while several of the staff officers had to spur their horses to catch up and then rein them in to keep them in line. My mount behaved perfectly, and when there was another trumpet call I was not surprised when it smoothly moved into the trot with all the other cavalry troopers. It was the next trumpet call that caused the problems.

The strident tones of the charge rang out and the horses picked up speed again. The drumming of the hooves was thunderous now and dust was being kicked up by the rank of horses ahead. Looking down the line, troopers had the reins held loosely in their left hands and were now stretching their sword arms out in front for the attack. I, on the other hand, was struggling to control my mount, which had decided that its proper place in any charge was the front rank. It surged forward and I yanked on the leather to haul it back, only to feel something give. One of the reins must have been partly cut through in the melee that had killed Fairfax and it had now snapped. If the horse obeyed a pull on the remaining strip of leather, it would veer into the path of the second rank, bringing us all down in a mess of flailing hooves. With horror I realised that I was a passenger on this dammed horse which even now was pushing itself between two horses in the front rank. Riders on either side moved to make room and Carstairs, who was two horses away, saw me join his line and grinned. He shouted something that I could not catch above the noise. Doubtless the harebrained oaf thought I could not wait to get to the enemy.

Now I was at the front I could see the begum's forces clearly. We were coming up at them on a diagonal line to theirs but they were making no attempt to get into squares. Instead they had stopped marching and had formed themselves into a long line of mostly green-jacketed troops, the front rank kneeling and the other ranks standing, interspersed with galloper guns. They did not seem to have read the manual explaining that infantry in line is always beaten by cavalry. God knows how the front rank found the courage to kneel in front of two thousand charging horses but they did. Imagine yourself kneeling at the finishing post of the derby with the horses a furlong to go. Then imagine the jockeys with swords and malicious intent. You would need nerves of steel to stay there even with a musket in your hands. But the begum's troops stayed there all right. As I watched they brought their weapons to the shoulder and suddenly the whole world seemed to slow down as dozens of things happened at once.

We were just a hundred yards away now and I noticed the begum sitting on her horse a few yards behind her men, watching us. In fact she seemed to be looking straight at me. We would smash into their line in the next few seconds. Nine hundred and ninety-nine men in the front rank let out their charging roar or yells while one man let out a shriek of panic-stricken terror as he saw the enemy officers' swords slash down as they gave the order to fire. The enemy line disappeared behind a triple row of orange dots that were instantly obscured with musket smoke. Then I was hit.

One moment I was screaming my head off and the next something slammed into my chest and I could not breathe; it was as though I had been punched in the solar plexus. Horses all around me were going down; the rider next to me was plucked clean from the saddle by the impact of shots. Incredibly the Mahratta line still stood, and while some horses got close enough to suffer bayonet wounds, Maxwell appeared to give the command to wheel away and most of the troopers did. Only later did they discover that he had been killed in the attack and the outstretched right arm was probably the result of the bullet impact. The remaining riders were starting to veer away. My horse tried to follow. Whether it was hit or tangled with the legs of the other thrashing horses I don't know, but it went down amongst a pile of downed men and mounts. I dropped my sword as it stumbled, got my leg out of the stirrup and managed to fall clear. There were screams and yells all around and the thunder of hooves as the second rank veered right almost over the top of us.

I hit the ground hard and gasped for breath with an intense pain in my chest. Terrified, my shaking hands began to search my body for the wound. A bullet to the chest was nearly always fatal; was I to end my life in this dusty field? I had a horrid vision of that lieutenant I had met, it was just an hour or two ago, desperately trying to hold his guts in his body. Would that be me now? I scrabbled about the folds of my shirt, searching for the hole and the wound, and then found it. There was some blood but not a lot, and just as I found something small, hard and hot in the wound a horse whinnied behind my back and a hoof slammed into my head, sending me to a peaceful oblivion.

Chapter 22

Wellesley once said that the aftermath of a battle won was the second worst sight in the world, and he is not wrong. As I came back to consciousness it was night and it took me a full minute to remember where I was. Memories of the previous day came in waves, not all in the right order, but gradually I came to my senses. Tentatively my hands searched again where I remembered the wound to be and I could have cried with relief. I found now a cold musket or grape ball that must have struck something else on the way to me. Whatever it had hit took the brunt of its force but left a jagged edge. That edge had scored a deep cut in my chest almost exactly opposite the one in my back, but it was no worse than that.

My head still throbbed as I sat up and looked about. The begum's troops had long since marched away but their former presence here was marked by a line of fallen men and horses. Some still moved and moaned in the darkness. I slowly pulled myself to my feet and stared across the battlefield. There was a startled shriek from nearby and two villagers from Assaye, who had evidently crept over in the darkness to plunder the bodies, suddenly leapt up and ran away into the gloom. I had no idea how many more there might be and, looking around for a weapon, I saw something glinting in the moonlight. There was the jewelled sword, worth a fortune to me, never mind a poor Indian farmer. I picked it up and felt slightly more secure. There were some men with burning torches moving around the battlefield but they seemed to be in uniform and a couple were heading my way. I staggered to meet them.

"'Who are you then?" called one who levelled his musket at me while his mate held the torch higher.

"I'm British. I charged with the cavalry but must have got knocked out."

"Where is your uniform then?" asked the soldier suspiciously.

"Leave off, George," said his mate. "'e is hardly a Mahratta with a voice like that,"

"They had European officers," said George defensively.

"Yes, but 'e is walking towards us, isn't he. If 'e was a bleedin Mahratta, 'e would be running hell for leather the other way."

"I am not sure I could run hell for leather in any direction at the moment," I said. "Where is everybody?"

"Well," said the soldier with the torch, "it depends on who you are looking for. The cavalry are mostly at that large ford by the south river. Those two big fires, that is where the surgeons are. The general and lots of the officers are there too. Most of the infantry have just laid down where they stopped."

"What are you doing then?" I asked.

"Patrolin' to keep jackals and vultures off the wounded," said George importantly, "and stop any looters," he added, looking meaningfully at my jewelled sword.

"There were a couple of villagers searching bodies, but they ran off when I got up."

"You were lucky then," said George. "They would cut your throat to get a sword like that if they found you. There are stretcher parties out too looking for wounded. Are there many wounded 'ere?"

"I have heard the odd groan but I have only just got up. Did the Mahratta get away?"

"Oh aye," said the soldier with the torch. "They marched off with their banners flying, but I doubt that they will pick a fight with us again. They had to leave all their big guns behind, see. There must be a hundred of them spread over the field. Great big buggers they are too, and they were well served. We should know, we spent long enough marching towards their muzzles. You best get off, sir, head towards those big bonfires."

I staggered off as he suggested. It was a grim walk punctuated by the occasional screams and yells from wounded men and barks and yelps from jackals that were now prowling for meat. I heard the odd shot too; whether they were from guards shooting jackals or despatching the hopelessly wounded I did not know and nor did I want to.

As I got closer to them, the fires revealed a scene like one of those religious paintings of hell. Four tables had been set up between the two fires to give the surgeons light and more orderlies with burning torches stood around them. There were rows of men lying on the ground waiting to be seen and other rows of men who, judging from the bandaging, had been treated, and in between were those awful tables. There was the odd bubbling scream or whimper from the men on those altars of pain and grunts of exertion from the surgeons or men that were holding the patients down. By far the worst noise, though, was the sound of the saws as they cut through human flesh and bone. It wasn't a loud noise, just grating when they hit bone, but because you knew what it was it made every fibre of your being clench in revulsion and relief that it was not you on the table.

I was going to walk past to the tents beyond but a voice called out to me from nearby: "I say, could you give me a hand?"

I looked round and saw two heavily bandaged men sitting against a log nearby.

"He can get you one from the bucket," said the second man, who chortled with laughter at his own joke. I turned to where the laughing man was gesturing and was sickened to see a large pail by one of the tables that was full of severed arms, legs, hands and feet.

I moved towards the two men. "What can I do for you?"

"There is a chap over there cooking horse. Could you get me some? I am famished."

"Me too," said his mate, who was wearing a cavalry trooper uniform. "I just hope it is not my nag we are eating."

I had not thought about food all day but now realised that I had not eaten anything apart from a handful of rice at breakfast. I went over to the enterprising soul who was now cooking strips of horse in a Mahratta breastplate balanced on some half-buried bayonets over a small fire. There was a group of men sitting around the fire and they were happy to give me three strips. I went back and shared them with the other two and sat down next to them. The man who had first spoken to me was an infantry officer and he had lost a leg at the knee while the trooper had bandages around his shoulder.

"You're that gentleman who joined us with Major Malcolm for the last charge, aren't you?" said the trooper.

"That's right but I did not last long. The horse went mad and pushed into the front rank and then we were hit and it went down."

"Ah, Lieutenant Fairfax always rode in the front rank, so that is where the horse thought it should be," said the trooper. "I still don't understand how we did not ride right through them, though. They were brave bastards, I'll say that for them, but if the colonel had not signalled to wheel away we would still have had them."

"Maxwell is dead," said the infantry officer. "Half his chest shot away. I saw his body. God, it was a close run thing today, though, wasn't it? If their cavalry had half the balls of our old seamstress, we would have been slaughtered."

"Your old seamstress had balls," laughed the trooper.

"She did too," confirmed the officer. "Worked for the family for twenty years, damn good seamstress too – she made all my early clothes. Then when she died the undertaker told us she had a cock and balls."

"Get away!" said the trooper, astonished.

"You are not half as shocked as Mother," said the officer. "The seamstress had been measuring her for underwear for years!"

We laughed and told tales and I began to relax, helped by a flask of brandy that the infantry officer passed around. We did not even notice as much the odd scream or wail that came from the surgeons' tables. Even in that hellish scene there could be humour; it was a relief valve for those who were just desperately glad to still be alive. I remember being greatly amused when a surgeon got a shock looking for more bandages. The fires had been set up near where the 74th had been slaughtered as that was where most of the wounded were, but the ground was well littered with Mahratta corpses as well. Running out of cloth, the surgeon looked around and saw a Mahratta with a long white sash around his waist. He went over, untied it and was yanking it off the body when the 'corpse' came round. Both the Mahratta and the surgeon shrieked in alarm. Then the Mahratta, minus his sash, leapt to his feet and ran into the darkness while the surgeon sank to his knees, clutching his heart. No one moved to stop the Mahratta, we were all too busy laughing, and for the rest of the night the surgeon was ribbed about how he was now a resurrectionist.

The good thing about being frightened out of your wits is that when the danger is past you feel a strong sense of elation. This was my first land battle, although God knows it was not the last. I felt ebullient as I sat there with my comrades in arms – well, they had probably used their weapons, though all I had done was drop mine. The battle was definitely over now and I had survived. I was going home, and with that happy thought I must have settled down on the ground and gone into a deep sleep.

I was shaken awake by the cavalry trooper in the morning. "He's dead," he whispered to me, pointing to the infantry officer who was now slumped to one side. Sure enough, he was. I found out later that people often went like that when they lost a limb. The shock, I think, kills them. Still, it was a bit of a shock to us too as he had seemed fine joking and telling stories earlier. It was an unwelcome reminder of how fragile the strand of life can be.

The sun was well over the horizon by then and so I helped the trooper to his feet and walked with him back to his troop. I had to return the jewelled sword; it was tempting to keep it as it must be worth a fortune but for that reason it was a loan that would not be forgotten. I did not want a pack of angry British horsemen on my tail. The battlefield looked little better in daylight. Stretchers were still moving the wounded to and from the surgeons and vultures still circled in the sky. Now that the dead were being gathered each regiment was preparing its own burial, but the Mahratta were mostly left where they lay. By the river, very much with the living, was bloody Carstairs, still without a scratch from the battle and full of his schoolboy enthusiasm.

"Hello, Flash, I wondered what happened to you," he cried, beaming with delight when he saw me. "What a day, eh? Did you enjoy your first cavalry charge?"

You can imagine I was less enthusiastic in my response and most of the other cavalry officers were sombre too: Maxwell had been a popular commander and they had lost lots of others too. This included the fellow who had lent me the sword, but his effects would be auctioned for his widow and the jewelled sword would raise a tidy sum.

Over the southern hills men and wagons could be seen coming towards us. It was the baggage train that Wellesley had left behind the previous day.

Wellesley had set up his headquarters in an abandoned Mahratta tent near their original position. I wandered over but was intercepted by a gruff sergeant who poked me in the chest with a finger like a marlinspike and asked what my business was. I was still in my Mahratta uniform breeches and shirt with holes and bloodstains front and back.

"My name is Thomas Flashman. I am here to see the general."

"Aye well," he said, running a suspicious eye up and down my attire, "we will see about that. Wait here." He went into the tent and a few moments later Wellesley himself came out to welcome me.

"Thomas, I heard you had reappeared, back from the dead indeed. Are you wounded? No? Good. Come and meet my staff."

I stepped into the tent in which the rich Oriental carpets and silk hangings contrasted strongly with the haggard and dirty officers all still wearing the same clothes that they had fought in the previous day.

"Gentlemen," introduced Wellesley, "this is Thomas Flashman, who brought the letter from the begum we have just been discussing."

There were nods of greeting from the officers present including Jock Malcolm and Major Swinton.

One of the officers I did not know asked, "Is it true Scindia considered murdering all of his officers?"

"Well, he only originally planned to kill the Europeans, but once Perron heard about the plan he brought all his officers to a meeting, and yes, Scindia still considered it."

"You are being too modest, Flashman," said Malcolm. "From what I read in the begum's letter you worked with her to create considerable dissent amongst the officers against Scindia. Did he not sentence you to death for it?"

"Yes, a particularly grisly death too," added Wellesley.

I knew that people who downplay their achievements generally earn more credit than those who brag about them, but I was being diffident because I did not know precisely what was in the begum's letter. I had to tread carefully as if I contradicted it then things would unravel pretty quickly.

"Oh, she did rescue me so all ended well on that score," I said airily. I knew that the rescue at least was in the letter as she had told me that on the rooftop.

"Well, I think you have achieved far more than we expected when we sent you into Mahratta country," declared Wellesley. "The morale of their officers must have been affected and possibly that was why most of their cavalry avoided battle."

I knew that this was more to do with the fact that most of their cavalry were *pindaree*, who judging by recent performance would avoid battle with a blind orphan boy if he was armed with a sharp stick. So I just gave another modest shrug and moved on to what was for me the point of the visit.

"I am glad to have been of service, but now my mission is done I had better be heading back to Madras. Would you be able to lend me a horse and perhaps a few men as an escort?"

Wellesley reacted as though I had goosed him with a red-hot poker. "You are not serious, surely?"

The others looked equally surprised at the request.

This was not quite the reaction I had been hoping for. By their own admission I had done all I could, so now I thought they would let me go. "Well, I don't see what more I can do. I am too well known to go behind enemy lines again and I am not army, you know."

"On the contrary," cried Malcolm. "You spent a couple of months with a Company cavalry troop, then you were, according to the begum, a very capable officer in Scindia's army before you spent six months in her forces, again serving with credit. You probably know more about the enemy than anyone. You are far too valuable to be allowed to go home in the middle of a war."

"And we can solve the problem of you being *'not army'* right now," said Wellesley, smiling. "I can give you a battlefield commission of lieutenant, no, captain, backdated to when you were first sent to the Mahratta. The 74th are desperate for officers. Major Swinton, would you put Captain Flashman on your regiment's strength?"

"I would be glad to, sir," cried Swinton and, turning to me, he held out his hand to shake. "Welcome to the 74th Highlanders, Captain Flashman."

There are times when you just know it is not worth arguing, and they may have had a point about my unique knowledge of the enemy.

While they were press-ganging me into the army I remembered one important fact I needed to pass on. "Before we go any further I must tell you that your guide and Stevenson's both work for the Mahratta."

"That explains why he has disappeared," growled Wellesley. "I was beginning to suspect as much yesterday when he insisted that the only ford was in front of the Mahratta position. See, you are showing your value already. Now, gentlemen, to business."

There then followed what seemed to me to be a very tedious conversation on supplies, ammunition levels, bullock trains, wounded lists, burial arrangements and other administration details that would have sent me to sleep had I not been sitting on an uncomfortable camp stool. I remember a Lieutenant Serle of the 19th Dragoons was let off a court martial due to his gallantry, while the commissary of cattle for the army, a Captain Mackay, would have been reprimanded for leaving his post with the supply chain to join the battle were it not for the fact that he had been sabred to death by the Mahratta for his trouble. Of course in the months and years to come I was to learn that maintaining supplies and discipline in an army was at least as important as the army's placement in a battle, but back then it just seemed a boring frost. As Wellesley went through his written list of issues in his usual brusque style I found myself watching some flies circling the tent and reflecting on this most recent change in my career.

When I was eighteen I had wanted to join the army, not to take part in battles but because Teddy Carstairs had written to George Berkeley to say what fun it was. Mess parties, plentiful women and back then there seemed little chance of seeing action, which suited me fine. But my father had intervened. He had been in the army and convinced me that survival was a fairly random affair and so since then he had been trying to get me safely into politics. Well, so far I had done a bloody poor job of keeping myself safe. While I had a patron in Lord Castlereagh, I had spent my first year sailing with Cochrane in the Mediterranean and now over a year risking life and limb in India. To cap everything, I now found myself in the army, the one place my father had engineered my career to avoid.

I could see that there was no way I was going to get an escort to Madras and the country was still too wild to risk going it alone. To run now would also ruin my enhanced reputation and risk a charge of desertion. Whether I liked it or not, I was in the army, and so I should probably make the best of it. After all, the Mahratta had been given a proper beating at Assaye, the begum would not put her forces up against the British again and most of the Mahratta cavalry was much more interested in looting than fighting. Hopefully Pohlmann had got away as I liked him, but Scindia would hold other infantry officers responsible, doubtless with more executions, and their morale would sink even lower. To my ignorant mind this campaign seemed all over bar the shouting, and so joining the army now might not be so bad. The enemy was on the run and there would be towns and opulent palaces to capture, which meant loot for me. If that bastard Scindia fell into our hands then perhaps I could suggest a rocket crucifixion for him too.

Looking back, I sometimes wonder how I have managed to live so long as my ability to foretell the future is truly shocking.

Chapter 23

"What do I have to do as a captain?" I asked Swinton as we walked back to the part of the battlefield where the 74th Highlanders were based. It was also the part where most of them had died and the bodies were now being collected in grim rows.

"Do?" queried Swinton. "Oh, very little. The sergeants do most things, but you will need to sign off the company records and carry out inspections, that sort of thing. Sarn't Fergusson is a very capable man. He will run a smart company for you."

"How many men are in the company?"

"Well, we only have eighty-nine men listed as fit and that is roughly the size of one company. So I will leave you in charge of company affairs while I will look after the regimental matters."

As we walked I noticed that the baggage train was crossing the ford and the first wagons were beginning to spread out towards their regiments.

"Ah, here is the only other surviving fit officer of the 74th," said Swinton as we approached another grim officer coming to meet us. "Mr Grant, our quartermaster who was with the wagons. Mr Grant, can I introduce you to our newest and only other active officer, Captain Flashman."

Grant shook my hand automatically but he was still looking around the field. "It is true then about the casualties," he said in a strong Scottish accent. "We heard the gunfire but had nae idea it would be this bad."

"Yes, Grant," replied Swinton, "one hundred and thirty-four dead and two hundred and seventy-seven wounded, but many of those should recover in time."

"One hundred and thirty-seven dead, sir," said a voice from behind us.

Turning, I found myself looking into the flinty blue eyes of the sergeant I had seen gutting the Mahratta rider with his spontoon the day before.

"Captain Blakeney and two privates died of their wounds earlier, sir."

"Ah, poor George. At least he was not married with children like some," said Swinton. "Given the number of wounded I suppose we had better brace ourselves for more. But I still hope most will recover. Sarn't Fergusson, I would like to introduce you to our new officer,

Captain Flashman. The general has just given him a battlefield commission but he is unfamiliar with our ways, so I will leave you to show him the ropes, eh?"

Swinton finished with what he thought was an encouraging smile to both of us. It was wasted on the sergeant, who shot me a look of pure venom before turning back to the major.

"This is the same..." Fergusson paused as though struggling to get his tongue around the next word "... gentleman, who was fighting for the Mahratta yesterday, is it not, sir?"

"Ah no," said Swinton, trying but failing to sound firm with the sergeant. "I have just been with the general who confirmed that he himself sent Captain Flashman into Mahratta territory to cause dissent among their commanders. Indeed, Captain Flashman was sentenced to death by Prince Scindia himself, but managed to escape with the help of another of their leaders. He is quite loyal."

"As ye say, sir," growled the sergeant, giving me a look that showed he was far from convinced.

Swinton moved off, leaving the two of us alone, and for a second or two there was an awkward silence. I was trying to think of what I could say that would maintain an air of authority without antagonising him when the sergeant spoke.

"There'll be an auction of officers' effects this afternoon, sir. You can buy uniforms and officer kit. It would be best for you to be in uniform before you are introduced to the men."

"Thank you, sergeant," I said, but he just nodded and walked off without saluting. I noticed that he was heading to the general's quarters and wondered if he was going to confirm Swinton's story with the sergeants in the general's guard.

I may have been new to this army but Malcolm was right, I had spent most of my time in India in three different armies. There was one universal truth in all of them: the sergeants really ran things. Whether they are called havildars, daffadars or sergeants, you can be sure that their mess will be the best equipped and served as between them they know every trick in the book. The officers' mess may run out of wine but the sergeants' mess never runs out of grog. I remembered my time with the Company cavalry and Lal and the others talking about their officer whom I never saw. Poorum had been a havildar-major or sergeant major and had been left to command the patrol on his own. Officers may think that they command the army but they do it on the information given to them by the sergeants and lots of what happens never reaches an officer's ears.

Now that I was left on my own I had nothing to do. I wandered around for a bit and found myself walking the few hundred yards to the village of Assaye. Once there I climbed up to the rooftop from which I had watched the battle. Most of the wagons had now crossed the ford and were spread out amongst their regiments, being unloaded. The big telescope was still on the roof and I was watching through it the last few wagons cross the ford when I heard footsteps coming up the stairs. I turned and saw Fergusson with a grim expression on his face.

"Ah thought ah might find ye here," he said. He had dropped the anglicised respectful tone of a sergeant and spoke in his broad Scots accent with more than a hint of menace.

"Why is that, Sergeant?" I replied, trying to sound unconcerned.

"Ah saw ye on this roof during the battle, didn't ah. You in your Mahratta uniform, and then with their general and some wee fella."

"Yes, I was here," I confirmed. "I saw you too, killing two horsemen with your spontoon."

Another awkward silence followed. I was uncomfortably aware that I was still unarmed and we were alone on this rooftop. The sergeant did not have his spontoon but I did not doubt that there was a blade on him somewhere and that he knew how to use it.

"Ah saw ye watching as we wus killed. Did ye get a good view through yon glass?" He took a couple of steps closer and hissed angrily, "Spy or no, ye did not seem to be doin' much to stop it."

There was no mistaking the menace now as he looked me in the eye. He was directly between me and the stairs, deliberately I was sure.

"The wee fella," I said, trying to sound unconcerned at the threatening tone, "was the begum of Samru, a lady and a very capable commander." I decided that attack was the best form of defence. "What did you think was going to happen when Colonel Orrock marched his men on their own directly towards her lines, which were the strongest the Mahratta had? Of course she was going to attack." I decided to embellish my role slightly and added, "I only just stopped her from a second attack which would have wiped you out entirely."

He thought about that for a moment, looking across to where the 74th had made their stand. He must have been recalling the slaughter and the people watching him from that distant building.

"Aye," he murmured after a moment. "The colonel had nae idea what he was doin'." Then, looking at me again, he added, "But ah'll be watching ye." With that he turned and headed off down the stairs.

I breathed a big sigh of relief. I felt I had passed some sort of test but I was still clearly on probation. I had seen what he could do to the enemy but he was almost as frightening to his own side. There was no point complaining to Swinton about his attitude as I sensed that Swinton found him as intimidating as I did. But Fergusson was protective of his 74th Highlanders, there was no doubt of that. Woe betides anyone whom he thought had betrayed them.

I loafed around the camp for the rest of the morning and then headed over to the auction of officers' effects. It would be fair to say that it was a buyer's market, particularly for kit owned by the 74th. There were the effects of eleven officers to sell and only one potential bidder, yours truly. Looking through the lots in advance, I had discovered that the late Captain Blakeney had been my size and a very wealthy young man with an opulent mahogany campaign chest full of everything a young officer might need in the field including dress uniforms, silk shirts, linen shirts, silver-mounted razors and bowls, cutlery and crockery. It must have cost a fortune, I bought it for five guineas and could probably have got away with one if I had not minded appearing like a thief to those watching the bidding. I also bought a spare uniform coat for everyday use (the one Blakeney had been wearing had a large hole in it), some spare boots my size, a good sword, some pistols and a handsome horse, again all at bargain prices. As I had no cash this was deducted from my pay and delivered to my new quarters, a tent to myself in the 74th company lines.

A short while later I was alone in my tent pulling on my army officer redcoat for the first time. Sadly none of my late comrades had thought a full-length mirror necessary for a military campaign and so I could not view the effect myself. But when I stepped outside the tent it had the desired effect on the men nearby, who stopped and saluted at the new officer with a silver '74' badge in the tall black leather hat that I now wore.

"Do ye want the men fallen in for inspection, sir, to announce yerself?" Fergusson growled from behind me. He had evidently been waiting for me to emerge from the tent.

I looked across the field. The soldiers were busy digging a mass grave for their comrades and there were similar excavations by other regiments around the field. Some of the sepoy battalions were breaking down wood from the village that was now largely abandoned and others were chopping down trees to cremate their dead according to their Hindu customs.

"No, leave them be, Sergeant. I will introduce myself later."

Walking across the field, I saw that the 74th had so few fit men and so many dead to bury that a company from the 78th were helping dig the long pit and other men with handkerchiefs over their noses were collecting the dead, who had already started to swell and smell in the heat. The handkerchiefs were not necessary just for the stench but to avoid breathing in the flies which swarmed over the bodies. It was a hellish scene, but the sooner it was done, the better. I wandered away from the trench, retracing the march the 74th had taken towards the begum's lines, and saw the surviving drummer boy coming towards me with a human leg in his arms. He saw me and put it down to salute.

"John McTavish, sir. They call me Wee Jock. I am a drummer boy," he added unnecessarily; he was only twelve or thirteen and so he could hardly be anything else. He wore a red uniform coat cut to his size and on his belt he had a long case for his drum sticks on one side and a viciously sharpened bayonet on the other. As he was too small to carry a musket I was not sure he was supposed to have a bayonet which hung down his leg like a sword, but I was not going to take it off him. I heard later that drummer boys would sometimes be interfered with by the men, particularly if there were no women about, but I doubt that happened in the 74th. For a start Fergusson would probably find out and punish the offender, and Wee Jock had a belligerent look in his eye that indicated that he knew how to use the blade at his hip.

I glanced down at the leg; it was a boy's with a boot and part of a trouser leg still wrapped around it. I had a sudden memory of a leg spinning away during the battle when a cannon ball killed one of the drummer boys.

"Is this from the other drummer?" I asked.

The boy wiped his nose on his sleeve before replying, "Aye, it is Jimmy, sir. Ah have found most of 'im but ah cannae find one o' his arms. Ah reckon that the fookin' dogs got it."

With that he saluted, picked up the leg and marched off towards the pit to put Jimmy's leg with what other bits of his body he had found and then bury them with his comrades. Children can be quite callous of death; many do not fully understand it. But Wee Jock understood all right. He must have seen enough of it in his short life. He was mourning in his own way, and among the rest of the men there were few tears, just a quite stoicism as they collected and buried their friends. The only person I had seen weeping uncontrollably was Orrock over his damned horse. He had suffered some kind of breakdown and since disappeared.

With little else to do, I tooled over in the direction the march had come. I searched for a while for the missing arm, roughly where I remembered that the cannon ball had eviscerated the drummer boy. The grass was long but trampled flat. All I found were a few gobbets of flesh and entrails in blood-smeared patches that no one, including me, thought worth picking up.

Having walked all the way to the ford the British had used to cross the river just the previous day, I walked back to where the men were piling a layer of earth back over their mass grave to trap the flies and the stench.

"Did you find it, sir?" called out a high-pitched voice.

"What? Oh, Jimmy's arm. No, sorry, I didn't."

"That is what ah thought, sir. Fookin' dogs eh?"

Now I might have been new in the army but I was pretty sure that was not how a drummer boy should address an officer. On the other hand he seemed to be the only friend I had at the moment, and so as Fergusson watched with a curious look on his face I decided to let that pass.

"Sarn't," I called, copying the pronunciation I had heard Swinton using, "will there be a burial service for the men?"

"Yes, sir. Major Swinton is just trying to find a padre to do it now."

I looked at the men. Apart from Fergusson, who always looked smartly dressed, the rest were covered in mud and worse and had dust-covered faces broken with streaks of sweat.

"Perhaps you could get the men smartened up first, Sarn't."

"Yes sir. You heard the officer, prepare for inspection in ten minutes."

There is something satisfying in seeing ninety men leap into action at your order. Not that I discovered it then, for the soldiers just stared in astonishment at this new officer. Then, after a moment, they reluctantly started to shamble off to where their kit was stored, muttering mutinously as they went. Some were speaking Gaelic so that I could not understand but the words 'bastard English' I did pick out, as I was supposed to, from one crowd of men.

"You move yourselves and smarten up to show proper respect to the dead," barked Fergusson. "And show respect to the officer," he added as a surprising afterthought.

I retired to my tent but Fergusson called me out a short while later to inspect the men.

"This is Captain Flashman," he shouted out to them. "He is your new company captain."

They were drawn up in three ranks of around thirty. Their jackets, which had faded to orange in the harsh Indian sun, were all straight and belts were on, although hardly any were properly white. Most had given their faces a wipe rather than a wash, which had just re-arranged the dirt. Above all I noticed, as they stood in a compact group in front of me, they stank. Compared to the Indian Company sowars I had ridden with for two months who washed most days and kept themselves and their kit spotlessly clean for a daily inspection, this lot were filthy. They could fight, though, and their weapons were at least in working order.

I walked along the front rank, glancing over their shoulders at the rows behind as I went. For an inspection I did not know where to start. They looked a shambles compared to the smart guardsmen I had seen marching in London. But then those guardsmen had not marched twenty miles the previous day, fought and won a battle against massive odds, seen most of their comrades slaughtered and then spent the day burying them. On the whole I felt some leeway was justified.

Most were tall, broad-shouldered men with hard faces but there were some wiry types too. In the middle of the back rank was a giant of a man, a full head and shoulders above the rest, who stared back at me with a look of benign amusement.

"Private Campbell, sir," said Fergusson, who had walked beside me and saw where I was looking. "He is known as Big Jock compared to Wee Jock, who is..."

"... the drummer boy," I finished for him. "And who is that?" I asked, pointing to a figure that could only be described as skulking in the middle rank. Since I had been in India I had heard tales of half-human half-ape figures that lived in the northern mountains; yetis they were called. We seemed to have recruited one, as this character hunched even further under my scrutiny to hide behind the men in front. He was without doubt the scruffiest and dirtiest. His buttons were done up but misaligned, his belt twisted and his bayonet covered with a combination of rust and dried blood.

"Private McFarlane, sir," Fergusson muttered, sounding embarrassed that I had noticed this pariah of the regiment whom he had evidently been trying to hide behind two tall men in the front rank. "He fights better than he looks," he added.

I could see Swinton coming towards us with a harassed padre and a piper he had borrowed from the 78th. I turned to Fergusson and told him to march the men to the graveside. Some of the walking or hobbling wounded were also coming across from where the surgeons still had their camp.

"Ah, Captain Flashman, I see you are settling in," called Swinton as he approached, sounding slightly relieved, as he glanced at Fergusson. He turned to his companion, dressed in church robes. "This is Mr Dacre, a regimental padre attached to the army."

Dacre nodded in greeting. He was bald, sweating and seemed slightly intoxicated as he took a pull on a huge silver hipflask.

It was not an impressive service. The padre evidently knew the words of the burial ceremony by heart and seemed determined to get through them as quickly as possible. At the end Swinton turned and asked me to fire the salute. Not having been to a military funeral before, I was completely unprepared. But before I could even look round I heard Fergusson giving the order and in a moment a volley of musket fire rang out. I was about to dismiss the men when the piper started up with something I later discovered was called a lament. Well, I certainly lamented being there to listen to it. It went on for ages, droning and wailing. While I fidgeted impatiently I saw several of the men with tears now going down their cheeks.

Eventually the awful din stopped and the men fell out and I walked back to our tents with Swinton alongside me.

"I have what is left of our regimental bagpipes in my quarters. Can I give them to you to see what can be done about repairing them? We also need to appoint a new pipe sergeant to play them. Perhaps once the pipes are repaired we can hold some trials, eh?"

"Certainly," I agreed, shuddering inwardly in dismay at the thought. "Any news about enemy movements from the general?" I added.

"Oh, your friend the begum is marching steadily north back to her own lands. The rest of Scindia's men have dispersed and are no threat either, although our cavalry patrols make sure that they keep marching away from us. Stevenson's column should be here in the morning. Apparently he worked out himself that his guide was working for the

Mahratta and hanged the chap. One of our cavalry patrols found him and his men in the hills and is guiding them towards us."

That evening I joined Swinton for dinner, which was a surprisingly formal affair in his tent, with table and chairs and a soldier he seemed to use as his personal orderly serving the food. We ate part of a vulture that had been shot earlier in the day, not a meat I could recommend. He had even found a decent wine and cigars from somewhere, possibly the unsold personal effects of the officers.

As I left he handed me the tattered remains of the regimental bagpipes. The bag bit was torn to shreds and covered in bloodstains from its last player and three of the pipes had also been broken. Highlanders may love their pipes but I did not. Having to listen to their awful din on a regular basis would be intolerable, and so as I walked back to the small campfire outside my own tent I came to the conclusion that they were beyond repair and dropped them into the flames.

The next morning I was awoken by a corporal with a bowl of what he called porridge for breakfast. I upturned the bowl onto a plate and the contents remained in a perfect greyish-white dome. It reminded me that I needed to write a letter to Runjeet to reassure him that I was still alive and to organise one of his more capable cousins to come and serve as my orderly. The letter could go with the despatches being sent to Madras, followed by wagons of wounded that were preparing to leave that day. Stevenson's column was already in sight coming from the south.

Later, Fergusson came to my tent to tell me that the general was planning a parade of the whole army that afternoon.

"Ah will get the men smartened up, sir," he promised with what seemed rash optimism. "Do ye have the bagpipes?" he added. "One of the *bhinjarries* reckons he can repair them."

"Oh," I said, beginning to regret the wine-fuelled impulsiveness that had prompted me to cremate them the night before. "Well, Sergeant, they seemed far beyond repair and so I got rid of them."

"Got rid of them?" he repeated, sounding aghast. Then, as if reading my mind, he looked down at the ashes of the fire and with the stave of his spontoon he stirred them around and there among the burned embers he uncovered four white rings. They must have been made of bone or horn that withstood the flames better than the rest. They seemed to stare up at me like four accusing eyes.

"Aye," he growled at me as he bent to pick them up. "They certainly are beyond repair now." Giving me a look that would chill an Eskimo, he turned on his heel and stalked off.

I was about to learn the first rule of being a junior officer: never infuriate the sergeants, for they have myriad ways to get their own back.

Fergusson's revenge appeared in the form of the yeti-like Private McFarlane later that morning. "Sarn't Fergusson says ah'm to be your orderly," he announced firmly while wiping his nose on his sleeve. He stood there at the feral stoop that he called attention with a small swarm of flies buzzing like a cloud around him and genuinely thought I was going to let him play a part in smartening me up. Well, it was as plain as a pike staff what Fergusson was up to and it was not going to work.

"You step one foot inside this tent and I will have you shot, is that understood?" I told him firmly.

The former owner of my kit, Captain Blakeney, obviously had employed an excellent orderly and everything was in prime condition, something that this ape-man could destroy in moments.

"But ah'm to be your orderly," he persisted, looking dejected.

I cast around for something I could give him to do that would not require him to enter the tent. In the corner were a pair of brown boots that I had worn with the Mahratta. They were filthy from the days of marching to Assaye and as they were brown I would not need them in the army because their boots were black. "Here," I said, giving them to him. "You can clean these."

McFarlane shambled off with the boots and I got on with other things. Looking back, I think Fergusson must have got someone to help McFarlane with the boots for he came back an hour or so later and they were absolutely gleaming. Sure, they were now black rather than brown, but I guessed that the army only had black polish. I was pleased as these boots were more comfortable than the army ones and so I could now wear these with my uniform. I looked at McFarlane and began to wonder if I had misjudged him. Perhaps he could clean but just did not take any pride in his own appearance?

All of the best uniform I planned to wear for the parade was Blakeney's pristine kit, apart from the shako hat. I had a bigger head and the only hat I could find that fitted was one that had been worn by another officer in the battle. It would have been acceptable for the parade despite being a bit dull and dusty, but as I looked at the boots I thought McFarlane could shine it up a bit. It was like a tall leather top hat but with a rounded top, the regimental number in silver on the front and a red-and-white cockade that went in a brass socket on one side. The cockade was only worn for battles and parades. Of course I know now that asking McFarlane to clean the shako was a mad decision. Even today as I write this I could knock my head against the wall at my own stupidity, but back then it seemed sensible, given the shine he had put on the boots.

McFarlane seemed delighted and honoured to be given this task and carried the hat off in both hands as though it was a precious Greek urn. "Ah'll get it reet proper-looking for you, sir," he muttered in hushed tones as he bore it off.

I got on with other jobs such as checking supplies with the quartermaster – Wellesley was always a stickler on logistics. I did not think about the hat again until I was preparing for the parade. I had gone back to my tent and carefully got dressed in my smartest finery. This was my first parade and I wanted to make a good impression. I suspected that many of the officers would not see me as 'proper army' with my battlefield commission. Even without a mirror I thought I looked damn fine, and when I stepped out of the tent I saw that Fergusson had worked similar magic with the men. Eighty-eight of them stood there, jackets brushed clean, belts whitened and boots gleaming. They were a credit to the regiment.

"Where is McFarlane?" I asked as I scanned down the ranks and did not see him.

"As he was working as your orderly I have excused him the parade," said Fergusson primly.

I knew his game: there was no way that McFarlane would pass muster on a general's parade and so the crafty devil had given him duties that would keep him out of the way.

"But he has my shako to clean, and I need it now."

"Doan worry, sir, ah'm here," came a voice and a small cloud of flies could be seen moving down the left-hand side of the neat files of men before McFarlane appeared, running and breathless. In his hands was a shako that was every bit as gleaming as the boots had been. It was perfect, and even Fergusson looked surprised and impressed. I felt that my trust in him had been justified and was just congratulating myself on my good judgement of men when I noticed that the cockade was missing.

"Doan worry yerself, sir," said McFarlane when I pointed this out. "It is jist drying oot. I gave it a wee wash."

"Well, go and get it, man. The parade is in five minutes."

McFarlane turned about on the run and headed back in the direction he had come while I looked closely at the shako. It really was a good piece of work. The rim seemed a bit sticky with un-buffed polish when I put it on my head, but I did not worry about that as we set about getting the men marched to their position in the parade. All of the fit men from Stevenson and Wellesley's columns were to be drawn up. It was an impressive show of strength. The villagers from Assaye were watching and would doubtless pass word of our strength to the Mahratta, which was probably what Wellesley intended.

The sudden arrival of flies announced the return of McFarlane. "Here are yer feathers, sir," he said, reaching up to place the cockade in its brass holder.

"Now get out of sight until the parade is over, McFarlane," barked Fergusson from behind me.

"Ah'm goin', ah'm goin'," muttered McFarlane, shambling away.

I stood there with my back to the men and waited for the general to appear. It was a hot day and I was soon sweating. There was a strange burning smell from somewhere but I thought nothing of it. There were more cremations for injured sepoys who had died of their wounds on the far side of the field and a gentle breeze was blowing the smoke slightly in our direction.

Soon the general's party could be seen coming down the line. Wellesley rode imperiously alone in front of his staff and was notorious for staring coldly at any officer who caught his eye. A gaggle of staff officers including Swinton trotted on some distance behind. I used the back of my hand to wipe away the rivulets of sweat that were running down my forehead and down my cheeks. I turned to look at the men to ensure that they were ready for inspection and if any looked alarmed at my appearance then I did not see it.

As Wellesley approached I threw up my smartest salute as I had seen the other officers do and braced myself for his chilly glare. But when I looked at him he seemed to be fighting his emotions. I thought at first he was moved by the paltry size of our dwindled ranks and then I saw that the edges of his mouth kept curling up and that he was suppressing a smile.

It turned out that thanks to McFarlane I was indeed making a memorable first impression to the officer corp of the army. If he had ever polished his own shako, McFarlane would have known not to put polish on the inside rim of the hat, certainly not whatever polish he had been using. As I discovered, it became more liquid with heat and mixed easily with the sweat of the wearer on a hot day, to send rivulets of a black polish and sweat mixture down their face. If the person wearing the hat inadvertently used the back of his hand to smear the mixture all over his forehead and cheeks just before the approach of a general then the effect was greatly enhanced. I only noticed that the back of my hand was black when the other officers rode up and started guffawing with laughter. It was also then I discovered that for a *pièce de resistance* effect McFarlane had also managed to set fire to the cockade when he had been drying it over a fire. Even then it was still smouldering gently in the breeze with a steady wisp of smoke like an incense burner.

Chapter 24

The day after the parade Stevenson's men set off again in pursuit of
Scindia's forces, while our part of the army marched for a nearby hill
fort where a more comfortable field hospital could be created for our
wounded. For a while I was angry at the embarrassment I had
experienced at the parade, but that did not last long. For a start the
other officers viewed it as an amusing jape, an initiation into their
brotherhood, and I began to feel more as though I belonged in their
company. Most had similar tales of humiliations to tell. Fergusson
became almost civil. I think the prank had gone much further than he
expected; he hated to cause any embarrassment to his beloved 74th. As
for McFarlane, he was keeping a very low profile. The simple fact was
that I needed Fergusson at that time far more than he needed me. If I
was to really antagonise him, well, I would not be the first young
officer killed by an 'accidental' shot from my own side in the heat of
battle.

I was invited to join a staff meeting with Wellesley a week later
when he received a message from Scindia looking to open negotiations
for peace. Scindia was requesting that emissaries from Wellesley and
the nizam of Hyderabad visit his court to discuss peace terms and an
armistice. It was a classic face-saving delaying tactic: Scindia would
prolong negotiations until British supplies started to fail while he built
up his army again for another attack. Wellesley agreed with my view
and sent a message back to say that he would continue to attack until
Scindia sent representatives to his camp to agree to peace terms.

To drive the point home to Scindia, the army started its march north
again. Stevenson's men had crossed the river Tapti and captured the
town of Burhampoor. He then opened a siege of Asseerghur, a strong
hill fort belonging to Scindia. After some delay we moved forward so
that we could support Stevenson if necessary and also headed to
Burhampoor. Compared to the *pindaree*-ravaged plains the British had
come from they were most impressed with the much more fertile
regions they now found, with ripe harvests everywhere they went. Both
men and beasts of burden could eat their fill. The country was not
completely benign, though, as I nearly found out to some cost.

When marching I generally rode on my horse in front of the men.
As they marched the stench from them ripened even further as they
sweated in the sun. Downwind of them when they were massed in tight
ranks it was enough to make your eyes water. Compared to the daily

washing of the Hindu soldiers, the Highlanders did not seem to wash at all. When we came to the Tapti river we had to wait for boats to ferry us across, which gave me an opportunity change things. Having had enough of the stink, I gave the command that the 74th Highlanders were going to bathe. The order was greeted with dismay and revulsion by some who thought it was a gross abuse of my position as an officer to suggest such a heresy, but Fergusson, trying to regain favour, enthusiastically backed me up.

Soon clothes and kit were being abandoned by the riverbank and nearly ninety men were hesitantly approaching the water in various degrees of undress. While their faces and hands had been browned to a mahogany colour, the skins of their now-exposed backs and chests were a whitish grey. Some still wore their breeches and others took shirts and other clothes to wash in the river while they were there. I noticed that Wee Jock, the drummer boy, had gone away from the rest of the men to immerse himself. He was going through puberty and was more conscious of his body than the others. As well as his breeches he even kept on his bayonet belt; perhaps he was worried the others would try to duck him. Amongst the last into the water was McFarlane, who was struggling hard as he was half-carried in by four others including Fergusson while wailing, "Ah'm no dirty, ah'm no dirty!"

I sat on my horse, watching them soak and wash in the water, feeling well pleased with myself. No more stink. They seemed to be enjoying themselves splashing about and I began to feel like a dip myself, but it would not be seemly for an officer to bathe with the men. I was trotting the horse down the bank when I saw it, a slight flick in the water a hundred yards beyond Wee Jock, who was standing chest deep. It meant nothing to start with and then a small log surfaced about fifty yards beyond the boy. I squinted at it in the sunlight and then a chill ran down my spine. The log had a wake, it was moving towards Wee Jock and it could be only one thing.

"Crocodile!" I yelled, spurring my horse towards the boy in the water. "Crocodile!" I yelled again as the horse picked up speed.

I was pointing now and shouting at the other bathers in the water, although what I expected them to do about it I don't know. Come to that, I was not sure what I was going to do either. I certainly was not going to tackle a crocodile in the water. Not that it mattered anyway, as the great scaly beast was nearly on the boy.

"Crocodile!" I yelled a third time, pointing at it. Wee Jock just stared at me with a puzzled look on his face. I realised as the great jaws started to open behind him that I had simply distracted him from his fate. But suddenly he sensed the attack and turned. The calm brown water suddenly seemed to explode with a flurry of splashing, with small white arms and a flailing reptilian tail visible in the spray. It was a hopelessly mismatched conflict: a primeval predator perfectly designed to hunt and kill all manner of prey in water against an urchin from the Glasgow slums. The crocodile did not stand a chance.

I watched, aghast, expecting to see the reptile drag the boy under and leave just a whirl of disturbed water, but instead I saw the frantic thrashing of the beast. My horse reared in panic, and as I struggled to stay in the saddle to my astonishment I heard a plaintive cry of, "Help me wi ma big lizard."

By the time I had the horse under control men were rushing across to help Wee Jock as he tried to haul the beast ashore by his tail, its death throes now almost over. As the men got it onto the bank it was clear what had happened, as sticking out of the reptile's eye was half a bayonet, the rest pushed by the boy into its brain. He must have been lightning-quick. The survival instincts required to live in a Scottish slum were evidently sharper than those needed by a river predator. The boy had taken deep gashes across his chest and an arm in the struggle, but he did not seem to mind as one of the corporals was assuring him that the *bhinjarries* would pay handsomely for crocodile skin.

Perhaps the final word on this incident, though, should go to McFarlane. He shambled out of the water as soon as he could and, with rest of the men, edged over to look at the dead beast. As he got to the front of the crowd and looked down at it I saw him shudder with horror and then shake the water off himself like a dog. His face was filled with disgust, whether at being wet or at the tooth-filled jaws on the ground in front of them I could not tell. But as he turned to go away I distinctly heard him say, "Ah'm no gettin in the watter agin."

The army settled into a routine as it marched, much as it had been with the Company cavalry before. I was awoken in my tent well before dawn. Breakfast would be tea and rice eaten while orderlies took down the tents and loaded everything onto to carts. Then, in the cool of the morning, just as we could start to see where we were going, the march would start. There would be a cavalry screen to the front, followed by most of the infantry marching in column, then artillery and their wagons with the rest of the baggage train. Bringing up the rear would be another battalion of infantry as a rear guard and there was also a heavy cavalry presence around the wagons to deter any raids by *pindaree*. The march stopped after around six hours just before noon so that men could be in the shade for the heat of the day. They mostly dozed in the afternoon before a dinner of spiced meat stew and rice.

In an area with plenty of food for us, fodder for the animals and no sign at all of the enemy, it was not unpleasant work. Every step we took deprived some Mahratta warlord of his lands and put more pressure on Scindia to settle with the British. He had already sent some representatives to open negotiations and they had returned with terms for Scindia to consider while we continued into his territory. The raja of Berar was also expected to start peace talks, but was still delaying.

"Do you think we will have to fight again?" I asked Wellesley one morning as we rode along together. Compared to the starchiness of staff meetings, he could be quite informal when there were just the two of us.

"I am not sure. There seems to be a power struggle now between Scindia and Berar for leadership of their confederation. They are both talking about peace, but either could try to make a last stand somewhere."

"Do you think it will come to that then, a last desperate stand?"

"No, I think they will come to terms. I don't think Berar is foolish enough to challenge us on his own, and every day Scindia is getting weaker as we are putting more pressure on him to settle."

We rode on in silence for a few minutes, each pondering the future. I was hoping for a quick and bloodless end to the campaign followed by a return to Madras and home. Wellesley was clearly hoping for more victories.

"I would like to defeat them on the field of battle," he said quietly. "Subdue the Mahratta once and for all, otherwise someone may have to come back and do it all over again."

I smiled at him in the early dawn light. "Do you remember in Eliza's garden when you said that you needed a victory in battle to be taken seriously as a general? Well, now you have had one, a historic victory against far greater numbers. You are now a proven general. You don't have to destroy every last enemy you see. The Mahratta are like the Hydra, a many-headed monster: cut off one head and more will spring up. It might be better to leave a weak head that we know."

Wellesley thought about that for a while and then gave his short bark of a laugh. "There is a lot of truth in what you say, Thomas. I am seen now as a successful general, but I do not believe it myself yet. You know yourself that I had to fight when I did. I lost two horses under me that day, and if it were not for some savage sergeant saving me at the line of guns, I would not be here now. I am not sure if I won that battle or if the Mahratta lost it."

"There is a difference?" I asked, puzzled.

"There is to me, Thomas, there is to me," he repeated as he spurred away to chat to the commander of the next battalion.

A few minutes later Swinton rode up and joined me. I think he was intimidated by Wellesley and he tried to avoid his company where possible. I had discovered that he was also a third son of a landowner. As his family could not afford to buy him a decent rank in the regular army, he had been sent to India to join the Company army instead. Here promotion was much more to do with length of service than the size of your purse. It had taken him twenty years to make major. He had kept his nerve at Assaye but I think blamed himself for not stopping Orrock's march across the battlefield. He was too timid to be a natural leader, but after the McFarlane parade fiasco he had allowed his orderlies to look after me as well and he seemed pretty fair, so I could not complain.

The only downside to the march was that Fergusson had persuaded the *bhinjarries* help him find a new set of bagpipes. He presented them one afternoon. The bag had some Oriental silk covering rather than the traditional Scottish cloth, but other than that the bagpipes were the same as other examples of this awful instrument I had seen.

"It has the original bone tops on the pipes," he explained proudly. "Ah am thinking of holding trials to appoint a new pipe sergeant this afternoon."

"Oh God, must you?" I asked, thinking of various people with no skill trying to play the thing. They were bad enough in the hands of an experienced player.

Fergusson smiled. "Ah saw ye twitching impatiently through the lament at the burial. Ye may not like the music, but ye must understand that the value of the pipes lies in what it means to others." He looked more serious. "A set of pipes can be worth a hundred men in battle for what they do to our folk and the enemy. The skirl of the pipes will remind our men of their homes and clans and the reputation of the Scots as fighters that never give up." He paused and then added, "It does the same for the enemy, who know that before the day is out they will face a Highland charge of cold steel. They rarely stick around for it as ye have seen for yerself."

He may have had a point, but I went for a ride that afternoon and forbade any practice to start until I was at least a mile away from the camp.

Chapter 25

You may think that seeing the enemy army arrayed before you at the start of the battle is a frightening sight, but as I discovered at Argaum, it is not half as frightening as not being able to see the enemy in front of you. It was the middle of November 1803, two months after Assaye, and until few hours before I had been convinced that I would end up safely in Madras without having seen another shot fired.

Scindia had eventually agreed to peace terms, but his ally, the raja of Berar, had been slow to follow suit. After Assaye many warriors had left Scindia's service and Berar had seen the opportunity to capitalise on his ally's failure. Berar had a strong army and he also had a thousand crack Persian troops called the Pharsee Risaulah. These fearless warriors were unbeaten in battle and the raja of Berar used their reputation to promote himself as the new military leader of the Mahratta and to encourage more of Scindia's former troops to his flag.

To meet this new threat Wellesley had combined his army with that of Stevenson and marched towards Berar. The raja at first seemed to recognise the danger and had started negotiations, but then inexplicably he formed his army up in battle order just a few miles away from where the British were camped. I suspect that this was just face-saving bravado on his part. They would have stayed for a few hours and then dispersed, spreading the rumour that the British had been too frightened to take them on. What they did not appreciate was that Wellesley was looking for another battle and this was too good a chance to miss. He now had nearly twice the men he had commanded at Assaye and the enemy was half the size of the one he had beaten before.

I was with the newly enlarged British army camped at the village of Paterly. We knew that the enemy were a few miles off and had agreed to withdraw under a truce. No one thought that they would be stupid enough to offer battle. Many had resented the fact we had agreed to the truce, for rumour had it that the raja of Berar was with his army, which meant that the luggage would be loaded with loot. When word came through that Berar was indeed a fool and had drawn his army up for battle in front of the village of Argaum, preparations for dinner were hastily abandoned and the men eagerly formed up.

The enthusiasm was not universal as you might imagine. War is a damn random business and I could not imagine a thousand Persian fanatics giving up without taking a few redcoats with them. As company captain I was expected to lead my men from the front, which was an unwelcome prospect as the Highlanders were bound to be in the centre of the line.

In half an hour we were formed up and marching towards the enemy. The much larger 78th Highlander regiment was the vanguard with the remnant of the 74th, led by yours truly, just behind. More sepoy regiments followed us with bullocks pulling cannon and ammunition carts. Stevenson's division marched alongside. The men were in high spirits, even when we crested a hill and saw the dark mass of the enemy on the opposite ridge. There were around ten thousand of them, with forty cannon along their front and cavalry on their flanks. Half a mile in front of their position was a small village and Wellesley's division was to pass to the right of it and make up the right-hand side of the line. Stevenson, who was ill and commanding his troops from the back of an elephant, was to form his men up on the left.

While Stevenson may have been able to see the enemy from the back of his elephant, for the rest of us they disappeared from view as we approached the village. The slope up from the village towards the enemy was planted with millet. It is not grown in Hampshire or even the New Hampshire in the new United States, and so if you are not familiar with the crop I should explain that the stems of the plant can grow up to four yards tall. As we entered the field we entered a world of tall, golden stalks. The foot soldiers could see no more than a few feet ahead of them. Mounted on my horse, if I stood up in the stirrups I could see further over the fluffy millet heads. It was still hard to see what was happening on the ground, but the movement and sudden disappearance of stalks as they were trampled gave an indication of where the troops were moving.

The 78th began to form a line in the field facing the enemy directly in front of the village, and I joined the 74th to the end of that line. As we cut and trampled our way into the crop we slowed and the sepoy troops behind us who were set to continue the line began to build up in the village. The bullock-drawn guns and ammunition carts were mixed in with them, creating a jam of animals and humanity between the huts. Given time they would have sorted themselves out, but they did not get the chance.

From the hilltop in front of us there was a rumble of gunfire. Berar's artillery had chosen this moment to open fire and they were good. Instinctively I ducked, but the shots were all going over our heads. I wheeled my horse around to see what was happening in the village through the edge of the crop. Berar's gunners had the range and with such a close-packed target they could not miss. Balls smashed into the crowds of soldiers, killing dozens of them. The cannon fire also smashed gun carriages and killed oxen. The remaining animals started to panic and bolt from the village, dragging whatever was still attached to them.

Rockets were being fired from the Mahratta lines now. Normally they were wildly inaccurate, especially at that range, but by chance two managed to reach the village and ricocheted between walls before exploding amongst the sepoys. The rout spread quickly. The front ranks had started to edge back, compressing the middle, which pushed against those behind them. As more cannon balls smashed into the crowded mass the rear ranks did not need much persuasion to start pulling back themselves. Once the movement had started, the edging back became a walk and then a run in a matter of moments. Suddenly the right-hand half of the British line consisted of just the 78th and 74th Highlanders, around six hundred men. I could not see Stevenson's men but could only hope that they were still making up the left of the line. This battle suddenly did not seem like it was going to be the walk in the park that everyone had thought minutes earlier.

I rode my horse over to the nearest captain of the 78th. "What do we do now?" I asked, gesturing at the now fast-retreating sepoys.

He was another flinty-faced Highlander with a thick beard, who looked at me with a slightly puzzled expression. "We stay here until we are ordered to advance," he said firmly.

I turned my horse back down the trampled strip of crop to stand it in front of the middle of the short line of men of the 74th. To my right I could see lance tops of our cavalry moving through the millet, but some way off: they were leaving space for where they thought the sepoys were coming.

The crop surrounded us like a tall green cage, but I knew from the journey into the valley that in front of us there was half of the enemy line comprising five thousand men and around twenty well-served guns. With no targets remaining in the village, those guns now turned their attention to the enemy whom they could not see in the field. There was another rumble of gunfire and for a second I wondered if the sepoys were coming back, but then I heard the thuds and the rustling of the crop. Two balls bounced straight over us but the much longer line of the 78th was not so lucky. There were screams as two balls smashed into their double rank, taking out men in both lines. It seemed the

Mahratta gunners were playing skittles with us as the pins, firing into the field short so that the balls bounced along the ground. With a continuous line of standing redcoats in front of them they could hardly miss. Already I could hear the sergeants of the 78th getting the men to close up the gaps.

We couldn't just stay there. If we had to wait too long then there would be nobody left in the ranks to make the attack. Equally I could not withdraw the men on my own initiative, because we had been ordered here by the general. I needed Swinton to order a withdrawal, but he had gone forward with Wellesley and some of the other colonels to survey the ground ahead. Wellesley wanted every one of his colonels very clear on the plan of attack so that there would not be any confusion in the tall crop, with lone charges like Orrock's at Assaye. There was no way I was going to die unseen in some bloody Indian field. The solution to the problem came when I saw a cannon ball coming with my name on it.

When a cannon is aimed directly at you, if you look you can see a briefest glimpse of a black line in the sky which is the ball's trajectory when it is fired. I had seen this back in 1800 when sailing with Cochrane. I had also seen it once earlier that afternoon, but then I knew that the ball would be aimed well over my head. This time I knew that one of their guns was aimed directly at me and in a second a ball would be crashing through the crop.

Some officers imbued with traditions of military honour and demonstrating courage to the men might have hesitated, but I am proud to say I did not. When saving the precious Flashy skin, I act first and think about the consequences later. This explains why the soldiers of the 74th saw their gallant officer leap off his horse and dive onto the trampled crop, shrieking, "Get down!" A split-second later a cannon ball smashed its way out of the crop, bouncing just a foot over the saddle of my confused mount.

It was as I lay sprawled and slightly winded amongst the stems that the answer to the problem came to me. "Have the men lie down, please, Fergusson," I gasped as I got my breath back.

The sergeant just stared down at me, aghast. I don't think he would have been more appalled if I had ordered him to get the men into an orderly queue to bugger the archbishop of Canterbury. In fact as the good bishop is an Englishman he would probably have found that more acceptable. Eventually he drew himself up to his full height and in clear, ringing tones said, "A Highlander does not get down on his belly in front of the enemy."

At that moment fate again intervened and another ball smashed out of the crop just a few yards away. This one was pitched perfectly from the Mahratta point of view to hit the line at chest height. A soldier whose name I had not yet learnt simply disappeared. One moment he was there and the next he was snatched away in a spray of blood and offal, taking down the two men behind him too.

"Lie down!" I shouted directly at the men. "That is an order."

Some glanced at the sergeant for his confirmation, but most dropped to their knees and then down on the ground. As the majority began to lie down, the few looking at Fergusson followed suit. Soon only the sergeant was standing.

I crawled along the line to where the two wounded men from the second rank were lying. Both were covered in blood, although it was not clear whose it was. One wiped blood from his eyes and started getting on his hands and knees, but the other seemed to have had his chest laid open and a bloody rib was protruding from his abdomen. I recognised him as the man who had stuck a bayonet in my back when I had first come over from the Mahratta lines.

"Lie still, Gilray, you are in a bad way. Sergeant, if you are going to insist on standing, perhaps you can get some stretcher bearers."

"Aw, I am not so bad, sir," gasped Gilray, trying to sit up and wincing a little.

"Lie down, you fool. One of your ribs is poking out of your chest."

Leaning on one elbow, Gilray looked down at the bone with a puzzled expression on his face as though he could not comprehend how he had been so badly hurt. A wound such as this would invariably be fatal as there would be massive internal injuries. He used his sleeve to wipe blood that was dripping into his eyes from a cut on his forehead and then he gingerly moved his hand down to touch the bone. Before I realised what he was doing, he had gripped it and pulled the bone free from his own body. I gasped in disgust before he looked up and grinned at me. "It's all right, sir. Its nae my rib."

Any further discussion was interrupted by the clatter of hooves. For an instant I thought that the enemy had launched their cavalry against us, but then a small group of British officers emerged from the crop, some of the horses wheeling around to avoid tramping the men lying on the ground in front of them.

"Flashman, what on earth are you doing?" asked Swinton, seeing his regiment prone before him.

"The sepoys have broken and run and the Mahratta are bouncing balls through the crops."

Wellesley was giving me his usual icy stare but his head whipped around to where the sepoys should be when I told him that they had run and I saw him curse under his breath.

I got on my knees and continued. "I thought lying the men down would be best to ensure that they are still alive here and ready to fight when the time comes."

"Ah told him Highlanders do not lie down in front of the enemy, sir," cried Fergusson, the peaching bastard.

But he was backing the wrong horse here. I had been looking at Wellesley when I had spoken and I had seen him give a slight nod when I had used the words 'ensure that they are still here'. He would have to regroup the sepoys, which would take some time, and he needed to be sure that the Highlanders were not decimated by cannon or edging back themselves in the meantime.

"Have the whole line lie down until we are ready to attack," he said in clipped tones to his colonels. "Now back to your regiments, gentlemen," he said. "I need to re-organise the sepoy battalions."

With that the horsemen dispersed.

If you read the history books, they say that Wellesley's decision to lie the army down at Argaum was an example of his military genius. Of course, yours truly who started it does not get a mention. Wellesley used the tactic repeatedly after that both in the Peninsular War and even at Waterloo, but as for me, I was just happy to still have my head on my shoulders at the end of the day.

Chapter 26

It took Wellesley over an hour to regroup the sepoys and then they started to sheepishly appear at the end of our line and extend it further into the field, before lying down themselves. The Mahratta had kept up a steady fire on our lines and must have thought that they were killing hundreds of our men, but in the 74th we did not lose another man. Of course that is easy to say with hindsight, but at the time every time we heard a cannon ball crash through the crop we had no idea where it would land. I saw one smash its way out of the stems just in front of me and whistle just a few inches over my head. The 78th had three casualties when a ball pitched to bounce right on top of some lying men, but that was it from an hour's cannonade. Fergusson had refused to lie down and so Swinton had sent him and Wee Jock with the regiment's flags back into the village, telling them to wave them about a bit as though we were retreating and then stand behind the thickest wall they could find.

Finally the order came to start the attack. A couple of horse-drawn galloper guns appeared at the end of the line, Fergusson, Wee Jock and the flags were recalled and suddenly the British and sepoy line was ready.

"Check your priming," called Fergusson and down the line men checked that their muskets were loaded and primed with powder to fire.

I swung myself back into the saddle next to Swinton, Colonel Chalmers of the 78th gave the order to advance and Swinton followed suit. Wee Jock started beating the time on his drum and then Fergusson said the words I least wanted to hear: "Shall ah start the piper, sir?"

"Yes, yes, of course," replied Swinton eagerly, for at that moment a caterwauling screech had started up from the pipers of the 78th. A few moments later the racket was enhanced by the rising drone of our single piper, who naturally seemed to be playing an entirely different tune to the others. The pipe tunes all had stupid names; the 78th were playing something like 'Stealing the Campbell's Sheep' while our piper was giving wind to 'When McDougal Got Stuck in a Bog'. The noise alone should have been enough to send the enemy running.

I turned my mind to more important matters. In a few minutes we were going to emerge from this field into open ground and facing us would be a thousand of Berar's unbeaten fanatical Arab soldiers intent on our slaughter. I needed to determine the safest place in this attack for T. Flashman Esquire. The double rank of infantry now in front of us appeared to offer even protection along the line. Swinton and I were the only officers on horseback and we were either side of the party carrying the regiment's colours, which included Fergusson with his vicious spontoon. In theory we were supposed to fight to the death to protect these flags, but some Arab could have them for his underdrawers for all I cared. My priority was to emerge from this battle intact.

Looking along the line, I saw that the man mountain known as Big Jock was lumbering away in the second rank a few yards to my left and so I eased my horse behind him. Any Arab that took him on was likely to be brave and dead in short order, for I had seen him perform amazing feats of strength in the few weeks I had known him. But just to be on the safe side, I checked again the priming in my two pistols and that my sword was loose in the scabbard.

The line moved forward steadily. As I looked left and right I could now see a solid line of red jackets moving with grim determination. The beat of the drums and even the ceaseless drone of the wretched pipes gave off a martial air, and looking ahead from my higher vantage point on horseback, I could see that the crops were starting to thin. The galloper guns accelerated ahead and I heard their officers shouting orders to unlimber the guns so that they were presented at the enemy when we emerged a few seconds later.

I don't remember the enemy guns firing as we marched through the field, maybe the pipes drowned them out, but certainly they did no damage to the 74th. The guns had a much wider target area now with three regiments of sepoy troops making up the line to our right. I had half-expected a fresh cannonade from them as we emerged from the crop, but as soon as we appeared the Arab troops rushed forward to block the Mahratta cannon's line of fire. They paused in a long line some two hundred yards ahead of us. Their drums were beating loudly and they had a high-pitched, ululating war cry, similar to the sound I heard an Iroquois squaw make in North America during the 1812 affair. They were dressed almost entirely in white, with robes and turbans. Some had some ornately decorated muskets, but most had scimitars and small metal buckler-style shields. If the effect of the war cry was to intimidate us, it failed miserably.

"Look at those stupid bastards," I heard Big Jock say to the man alongside him. "All that fancy work on their guns but hardly a bayonet between the lot of them."

"Aye, we will make short work of them right enough," said his mate.

This was just the sort of comforting view a chap like me wants to hear, although it did seem a tad optimistic given that there were over a thousand Arabs and only around six hundred Highlanders.

"Fix bayonets!" called Colonel Chalmers, who had overall command of the Highlander brigade, and the order was repeated by sergeants down the line. Six hundred seventeen-inch steel bayonets flashed in the sunlight as they were fixed onto the lugs at the end of the musket barrels. Even a military novice like me knew that this signified we would be firing just one volley as it was awkward to reload with the bayonet attached.

The bayonets seemed a provocation to the Arabs, for with an even wilder yell they started their charge down the hill. More Mahratta took their place in the line, but most stood back to watch the outcome of the confrontation between their best troops and the feared Highlanders. The contrast between the two groups of soldiers was startling. The Arabs came at the run, screaming their shouts and challenges. The ones with guns started to fire their muskets at us as they charged. God knows where the shots went as some even fired one-handed. The redcoats were still and silent, watching their enemy with the appraising look of the professional soldier.

"Present."

Six hundred men angled their bodies slightly to the right and raised the musket buts into their shoulders.

"Aim low, lads, aim low," Fergusson called as the musket recoil on firing would make the muzzle rise. "Make every shot count, then there will be less to kill later," he added in a ringing tone that could be heard down the line.

They were a hundred yards away now. I knew that a musket's optimal range was about eighty yards, but they ran past that point too. I looked across at Swinton. Had he frozen? Was he going to leave it too late? They were now just sixty yards off and I saw Swinton lick his lips in preparation for giving the order. If he had not, I think I would have shouted it myself.

"Fire!"

Six hundred muskets crashed out at what was almost point-blank range and the enemy was completely obscured behind a wall of musket smoke.

"Forward now, lads," called Swinton. "Go and get 'em."

Only now did the Highlanders make any kind of sound, a low guttural growl as they paced forward in a solid rank with their bayonets extended. The odd shriek indicated where an Arab still coming in the opposite direction had encountered seventeen inches of steel in the wall of musket smoke as he tried to run through it. I followed them through the smoke, and as it drifted away it revealed a scene of total carnage. At least half the Arabs had been hit with the opening volley and the rest were disentangling themselves from the bodies or climbing over them to continue their attack. Despite the slaughter they had already seen, none seemed ready to retreat. Big Jock was right: they were damned fools.

The Highlanders knew their business and, staying in disciplined ranks, they moved swiftly over the ground. Any man who tried to stand against them soon found cold steel jabbing at his front or sides, while the second rank finished off any of the fallen who looked still inclined to put up a fight. They moved forward like a machine of death and Swinton and I followed on behind with nothing to do. Soon even the Arabs could see that the day was lost and they began pulling back over the hill. It was an awesome display of disciplined fighting and as we crested the ridge the Mahratta infantry could be seen milling around on the reverse slope in complete disarray.

"Don't let them stand," came a voice from somewhere, I think it was Wellesley's. Suddenly the men were released into a full Highland charge down the hill with the sepoys joining in enthusiastically alongside.

There are few things more exhilarating than chasing a broken enemy. Why, in Spain I have seen an army padre, who is now very senior in the church, chasing the fleeing French, laying about them with his cane while shrieking some very unchristian oaths. Flashy's first principle of warfare is lie low when under attack and go for them when they are defenceless and on the run. It makes good sense: you don't want to give them time to think or they might stop and fight back. In this case, after pressing myself into the dirt for over an hour with cannon balls crashing through the crops around me, I wanted revenge. Having experienced fear and terror, helping to inflict it on someone else kind of redeemed my manhood somehow. Finally as the commanding officer of a bunch of murderous Highlander savages who were at the vanguard of the slaughter, it seemed at the very least polite to be there to cheer them on. From a safe distance naturally.

This brings me to Flashy's second principle of warfare. In retreat there are two kinds of people. There are those that will be driven by terror to run as though the hounds of hell are at their heels and regardless of the slaughter about them they will hang on to the hope that somehow they can win through to safety. I am of course in this group, and my ability to write this account in my old age is a testament to the fact that with a little ingenuity you can win through against enormous odds. Unfortunately there is also a tiresome second group who have ruined many a good rout. They come to a point where they see that there is no hope for survival and decide that it is better to die with a weapon in their hand and facing the enemy than with a sabre in the back. They are a most dangerous foe for they appear suddenly and are not looking to survive but just to take you to hell with them.

As I spurred the horse to follow the Highlanders down the reverse slope a knot of this second type gathered halfway down the hill. A group of Scots fell on them with enthusiasm, but one of the Mahratta had a long spear and quick arms and with a longer reach than their bayonets he was keeping them at bay. The now bandaged Gilray had broken away from the fight and was busy loading his musket. "Ah'll shoot the bugger," he called to me as I rode up. But with loaded pistols in my belt, I thought I could help out. So I drew one, aimed carefully for his chest and shot him in the head. It is true, the recoil really does raise the aim. With a roar of delight the Highlanders piled in and I wheeled my horse away, feeling pleased with myself.

When I first saw the horseman coming towards me I assumed it was one of ours. No enemy in his right mind with a horse should still be on the slope. They had the means to make their escape while our army was distracted by pursuing their poor bloody infantry and looting the baggage. He was dressed in white robes, though, like the Arabs, and as I watched I saw him spur his horse into a run and something glittered in his right hand. It took me a second to realise that the glittering thing was a sabre pointed in my direction and that despite my very best endeavours I was being attacked.

I looked around. The nearest Highlanders were busy chasing the Mahratta and even though I shouted none looked round. There was no other cavalry nearby to give me assistance. It was already far too late to run as my horse was standing still. I dropped the fired pistol in my coat pocket and drew out the ungainly sabre as I spurred my horse forward. I hardly had time to think about what I was doing; I had a feeling of disbelief as the stranger charged in. What the hell was he still doing here and why was he trying to kill me? The white-robed horseman was already whirling his sword above his head for a killing cut as he swept past, and then some remnant of a memory from Poorum's training sessions with the sabre came to mind and I managed to move my weapon to block the blow and the twisting back cut he tried next.

We both wheeled our horses around to face each other, mine now moving at the same speed as his as we closed again. We were due to pass down our right-hand sides, but I remembered Poorum talking about crossing in front of the enemy horse at the last minute and hacking down on their unprotected left-hand side. It was the only other bit of sabre training that I could remember, so I had to give it a go. With a few yards remaining, I yanked on the reins to haul my horse to the right and prepared to slash to my left, but my opponent had planned the same tactic and so we passed well out of reach of each other.

I sensed he was turning tightly and so I did the same. He was obviously a skilled horseman while I was now out of ideas. Looking around, I saw there was still no sign of anyone who could come to my aid. I could not run; his fast, nimble horse would enable him to slam a blade in my exposed back in a moment. My only chance was to try to hold him off until help arrived. Already he was coming at me again and I launched a massive haymaker swing of the sabre at him with all my strength. But he easily saw it coming and moved wide to cross in front of my horse.

What I did not realise was that my wild sabre cut had sliced off the top of my horse's right ear. The mount took exception to this and decided that we should part company. I was already overbalanced, leaning out of the saddle to make the cut, and the horse kicked out with its back legs to launch me into the air. My feet came out of the stirrups and the next thing I knew I was flying high over my horse's head and the Arab was below me. Not expecting an airborne attack, he just managed to look round as he heard my surprised yell, but could not bring his sword up in time. I desperately slashed with my sabre and more by luck caught him in the neck a split-second before I landed on top of him and we both tumbled from his saddle. Luckily he landed underneath me and I rolled away to come up, I am proud to say, with the sword still in my hand. One glance told me the Arab was finished. He had got into a kneeling position but the front of his robes was already crimson and blood was gushing from a deep wound down the side of his throat. He reached for his sword but did not make any attempt to attack, he just held it against his chest and seemed to be mouthing some prayer.

I stared around me but nobody seemed to have seen my novel method of attack. The Highlanders had their backs to me as they steadily drove the Mahratta on and the Mahratta were far too occupied with self-preservation to notice a British officer getting thrown from his horse. The battle was moving swiftly away and I was left with just the dead and dying.

I watched the Arab for a moment but then he made the most awful choking noise and started to shake. He was drowning in his own blood and went down on his hands and knees with his fingers digging deep into the dirt. He appeared to be in a lot of pain and I wondered if I should put him out of his misery. I got the second pistol out of my belt and was just cocking it when his head rose as he sat back on his haunches and glared up at me. His face was contorted in agony but he looked me steadily in the eye before gasping the single word "Solomon". Then he looked at the pistol in my hand and seemed to nod his agreement before looking down again at his lap. I was not sure I could kill him now, but then he made another horrible gurgling noise and I realised that it would be better than watching him linger in pain. He now looked up with his eyes closed and his face towards the sky. With a shaking hand I raised the pistol. This time I managed to successfully shoot my target in the heart, having aimed just above his balls.

I sat down on the ground amongst the dead for a moment to let my nerves recover. After several minutes I heard another horse trotting up and turned to face it. If it was another enemy horseman, I would be finished, but luckily the rider was wearing a red jacket.

"Hello, Flashman, it looks like you have been busy," said Jock Malcolm as he rode up. "I say, that is Abu Saleem you have killed there. He is, or should I say was, the commander of the Arab troops. He was supposed to be quite a horseman too. I see you got him with a sabre cut. You must be a sharp hand with a sword. Good work, man." With that he rode off without waiting for any kind of answer to keep pace with the troops.

Looking again at the corpse, I saw that the sword this Abu Saleem had been holding when he died was a thing of beauty. The hilt was gold and had an astronomic design with a moon made of mother of pearl and a star constellation picked out in diamonds. There was also an inscription in Arabic which I did not understand. The blade was slim but intricately engraved in blue Damascus steel. I picked it up. It was perfectly balanced and fitted easily in the hand, much better than the one I had been using. I unhooked the scabbard from his belt and, putting the sword back in it, I exchanged it on my belt for my old sword.

His horse, a white gelding, stood passively nearby. I walked over and held the bridle and then swung up into the saddle to examine the saddlebags. There was an Arabic book, which I took to be the Koran. I dropped it next to its former owner. There was the usual food and some clothes, but burrowing down beneath these I found a substantial bag of gold coins on one side and a small leather bag on the other containing a handful of diamonds, rubies and sapphires. It was a handsome haul.

The Arab horse responded to the lightest of touches and I rode over to where my old horse stood with what was left of its ears pointing back and looking at me malevolently while the blood trickled down one side of its head. Well, you don't say sorry to a horse, do you... or at least you don't admit it if you have. But I reckon that nag saved my life that day. I would never have beaten the Arab if I had stayed in the saddle, so I don't lose any sleep over cutting its ear. There have been a number of times in my career when my wrinkled carcass has been preserved due to some insignificant trifle, be it recalling the name of a distant Spanish relative I had never met, the twisted flight of a feather stuck to an Iroquois war arrow or the glint of sun on a weapon warning of an ambush. But perhaps the strangest is the tip of a horse's ear. Mind you, since it happened I discovered that it is not that rare an occurrence. Novice troopers often slice a horse's ear in training. Look for yourself next time you see a troop of cavalry in the park and more often than not you will spot that one of the mounts does not have all of an ear.

Chapter 27

With my old horse in tow I slowly followed my Highlanders as they worked their way forward until greed overtook their more violent instincts. Gradually more began to spend time looting the dead than pursuing the enemy. The last enemy soldiers were able to make their escape as the redcoats, both sepoys and Highlanders, began to retrace their footsteps, searching the dead with industrious efficiency. Bodies were stripped, clothing searched, turbans unravelled and anything of value was taken. Not that I could blame them, for inadvertently I had done quite well out of the battle myself. I was not the only one, though, for the baggage included elephants laden with treasure and one cavalry officer was made spectacularly rich by capturing one with a casket of priceless jewels.

It was nightfall by the time I made my way back to our camp where another surprise was waiting. I went to where I had left my shabby little campaign tent but it had gone. Instead there was a much larger tent and through the pinned back door I could see a rug, comfortable bed and chair. Behind this new tent stood two new bullock carts, one still half-loaded with provisions. As I started to look round in puzzlement from inside the tent stepped Runjeet.

"Greetings, sahib," he said, grinning broadly. "I receive your letter after the big battle and rush to bring your house to you. I also bring my cousin Jamma, your favourite cook."

Here he gestured at another man who looked familiar from those few weeks a year ago when I had enjoyed my bungalow in Madras. Those memories rushed back at me and I could almost smell the delicious food they used to serve. Then I realised that they were not just memories and I could actually smell it. I hadn't eaten since breakfast and was starving. In a few moments I was sitting down at my new camp table, eating one of the best meals I had consumed in months.

It is true what they say about an army marching on its stomach, and after satisfying their bloodlust and then filling their pockets, the thoughts of many of my fellow officers turned to filling their stomachs. The smell of Jamma's cooking acted like a magnet, which fortunately he had anticipated by preparing a feast. Soon my tent was full of officers excitedly recounting their parts in the battle and showing off their spoils. My new sword was much admired, particularly when Jock arrived and explained I had taken it by going sabre to sabre with the

Persian commander. I played down this achievement, suggesting I just managed to get in a lucky blow and not mentioning my novel method of aerial attack. Nobody likes a bragger, and downplaying my achievements earned me more credit with these men who now seemed to fully accept me into their brotherhood.

I was modest for another reason too. I had already learnt from my first meeting with Wellesley that if you overplay your abilities then people get unrealistic expectations of what you can achieve. Trying to claim that I was more than a courier to Carstairs had seen me sent on a near-suicidal mission behind enemy lines. I did not want my new undeserved reputation as an expert swordsman landing me in more trouble, but it was actually my errant cowardice that earned me praise from Wellesley.

"It was quick thinking to get the men lying down," he told me later when he came by my tent just as the other officers were leaving. "It was unconventional, but you have not been influenced by army traditions. You realised that there was a chance the men could run with prolonged bombardment and solved two problems at once. We are fighting new enemies and must use new techniques; we cannot always fight by convention. Yes," he mused, "you seem a very capable officer indeed, Flashman. Quick thinking, and you know the Mahratta as well as anyone on my staff."

Coming from Wellesley this was enough to send the hair on the back of my neck prickling with alarm. "Oh, it was no more than anyone would do in the same circumstances. I have just been in the right place at the right time. Your other officers are just as capable and I have had no proper army training."

Runjeet interrupted with glasses of Madeira he had found from somewhere. The other officers had gone and the two of us sat down at the camp table with the tent lit by the flickering light from the fire beyond the doorway and a dim lantern hanging from the roof.

"Really?" said Wellesley, raising one eyebrow in mild amusement. "I suppose that Arab commander just threw himself on your sword point as he rode past, did he?" He gave another of his barks of laughter. "Your reticence goes too far, Thomas."

It was time to change the subject. "You must feel like this time it was a battle you won. You regrouped the sepoys, led the army in good order and routed the enemy as well as capturing all of their cannon. Are you satisfied with your victory this time?"

"Yes, I feel I can look other commanders in the eye now. Of course back home the Mahratta are not seen as being in the same league as the French. Victories in India will only go some way to helping me get a command in the war against France. While a defeat here could destroy my recently earned reputation entirely."

"Is that what you want, to command an army against the French?"

"Here a man can get rich if his health lasts, but he will get little recognition back in Britain. On my achievements so far I would be just known as a sepoy general. Europe is where reputations will really be made, and that is where I need to prove myself."

"So you are going to return to Europe then?" I asked.

"Not until the Mahratta are properly subdued. I need to finish this job first."

"But surely they are subdued now – you have beaten Scindia at Assaye and he is suing for peace. You have just routed most of the raja of Berar's forces and he was talking about truces before the battle. He is bound to sign a peace treaty now."

"Maybe, but Jock Malcolm thinks that the hardcore Mahratta will withdraw to a place called Gawilghur and hold out there. Have you been there when you were with the Mahratta?"

"No, I have not heard of the place. But what makes them think that they can hold out against us at this Gawilghur?"

"Quite simply because it is an impregnable fortress that has never been captured in hundreds of years. Legend has it that a child with a pile of rocks could hold off an army from its walls."

"I don't believe that. It has not come up against modern artillery. We could pound it into submission."

"That might be difficult in this case as apparently the fort is built on the top of a high escarpment overlooking the Deccan Plain. There is a sheer drop around three sides of the fort and on the fourth side there is another outer fortress, with a ravine between that and the inner fort. In short, it will be something of a bastard if we have to capture it."

"Let's hope that Berar's people decide to give up then," I said with feeling.

Suddenly I felt a chill in the warm evening air. A few minutes ago I had assumed that the war was now largely over, but now I had a sinking feeling that this was not going to be the last I heard of Gawilghur.

I have always thought that the best alarm clock in the world is a pig. Not alive, of course, but in slices frying in a pan, as the smell of bacon is a wondrous thing to awaken to. I had gone to bed with worries but awoke on my new soft bed in my new large tent with delicious aromas on the air and suddenly the world seemed a better place. After the battle the previous day no one was getting up early and the sun was well up when I sat at a crisply laundered table to break my fast. After bacon and eggs and proper raised bread I was in high spirits, which were enhanced when Runjeet brought in letters that had been sent to me over the last year from England. Even though he feared I was dead, he had kept them and maintained the bungalow, using the funds I had left him. He needed more money now, of course, but I was able to pay him from some of the gold I had just captured. Later I deposited the rest on account with the paymaster, but the gems I kept. Paymasters can give receipts for weighed gold but gems are too easy to lose or switch, and so I spent an evening sewing those into the lining of my jacket so that only I knew I had them.

When I looked through my letters there were the expected ones from my father whom I had asked to manage my affairs while I was away. He updated me on my finances – healthy as I was not spending; on family – I was an uncle again; and politics – war had resumed with France. One letter I had not expected to receive, though, was from Louisa Berkeley. She wrote to tell me that Sarah had given birth to a ginger-haired baby six months after the Paris trip and had confessed that she had tried to seduce me to incriminate me as the father. The actual father seems to have been a ginger-haired coachman. She had been terrified of admitting to her aristocratic father that she had been rogering the servants – not that she was pregnant, mark you – which gives you some idea of scandal and snobbery in Georgian England. Berkeley had long since called off his thugs, who were now searching for the ginger coachman. She finished the letter by asking for my forgiveness and begging me to write if I had still had feelings for her. The letter was nearly a year old.

The streets of London and Paris seemed another world away and suddenly I was feeling very homesick. I wanted to get back to Madras and board a ship more than ever. But India had not finished with me yet. The outcome of a battle, a campaign and Wellesley's career was about to depend on me stumbling around in panic and, of all things, a bagpipe.

I got the first inkling of this around three weeks later. The army had been marching east and had reached the town of Ellichpoor when I was summoned to Wellesley's tent for a staff meeting. This in itself was worrying, as humble captains were not normally asked to join the general and his senior officers as they planned out their strategy.

"Ah, Flashman, I think you know everyone here," said Wellesley brusquely as I walked into his tent. Around a dozen other officers were standing around a map table, which was covered in maps and drawings.

"Yes, sir," I replied, looking around. Swinton was not here as the 74th now had a new colonel called Wallace, a gruff but capable Scot who gave me a nod of greeting.

"As you know," said Wellesley, looking around the gathered faces, "a good number of the raja of Berar's forces have retreated to their fortress at Gawilghur. There they seem to be being reinforced by some of Scindia's chieftains, who are not happy about the truce we have agreed with their master. They believe that the fortress is impregnable and they can hold out there until our supplies fail and then recover their lost territory. Gentlemen, to finish this campaign we must take Gawilghur and destroy this last pocket of resistance."

"We have taken other fortresses that they thought were strong without difficulty," said the new cavalry commander. "I am sure that we can take this one."

"That is easy for you to say, with your horses," growled Chalmers of the 78th Highlanders. "You are not going to be the ones storming the breaches. This fortress is not just hard to take, it has never been taken."

"Gentleman," said Jock Malcolm, "let us concentrate on what information we do have about the fortress. There are in fact two forts, a large inner one which contains the town and which is protected on three sides by a near-vertical drop, and an outer one on the flatter approach. If we can get guns up there then we should be able to take the outer fort, but the real nut to crack is the inner fort. In between the inner and outer forts is a ravine with a narrow path around the edge, allowing access to the inner fort. There is another path up from the plain below which winds up the ravine and joins this path, but it is covered by the guns of both the inner and outer forts at the top. There is also a path from the Deccan Plain to the south directly up the cliff itself to a gate in the inner fort wall, but this is down to single file in some places and when you get to the top there is a fifty-yard flat expanse of land covered by several cannon to deter anyone trying to break down the gate."

He paused to allow us to absorb this and look at the plan he had been pointing at.

Gawilghur 15 December 1803

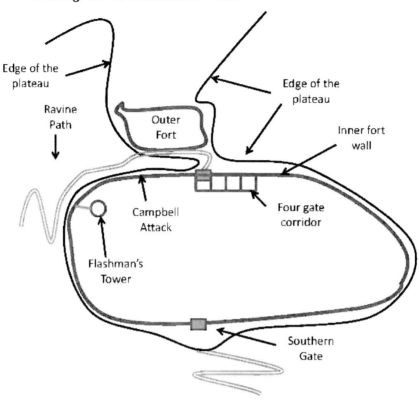

Edge of the plateau

Ravine Path

Outer Fort

Edge of the plateau

Inner fort wall

Campbell Attack

Four gate corridor

Flashman's Tower

Southern Gate

"So," said Chalmers, "we storm the outer fort, get a cannon to blow the gate off the inner fort and then we will have to go along the path that joins the forts to storm that gate. It will be bloody work, but we can do it."

"It is worse than that," said Malcolm. "We think that there is a second gate in the inner fort. When people enter the fort there is a blank wall in front of them and they have to turn left. If there is another gate there then we will not be able to hit it with cannon and so it will have to be broken down with axes under fire."

"Christ, it will be hot work indeed," muttered a Colonel Wallace.

"Not for you, Wallace," said Wellesley. "When we attack I plan to send the 74th up the cliff path directly to the southern gate of the inner fort. You can attack when the gates are opened, but I want you to distract the enemy into protecting that gate – we need to spread their forces. You can also stop any who try to escape that way. Your small numbers will not matter there, as only a handful can fight on that path at any one time. I am sending the 78th Highlanders up the path into the ravine, but the main attack will have to be through the outer fort."

"That is all assuming that we can get some guns up there to make the breeches in the outer fort," said Captain Johnston of the engineers.

"Yes," said Wellesley. "That is our first objective; we need to reconnoitre the road up to the outer fort. If it cannot take guns then we will have to build a new road. Then we will need to site breaching batteries. Johnston, I want you to go up to the fort with young Blackiston. You must assess the road and, if you can see them well enough, the state of the walls. Meanwhile Blackiston is to prepare some drawings of the fort to help plan the attack. Don't worry, you will have a cavalry escort to see you are not captured. Flashman, I would like you to go with them too. The escort commander suggested that you might be useful to talk to any Mahratta they meet."

"Did he?" I asked with a very forced smile. "I will be sure to thank him when I see him."

An hour later Johnston, Blackiston and I met our gallant escort commander at the front of a squadron of around eighty mounted troopers.

"Hello, Flash," called Carstairs from the head of his men. "This should be fun, eh!"

Chapter 28

In hindsight riding my captured white horse on the trip was a mistake. When we were travelling through dark forests it stood out and was easy to see. But it was fast, damned fast, and if we needed to make a run for it then it would go like the wind. There was every chance we might need to make a fast escape too for most of the country between Ellicpoor and Gawilghur was covered in tall crops and jungle so that we could not see far ahead. Remembering my time with Poorum, I suggested that we put small groups of riders on our flanks and in advance to scout for us. Only once did they see a Mahratta patrol, but that had over two hundred horsemen, armed to the teeth. Carstairs was all for attacking it; odds of nearly three to one seemed quite fair to him. It was only with some difficulty that Johnston and I were able to remind him of the secret nature of the mission.

Carstairs was without doubt one of the most annoying people I have ever ridden with. I was already furious with him for roping me into this adventure, but he did not seem to notice my acid retorts. Instead he prattled on about our school days together and how pleased he was to join me on one of my adventures. He bounced around like a puppy that had been eating sugar and generally got on everyone's nerves.

"Your friend seems a little highly strung," said Blackiston to me on the second morning while Carstairs held an impromptu kit inspection for his men.

"He damn well would be if I had a rope," retorted Johnston before I could respond. "Can't we send him with the forward scouts this morning? With a bit of luck he will be captured."

"God, no," said Blackiston, "he would probably attack any patrol he came across with just the scouts."

If they expected me to leap to the defence of Carstairs, they were disappointed, because I thought they were right. Carstairs was an incredibly dangerous man in one respect: he did not seem to have any fear. Remembering him at Assaye, he had talked of charging the begum's infantry with the same concern as going into bat at cricket. He had gone out of his way to volunteer for this dangerous mission behind enemy lines because he thought it would be fun. Then he arranged for me to join because he genuinely thought I would not want to miss out. I began to wonder how we had been friends at school.

It took us three days to reach the bottom of the broad track that led up to the outer fort. As well as maps we had a local guide who could be trusted and who knew the country around Gawilghur. He led us across the plain in front of the inner fort far above us at night and told us of a massive cannon in the fort that could terrorise all the villages for miles around. It did not fire and as far as we could tell we had not been spotted. By dawn we were safely back under cover. Now we started up the track, which was little more than a footpath and rugged going. Halfway up we had to dismount and, leaving the horses with some troopers hidden in some nearby jungle, we proceeded on foot until we reached an outcrop that finally offered us a view of the outer fortress. There was a broad expanse of land some three hundred yards wide approaching the large gate of the fort. Johnston, studying the walls through his telescope, reported that they looked several hundred years old and would offer little resistance to cannon. There were good places to site the siege guns nearby too. Looking beyond the outer fort, we could see the tops of some walls and a tower from the inner fort and remembered the hidden ravine between the two. It looked an intimidating place and I wondered how many others had sat there on that hillside over the centuries, making plans to capture it which had failed. As soon as Blackiston had finished his drawings we started on our way back down.

It was close to dusk by the time we reached the place we had left the horses in the trees. Across the uneven ground we walked the horses towards the main path that led back to the plain. It was a half-mile walk and we were scattered through the trees as we picked our way around trees and rocks. Carstairs was walking beside me, chatting away about a fakir he had seen who had passed a spike through a hole in his leg when suddenly he was interrupted by shouts from ahead. A moment later there was the unmistakable crackle of musket fire. Through the trees we had no way of knowing if it was a small patrol or a regiment that our forward scouts had blundered into coming up the path.

"Mount up," called Johnston in the darkness. "But for Christ's sake, don't do anything until we know what we are up against." This last comment was directed at Carstairs, who was now climbing onto his horse alongside me.

"Well, Flash, it looks like we might see some action again, eh?"

"Shh, I am trying to work out how many men they have. There must be at least twenty."

"Don't worry, Flash, however many they have we can ride 'em down. Why back at..."

His words were interrupted by a trumpet call from behind us. Looking over my shoulder, I saw horsemen silhouetted against the sky as they rode over a ridge a hundred yards to our rear. They had shields and lances, which our men did not. They were Mahratta and there were lots of them.

"It's a trap!" called Blackiston. "Ride for it down the hill."

Well, I was ahead of him there, spurring my horse before the sentence was completed. It is not often that a Flashman bolt is sanctioned by army orders but I was making the most of it. I lay low in the saddle as more muskets flamed to my left, and while some of our troop charged the guns, drawing their sabres, I veered to the right where there were more trees and cover. Carstairs was with me along with five British cavalry troopers as we charged our horses, half-blind in the gloom down the hill. It was rough terrain and if a horse missed its footing it was likely to be fatal for both horse and rider. I glanced wildly around and the Mahratta horsemen seemed to have broken up to chase our scattered force and I saw a dozen heading in our direction. A big rock loomed out of the darkness in front of us, blocking the way down.

"This way," shouted Carstairs, pulling his horse round to the right and instinctively I followed him. A second later I realised that the rest of the troopers with us had gone to the left, but there were trees ahead and there was no time change my mind. My white horse must have stood out like a beacon to the Mahratta behind, for when they came to the rock all of them took the path to the right. We ploughed into the trees with arms over our faces to protect against low-hanging branches. I wanted to go to the left to rejoin the other troops, but there was a ridge of rock blocking the way.

Looking behind, I saw the Mahratta were gaining on us. I followed Carstairs as we ran down what seemed to be a dry stream bed. It twisted and turned and I lost all sense of direction, but what I really needed was some open ground so that my horse could show its speed. If Carstairs could keep up, fine; if not then at least he would buy me some time as the fearless ass was bound to charge them single handed.

Suddenly my prayers were answered for through a break in the trees I could see a smooth plain to our right.

"Come on," I shouted. "This way!" I reined my horse to the right and we burst out of the trees and onto the plain and then we were really flying along.

"Well done, Flash," called Carstairs. His horse was keeping up pretty well. He stared over his shoulder and added, "We are leaving them behind already."

I looked back too and the Mahratta had galloped onto the plain but were making no real effort to catch us; perhaps their horses were already blown in the search for us, I thought. The reason did not matter. We were leaving them well behind.

We rode on for a mile and by then they were way in the distance.

"They will give up soon," I panted at Carstairs. "Once we reach the end of this plain we can slow down and get our bearings."

"Yes, I hope the others got away," gasped Carstairs from his horse, which was still alongside me. Then he suddenly shouted "Bloody hell!" and frantically started to rein his horse in. I followed his gaze and was then desperately hauling on my reins too, for we had just found out why the Mahratta were not rushing to catch us.

We both came within a couple of yards of just galloping off the edge, for the plain ended suddenly in a sheer drop. We could not see the bottom, just blackness, and I remembered that a massive cliff protected the inner fort and wondered if this was part of the same precipice. We could not go back and so we rode our horses along the edge, but more slowly now so that we would have time to stop. When I looked back again I could see the Mahratta still riding towards us but spread out now in a line. The cliff edge started to turn back towards the Mahratta, and with a sinking feeling I realised that we were trapped. That was why the Mahratta had not chased us. They knew that we would either ride over the edge to our deaths or that we would be up against their lance points.

"Shall we charge them?" asked Carstairs, drawing his sabre.

"There are twelve of them, with lances," I replied resignedly. "They would spit you on a lance point long before you were able to use the sabre."

"What do we do then?" he asked, seemingly puzzled as though the obvious solution had not occurred to him.

"We surrender, of course."

I had not had three months of liberty since my last captivity but here I was a prisoner again. Once they saw that we were not going to try to run the Mahratta slowed to a trot with their lance points lowered. Then two dropped from their saddles to take our swords, pistols, tie our hands and grab the reins of our horses. We were led back the way we had come. As the night got truly black the leading horsemen lit torches to see their way and we pressed on, following the horses in front. Four Mahratta rode behind us in case we got any ideas of escaping in the night.

We had ridden the previous night across the plain and then spent the day climbing to the fort either on horseback or on foot. We were already exhausted, but there was to be no rest. Our captors evidently wanted us in the fort by dawn. A couple of times during that night I saw other torches flickering on the hillside, but for the most part I half-dozed in the saddle. Perhaps it was the tiredness, but unlike my previous captivity, I was feeling more relaxed. Being a prisoner was a lot better than being a pile of mashed bones at the bottom of a cliff or being skewered on the end of a lance. I also thought that the Mahratta would be less likely to mistreat prisoners as they knew the British were coming.

"Do you think they will kill us?" asked Carstairs at one point.

"No, we are more use to them alive as messengers or hostages. They must know the British are planning to besiege the place."

"Will they torture us for Wellesley's plan of attack then?"

Carstairs was a ray of sunshine in a tight spot; I had not thought of that. For a moment my nerves jangled as I thought of a previous time I had narrowly avoided being tortured, but then I relaxed as I thought it through.

"No, they won't need to torture us because I will tell them the plan if they ask."

"You can't do that," gasped Carstairs. "Hundreds of our men could be lost if they know what to expect."

"Nonsense, there is only one way to attack: through the outer fort. A child could work it out, and our presence surveying the ground has confirmed it."

He was quiet after that. What I had said was true, but I had also seen what torture could do and I knew I could not have withstood it. Most people think that they would not talk, but trust me, when you are tied up in a dank cell with a sadistic bastard and no hope of rescue, you tell him anything to stop the pain.

My mood was not brightened as we rode in the grey light of dawn through the gate of the outer fortress. There we saw the bodies of ten of our troopers lying in the courtyard. Two more wounded men were being bandaged against a wall and I called out to them about the rest of our party.

"They got away, sahib," called back the sowar before he was cuffed and told to keep quiet.

That was a relief; Johnston was our best engineer. His capture would have extended the siege and our captivity. I had no doubt that the fortress would be taken, but back then I did not know its secret.

I had spent so long in the saddle that I virtually had to be helped off the horse.

"What are your names?" a court flunkey asked us.

We told them while guards searched us for hidden weapons. It was not a thorough search as they did not find the gems sewn into my coat lining, but they took my small fruit knife.

Carstairs and I were taken to a small cell in the gatehouse and left with a water jug and a bucket. Immediately after the door shut Carstairs started asking inane questions and talking of escape, but I told him quite sharply to shut up. I needed some sleep and made myself as comfortable as I could.

Chapter 29

"How did you get this sword?"

I was being roughly shaken awake and as I opened my eyes I saw
my previously confiscated gold-hilted sword being held in front of me.

"I killed its previous owner," I mumbled and then immediately
regretted it as I saw a look of fury cross the face of my questioner.
Now I saw he was wearing a white robe and it was, I admit, stupidity
of the highest degree. My only defence is that I had slept for just two
hours in two days.

Before I knew it I was being half-dragged and half-thrown out of the
cell, blinking in the bright sunlight of the morning.

"You are a liar," snarled my new guard. "Abu Saleem would never
allow himself to be killed by a worm like you, unless you shot him in
the back."

"I took him with a sword," I shouted back as I struggled to get to my
feet and look around. My new captor was a big man, an Arab by the
look of him, and I guessed he must have been one of Abu Saleem's
officers. There were four other soldiers with him, also in the white
robes I had seen at Argaum.

"We will see," said my captor and then to the soldiers he added
"Bring him" before marching off.

I was grabbed and hauled after him none too gently. After a moment
I realised that we were heading towards the gate for the inner fort. We
stepped through the archway and onto the ravine path and I began to
understand why Gawilghur would be so hard to capture. To my left the
path twisted down slightly into the ravine before going up again to the
gate of the inner fort. To my right the path went past the wall of the
outer fort and down into the ravine itself, leading all the way to the
plain below. It was a narrow path, just big enough for a small cart, and
had a cliff face on one side and a sheer drop into the ravine on the
other. Any enemy coming up this path would only be able to march
three or four abreast and would be directly opposite the guns of the
outer fort, which could sweep the path clear with grape shot.

I thought I understood now why the place had never been taken, but
what I had seen was just the start of the obstacles. The big secret was
just inside the gate. As Wellesley had heard, when you went inside the
gate of the inner fort you had to turn left, where there was a gate that
was protected from cannon. He thought he would have men with axes
take care of this, but when I looked up the walls were covered with

embrasures to protect men who would shoot down at the poor bastards doing the chopping. But once through that gate there were another three more massive gates in a long passage packed with more gun embrasures. In short, it was a huge trap. Our men would, if they were lucky, hack their way through the first gate just to find another, and then another. The casualties would be enormous. The passage would be blocked with our dead long before they reached the fourth gate.

Of course, now the gates were all open and we marched straight through and on up to a building that I took to be the palace. It was not a grand residence like some I had visited. The walls were mostly plain and there were no rich hangings or furniture. It was the home of a person with either little money or simple tastes. In a few moments we were entering an audience chamber where half a dozen men lounged on couches or cushions at the far end. As we walked towards them the captain of my little guard grabbed me by the scruff of the neck and pushed me so that I fell, sprawling, to the floor.

"This is the man who had Abu Saleem's sword," he called to the assembled company. "The worm claims he took it in a fair fight."

Well, I have made better entrances. I looked up at the quality, which was staring at me in curiosity, and I decided to try to recover some of my dignity.

"Now look here," I said and I started to get back on my feet. "I am a British officer and I demand..."

The next thing I knew I was back on my knees and there was a blade at my throat.

"You demand nothing," my guard commander said in my ear. He pressed the edge of his blade deeper into my skin, which was a persuasive argument. "You are in the presence of Manu Bappoo, brother to the raja of Berrar and the commander of his army. You will address him as Excellency."

I looked up. In the centre of the group in front of me a man was watching me closely with dark eyes. He wore richly embroidered robes and a turban and had a neatly clipped beard; I guessed his age at early forties because his beard was starting to go grey. The others glanced nervously between him and me and so I realised he must be the raja's brother.

"Your Excellency," I began. "I am a British officer and..."

"How did you kill Abu Saleem?" interrupted Manu Bappoo. He spoke quietly but with unmistakeable authority. "He was one of my closest friends and the finest swordsman I have ever known. Yet my men tell me you carry his sword and ride his horse but gave up without a fight." As he spoke one of the guards handed the golden sword to Manu Bappoo, who put it on the floor by his stool.

"I killed him at Argaum, Excellency," I said, sensing a sudden chill in the room despite the sweat trickling down my spine.

"I know where he died. I commanded my brother's forces at Argaum. I asked you how he died. Be warned, if you lie I will get Khaled there to cut out your tongue before he arranges a slow death for you."

"He shot him in the back, Excellency. It is the only explanation."

"Be quiet, Khaled. Let him speak."

You can imagine how my mind was spinning. The way I had killed Abu Saleem was so implausible no one would believe it, but they would never believe that I had beaten him in a fair fight either. I stood frozen, unsure what to say. A few minutes before I had been asleep in a cell, expecting that I would be released in a few days. Now I knew that any attack on the inner fort was doomed and that I would be lucky to survive the next hour. Twice I opened my mouth to say something, but I did not know how to start.

"Did you shoot him?" prompted Manu Bappoo, watching me closely.

"Only at the end," I blurted out. Khaled, beside me, started to growl in anger and I hastily added, "In the chest, to speed his end, and he wanted me to do it."

"So how did you beat him with a sword?" asked Manu Bappoo again.

I took a deep breath and decided that the only way forward was to tell the truth. "It was towards the end of the battle. The Highlanders were driving the last of the Arab mercenaries back over the hill. I looked up and I saw a man on a white horse charging with his sabre pointing right at me."

Manu Bappoo nodded. "He had sworn to avenge his dead by killing an officer of the white troops who had destroyed his soldiers. So what did you do?"

"I did not have time to do much, just parry his blow and his back cut, and then we were turning to each other again. We both crossed in front of each other's horses and then I managed to get a lucky blow that caught him in the neck."

Manu Bappoo's eyes narrowed slightly as he asked, "How exactly did you get this lucky blow?"

I paused nervously, wondering if these might be the final sentences that my tongue would ever be able to utter. "I took a big swing at him but missed. He was riding his horse in front of mine." I took another breath and then added the fateful words: "I had accidentally cut off the top of my horse's right ear and the horse threw me into the air over Abu Saleem. I cut him in the neck before he could get his sword up and then landed on top of him."

There was a stunned silence; you could have heard a pin drop and I could certainly hear my heart pounding. Manu Bappoo was watching my face closely, looking stern, but then slowly he smiled and let out a great guffaw of laughter.

"The greatest swordsman Abu Saleem, killed by a man falling from his horse," he gasped between laughter. "It is a poetic death indeed."

"You surely do not believe this dog, Excellency," called out Khaled, astonished. "Give me half an hour with him and I will get you the truth."

"Come now, Khaled, you knew Abu as well as me. Would he not have found this funny if it had happened to someone else? Surely this is a story that no one would have made up."

"He lies, Excellency. I have found out he is the British spy Iflassman whom Lord Scindia hunted because he told lies about the death of the Old Patiel."

"Really," said Manu Bappoo, looking interested again.

I wracked my brains for some detail that would prove what I said, and then I had it.

"Was Abu Saleem Jewish?" I asked.

Manu Bappoo gaped in astonishment. "Of course he was not Jewish. He was one of the most devout Muslims I have ever met. What on earth makes you say such a thing?"

"It is just that when he died the last thing he said before he gestured for me to shoot was 'Solomon'."

Now it was Khaled's turn to look surprised and he stared at Manu Bappoo as though this meant something to both of them.

"I think perhaps," said Manu Bappoo gently, "that the word was 'Salome', could it have been that?"

"Yes, it could," I admitted. "He was gasping in pain at the time and it was hard to hear."

"So he loved her to the end," said Khaled thoughtfully.

"It seems so," agreed Manu Bappoo. He saw me looking puzzled and explained. "Many years ago in Arabia, Abu Saleem fell in love with the daughter of a rich and powerful merchant. Her name was Salome. The merchant forbade the match but the couple eloped over the mountains and across the sea to India. Unfortunately the girl died of fever a few months after they arrived here. Abu stayed as a penance and had mourned her ever since."

"Is that what the inscription on the sword is all about?"

"Ah, yes." Manu Bappoo reached down and picked up the golden sword. "The inscription is from a famous Arabic poem, which talks about people who are apart looking up at the same moon and stars." He paused, weighing the sword in his hand and looking at the words. "I think you should have this sword back. You may have done my friend the greatest service in returning him to his love. You clearly had divine help to beat Abu, and I cannot think of anyone else who should have it."

"Excellency!" said Khaled, who seemed set to protest.

"Do you know of anyone else who deserves Abu's sword?" asked Manu Bappoo sternly. "Abu would want it to go to the man who beat him. Now that this Iflassman officer knows its history, I am sure he will treat it with respect."

I nodded eagerly in agreement. I was happy to escape this encounter with my tongue and my life – the sword was an unexpected bonus.

"Now take him to stay in a room in the north wing. He has seen the inner gateway; I want him kept in the inner fort. Mr Iflassman, I would be grateful if you would join me for dinner later.

"It's Flashman, sir, and I would be honoured."

I had to wait five days for that dinner, but I was kept in comfortable lodgings, a lot better than the guardroom cell I had shared with Carstairs. I did wonder if he would be allowed to join me, but they evidently decided that the fewer Englishman who knew the secret of the gates, the better. The sword was returned and I kept it on the small table in my cell, but I noticed that every time the door to my room was opened there were two guards with pikes on hand in case I was tempted to fight my way out. Khaled looked in on me once each day, and on the second day he asked me if Abu Saleem had really died as I had described. I looked him the eye and confirmed that he had. He stared at me for a while and then nodded and went away without saying another word.

I was left to ponder my fate. Call me the eternal optimist, but I did not think they would kill me or they would have done so already. Equally I could not understand why they thought it worthwhile to keep me in comfortable lodgings. I found out on the fifth day when I was summoned to join Manu Bappoo for dinner. I was told to leave the sword behind and was taken down various staircases and corridors until I was shown into a large but plainly decorated room with a table and chairs set for dinner in the European style, instead of the couches and lower seating that would be normal for a meal in an Indian palace.

"You see, I am trying to make you feel at home," called Manu Bappoo, smiling as he got up to welcome me.

I was instantly on my guard: why should he make such an effort when he held me prisoner and was in an impregnable fortress?

"There was no need to go to so much trouble, Excellency," I replied, shaking his offered hand.

"On the contrary, you are an honoured guest and we have much to talk about." He gestured me to sit down and sat himself.

"We do?" I replied, sounding puzzled.

"Of course." Manu Bappoo laughed. "I have found out a lot about you since we last met Mr... Flashman, is that how you say your name?" I nodded in reply before he continued. "For example, I am now aware that you are a trusted confidant of the begum of Samru."

"I would not go that far," I replied. "The begum plays her cards close to her chest. I don't think anyone is her true confidant."

"She plays her cards..." said Manu Bappoo, looking confused, and then his brow cleared. "Ah, I understand your meaning. You think she does not tell anyone what she is really thinking. You are probably right, for she is a great survivor as the ruler of a small state amongst the more powerful Mahratta princes." He paused to take a drink from a gold cup on the table. "But from what I hear she values your judgement. Did she not take you to Assaye and ask your advice on what Wellesley would do? And alone, amongst those advising the Mahratta commander, did you not correctly predict that Wellesley would attack?"

So that is what this is about, I thought. "Do you want to know if Wellesley will attack you here? Is that why we are meeting?" If he wanted to know, I would tell him, for it was no secret. But I was surprised that he could not work this out for himself and wondered if the preparations had been delayed for some reason.

"Of course not." Manu Bappoo smiled. "We can see the British siege guns coming across the plain and your engineers are widening the road up to the outer fort ready to bring up the guns to pound down a breach in the outer fort wall. But we are not worried. You have seen the gate to the inner fort. The British will die there and my brother will be acclaimed as the man who succeeded where Scindia failed in beating the British. I am looking beyond the defeat of the British, for that is inevitable. When the British are gone there will be war amongst the Mahratta princes, with Holkar on one side and my brother, supported by Scindia's forces, on the other. I want you to watch the British defeat and then take news of it to the begum. I want you to persuade the begum to join her army to Berar's forces."

So that was it, I was to witness the destruction of the British army and then become a messenger again. My first reaction was relief; I had feared something much worse. I could do this and survive, which was more than those poor bastards assaulting the inner gate were likely to do. The begum would take no notice of my recommendation of course; she would weigh the odds herself. I would not be surprised if she had her own spies in Berar's forces. But Holkar could not afford her army and Berar and Scindia's lands were closer to her own, and so I thought that there was a good chance she would decide to go with the raja. But there were still a lot of loose ends to the Berar plan, Scindia for instance.

"Scindia is used to leading the Mahratta confederation," I said. "He seems a proud man and his army must still be bigger than yours. Has he agreed to let the raja rule the confederation now?"

"That is very astute, Mr Flashman. I see you are asking the questions that the begum herself would ask when you talk to her. I think it is time I introduced you to a man you already know a lot about."

With that he rang a bell and a moment later the door opened and a sleepy-looking man walked in carrying a large earthenware pot. He put his pot on the table and then looked around with glassy eyes.

"I have never seen this man before," I said.

"No, but you have certainly heard of his exploits." Manu Bappoo turned to the man and said simply, "Show him."

The stranger took the lid of the pot and his hand hovered over the opening for a few moments before darting inside. It emerged holding a small snake. In a second a small knife appeared. There was a slight crunching sound as the snake was held down and then the head was tossed on the table in front of me. I looked down. It was the head of a small cobra. Its mouth was open and its tongue gave a final flick as I watched it. Suddenly I was remembering those two dried-up snake heads I had seen on de Boigne's table back in Paris.

I looked at Manu Bappoo. "So was it you who ordered the killing of the Old Patiel and then de Boigne?"

"No, this man, who calls himself The Cobra for obvious reasons, was hired by Scindia then. Now he is employed by us. But importantly Scindia thinks that The Cobra still works for him, which means he will be able to get close to do his work. I was going to give Scindia the chance to retire with his concubines, but he cannot be trusted – he would try to regain power. This man will ensure that Scindia does not dispute the leadership of the confederation." Manu Bappoo looked me clearly in the eye as he added, "He will take care of any Mahratta leader who blocks our ambitions."

"Including the begum?" I asked.

"I would not dream of threatening such a valued and trusted friend as the begum," he said, still looking me in the eye in a way that indicated that threatening the begum was exactly what he was doing. "And in case you are thinking of just fleeing back to Madras and then to England, I should mention that your friend Carstairs will be staying here and things will not go well for him if you do not do as we say."

"You seem to have thought of everything," I said grimly and looking aggrieved. Villains, and Manu Bappoo was certainly one of those, always like to be complemented on their plans. He looked pleased with himself, but I wasn't sure he had covered all the angles here. It was not the first time that I had heard a Mahratta leader take the defeat of the British for granted. At Assaye they had been arguing over who got the loot instead of whether they would win, but at the end of the day the Mahratta army had been routed. I could not see how the British could fight their way through those gates, but I knew enough about the British army now not to bet against them. I was also glad that, unless Wellesley's plans had changed, my 74th Highlanders would not be in that maelstrom for they were supposed to be coming up the cliff on the narrow path to the only other gate that led directly into the inner fort.

Manu Bappoo's biggest mistake was thinking that imprisoning Carstairs would get me to do as he wanted. Carstairs was bloody annoying and a danger to himself and those around him. On top of that, the chances of Manu Bappoo ever letting him go were slim. He could use Carstairs to get me to do his bidding and then kill both of us at the end. I decided I should view Carstairs as already dead and high-tail it for safety the instant I got the chance. And yet... I had known the irritating little squirt since we were at school together, and how easy would it be to head south if the country was overrun with marauding Mahratta? Manu Bappoo was bound to give me an escort to get to Sardhana and the begum, which would stop me escaping. Perhaps I could make the release of Carstairs a condition of her support?

I spent the rest of the dinner thinking through my options while listening to Manu Bappoo talk on about his plans for a Berar's leadership of the Mahratta. It was clear that it was not the raja making the decisions; he was just a figurehead. Manu Bappoo planned to rule through the army and that was firmly under his control. He talked of his plans for glory while I thought about my plans for escape. But we were both wasting our time, for what happened in Gawilghur defied everyone's expectations.

Chapter 30

The cannons started three days later. I had spent the days since the dinner fretting over what to do next. These days had been interrupted by a daily visit from Khaled, who would take me out for a stroll around the walls of the inner fort. I was allowed to wear my sword as befits a soldier but he had guards with pikes to ensure I was not tempted to do anything silly. Quite what he expected me to do with a sword against the entire garrison was beyond my imagination.

On the first day he pointed out on the plain far below what looked like a red snake slowly moving towards us. It was one of the British regiments marching towards the road that led to the outer fort for the assault. The garrison had tried firing their cannon at the British in the plain, but from such a height when the balls hit the ground their momentum was governed more by gravity rather than gunpowder and accuracy was impossible. I looked for the path that I thought my Highlanders would take and found the gate on the south side of the inner fort wall, but in front of it was a small flat triangle of land and a well-trodden path leading to the cliff edge.

The guns had little to do until the third day when the British revealed their siege batteries, which they had been carefully constructing under cover of night. The fact that they had got the guns up there meant that they had also evidently repaired the road we had surveyed. On the first day of the cannonade the British guns did little damage as far as I could see, but they were aiming for the northern wall on the outer fort. A cloud of dust rose from where each ball impacted to show that they were all aiming for the same point to create a breach in the wall for the troops to storm over. They seemed to have only three big guns and progress was slow.

When I awoke on the fourth day I could hear that the guns were firing more regularly, meaning that there were more of them. Khaled came to take me on our walk and this time I saw that there was already a breach in the north wall of the outer fort. Some of the guns were still firing at it to lower it further, but more of the guns were firing through the gap to create breaches in the southern wall of the outer fort, the one that faced the inner fort. Clouds of dust showed that they were trying to create two breaches in that wall. The Mahratta were returning fire from their cannon in embrasures on the northern wall of the outer fort, but the British cannon were protected behind big baskets of stone and covered when they were not firing. Other British cannon were also systematically destroying the Mahratta gun embrasures. The day before the Mahratta had been swarming around the courtyard of the outer fort with wooden battens, trying to shore up the wall being attacked, but this time they were doing nothing to hinder the bombardment. The men I could see in the courtyard were sheltering in the corners.

"Why are they not doing anything to rebuild the walls around the breaches or put up obstacles for the attackers?"

"Watch, huzoor, you will see."

A few moments later, in between all the sharp bangs from the cannon and the crack of the impact of the balls, I heard a *whoomp* sound. A black ball could be seen arcing slowly a fifty yards into the sky before dropping into the centre of the courtyard. It bounced a couple of times and then span to a stop for a few seconds before exploding with a loud bang that sent shards of iron whistling around the courtyard of the outer fort. The British had brought a mortar with them.

"It does not matter, huzoor. We know that they will take the outer fort. We will have men there to defend the breaches. At the last they will retreat to the inner fort with our men here giving covering fire. The British will think victory is in sight but then they will die in the gates."

Over the walls you could catch glimpses of the redcoats as they moved about their batteries. It reminded me of the time that I watched Wellesley and his cavalry before the start of Assaye. I had been feeling hopeless despair then as I could not see how the British and sepoy army would fight their way through. But as I watched that mortar slam into the outer courtyard and the Mahratta keeping their heads down, I took hope. Wellesley and Stevenson's columns had already fought sieges against tough fortresses and had taken them without difficulty. Granted, the others had not involved ravines, cliffs and multiple gatehouses, but while the Mahratta were warriors, the British and sepoy troops were professional soldiers who would carefully plan each stage of the attack. Well, that is what I thought at the time. How was I to know that the British would almost certainly have been beaten were it not for the impulsive decision of a brave Scottish captain? Oh aye, and the spontaneous action of a very irritating Englishman with no fear of heights.

On the fourth morning after the cannons started Khaled came for me early, and instead of taking me on our usual walk around the walls he went to a tower close to the west wall. We climbed a narrow spiral staircase to emerge on the top, which had excellent views of the outer fort and some of the ravine path between the two strongholds. A group of Mahratta leaders were there looking across with telescopes at the British and sepoy lines. One of them turned around at our arrival and I saw it was Manu Bappoo, this time dressed in gleaming armour.

"Welcome, my friend." He smiled at me excitedly. "You are just in time to see the fruition of all of our plans. The enemy is preparing to attack." He held out his telescope. "Do you want to look?"

I walked over and took the glass and focused it on trenches near the guns where large numbers of men could be seen moving. The Mahratta cannon facing the assault party had all been destroyed now, but the men in the outer fort were firing rockets which fizzed around the trenches before spinning off in random directions. I moved the glass over the outer fort and could see maybe a thousand men waiting in each of the more sheltered sides of the courtyard to meet the assault. British cannon and the mortar were still firing at the breach to deter any defenders from gathering there. Along the damaged walls of the outer fort more soldiers stood with muskets to fire at the attackers. In all there must have been several thousand in the outer fort. Looking around the inner fort, I did not need the telescope to see that at least a thousand more men stood on the ramparts of the four gatehouses and the walls between them. They would be able to fire down with impunity at the attackers trapped in the narrow passage between the gates, creating a corridor of death that the Mahratta expected would bring the British and sepoy attack to a bloody halt. The rest of the walls facing the outer fort were lightly manned as beneath those walls was a vertical cliff forming the sides of the ravine.

Manu Bappoo ordered his lieutenants to their posts and the men dutifully set off down the steps of the tower, leaving two guards, Khaled, Manu Bappoo and myself, on the top.

"I have brought your friend to join you," said Manu Bappoo, pointing behind me. "I would not want you to forget your friendship and it was not safe for him in the outer fort."

I turned to look as he spoke and there, crouched against the ramparts, was Carstairs. I had not noticed him when I first came up the steps as he looked like a bundle of rags and was hunched down below the level of the rampart. He had not been well treated. He was dirty, his clothes were torn and there were cuts and bruises around his face. But more alarmingly it seemed his irrepressible enthusiasm had finally been repressed. He just gazed blankly down at the stone between his feet, taking no notice of his surroundings.

"Khaled and the guards will stay with you," said Manu Bappoo. "Watch our victory closely, Flashman. I want you to be able to report all the details to the begum." With that he followed his lieutenants down the stairs.

Khaled and the guards turned to watch the outer fort and ignored me as I walked over to where Carstairs was crouching. I was shocked at the transformation in him. While I had been in several prisons before, this must have been his first time and some people struggle to cope. Evidently the conditions I had been kept in with decent food and a comfortable bed were a lot better than he had been enjoying. I was not quite sure what to do. I couldn't leave him like this. I needed him to pull himself together. He had spent years being shouted at by drill sergeants and riding majors and so I decided to use their approach.

"Lieutenant Carstairs," I called sharply down to him, "get on your feet at once."

He looked up at me for the first time and recognition crossed his face and then slowly he started to get to his feet.

"You are a British officer, God dammit," I hissed at him. "How dare you look so disreputable in front of the enemy?"

He pulled himself to attention and at last put his chin up and stared straight ahead. The irony was, of course, that it had taken me just a night to get to the same state in Scindia's jail, but Carstairs was not to know that.

"Sorry, Flash," he whispered. "I am just not used to this like you." I saw him look at my relatively clean and straight uniform and then surreptitiously pull at his own jacket to straighten it out.

"That is better," I said, suppressing a smile. "Now stand easy and stay alert."

"Are we going to escape?" he whispered at me, sounding a bit more enthusiastic.

"Escape?" I asked incredulously. "We are in a fortress on the edge of a cliff guarded by six thousand Mahratta soldiers – how far do you think we would get?"

"So are we going to help the British attack?"

I looked at him and bit back my initial response, that we were just going to try to stay alive. That would see the poor devil thrown back into his dungeon, and any fool could see that he was desperately looking for some hope to hang on to.

"Yes," I said at last. "If the opportunity arises to help the attack, we could look at it."

"Flash, I won't let you down." There was a gleam in his eye now and he started to pace around the top of the tower, looking over the edge.

I was not worried; there was not a lot we could do to help the British here. There was only one way up to the roof through the tower itself. It was not joined to any of the other battlements apart from with a stone arch over a street below which stretched from near the top of the tower to the west wall, and that was less than a foot wide.

Anyway, initially it did not look like the British would need any help. A sudden crash of musketry from the outer fort indicated that the attack was underway, and looking up, I could see a large crowd of redcoats running for the breach. The British cannon maintained their fire as the men ran in, shooting balls over the heads of their own soldiers in front to crash into the ramparts. The Mahratta swarmed to the breech to meet the charge and their shouts and yells almost drowned out the double *whoomp* sound as two perfectly aimed mortar shots landed in their midst. The carnage that these shells caused in such a tightly packed mass of men was truly appalling, and as the survivors staggered, stunned and shocked, in the smoke they found the first attackers tearing in at them. The redcoats were mostly sepoy soldiers from Madras and they streamed into the fort, fighting their way through the defenders like a hot knife through butter. Avenging hordes of red-coated demons flew up the steps leading to the top of the walls to rout the men who had fired down on their approach, and within a few second it seemed that thousands of Mahratta were running towards the gate leading towards the path to the inner fort.

Even though they had clearly expected the attack, the Mahratta were taken completely by surprise by the speed of the collapse of the outer fort. It was all over in a couple of minutes and the fastest redcoats were running amongst the retreating defenders towards the gate of the inner fort. Other redcoats had already started to fire up at the battlements of the inner fort, making the defenders keep their heads down, and the men at the gates of the inner fort must have panicked and slammed them shut. The gates were key to their defence and they could not afford to let the sepoys through with their own men as the redcoats could then hold the gates open for their comrades to storm the inner fort as well. I could not see what was happening in the gatehouses from the tower, but suddenly I saw that instead of running towards the gate, the Mahratta were now streaming along the narrow path that led down to the ravine floor. Those Mahratta defenders who had run towards the

254

inner fort gate were now also running back to go down the path and the sepoys were opening fire on them from the ramparts of the outer fort as they passed. More sepoys came out on the path and, forming themselves into ordered ranks, began to follow the Mahratta down the path, firing volleys as they went... and then the screaming began.

I could not see the bottom of the ravine but I could guess what was happening. When I had been briefed by Wellesley on the plan of the attack, the 78th Highlanders were set to come up the ravine path. The Mahratta defenders of the outer fort were now trapped between the Highlanders in front and the sepoys behind. The sepoys I could see following the Mahratta down the path formed themselves into a tightly packed wedge shape designed to force the Mahratta to the precipice edge. They now marched steadily forward, jabbing the Mahratta with their long bayonets. Those in front of the stabbing blades pushed desperately at their comrades to get away, but there was simply no room on the slowly shrinking space on the ravine path. Hundreds of men were being forced over the edge. Some grabbed for friends to hold them back, but more often than not both were pushed over instead. Sometimes they would go in ones and twos; other times whole groups of men who had been trying to hold on to each other would be dragged or pushed off, screaming in terror. Many of the desperate men tried to climb down the rough stone of the cliff, searching for hand and foot holds either to stay just below the path or to attempt a descent to the bottom. Some made progress, but others were dislodged by bodies falling from above so that they also fell to their doom.

"My God," breathed Carstairs from beside me as we both watched.

From the top of the tower and beyond musket range from the outer fort we had probably the best view of the unfolding drama. It was awful to watch, but you could not take your eyes away either. Those on the inner fort ramparts would look over the battlements occasionally, but their glimpses would be met by a hail of musket fire from the outer fort opposite. Most of the garrison could only gauge the scale of the tragedy outside their walls by the continuous shrieks, screams and yells. They knew that the outer fort garrison was being horribly slaughtered and it filled most of them with fear. The sepoys and Highlanders continued their slow, prodding march and hardly lost a man, while hundreds more of the enemy were killed. It was the panic and terror that killed the Mahratta, not the bayonets. The British commanders must have been torn between a sense of humanity and the wish to destroy an enemy at little cost to their own men. Even if they had wanted to let the Mahratta escape, they were blocking the only escape routes. As we watched, the sepoys prodded the remaining Mahratta further down the cliff and mercifully beyond our line of sight so that now all we could hear was the screaming too. I turned to Khaled, who along with the guards had been frozen and silent as they had watched the sickening scene unfold. I noticed that the hand that gripped his sword hilt had white knuckles and I remembered seeing earlier many of the white-robed Arab troops in the outer fort garrison. Their courage would have been no use them in the tightly packed crowd that slowly descended down the ravine.

It is easy to read these words in black and white, but when you have been two hundred yards away from several thousand men struggling desperately just to live, climbing over each other, trampling people or pushing others off to save themselves, well, it is a sickening sight. You forget for a moment about enemies and allies and just think of them as men, and so without thinking I put out a hand and gripped Khaled's shoulder in a gesture of support. He shook my hand off angrily and turned around with his eyes glaring furiously.

"I don't need your sympathy; the battle is not over yet. When your foul red-coated dogs try to enter the inner fort we will show you what real slaughter is!"

I stepped back to look at him. He was angry but he was also shaken, I could see that. If I was unsure then the guards standing behind him were definitely looking shocked, glancing nervously between Khaled, Carstairs and me as though unsure what would happen next. I didn't reply as I could not think of anything helpful to say. Carstairs and I retreated to the opposite side of the tower while Khaled and the guards stayed where they were.

"God, Flash, did you know that the Mahratta would be trapped like that?" whispered Carstairs.

"I had an idea," I lied, for I had only remembered about the 78th coming up the ravine when the screaming started. "The 78th Highlanders are coming from the ravine and the 74th should be coming up the cliff path to the southern gate."

Carstairs looked impressed that I knew the general's plan. "What are they going to do about the gates?" he asked quietly. "The general does know about them, doesn't he?"

That was the all-important question. Wellesley had certainly not mentioned them at the one briefing I had been at, but that may have been deliberate. If he knew we had to fight our way through them, he would not have wanted to worry his men early. But if he had known that there were *four* gates to fight through, surely he would have made alternative plans. For example, bring his siege guns into the outer fort and spend a day or two creating a new breach near the first gate. There was no mention of this in the briefing, but that was two weeks ago. Jock Malcolm must have been speaking to prisoners who had been at the fort, so perhaps one of them had revealed the presence of the gates. They were not new; they had probably been there for centuries. I stared anxiously at the outer fort and beyond for any sign that the plans had been changed, but there seemed to be no activity to move the siege guns at all.

"I hope so, Teddy," I replied. "I really do hope so."

Even the bloodthirsty Highlanders were finally sickened with the slaughter on the ravine path, and so a while after the trapped Mahratta had disappeared from our view Colonel Chalmers called his men and the sepoys opposite to a halt. Both units stepped back ten paces and called on the Mahratta to surrender and throw any weapons down. Most of the trapped men had already abandoned their swords and muskets in the struggle to stay alive. Single files of shaken prisoners were then allowed to pass the redcoats, some going to the top of the ravine and through the outer fort and some going to the bottom. The first we knew of this was when the screaming stopped. Then we saw the sad trail of prisoners coming up the path, some weeping, some being sick and the fight taken out of all them. Several wore the white robes of our guards and one of the guards tried shouting at a friend he saw on the path, but the man just stared back and did not respond.

"Quiet," snarled Khaled at the guard. "We will avenge them, brother. Now it is our turn to do the killing."

It seemed he was right, for as the redcoats appeared back up the path from the ravine they began to gather by the gate of the outer fort as though preparing for the assault on the inner fortress. No siege guns had moved, but I saw some gunners around a cannon in the outer fort bringing it round to bear on the first gate of the inner fort. This gate would be easy to destroy, but it just opened the way to the corridor of death that stretched around a corner and out of reach of further artillery support. With a sickening feeling, I realised that the British were about to walk right into the Mahratta trap

The musket fire between the two armies, which had died down during the conflict in the ravine, now increased. Mahratta were firing over the battlements at the mass of redcoats by the outer fort, while redcoats from that fort fired back to keep the heads of the defenders down during the assault. Some rockets were fired at the British defenders, but the Mahratta were not really trying to stop the redcoats from attacking. Instead, they gathered around the gatehouses and the walls between them and readied themselves to create their own bloodbath.

Carstairs and I watched in dismay as the cannon in the outer fort opened fire on the gate, for it seemed that we alone among the British knew what waited on the other side of that entrance.

"We have to do something," said Carstairs urgently as the assault party started to work its way around the ravine path towards the inner fort gate. I saw some were carrying axes, but it would take forever for them to chop their way through four gates and they would never be given the chance.

"What can we do?" I asked. "They would never hear now if we shouted a warning, and we can't get out of the fort to tell them. We cannot even get out of this tower. Khaled has more of his white-robed men gathered at the bottom if we try to make a run for it." While my hopes had risen at the fast fall of the outer fort, now that the redcoats were about to charge into the Mahratta trap I could see myself taking that message to the begum after all.

"I am not going back to that prison cell," said Carstairs firmly. Of course he did not know that his incarceration was as a hostage to ensure that I would do as Bappoo wanted – or that I had been weighing up the odds of running out on him.

Thoughts were interrupted by the booming of the cannon opposite, which punched its first hole in the inner fort gate. The assault party standing on the ravine path to one side cheered but did not move as through the dust they could see that the gate was still standing. I watched as the gun crew rushed to reload and in a few moments the gun crashed out again, this time with its aim slightly adjusted. This shot must have worked, for while I could not see the gate I could see the assault part rush forward, cheering again, and then all hell broke loose.

While the redcoats in the outer fort maintained a covering fire they could not see the Mahratta on the inner walls of the corridor between the gates and these men now fired down with impunity on the first redcoats through the broken entrance. Rockets were also thrown down, and while notoriously unreliable, in a confined space they were lethal, bouncing off the walls and hitting and scorching men until they exploded. The roar of gunfire as the first troops entered was terrific. Every Mahratta there seemed to want to exact revenge for the slaughter that they had been forced to listen to earlier. The commanding officer of the assault, Colonel Kenny, had been killed early on, but I heard later that several of the axemen had got through to the next gate before they were cut down. The rest saw quickly that they could not survive in that maelstrom and pulled back out through the gate, taking as many wounded as they could with them.

The redcoats milled around on the ravine path in confusion. I could see officers running to and from the assault party with news and orders. There was no sign of Wellesley; it was Stevenson's column that was to make the assault and the general had evidently decided not to interfere in its command. We watched as they tried to manoeuvre a gun onto the path to the inner fort, but the wheels of the gun carriage were too wide for parts of the path and as it was then blocking the way it was deliberately wheeled over the edge to crash down into the gorge below. More men came forward with axes and this time they also had bundles of sticks and torches; they were evidently going to try using smoke to give them cover. If there was just one gate that might have worked, but not with four. Once more the redcoats began to gather outside the gateway. Some leaned around to fire up at the Mahratta waiting for them on the inner wall while others lit and threw in the bundles of sticks as far as they could. The sticks began to burn. Some must have been damp, for the smoke was thick as it rose up out of the gap between the walls leading to the first gate in the corridor. I could not see as the men went in again, but I heard the effect for there was a sudden increase in gunfire from the Mahratta and the fizz and crack of more rockets. The British had the cover of the smoke but it hindered them too as they tried to cough their way through to the first gate in the passage. For the Mahratta, while they could not see, it was still like shooting fish in a barrel.

Chapter 31

It was Carstairs who saw it first. I was staring towards the battle at the gate when he nudged me and pulled me back, away from where Khaled and the guards stood also watching the gate. He nodded to a stretch of wall that faced the outer fort but was on the opposite end of the wall from the corridor of gates. There, looking through a gap in the battlements, was a face, an unmistakably white face, where a face had no right to be. For beneath that face and the wall it was on was a cliff that led down into the ravine, and consequently the wall was hardly manned at all. In fact, there were just three Mahratta guards on that stretch of the wall and they had gone much closer to the gate to watch what was happening there, confident that no one could reach the top of the wall behind them.

I found out later that the face I was looking at belonged to a Captain Campbell of the 94th regiment, part of Stevenson's division. When the first attack on the gateway had been repulsed he had looked for another way in. He had done some climbing in Scotland and thought that the cliff to the right of the gate was rough enough to be climbed. On his own initiative he had found a rope and a light bamboo ladder and led his light company along the path past the gate. Then he had started to climb, the rope tied to his waist and the ladder over his shoulder. Two men had gone with him to help and they had made it to a small rocky outcrop at the base of the wall. They tied the rope to a large rock so that it could support those who followed and then Campbell had put the ladder up against the wall. As his men swarmed up the rope behind him, he climbed the ladder to see what strength of enemy waited at the top of the wall. This was when we noticed him.

Carefully the captain slipped over the wall and, clever lad, he took off his shako and stood staring out over the wall as though he were on guard – far less conspicuous than if he had crouched down, looking furtive. Soon two more redcoats had appeared, adopting the same casual pose, then a steady stream of redcoats were coming over the wall. There must have been eight or nine standing there in their faded red coats and with their hats under their arms, but still the Mahratta guards further along the battlements had not seen them. Someone noticed them, though, for with a sudden Arabic oath Khaled pointed them out to the guards and then leant over the parapet to speak to his men waiting outside the tower. They were among the nearest to stop the redcoat incursion and I leant over the parapet to see how many there were. Twenty of the white-robed elite soldiers were staring up at Khaled.

The Persian commander had barely got the first words out when he emitted a shriek and started to lean out even further. I turned my head just in time to find that Carstairs had got behind Khaled and was in the act of lifting the man's ankles high above his head and the Persian was sliding over the edge. He flailed wildly for a grip but his body was over the tipping point now and Carstairs gave him a final shove with one hand while grabbing Khaled's sword from its scabbard before that disappeared from sight. The two guards who had been staring with astonishment at the British troops were for a moment stunned at their master's disappearance. Khaled's final scream terminated in a wet splat sound as he hit the stone-paved street below. Before they could recover their wits, Carstairs charged the guards with his captured sword, but the nearest one did not get chance to lower his pike before Carstairs was on him and jamming the captured sword in the guard's guts. The second guard, now outnumbered, did not stay around to contest the issue, but instead fled to the stairs down to the ground.

"What the hell have you done?" I shouted at Carstairs as I looked back over the edge of the tower. Instantly two muskets flashed and a ball chipped stone from the parapet inches away from my head. There were yells of outrage as the white-robed soldiers looked down at their fallen leader. Already several were running for the door of our tower.

"But you said we should look for chances to help with the attack," said Carstairs with what seemed childlike simplicity. He was bending to jam the shaft of the wounded guard's pike into a bracket to block the trap door. We could hear more shouts and yells coming from the floors of the tower below us as the Persians charged upwards.

"And listen," continued Carstairs with a note of pride at his own ingenuity, "they are coming up the stairs of the tower now rather than attacking our men."

This was true as the redcoats were now running along the wall to start attacking from behind the Mahratta in the gatehouse, killing the three sentries on the way. All this was fine, but it seemed to miss the more pertinent point.

"You bloody idiot," I shouted at him. "What do you think is going to happen when they get to the top of the tower? That stick isn't going to stop them. They are going to chop us to pieces. We are trapped up here!"

"Don't worry, Flash, we are not trapped." Carstairs was still talking calmly as he ran across the tower. "We can escape along the top of this wall."

With that he swung his legs over the top and dropped until just his face was showing over the parapet. That wall was far too narrow to walk across as I remembered it, but as I ran to him I saw his head moving towards the unoccupied eastern rampart. I looked down at the top of the wall again. It was bloody narrow, just a double course of bricks. That is fine if you are walking down a strip of bricks in the street to keep your boots out of the mud, but when there is a two-storey drop on either side it is a different matter. The trap door rattled behind me as a shoulder slammed into it from the floor below to remind me that I did not have long to make a decision. The chances were I would either be chopped up by a vengeful Persian or fall to my death on the street below, but at least there was a chance of survival walking along the wall. I swung my legs over and gingerly dropped down as once more there was a slamming sound behind me, but this time the noise of splintering too as the pike shaft was giving way.

Carstairs was now at the rampart and he turned and called, "Come on, Flash, just look at the bricks in front of you and don't look down."

Of course when someone says that to you the first thing you instinctively do is look down. For a moment I was frozen with fear. If I had not heard the trap door behind me finally smash open my nerve might have failed me completely, but then I knew it was now or never. Gingerly I started moving forward with my eyes fixed on the bricks ahead of me.

"That's the way, Flash," called Carstairs encouragingly and now I was taking bigger steps. I could hear shouting behind me but I blocked everything from my mind but that short stretch of wall. Soon I had just three steps to go, but then disaster struck. I stepped on a brick but the wall was old and evidently this one was a loose stone and it just tipped and fell away with my foot suddenly slipping into thin air. I could feel myself start to topple and flailed my arms desperately. I remember looking down and seeing a stone trough in the street below, which I seemed about to fall onto, but then I felt a strong hand grip my shoulder and steady me. I looked up to see a smiling Carstairs, who had come back out onto the wall.

"Come on, Flash, two more steps now," he said, stepping back to lead the way.

"God, I thought I had bought it just then," I said as I leant against the eastern rampart, feeling myself start to shake. "If we survive this, Teddy, I might kill you myself."

He was reaching forward with his sword to prise away more bricks from the top of the wall to make it harder for the Persians to follow us, as one of them was already lowering himself over the wall.

Carstairs laughed. "I never have been frightened of heights. It is no worse than running along the top of the chapel roof at Rugby."

"Yes, but you were the only one mad enough to do that too. The rest of us were watching from our dormitory windows or dodging the schoolmasters."

I had a sudden memory of the fourteen-year-old Carstairs flitting across the moonlit roof, but the crack of a musket brought me swiftly to the present. A Persian had fired at us from the tower roof but had missed. His comrade was now edging his way across the bricks towards us. I looked to the north and could see a steady stream of redcoats still coming over the northern rampart and following Captain Campbell towards the gatehouses. There must have been thirty or forty across already, and judging by the screams and yells from the gatehouse, their muskets and long bayonets were already having a lethal effect.

Carstairs hefted his captured sabre and prepared to meet the Persian on the wall. "I will hold them off here, Flash," he called. "You go and see if you can open the southern gate and let your Highlanders in." I hesitated, trying to work out the best course of action. Part of me wanted to join the safety in numbers of Campbell's men, but they would have a hard fight through the gatehouses. We couldn't hold the Persians off for long here and so perhaps going for the southern gate was the best course of action.

"We should both go together," I called back.

Carstairs' sword flicked out at the Persian. Crossing the bricks was hard enough, but getting past a swordsman at the end was near impossible, especially when more bricks were missing from our end of the wall. The Persian, who had been watching his footing, saw Carstairs lunge too late and his own parry was enough to unbalance him. With a scream, he toppled over and we were close enough to hear the crunch of broken bones as he smacked into the street below.

"Go!" shouted Carstairs. "I'll follow but I have score to settle with some of these bastards first." Another Persian was already lowering himself onto the wall.

I pride myself on the fact that I never need to be asked more than twice to save my own precious skin. Shouting "Don't be long" over my shoulder, I started running down the eastern rampart. It was empty as it was on top of a part of the ravine that no one could climb, at least not without half a mile of rope. As I ran past an unmanned cannon on the rampart a hundred yards further on I looked over my shoulder. Carstairs was there at the end of the wall and the second Persian was wobbling precariously on it. Another Persian came up some steps from the street below and again Carstairs' sword flicked out and the man went down. To give him his due, he was damn lethal with that blade and he was buying me valuable time to make my escape. To not waste it, I quickly ran on.

I must have got three hundred yards down it when I looked back again. I stopped, frozen, as I was just in time to see two Persians level their muskets at Carstairs from the top of the tower. The weapons fired and he went down. I remember screaming in anguish as several more of the white-robed figures then swarmed up the steps to attack him from the street. I thought they would hack him to pieces, but instead they decided to kill him in the same way he had killed Khaled. Picking him up, they carried him to the battlements. I could see he was struggling in their grip, but they just threw him over the top. He screamed, finally discovering his fear of heights, as he dropped into the chasm.

Grief affects us all in different ways, and seeing a boy you have known since you were ten being hurled to his death did strange things to me. I found myself with Abu's sword in my hand running towards those white-robed fiends, yelling obscenities. Thank God I came to my senses in time. It was as they noticed the lunatic charging in their direction and levelled their muskets that I skidded to a halt. My natural sense of self-preservation reasserted itself and I turned back in the direction I had come.

Muskets banged behind me but I was unscathed as I assumed Flashman's classic battlefield tactic: frantic flight running full tilt away from the enemy. Looking over my shoulder, I saw the white-robed figures were shouting and setting off in pursuit, some two hundred yards behind. The ramparts offered no cover and so I charged down the next set of steps and disappeared into the maze of alleys. I had no real idea where I was going, turning left and right, but I tried to head in a southerly direction and shake off my pursuers. It worked, because the voices behind got further away until at last I pulled up in a doorway, gasping for breath. I took off my faded red coat – it was a dangerous thing to wear in these streets – and put it over my arm.

I was still panting heavily when I turned the next corner and found myself at the southern gate, with twenty well-armed Mahratta soldiers all staring suspiciously back at me. I was stunned for a moment. What the hell was I going to do now? I stood there breathing hard, dirty and dishevelled and with a British army coat in my hands.

One of the guards came towards me with a lowered musket. Then inspiration occurred and I was shouting in my best Hindi, "The British are in the inner fort. Look, I have one of their jackets, see for yourself. The prince wants all soldiers to drive them back through the gatehouses."

Thank God I am good with languages, one of my few skills, and I pick up accents too, and in between the panting for breath it seemed convincing. The captain of the guard snatched the coat from me and looked at it suspiciously. But the metal buttons with the Company crest on each one proved it was a British coat and he took this as proof that my story was true. Barking a command at one of his men to stay, the rest ran back down one of the alleyways into the centre of town. I leant back against the wall and gave a sigh of relief.

There were still two gun crews watching me curiously from embrasures high up on the wall, one either side of the gate, with their cannon loaded with canister to sweep clear the small patch of land in front of the entrance. The one soldier left jabbered at me excitedly. I was not sure what he was saying but I don't think he knew either; it looked like one Indian village was missing its idiot. He pointed at my coat still in my hand and at the gate, evidently telling me that the British were out there too, and then he gestured for me to come close to the gate. As I walked towards him he opened a flap in the gate which covered a barred window at head height to allow guards to see visitors before they let them in. He peered round to look through the flap and there was the sharp crack of a distant musket from the other side.

The musket ball caught him in the jaw and he staggered back, holding his face and screaming in pain. The cannon either side of the gate both fired their lethal spread of shot and the gun crews threw themselves into the act of reloading their pieces. I realised I would never have a better chance. In a moment I had got my shoulder under the big wooden locking bar and was heaving it out of its bracket. The gunners did not have a clear view of the gate itself and only the idiot could see what I was doing, but he was far too distracted by his own injury. A moment later and the locking bar was out of both brackets and I was pulling furiously on one of the gate handles.

Slowly it started to swing open, but while the gate was moving with ponderous speed everything else started happening very fast. There was a cheer from outside, and looking around the gate I saw a dozen redcoats spring up from where they had been lying flat at the end of the path. They knew both cannons had fired and it was a race for them to cover the fifty yards and get at the gunners before they could fire again. I was pulling my coat back on so that I would not be mistaken for the enemy when I heard another angry roar from behind me. I turned to see the white-robed Persians coming out of an alley some forty yards away. They had seen me and the open gate and they were now also running towards me.

It was a race towards the gate and the outcome of the battle could depend on the outcome. The Persians, with a slightly shorter distance, looked like they were going to win. I looked around the gate again. The first redcoats were still some forty yards away but many more heads were rushing up over the cliff edge to join them. I stood there, looking at the running groups, and felt sure I should take some action, but was not sure what. I did not want to be trapped inside with the Persians, but if I ran out of the fort I would be exposed to the cannon, which would soon sweep the cliff top clear.

It was then I heard it, a droning wheeze followed by a high-pitched peal of squeals like an asthmatic wild boar caught in a trap: it was the damned bagpipes. But I also saw their effect. For the Persians could now see through the open gateway the redcoats rushing towards them. Then they heard that wretched droning and squealing and, shouting in alarm, they came to a sudden halt. Memories of the slaughter at Argaum with that same accompaniment were evidently all too fresh. So with a few muttered curses, they turned tail and disappeared back into the alleys.

"Bloody 'ell, it's the captain!" called Gilray as he charged through the gate.

He and several others ran straight up the nearby steps to carry their bayonets to the gunners, who even now were abandoning their guns and running for safety. Suddenly I was surrounded by friendly faces as the rest of the 74th started to run through the gateway.

Fergusson appeared and gave me a look of astonishment as he saw who had let them in. He flung me a sharp salute as he said, "It is good to see you again, sir."

I looked around at the familiar Highlanders as they entered the fort. They were grinning in delight at getting in so easily with some shouting "Well done, sir" and others shouting things in Gaelic which, judging by the accompanying grins, must have meant something similar. I might be one of the 'bastard English' but I sensed that in their eyes I had at last gone some way to be accepted in a Highland regiment. I knew most of them by name now and their lethal skills in battle gave a sense of security.

I had a sudden feeling of being back where I belonged and I turned to Fergusson and replied, "It's good to be back with you all again, Sergeant."

He looked me in the eye and gave a nod. I think we both realised that this time I bloody meant it. Then he grinned and added, "With your permission, sir, we'll start flushing the buggers out."

"Flashman, we thought you had been captured," said a smiling Swinton, as he pushed through the throng.

"I was," I said trying to sound as offhand as possible. "But a friend and I escaped and we thought you might need some help getting this gate open."

"Where is your friend?" said Swinton, looking around, and I felt a sudden stab of sadness as I remembered that struggling body going over the edge no more than five minutes ago.

"He didn't make it," I said curtly, not really wanting to talk about that now. I looked around for the 74th's new colonel. "Where is Wallace?" I asked.

"Dysentery," replied Swinton simply. "But I am not getting too much freedom of command as you will see in a minute. I had better get on, but it is really good to see you, Flashman." Swinton patted me on the shoulder and moved on to organise his men.

"I told you he wasnae fooking dead." The piping voice of Wee Jock was clearly audible and he grinned at me as he came through the gate. He was holding his drum to his body as he ran to stop it banging into his legs. Beside him was the lumbering bulk of his namesake, Big Jock, who also gave me a happy grin.

The next face I saw, though, was not smiling. It looked tired and strained and the lips were turned down in haughty disapproval at the familiarity of the drummer boy.

"Flashman, are Stevenson's men through into the inner fort too? How is the battle going at the north gate?" Wellesley barked the questions at me; he was desperate for news. He had spent hours climbing the cliff with the Highlanders and listening to the distant sound of battle without knowing how it was going.

"Some men have scaled the north wall and they are fighting their way along the gatehouses to let the rest of the army in. The garrison of the outer fort..."

"How many gates are there for the inner fort?" Wellesley interrupted.

"There are four; it is a death-trap. You would never be able to fight your way in without attacking the defenders from behind."

"Dear God," breathed Wellesley, looking pale. "We had heard rumours but we were not sure if it was exaggeration to deter us from attacking." Suddenly he was brisk again. "Major Swinton, never mind clearing the streets. Get your men into column. We must march straight for the northern gate. Put a skirmish line out in front, and a drummer and piper to tell them we're coming."

There had already been a couple of screams from women in nearby houses as hairy, horny Highlanders burst in on them with evil intent, but a few minutes of shouting from Fergusson got the regiment back in order. With a skirl of pipes and the rattle of a drum we set off down the widest street from the gate that led to the centre of town. An advance guard of a dozen or so men went in front to spot any ambush, but the doors and shutters of the surrounding houses stayed shut and the occupants silent. As we set off I decided that I had done enough to deserve a place in the rear, and so I was ideally placed to see what happened after we passed.

With the last British ranks still in sight down the street, Gawilghur residents were already charging towards the southern gate to make their escape. The British were in the inner fort, the town was lost and there was a battle raging around the northern gate. The locals were losing no time in saving themselves through the only other exit from the town, the south gate, before that was blocked again. Not all those escaping were civilians; I noticed there were also soldiers in the crowd. Houses that looked dark and closed up as the redcoats marched in front of them sprang into life after the redcoats were a hundred yards or so past. As we marched down the street I saw doors flung open further back and a stream of men, women and children emerge, looking nervously over their shoulders at us before running towards the southern gate, carrying bundles of precious possessions.

At a crossroads we could see through to a parallel street where there was a sea of humanity heading in the opposite direction to us.

Wellesley could see them too but he did not care. His battle was not with civilians, and if some soldiers wanted to run away too that was fine with him. He wanted to get to those northern gatehouses and help destroy the men who waited to trap and kill his army.

In the event we were not required, as Captain Campbell and the many men who followed him did the job without us. The Mahratta had heard if not seen the terrible slaughter of the outer garrison, and when the British appeared behind them many panicked and ran without realising how few the redcoats were. Only the final gatehouse put up any serious fight, but then the gates were flung open and Stevenson's men were in. We heard the roar of victory when the final gate was thrown open and Wellesley called a halt.

It was clear to everyone that the redcoats were now in the city, which meant that they would destroy any who tried to stand against them. The battle was won, and in the way of sieges and victorious armies, the raping, looting and slaughtering would begin. Wellesley had been clear before the assault that he would hang any soldiers caught looting or worse. With the general standing right in the middle of the ranks of the 74th, none of the soldiers felt like calling his bluff. Screams from the streets in front, though, indicated that other soldiers were taking a more cavalier approach to these restrictions as they claimed what they saw as the rights victorious armies had enjoyed for centuries. The inhabitants in the houses on either side of our column saw our men still standing in ranks and they heard the screams of their neighbours. First one or two started to emerge from their houses with bundles of possessions and run for the southern gate. Then, when they escaped unmolested, there was a general stampede of inhabitants all around us, heading south.

Wellesley decided to head for the palace and changed the direction of the march. The streets were pandemonium. Hundreds of people running from the rampaging redcoats in the north of the town panicked when they saw us and tried to fight their way down other streets, while those who had seen others escape past us fought their way to escape down the wide street we were on. Mothers and children got separated in the crush and screamed for each other. I saw Big Jock stoop to pick up a baby who fitted comfortably in one of his huge hands. He looked for someone safe to put it where it would not be trampled by the crowds and left it in the sagging awning over some shop. Possessions and valuables were dropped and some of the Highlanders behind the general would sometimes dart out to retrieve them. At a couple of shops I saw soldiers step quickly in to grab something, but they then got back in their place, usually stuffing something into a shirt or pocket. Sometimes we could barely move forward at all and then some muskets would be fired to clear the way, which resulted in even more screaming, shouting and panic in the surrounding streets.

Eventually we emerged in a square near the palace. There were more redcoats already there, sepoys from another regiment. Our men fell out from the column and stood jealously watching the sepoys, who were desperately trying to hide their loot when they saw that Wellesley was with us. An English officer came over and reported to the general that some of the Mahratta had retreated to a nearby building where they were making a last stand and shooting through the doorway.

"I expect they will give up soon," he added. "We have them surrounded, and as I came over they were starting to sing songs."

Wellesley looked at the officer. His uniform was torn and bloodstained and he had a bandage around one hand. The general turned to Swinton, whose Highlanders had so far seen no action at all, and said, "Sort out these last Mahratta, will you, Swinton, and if you find their commanders amongst 'em, bring them to me."

Fergusson shouted the commands and the men were once more into column and marching across the square and into a courtyard that faced the Mahrattas' final redoubt. It looked like some large hall, and judging by the noise there must have been at least a hundred men in there, all singing and chanting. Swinton brought the men to a halt as he considered the next steps and I went up to join him.

"What do you think, Flashman? It just don't seem right to charge in there while they are singing."

I was puzzled as the singing seemed strangely familiar, but I could not place it. Then I heard them sing a particular refrain and the memory came back and I realised the danger we were in. I did not waste time explaining to Swinton; there was not a second to lose.

"Sarn't Fergusson," I called. "Make sure all the men are loaded and get them in a line facing that door with bayonets fixed as fast as you can."

"You heard the captain," roared Fergusson. "Into line now and check your loads, flints and priming. Move it!"

"What is going on, Flashman?" asked Swinton, puzzled.

I pulled him back behind the fast-forming line of Highlanders as I explained. "The last time I heard that chanting I was with some hopelessly outnumbered Rajput cavalrymen in a hill fort."

"When you were trapped by the *pindaree*?" interrupted Swinton.

"Exactly. They sing it when they are preparing to die. There must be Rajput warriors in that building, and they don't do surrendering. Any minute now they will charge out and kill as many of us as possible before they are killed in turn."

"Good God," said Swinton, looking shocked. "Are we ready for them Fergusson?"

"Aye, sir." He turned to the men. "You will wait for the order to fire when they are all nicely spread out. Aim for the man in front. I don't want you all shooting the first bugger out of the door."

The men stood in a double rank of nearly fifty men each with their muskets held across their chests. Those nearest must have heard my explanation to Swinton but they looked resolutely to the front. Standing behind that line of backs covered in red cloth and white leather belts, I felt as safe as ever. These were the men that had marched into the cannon at Assaye. A few men, even Rajputs, charging from a hall would not trouble them. The chanting was getting faster and reaching a crescendo. Something was about to happen; you could sense it even if you did not understand the words they were shouting. I reached down and pulled my sword out of its scabbard.

The doors of the temple were suddenly flung back and the first men emerged, running straight towards us. They were bare-chested and they had removed their turbans so that their long hair trailed over their shoulders. More men spread out, running behind those leading as though they were in a race towards us. They were roaring a chant as they ran and holding weapons high in the air. Even behind that line of Highlanders I felt a chill of fright.

"Present," barked Fergusson and nearly one hundred steel-tipped muskets were pointed at the running men. "Aim low at the man in front."

Even more men were streaming out of the doorway; there were at least a hundred and the front runners were now no more than twenty yards away.

"Fire!" shouted Swinton, who seemed unsure if Fergusson would give the order and could not bear to wait any longer.

"Fire!" repeated Fergusson and nearly a hundred muskets spat death at a range that could hardly miss.

At ten to twenty yards a musket ball could pass through several bodies and those on the flanks of our line with no men in front of them had fired at an angle through the thickest mass of men. A wall of musket smoke obscured our view of the enemy and how many had survived. Normally the Highlanders would march forward, but this time the bodies were so close they could have tripped over corpses in the smoke and left themselves exposed.

Without waiting for an order, Fergusson gave the command: "Step six paces back."

The line moved back and Swinton and I stepped back with it. The distance gave our men a chance to react when the Rajputs burst out of the smoke, and burst out they did. Three came screaming with raised swords, aiming to split in two the head of the soldiers in front. In each case the targeted soldier raised his musket to block the blow while the man to his right jabbed out with his musket to take the attacker in the throat. It was cool, calm and disciplined as though they had done it dozens of times before, and they probably had.

"Second rank, reload," called Swinton, reasserting his authority over the regiment, while the rest of us watched the thinning skein of smoke in front of us.

There were groans and screams of pain from the hidden men in front of us, but just as we began to make out the shapes of the dead and dying lying on the ground there was a repeat of the chanted shout. Suddenly men were rising from the ground and coming on towards us, some obviously wounded, but others towards the back of the crowd sprang up unharmed and I think even more came out of the door behind. Perhaps the rattle of ramrods convinced them that all the British were reloading or perhaps it took them some seconds to recover from the devastating volley. Whatever the reason, there must have been at least fifty crazed Rajputs running in on us when half our men were partway through reloading and the rest had unloaded weapons.

Instinctively I looked for Big Jock, always a good man to stand behind in a tight spot, or so I thought. He swung his musket by the barrel as though it were a club and sent one of the Rajput flying back through the air. The front rank of the Highlanders seemed to holding their own against the rest too as they ran towards us, while the second rank continued to reload as fast as they could.

It was then that I saw the Mahratta giant running forward. I have seen it in countless battles since, even at Waterloo, but that was the first day that I discovered that a large man in a battle will invariably attract other giants to challenge him. Big Jock saw this one too late. He tried to swing his musket back to block the huge axe that the giant Mahratta was swinging, but the warrior was fast and reversed his swing to slam the end of the axe hilt hard into Big Jock's face. The Scotsman was off balance and screamed in pain as he fell to the ground. The giant Mahratta looked for a new target and found a British officer frozen in terror and holding a rather ornate golden sword just in front of him.

I had time to notice that the huge man already had two musket ball holes in his massive chest, but while both wounds were bleeding they did not seem to be slowing him down at all as he moved towards me. I tried to raise my sword, but he just swatted it away with his axe so hard that it flew out of my grasp. With his free hand he reached forward and picked me up by the throat and lifted me high into the air with a smile of triumph. He knew he was going to die, but he was going to have the satisfaction of taking the life of an enemy British officer as his final act.

I felt his fingers tighten about my neck as he started to crush it. With one hand I flailed for his face, but it was out of reach; with the other I tried to pull on his fingers, but it was like pulling on iron. I could hear shouts about me but his hand stopped me looking down. I couldn't breathe and the periphery of my vision started to get blurry. All I could see was his face as it suddenly contorted in pain and a slight squeal escaped his lips. The arm holding me started to lower but the grip on my throat did not diminish. As my feet reached the ground again I could see McFarlane slamming his bayonet through the giant's ribs on one side and Gilray ramming his bayonet up into the huge man's throat. But neither of those had created the initial injury that had caused the giant to lower his grip, which only now was slackening about my throat.

The last thing I saw before I passed out was Wee Jock. Amongst all this violence the boy, with his youthful innocence, looked almost angelic... and then I saw what he was doing. For with his crocodile tooth pendent hanging down across his chest he was pulling his bayonet out from the blood-soaked front of the giant's loincloth. He turned to me and grinned just before the blackness closed in, but clearly I heard him say, "Ah did for the giant fooker, didn't ah, sir?"

Epilogue

I came to in the shade of a wall, still in the courtyard I had passed out in. Along with several other wounded men of the 74th, I missed out on the grisly discoveries they made when they explored the palace. At the back they found a room full of the bodies of women and girls, most already dead but some still suffering a lingering death from the poison that they had been given. Those still alive revealed that they were the family members of the Rajputs who had died in that awful charge. On discovering that all was lost, these warriors chose to poison their womenfolk to give them what they felt was a more honourable death than being raped and used by the redcoats.

The British officers were sickened by the tragedy, although screams from across Gawilghur confirmed that rape was a likely prospect for any pretty woman found alive in the fortress by the invading army. I remembered James Skinner telling me about how his Rajput mother had killed herself because she thought her daughters had been defiled by being taken to school. There was a huge gulf between the cultures. Wandering later through the streets and seeing redcoats shooting helpless prisoners, fighting over captured women and loot or lying drunk in the streets, I was reminded of stories about the sacking of Rome. Quite which culture was the most civilised it was hard to say.

The most astonishing thing about the capture of Gawilghur was the butcher's bill. The Mahratta garrison was estimated at around eight thousand when the assault started, but the fortress was captured at the cost of just fourteen killed and one hundred and twelve wounded. All of the outer fort garrison were either lost in the ravine or taken prisoner, but many of those in the inner fort must have slipped away, either through the southern gate while it was unguarded or over the walls and down the steep sides of the ravine. The bodies of Manu Bappoo and the governor of the fortress were found amongst the corpses of those who had charged us out of the palace.

Captain Campbell survived and gave a glowing account of how Carstairs and I had distracted the Persians. He assured Wellesley that without our intervention he and his men would never have made it to the gatehouses. I genuinely tried to give Carstairs the credit, it was the least I could do, but such was my unearned reputation that this was taken as more modesty on my part and my standing rose yet further.

With Wellesley occupied elsewhere in the town, the 74th had scoured the palace enthusiastically for valuables, but there was little to be found. The raja and his brother had spent most of their wealth on recruiting soldiers. If you totalled the value of what they gathered, I probably had more in the form of the gems still sewn into my coat. I slept well that night, fingering the hard lumps in the garment's lining; I could afford to be well satisfied. The war was finally over, I had emerged with a greatly enhanced reputation, I had a small fortune in gold and gems and most of all I was alive and uninjured.

We stayed for a week around Gawilghur. I tried to find Carstairs' body to give him a Christian burial, but it must have been wedged somewhere up the cliff and I could not recover it. The ground surrounding the fort was littered with corpses, though. The bodies of the garrison of the outer fort who had been pushed off the ravine path were lying several deep at the bottom, while further round there were the remains of scores of men, women and children who had tried to escape down the cliff after the capture of the inner fort and who had evidently missed their footing. The vultures there were almost as thick as the flies.

I went back to the British camp where Runjeet still waited for me with his opulent tent. We stayed there for the rest of the week until Wellesley gave orders for the 74th to return to Madras. We were still by far the smallest regiment and desperately needed new recruits expected in Madras from Scotland. The journey took over two months and I am bound to say it was a pleasant trip. We marched to Bombay and there hired two large Arab dhows to sail all the way around the bottom of India and then back up the other side to Madras, stopping off at Goa and Cochin on the way.

Once more I found myself staring over the breakers at St George's Fort and soon those strange canoes were pulling us ashore. I noticed that with hard-faced Highlanders in the boat no oarsmen tried to renegotiate the fee on the way in. Runjeet hurried ahead to warn the household at the bungalow of their long-absent master's imminent arrival, while I called in at the fort to announce that the mission I had started over a year ago was complete. It took two hours to write a report of my activities for the governor general, who was away from the fort at the time.

When I finally emerged I was pleased to see my trusty syce waiting for me in the shade of the courtyard with a new horse; I had sold my old ones in Bombay.

"Welcome, sahib," he said, beaming. "The bungalow is all being prepared for your return and now your wife is here it will be a proper home."

"It is good to see you again and... eh... wife?" I was dumfounded. I thought perhaps he had misunderstood or misinterpreted. "This wife, she is a woman I have married, yes?"

"Yes, sahib," said the syce, now looking slightly worried that his master had spent too much time in the sun since they had last met. "Very nice lady," he added reassuringly.

Who the hell could it be? My mind rattled through various options. Had John Freese found out about his Eliza's infidelities and kicked her out? That was possible, but she would not pose as my wife in Madras where she was well known as the wife of someone else. There was Fatimah, my insatiable housekeeper from Meerut; had she tracked me down here? But surely there would be wealthy and energetic clients still in Meerut. Could it be the begum seeking refuge in disguise if Scindia had turned against her? No, she would fight to the death to retain her Sardhana.

"My wife," I enquired hesitantly to the syce, "is she an Indian lady or an English one?"

The syce's eyes boggled in astonishment – how can a man forget his own wife? He concluded that I had definitely lost my wits as he replied, "She is a very fine English lady, sahib."

"Well, we had better get home and meet her then," I said, climbing up into the saddle. Another name had sprung to mind now, but I hardly dared hope as it was virtually unheard of for daughters of the aristocracy to visit India.

A less welcome thought occurred: was Berkeley still on the run from the American? I shouted another question over my shoulder to the syce as we galloped out of the courtyard: "My wife has not brought her father with her, has she?"

"No, sahib, just her maid."

Lady Louisa Berkeley was waiting for me at the end of the bungalow drive where she had gone to get the first glimpse of me coming up the Madras road. We were in each other's arms in a moment and so began the happiest two months of my life. That pretty bungalow along the Madras road became paradise then. It was an idyllic time. Louisa wanted to hear all about my adventures and greatly admired the tiger-skin rug with the small bayonet cut still visible near one of the edges. In fact, one she evening she insisted that we make love on it, but even with her lying naked on top of it I struggled to dismiss the less erotic memories it brought back. As we writhed about at one point the skin's head flipped around and stared at me with its now glass eyes over Louisa's shoulder and with its teeth still bared in a silent grimace. That quite took my mind off the matter in hand. To make matters worse, as I suddenly moved back I felt a sharp pain in my left buttock and only then discovered that Runjeet had organised the skinning on the cheap with his cousin, who had left the razor-sharp claws in. I'll swear that wretched stuffed head was grinning as I hopped around looking for a cloth to staunch what was an inch-deep wound. That bloody tiger had got me at last.

Louisa explained that her sister had passed off the ginger sprog she had produced to an estate family and was now looking for a rich husband. Her father still hated me and had banned his daughter from any contact, but Louisa had felt betrayed by her family and had ignored him. After sending me the letter she spoke to Castlereagh, who put her in touch with Wickham, and between them I think that they helped arrange her passage to India. She posed as my wife to avoid her father hearing where she had gone, but when she arrived in India it was to discover that there were various stories about my fate. Some assured her that I had been killed in an ambush with the *pindaree* while others were sure that I had been seen at Assaye and was now with the British army. Somehow one of Runjeet's cousins had learnt of her arrival and offered her the use of the bungalow, Runjeet, Jamma and other household members having already set off to find me. 'Mrs Flashman' then immersed herself in the Madras social scene, eagerly learning every bit of news about the Mahratta campaign as it came in. She wrote, of course, but her letters only finally caught up with me some weeks after I had been in Madras.

After two months of enjoying ourselves, Wellesley and the rest of his army finally returned to Madras. We were invited to a formal ball in the town to celebrate victory in the campaign. All of Wellesley's officers would be there, together with local dignitaries and any unattached girls from the latest convoys. For the first time in ages I put on my captain's uniform, which had been pressed and cleaned. It no longer contained the gem stones in the lining. Some I had kept hidden elsewhere, others I had sold and one was on a ring on Louisa's finger. I buckled on my sword with the stars and the moon glistening on the golden hilt and looked at myself in the bungalow's full-length mirror. I realised it might be the last time I would wear the uniform. I had recently written to Colonel Wallace asking him to sell my commission for me, as I was not planning to stay in India with the regiment.

The ball was a glittering affair, hosted by the governor general to recognise the 'gallant heroes'. I was feeling very proud as I marched in with my smart uniform and Louisa on my arm. I had not seen many of the officers since Gawilghur and we were soon exchanging news and stories. Before anyone got too drunk the governor general proposed a minute's silence for the fallen, and as I stood there I suddenly realised what a lot had happened since I was last in this hall when I had first met Eliza Freese. There were a lot of fallen to remember too: Poorun, Lal, Flora, Daisy and all those other brave soldiers killed at the hill fort protecting me; that young lieutenant in the 74th at Assaye with his guts spilling into his lap but still friendly and polite; Abu Saleem finally ending his mourning for his Salome; and of course Carstairs, a man who seemed to have no fear at all until the end.

Over the evening I drank a toast to them all and plenty more besides. Louisa was impressed when the governor general came over to offer his thanks and congratulations on the service I had provided, but the person she really wanted to meet was Arthur Wellesley.

"My, isn't he tall and handsome!" she said as Wellesley emerged from the crowd and moved in our direction.

I introduced the pair of them and was concerned to note a leery glint in the general's eye as leaned over to kiss Louisa's hand. After the usual pleasantries Wellesley excused himself and asked for a word with me in private. Another officer swiftly moved in to escort Louisa to the punchbowl.

"Wallace tells me you are looking to sell your commission," said Wellesley, watching Louisa depart.

"That's right. I am not planning to stay in India with the regiment. It is time to go back to Britain."

"If you are sure, but your absence will be a loss to the army, which is why I have told Wallace to refuse your request."

"What? You cannot keep me here!"

"Don't worry, you are free to go, but I have asked Wallace to put you on the half-pay list so that you retain your rank and receive half-pay until you are called up again. You can sell your commission then, of course, if you like."

I was speechless. It was a very generous offer and would provide a regular income as well as the eventual sale value of the commission.

"Thank you, sir," I eventually managed to say.

"It was the least I could do after what you have done during this campaign," said Wellesley, still looking at Louisa. "You know," he continued, "there is a rumour going around town that you are not married to that woman at all. Someone is convinced that they have seen her before and that she is the unmarried daughter of Lord Berkeley."

"It must be a passing resemblance, sir," I said, keeping a straight face. Louisa, looking up and seeing us both staring at her, gave a broad smile back that seemed to light up the room.

"Well, she is certainly a striking woman," said Wellesley wistfully. "I don't suppose you would consider sharing her like Eliza, would you?" he asked with a grin.

"Absolutely not, sir," I said, grinning back.

"Well, if I were you," said Wellesley, reaching over to shake my hand, "I would ask the ship's captain on the way back to make sure you are married by the time you reach London. Then there will be little that Berkeley can do about it."

He moved on, casting a final lecherous glance in Louisa's direction, and I noticed that she gave a distinctly flirtatious look back. I decided that it really was time to go home. Wife or not, I was not going to let that randy bastard cock his leg over my girl.

We left India two weeks week later. With the army back and officers looking for lodgings it was easy to find a new tenant for the bungalow, and there was a convoy was ready to sail. I gave Runjeet a generous settlement to pay off the staff and on the morning of our departure he stood there, cuffing a tear, as Louisa and I stepped out towards a carriage on the drive with a cart of luggage behind. To my astonishment there was Sergeant Fergusson holding the carriage door open and saluting smartly.

"What are you doing here?" I asked, puzzled.

"The old company wanted to give their captain a send-off, sir," he said, gesturing down the drive. I looked to see nearly ninety men spaced a few yards apart all the way down either side of the long drive with their muskets at the 'present'. They were all there: Big Jock, Gilray, the new piper, even McFarlane who seemed less scruffy than normal.

"It has been an honour serving with you, sir," Fergusson added.

I thought back to his suspicion of me when he confronted me on that rooftop. Ironically his assessment of me then was probably more accurate than the one he had of me now. If they had known that all the feats that they seen or heard about were driven by fear or panic then they would probably have chased me down the street at the tip of their bayonets rather than stand in salute. But they didn't know and that was the point. It did not matter what I knew about my motives, it was what others believed that counted.

So I returned Fergusson's salute and climbed into the carriage, acknowledging the men as we passed them. At the end by the gate stood Wee Jock, who beat a tattoo on his drum as we passed.

"What a sweet-looking drummer boy," said Louisa as we went past.

If she only knew, I thought. I looked over my shoulder at Wee Jock, who grinned and gave me a wink back that was anything but innocent.

French Revolution and the 'Reign of Terror'

The facts around the period known as the Reign of Terror during the French revolution as described by the un-named sergeant to Flashman are largely correct. On the tenth of June 1794 a law was passed which was intended to simplify the judicial process. It was known as the Law of 22 Prairial. (It was passed on the twenty-second day of the month of Prairial in the year two in the French revolutionary calendar.) Its clauses included banning prisoners from employing counsels for their defence and suppressing the hearing of witnesses and it made death the sole penalty for guilt. It also included a clause empowering every citizen to seize conspirators and counter-revolutionaries and bring them before the magistrates. Citizens were required to denounce such people as soon as they became aware of them or they could also be found guilty of being part of such conspiracies.

The net result was a huge increase in the rate of executions. In the year before this law was passed around one hundred people were executed per month, but afterwards in the forty-nine days between the passing of the law and the fall of Robespierre, an estimated one thousand four hundred people were executed, over twenty-eight per day. This was mostly in Paris, but much greater numbers were executed elsewhere, particularly in western France where there was a strong royalist/counter-revolutionary uprising in early 1794. Estimates of those killed during the rebellion in the Vendee region range from one hundred thousand to five hundred thousand.

Benoit de Boigne

This general existed with a career as described in the book. Together with Mahadji Scindia, he helped create a European-trained army and Mahratta confederation that dominated the region. Benoit de Boigne did command an army of up to one hundred thousand men and was undefeated in a series of battles, showing great skill in controlling his forces. He retired to his native Savoy in 1807 and spent his remaining years managing his immense fortune and funding many state and religious organisations, particularly for the welfare of the poor and for education. He died having received many public honours in 1830 and left his still-considerable estate to his son from his first marriage with his Indian wife.

Life for the British in India 1802–3

In editing Thomas's memoirs I am deeply indebted to John Blackiston, a British army engineer who wrote a memoir called *Twelve Years Military Adventure in Three Quarters of the Globe*. This four-hundred-page account stamped *Univ of California* is available on the internet and confirms many of the facts mentioned by Flashman. The engineer was present at the battles of Assaye, Argaum and Gawilghur, and the information he provides is confirmed by other historical sources for these events, but it is the incidental details he provides that are the most valuable to the editor.

He provides anecdotes about the journey on the indiaman and may have even been on the same ship as he mentions a girl who confused a mosquito with an elephant. He talks about the arguments to hire a dubash on the beach, but is not lucky enough to find someone like Runjeet. There are references to food, customs, the formality of the fort, the balls introducing the new ladies to the community and regimental dinners, and he even mentions the major who was beaten by his own servant. He also describes the countryside of the campaign, villages after they have been ravaged by *pindaree* with the occupants left to die and incidental events during the battles. For example, he joined in the final cavalry charge with Flashman at Assaye, and saw the surgeon 'resurrect' the presumed dead Mahratta warrior when taking his sash for a bandage. In short, he confirms that Flashman's account of India during the period is entirely authentic.

Other information was confirmed by the author's own visit to the region, including the canoes with the v-shaped masts and the habit of ospreys to fly over wading elephants. The account of an elephant being left to babysit the mahout's child was something witnessed by the astonished engineer in 1802, but other sources have also confirmed this.

For those interested in the period, Blackiston's very readable account is recommended.

Wellesley and Mrs Freese

To confirm information about Arthur Wellesley, there is a variety of sources but notable is the definitive biography of Wellington by Elizabeth Longford. His time in India was obviously a pivotal period for Wellesley's career, turning him from an unproven commander to one who had demonstrated innovative tactics and a courageous approach, although luck certainly played a part in some of his early victories. He also proved himself a capable administrator first at Seringapatam and then managing the long supply chains during the Mahratta campaign, which were crucial to his success.

Flashman provides a rare insight into the insecurities he must have had at the start of the campaign, and due to their unusual intimacy over Mrs Freese, Wellesley seems to have been more willing to share his feelings. Elizabeth Longford's book confirms that some of Wellesley's officers had concerns over his close relationship with Mrs Freese while her husband was away, although her husband (promoted under Wellesley's command) never raised objections. Wellesley was godfather to their son (who had the red hair of John Freese) and supported the child when the boy was sent to England.

Biographies of Wellington also confirm that he felt that Assaye was his greatest battle and describe George IV's behaviour at the Waterloo dinners and the subsequent tour of the battlefield.

James Skinner
The autobiography of James Skinner provided another unique insight into the world experienced by Thomas Flashman, as James started his career with the Mahratta and finished it with the British. With his Rajput mother and Scottish father, he very much had a foot in both cultures and was well placed to understand their strengths and weaknesses. Skinner was clearly a very honourable man, refusing to fight against Scindia's forces even after he was expelled from Scindia's army, and fighting for the British. His autobiography is particularly useful for confirming the extraordinary circumstances of the meeting at Oojeine, which he does in some detail, with the exception of mentioning Flashman's arrest at the end. Perhaps he was embarrassed to admit his collusion in hiding Flashman's identity.

The Begum of Samru
The begum is an extraordinary character who is largely unknown in the west. She provides an exceptional challenge to biographers as she deliberately adapted and changed her persona to suit the circumstances. There are various theories about her parentage and her biographers cannot even agree on her name as she used several. She has also been associated with the massacre of some English prisoners by her first husband, which has soured the opinion of some contemporary English writers, to confuse the situation further. As the massacre happened in

1763 when she was aged around ten and almost certainly before she met her husband, it is highly unlikely she had anything to do with it.

The undisputed facts are that she was born around 1753 and whoever her parents were, they were not wealthy. As a result by her mid-teens she was living with a mercenary soldier called Walter Reinhardt Sombre, whom she married. Pronunciation of the French Sombre surname by Indians evolved it to Samru. She was just over four feet tall and later portraits of her in middle age show a face with a prominent nose. But clearly in her youth she was very captivating to attract and marry a wealthy and powerful mercenary general and later have a man kill himself for her.

It seems that she also had exceptional leadership abilities such that when her first husband died in 1778, when she was aged around twenty-five, the officers of her husband's army were content for this young woman to assume command. This was quite extraordinary given the male-dominated culture in both Europe and India at the time. She did not so easily inherit her husband's lands at Sardhana, as a son by an earlier wife of her husband contested the inheritance. There are accounts of her imposing her authority at this volatile time by having the two servant girls buried alive as she described to Flashman. She was baptised a Catholic in 1781.

In 1787 she supported the blind Mughal emperor Shah Alam in putting down an insurrection, and when the Shah's troops were wavering in their resolve to attack, it is said that she personally advanced with a force of a hundred men while ordering her artillery to open fire on the rebels. In recognition of her courage the emperor declared her to be his 'most beloved daughter', bestowed various honours on her and settled the dispute over the estate of Sardhana in her favour.

There are various accounts of what happened after her second marriage to Le Vassoult. Her troops did mutiny on hearing of the marriage and attempted to stop the couple leaving. The undisputed facts are that Le Vassoult shot himself and that the begum cut her chest with a knife. It will never be known whether she was actually trying to kill herself or tricking Le Vassoult into committing suicide so that she could regain power. Whatever her motive, with the help of George Thomas she swiftly regained control of her army and retained the Samru surname for the rest of her days, rarely mentioning her second marriage.

She remained an exceptionally astute political operator after that and played off the various Mahratta factions to retain her lands and influence during a very volatile period. When the British extended their influence she interacted with them too and became a very rich lady. Her estate was apparently valued at eighteen billion Deutsche Mark in 1953 by some descendants of her first husband who are still disputing the will to this day.

She died at the age of ninety in 1836 and her body was buried in the imposing Catholic church known as the Basilica of our Lady of Graces which she had built in Sardhana. Flashman's memory may be playing tricks on him if he remembered her priest called Julius Caesar during his visit in 1803. It is unclear when this man started in her service, but he would certainly have been in Sardhana for Flashman's subsequent visit. He was Bishop Julius Caesar by the time of her death and complaining that he had not been left enough in her will to reward him for many years of service.

The Battle of Assaye

The Battle of Assaye was an extraordinary event with Wellesley achieving victory against immense odds. It has to be said that the outcome would probably have been very different if the Mahratta cavalry had chosen to play a part in the battle with their vastly superior numbers. While there are many accounts in the west of the battle from the British point of view, Flashman's is the only account I have found of the build-up to the battle from the Mahratta perspective. He is also the only person to offer the intriguing insight that the begum may have worked with the *bhinjarrie* to bring Wellesley to Assaye and change the Mahratta plan of attack. Various sources do confirm that it was a cavalry patrol meeting a group of *bhinjarrie* traders that alerted the British to the true position of the Mahratta army.

The battle of Assaye is described in some detail in the book and the details Flashman provides match precisely the British historical records I have found. They viewed the Mahratta as a single mass and did not make distinctions between the troops of Scindia or the begum as Flashman did. All accounts describe that one group of Mahratta troops withstood the cavalry charge and marched off in good order, but few mention whose troops they were. It must be acknowledged that in at least one web-based account of the battle, the begum's troops were described as poor quality and guarding the baggage in the battle. I suspect that this account is rather biased against her, as it is hard to believe that Pohlmann would have thought it necessary to have half of his European-trained infantry guarding the baggage. Other sources confirm that it was the begum's men who held the line near Assaye and left the field unbeaten. In particular Skinner's autobiography, *The Recollections of Skinner of Skinner's Horse* by James Skinner with additional notes by J. Bailey Fraser, on page 147 confirms that: "It is a remarkable thing and much to the credit of the begum's troops that some four of five of her battalions were the only part of Scindia's army that went off unbroken from the field of Assaye." Remembering that James Skinner's brother, Robert, was one of the begum's officers, James Skinner should be a reasonably reliable source of information for what happened to the begum's troops at Assaye. Anthony Pohlmann seems to have followed the begum's advice as he disappeared after the battle.

The battlefield of Assaye is largely unchanged, as any reader can see by putting 'Assaye India' into Google Maps. You can clearly identify the space between the fork in the two rivers. Wellesley's ford is even marked, although there is a road bridge there now so you do not have to get your feet wet crossing the river. There are few remnants of the battle visible, but there is a white gravestone next to a giant peepul tree which is apparently that of Colonel Maxwell, killed leading his men in that final cavalry charge. Perhaps it is also the same peepul tree that Flashman rested beneath before he joined that charge.

Gawilghur

The final battle of the book was another extraordinary event but also a mystery for historians. According to contemporary witnesses, there were around eight thousand Mahratta soldiers in the fortifications before it was attacked. Yet it fell to the British with the official casualty figures as quoted by Flashman of just fourteen killed and one hundred and twelve wounded. Certainly a lot of the outer fort garrison died in the ravine, but that does not explain how the inner fort fell so quickly or so easily.

The fort still stands and has not been used as a stronghold since the battle. The breaches in the outer fort walls remain there to be climbed. The inner fort is still an imposing structure and traces of the four gateways survive. Historians have speculated that the defenders of the inner fort were thoroughly demoralised and so did not put up much of a fight. But these were the troops who had gathered to make a last-ditch stand and there was no easy escape from Gawilghur. You would have thought then that they had every incentive to fight hard to defend the inner fort.

The engineer, John Blackiston, who was there for the battle, is not particularly helpful. After describing the awful slaughter of the garrison of the outer fort he simply says: "The light company of the Scotch brigade placed their ladders against the wall and we were soon masters of the last defences of the fort." He does go on to describe the suicidal attack by the Rajputs and finding their womenfolk, but that is the only other resistance he mentions.

Of casualties, the engineer simply says: "Our loss on this occasion, and during the operations of the siege, were (sic) not as great as might be expected. That of the enemy must have been immense. Out of a garrison of 8,000 men, none escaped but such as dropped from the walls at the peril of their lives, all the gates having been stopped by our troops."

This imbalance of casualties sounds hard to believe, and so perhaps Flashman's account that the southern gate was for a while unguarded and that many escaped through it goes some way to explaining what happened.

Thank you for reading this book and I hoped you enjoyed it. If so I would be grateful for any positive reviews on websites that you use to choose books. As there is no major publisher promoting this book, any recommendations to friends and family that you think would enjoy it would also be appreciated.

There is now a Thomas Flashman Books Facebook page to keep you updated on future books in the series. It also includes portraits, pictures and further information on characters and events featured in the books.

Also by this author

Flashman and the Seawolf
This first book in the Thomas Flashman series covers his adventures with Thomas Cochrane, one of the most extraordinary naval commanders of all time.

From the brothels and gambling dens of London, through political intrigues and espionage, the action moves to the Mediterranean and the real life character of Thomas Cochrane. This book covers the start of Cochrane's career including the most astounding single ship action of the Napoleonic war.

Thomas Flashman provides a unique insight as danger stalks him like a persistent bailiff through a series of adventures that prove history really is stranger than fiction.

Flashman in the Peninsula

While many people have written books and novels on the Peninsular War, Flashman's memoirs offer a unique perspective. They include new accounts of famous battles, but also incredible incidents and characters almost forgotten by history. Flashman is revealed as the catalyst to one of the greatest royal scandals of the nineteenth century which disgraced a prince and ultimately produced one of our greatest novelists. In Spain and Portugal he witnesses catastrophic incompetence and incredible courage in equal measure. He is present at an extraordinary action where a small group of men stopped the army of a French marshal in its tracks. His flatulent horse may well have routed a Spanish regiment, while his cowardice and poltroonery certainly saved the British army from a French trap.

Accompanied by Lord Byron's dog, Flashman faces death from Polish lancers and a vengeful Spanish midget, not to mention finding time to perform a blasphemous act with the famous Maid of Zaragoza. This is an account made more astonishing as the key facts are confirmed by various historical sources.

Flashman's Escape

This book covers the second half of his experiences in the Peninsular War and follows on from *Flashman in the Peninsula*. While it can be read as a stand-alone novel, if you are planning to read both, it is recommended that you read *Flashman in the Peninsula* first.

Having lost his role as a staff officer, Flashman finds himself commanding a company in an infantry battalion. In between cuckolding his soldiers and annoying his superiors, he finds himself at the heart of the two bloodiest actions of the war. With drama and disaster in equal measure, he provides a first-hand account of not only the horror of battle but also the bloody aftermath.

Hopes for a quieter life backfire horribly when he is sent behind enemy lines to help recover an important British prisoner, who also happens to be a hated rival. His adventures take him the length of Spain and all the way to Paris on one of the most audacious wartime journeys ever undertaken. With the future of the French empire briefly placed in his quaking hands, Flashman dodges lovers, angry fathers, conspirators and ministers of state in a desperate effort to keep his cowardly carcass in one piece. It is a historical roller-coaster ride that brings together various extraordinary events, while also giving a disturbing insight into the creation of the Hunchback of Notre Dame!

Flashman and Madison's War

This book finds Thomas, a British army officer, landing on the shores of the United States at the worst possible moment – just when the United States has declared war with Britain! Having already endured enough with his earlier adventures, he desperately wants to go home but finds himself drawn inexorably into this new conflict. He is soon dodging musket balls, arrows and tomahawks as he desperately tries to keep his scalp intact and on his head.

It is an extraordinary tale of an almost forgotten war, with inspiring leaders, incompetent commanders, a future American president, terrifying warriors (and their equally intimidating women), brave sailors, trigger-happy madams and a girl in a wet dress who could have brought a city to a standstill. Flashman plays a central role and reveals that he was responsible for the disgrace of one British general, the capture of another and for one of the biggest debacles in British military history.

CPSIA information can be obtained at www.ICGtesting.com
Printed in the USA
BVOW05s0637280815

415118BV00002B/138/P

9 781782 990055